MW00744825

"Magic in the hands of a diab rorizes a pastor's family. Will their faith vanish when they need it most? Set against the backdrop of Lake Superior's magnificent shores, *Fatal Illusions* is chilling, action-packed suspense that will keep readers moored right up until the very last page!"

—Andrea Boeshaar, author and speaker

"Adam Blumer's debut novel is compelling and riveting, with a cast of well-defined characters and a plot as tight and action-packed as any best-selling thriller on bookstore shelves today. *Fatal Illusions* contains enough twists to keep even Harry Houdini impossibly bound! I can't wait to see what else this author has up his sleeve!"

—Thomas Phillips, author of *The Molech Prophecy*

"Every now and then I find an author whose voice I immediately fall in love with. Adam Blumer is one of those authors. In *Fatal Illusions* he weaves a tale so spellbinding and gripping, I couldn't wait to turn the next page. With characters I could identify with, a killer who had me looking over my shoulder, and an ending full of twists and surprises . . . just like that, I'm an Adam Blumer fan!"

—Mike Dellosso, author of *The Hunted* and *Scream*

"*Fatal Illusions* is a heart-thumping novel that not only kept me flipping pages, but impressed me with the Christian values it portrayed. Mystery reading at its best!"

—Bea Carlton, author of fifteen books

"*Fatal Illusions* is an engaging, fast-paced read with a captivating story line that grabs you from page one and doesn't let go. Adam Blumer has skillfully weaved the threads of grace, mercy, and forgiveness into this compelling suspense novel. Highly recommended!"
—Mark Mynheir, homicide detective and author of
The Night Watchman

"In *Fatal Illusions*, Adam Blumer has crafted a page-turner with characters that capture the imagination and a gripping plot from the first paragraph to the final sentence. An awesome ride!"
—Rosey Dow, Christy Award–winning author of
Reaping the Whirlwind

"Adam Blumer tells a fast-paced story that weaves together a serial killer, a physically wounded pastor, and his spiritually wounded wife. The twists and turns will keep readers guessing, and the idyllic setting will have non-Yoopers wondering when they'll be able to pay a visit to Michigan's Upper Peninsula."
—Rick Acker, author of *Dead Man's Rule* and *Blood Brothers*

FATAL
ILLUSIONS

Someone is watching . . .

FATAL
ILLUSIONS

A Novel

ADAM BLUMER

Kregel
Publications

Fatal Illusions: A Novel

© 2009 by Adam Blumer

Published by Kregel Publications, a division of Kregel, Inc., P.O. Box 2607, Grand Rapids, MI 49501.

All rights reserved. No part of this book may be reproduced, stored in a retrieval system, or transmitted in any form or by any means—electronic, mechanical, photocopy, recording, or otherwise—without written permission of the publisher, except for brief quotations in printed reviews.

Scripture taken from the New King James Version. Copyright © 1982 by Thomas Nelson, Inc. Used by permission. All rights reserved.

The persons and events portrayed in this work are the creations of the author, and any resemblance to persons living or dead is purely coincidental.

Library of Congress Cataloging-in-Publication Data
Blumer, Adam
   Fatal illusions : a novel / Adam Blumer.
      p. cm.
   I. Title.
PS3602.L87F38   2009   813'.6—dc22   2008055645

ISBN: 978-0-8254-2098-6

Printed in the United States of America

09 10 11 12 13 / 5 4 3 2 1

To my wife, Kim, my number-one encourager, for watching the kids while I disappeared into the basement to write.

To my parents, Larry and Rhoda Blumer, who pointed me to Christ and always said I could do more with my writing.

Masquerade!
  Hide your face, so the world will never find you!
      —From the Broadway musical *The Phantom of the Opera*,
          lyrics by Richard Stilgoe and Andrew Hart

All things are naked and open to the eyes of Him to
  whom we must give account.
                              —Hebrews 4:13

ACKNOWLEDGMENTS

WRITING A NOVEL IS often a solitary venture, but publishing a novel never is. My first feeble notion of what to put on the first page could never have evolved into a publishable novel without God's leading and a crew of dedicated folks who counseled and cheered me on as I ran this marathon called "writing a novel." Special thanks to:

Bea Carlton, Christian suspense novelist and Writer's Digest School writing instructor, who coached me through the planning and early chapters. Her encouraging advice and confirming words that I was headed in the right direction gave me the confidence to keep going when I was ready to give up.

My long-suffering early draft reviewers, who graciously told me what needed help: Aaron Blumer, Kim Blumer, Marilyn Blumer, Rhoda Blumer, Ruth Christison, Michael Coley, Philip Crossman, Natalie Everson, Andrea Koenig, and George Sooley. Thanks to Yahoo Groups—some of you actually read the whole novel online (what a crick in the neck!). You saw that I could publish this novel long before I did.

My Kregel friends for taking a chance: Steve Barclift, Miranda Gardner, Dennis Hillman, Cat Hoort, and Janyre Tromp. Miranda, Janyre, and freelance editor David Lindstedt especially opened my eyes to new possibilities and helped take my work to a whole new level. Thank you!

Others who provided expertise and advice along the way: Rick Barry, Andrea Boeshaar, Jason Curtman, Mike Dellosso, Rosey Dow, Craig Hartman, John Koenig, Steve Laube, Susan K. Marlow, Mark

Mynheir, Thomas Phillips, Stephanie Reed, Les Stobbe, Jamie Langston Turner, and Amy Wallace.

God, the Shaper and Enabler of dreams. May the Lord receive all the glory!

PROLOGUE

AS DUSK SETTLED OVER the suburban Cincinnati neighborhood, the sodium-vapor lights along the quiet street blinked and came to life on cue. They chased the shadows from the grade school parking lot, now littered with dried leaves that scraped across the pavement and swirled in their seasonal dance of joy.

Across the way, a man in a jet-black jogging suit eased behind a tree and checked his watch as the chilly breeze tousled his hair. He breathed deeply, noting the intoxicating aroma of burning leaves, and impatiently studied the faces of the pedestrians now strolling toward the school auditorium. Anxious children tugged at reluctant parents, their excitement barely contained.

"Yes, yes," he overheard a woman tell a child. "We'll get there in plenty of time. No need to rush."

He smiled. He had been that overzealous child once, but that was a long time ago. He'd grown up, things had changed, and not every change had been welcome.

His smile faded as he continued to search for a certain bespectacled face. He'd been watching her for weeks and knew everything about her: when she got up in the morning, when she went to bed, where she went each day, how she spent her time. He even knew she was failing English for the second time, even after her teacher had given her a two-week extension on her term paper. Going through her trash, he'd discovered her addiction to Snickers bars, her affection for Ruffles potato chips and cream soda, and her preference for Pantene shampoo, which added luster to the blonde hair she wore long and wavy.

A familiar red nylon jacket caught his eye, and he sucked in his breath. Concealing himself farther behind the tree, he waited for her to pass.

Hmm. She was so close. He could have reached out, could have touched her hair. But he steadied his breathing and let the moment pass, deciding that reason must win the battle with emotion. There were simply too many people around who might see him and remember his face. He watched as she strolled into the school with her two charges in tow, carefree and unsuspecting.

Just the way he wanted her.

He took another deep breath, surprised by how calm he felt tonight. He knew what he needed to do and realized he had the resolve to execute his plan. Now all he needed was the opportunity, but waiting had never been easy for him. He could hear his mother's chiding words strumming across the strings of his memory.

You're so impatient, Donny. So restless. Don't you know that good things come to those who wait?

Time to get inside.

＊　＊　＊

Someone was watching her. For weeks, she'd felt unseen eyes following her every move. Evaluating. Judging. But when she would whirl around, no one was ever there—just brittle leaves scudding across the empty sidewalks.

"C'mon, you two. Hurry up."

Clutching their hands with icy fingers, Erin Walker yanked Daphne and Thomas along to match her stride. It was bad enough that she was stuck taking care of these first-grade brats on a Friday night. Worse, the evening's entertainment promised to be a childish, elementary school musical, and she had better things to do with her time.

She'd been planning to give Sheryl a cut and dye job tonight. Her hairdressing service brought in more money than babysitting, but her mom had said she owed the Spensers a favor.

Yeah, whatever.

Erin wished for her father right now. Divorced from her mom and recently remarried, he had moved three states away, leaving them with the mortgage and a barely enough paycheck from her mom's job as a nighttime gas station attendant. Her mom had said he was a no-good lowlife, that they were better off without him, but Erin wasn't so sure. She had fond memories of her dad taking her ice-skating, just the two of them. He had shown her the spins he'd mastered as a young man, when he had almost qualified for the Olympics.

Almost. *Dreams are never easy,* he'd told her. *You have to work hard and never, ever give up.*

One more year and she would graduate from high school. Maybe then she could free herself from her mother's stranglehold and open the beautician's shop she'd always wanted.

The lights of Bridgetown Elementary glimmered against the darkening sky, the crisp wind swirling the leaves at her feet. She wished she'd worn her jean jacket instead of the thin, red windbreaker. She pushed her wire rim glasses up on her nose and glanced at her watch, realizing that in her reverie she'd slowed her stride.

"C'mon, we're going to be late if you two don't hurry," she said.

"Slow down!" Daphne cried. "We can't keep up."

Erin peered down into Daphne's frustrated hazel eyes. "Look, I'll let you wear my watch if you'll get a move on."

Daphne squealed. "Cool!"

Though they were five minutes late, the program hadn't yet started. But Erin realized that they should have come much earlier if they'd wanted to get a good seat. The place was packed, and she didn't see an open row anywhere.

Biting her lip, she spied a friend coming down the aisle toward her. Laurie was a stagehand—and, as it happened, she was also the solution to their problem. She had been saving seats for her mother and sisters, but they'd all been waylaid by food poisoning or something, and wouldn't be coming.

Three seats. Right in front. Perfect.

Erin couldn't help smiling smugly as Laurie escorted them to the front row like celebrities at the Academy Awards, minus the red carpet preshow, of course. She felt the indignant glares drilling into her back from those who had arrived a half hour early to get their seats. She felt a rush of pleasure at the realization that she was the cause of their indignation.

Let them sulk. Sometimes good things happen when you least expect it.

Her mind replayed a similar thrill she'd felt just a month ago, when she'd been summoned to give testimony in a big court case downtown.

＊　＊　＊

She'd done up her hair special, dry-cleaned her navy twin set, and worn her new high-heeled shoes, which made her short, lithe figure seem several inches taller. Approaching the stand, she had, for once in her life, felt important; felt as if every eye in the room was glued to her, mesmerized by this long-haired, blonde goddess with the porcelain skin and sapphire blue eyes. She hadn't realized until later how important her testimony had been.

"And you *saw* the defendants enter Margaret Stowe's house?" Stan Loomis, the prosecuting attorney, had asked.

"That's right."

"And you're *sure* it was Walter and Virginia Owens. You're *positive*?"

"Yes, sir."

"Remember, Miss Walker, you are under oath. You *saw* their faces?"

She had bitten her lip as she tried to remember.

She had just finished house-sitting for Mrs. Stowe, as another way to make some extra money. The old lady was loaded. She had said good night to Mrs. Stowe and had walked off, feeling giddy at the sizable check. Almost to her car, she'd dropped her keys and bent to pick them up. Hearing voices, she'd glanced back and had seen two people walking up the sidewalk to Mrs. Stowe's front door.

A man and a woman, wearing long, dark overcoats. They had looked wealthy. The man had placed his black-gloved hand at the middle of the woman's back.

"You don't think she'll mind?" the woman had asked, a musical quality to her husky voice. "It's late."

"You're right. It *is* late. Too late." The man's voice had sounded rough, like a smoker's. "She can't turn us away now."

Standing beside her car, Erin had watched as the man knocked.

When the door opened, a band of light had slashed across their faces for an instant before they disappeared inside.

Staring unflinchingly at Stan Loomis, she had said, "Yes, it was them. I'm sure of it." She'd pushed away the fact that the encounter at Mrs. Stowe's house had occurred the week before she'd gotten her new glasses.

"For the benefit of the jury, would you please point out who you saw?"

Her hand had trembled as she pointed to the pale-faced Owenses, who sulked beside their defense attorney. They didn't flinch. They didn't move. But their eyes—they hated her. They wanted her dead. Ever since, those eyes had stared back at her in her dreams.

Those dark, hateful eyes.

✳   ✳   ✳

The sound of a grade school chorus singing an upbeat song drew her attention back to the stage. She stifled a yawn and glanced at her watch, only to realize that Daphne was still wearing it. Well, no big deal. She'd get it back later. The musical version of *Winnie the Pooh* was okay, she supposed. She reminded herself that she'd worked more demanding babysitting jobs for even less than the paltry, sub-minimum wage she was being paid.

The musical was drawing to a close. In another five minutes, the show would be over, and she'd take the kids home. Maybe there'd even be time for Sheryl's cut and dye job.

A female voice sliced into her thoughts. Amid the waves of applause, the director was acknowledging the stage crew, who bowed awkwardly in their matching black jeans and T-shirts. Erin's gaze locked onto one of the crew members, who appeared to be staring at her. A look of recognition glinted in his black eyes before Erin glanced away.

Do I know him? He didn't look familiar. Unsettled, she rushed Daphne and Thomas home as soon as the show was over.

✳   ✳   ✳

Walking home from the Spensers alone, Erin kept to the edge of the roadway, away from the sidewalk and out from beneath the shadow of the trees, as her mother always insisted. She scuttled between the dim pools of light cast by the streetlights, which seemed to do a better job of lighting the tops of the posts than illuminating the street below; she walked briskly, though she was really in no hurry to reach her quiet, lonely house. Her mother would be working at the gas station, and Erin would have the rest of the evening to watch HBO, to see if Sheryl wanted to squeeze in that haircut, and maybe to take a long, hot bath.

A familiar prickly feeling crawled up the back of her neck. Someone was watching her again. She whirled around, but no one was there.

Exhaling a relieved sigh, she resumed her journey. A fresh blast of frigid wind cut through her thin jacket and set the leaves to dancing at her feet. Thoroughly chilled, she hugged herself as she walked along the shadowy street.

She heard the car before she saw it—a distinctive chirping noise above the sound of the engine as it pulled alongside.

"Hey, it's cold out there. Want a ride home?" the driver called to her through the open passenger-side window.

Erin glanced in his direction, but couldn't see his face. "No, thanks. I'm fine." She kept walking.

"It's me. From the musical."

She stopped and looked closer, recognizing the guy from the stage crew. He was the one who'd been staring at her. She'd felt uncomfortable then, but didn't feel uneasy now. He was attractive and friendly enough, but still she was cautious. "I don't think I know you."

"Well, maybe we could talk, get to know each other a little bit. I'm not so bad, if you give me a chance."

Her hands automatically moved to smooth back her hair. He had to be at least ten years older. "I don't know . . ."

"You look like you're freezing. At least let me give you a ride home. I don't bite. Honest." He opened the passenger-side door and swung it toward her.

Stepping closer, Erin peered in and studied his face in the dome light. He had a nice smile and white, even teeth. His black, curly hair was kind of cute, too. She wondered if his curls were natural. "Well, it is pretty cold out here . . ."

✷ ✷ ✷

Daphne Spenser tugged at her mom's arm. "Erin let me borrow her watch, but I forgot to give it back." She held up the too-large watch for her mom to see.

Washing dishes at the sink, Diane Spenser wagged her head. "How many times have I told you to return things you borrow? Hurry. Erin just left. Maybe you can still catch her."

Out the front door and pulling her jacket on, Daphne scampered down the steps to the sidewalk and peered down the road. Halfway down the block, Erin was standing beside a brown car and talking to someone through the open window.

"Erin!" Daphne ran toward her. "Erin, wait!" But the wind was howling, and Erin couldn't hear her. Daphne kept running, hoping Erin would see her.

She saw the passenger-side door open, and Erin stepped closer to the car. Just then, a hand shot out from inside the car and closed around Erin's arm. She screamed and tried to pull away.

Daphne's heart slammed into her throat. She froze.

A man was pulling Erin into the car in spite of her screams. Daphne saw his dark hair, but couldn't see his face.

The car squealed away. The passenger door slammed shut as the car sped around the corner and headed out of sight.

Daphne's heart pounded in her ears.

She wouldn't see Erin again until the funeral.

Part 1

WHISPER OF AN ACCUSATION

When lovely woman stoops to folly,
And finds too late that men betray,
What charm can soothe her
  melancholy?
What art can wash her tears away?
    —Oliver Goldsmith, "Woman"

CHAPTER 1

Four years later

ON THE MORNING WHEN everything in her secure, even-keeled life was about to change, Gillian Thayer picked up her Osmiroid fountain pen, leaned over her desk, and pressed the nib to a sheet of angled Strathmore document paper. With the first stroke and the accompanying bleed of Pelikan 4001 blue, something magical happened. Words became art, stimulated the eye, and made a memorable quote even more memorable.

The phone rang. Carefully placing her pen on a sheet of tissue to avoid dripping onto her project, she grabbed the receiver. "Thayer Calligraphy."

"Hey, Gillian. Got another question for you."

"Oh, hi, Christine." Gillian bit her lip in disappointment; she'd been hoping for more work, not a call from Christine Reynolds, manager of the frame shop where she did most of her business. Still, a call from Christine was always refreshing.

"Sorry to bug you. My son, Ruben, is doing a report on last words of famous people. I told him you'd know who these people are, but he doesn't believe me. Can you help me prove him wrong?"

Gillian laughed. "Sounds intriguing. Okay, I'll give it a shot."

"Here's the first one. 'Let us cross over the river and rest under the shade of the trees.'"

"Stonewall Jackson."

"'The fog is rising.'"

"Emily Dickinson."

"Here's the last one: 'Lord, help my poor soul.'"

"Poe," Gillian said. "Definitely Poe."

"Poe?"

"Edgar Allan Poe. You know, that horror fiction writer who was popular in the early 1800s. 'Quoth the Raven, "Nevermore!"'"

"Oh, yeah. *That* guy."

"And if anybody meant those words, it had to be him. From what I understand, he had one miserable life and died young under mysterious circumstances."

Christine chuckled. "Incredible. You really know your stuff, don't you?"

"People don't call me 'The Quote Lady' for nothing. I guess you can't be in my line of work and not become a walking encyclopedia of poems and famous quotations."

"I guess so. Thanks a bunch. Oh, hey, your framed John 3:16 is almost done. We had a few problems with the matting, but we got it fixed. Everything's okay now."

"Glad to hear it. When can I expect it?"

"Tomorrow afternoon. I'll have Jeremy drop it by."

"Sounds good."

"Hey, thanks again, and have a super day. And, Gillian, promise me you won't stay cooped up indoors all day, okay? It looks like it's going to be a perfect October day. Get out. Feel the sunshine. Promise me."

"Promise."

"Well, I've bugged you long enough. Talk to you later. Bye."

"Bye."

Gillian gazed out the window at her sunny garden and longed to feel the cool grass under her feet. She remembered a quote by Pearl Buck: "Order is the shape upon which beauty depends." In other words, her art wouldn't be its best until she'd spent some time ordering her world, and order meant sticking to her schedule. She eyed her flower garden again and shook her head.

Later. I've got work to do.

She turned back to Isaiah 41:10, her favorite Bible verse. She was painstakingly transcribing it from the traditional King James Version for one of her newly commissioned projects.

She heard a knock at the door but didn't look up, refusing to lose her focus. Crystal, her sixteen-year-old daughter, knew she hated to be interrupted when she was in the middle of a project. But she also knew that Gillian hated it when she left for the day without saying good-bye.

Crystal crossed the studio, waited until Gillian had finished putting the descender on a small letter *g*, and bent to kiss her mother's cheek.

It used to be that Gillian would be up at the crack of dawn, busy with her work long before Crystal left for school. But lately, she'd succumbed to a more leisurely pace and a later start. After all, it wasn't that she had so many projects to do that she had to work from dawn to dusk like a mad fiend under the pressure of deadlines. Certainly not. But her hands were most sure of themselves, more steady, in the morning; and steady hands made what she did possible. Sometimes, she imagined that she'd lost her hands in a car accident, or that they'd been crushed somehow beyond repair. The thought always made her shudder.

"I have choir practice this afternoon," Crystal said. "Just wanted to remind you."

"As if I needed reminding." Setting her pen aside, Gillian flashed Crystal a smile mingled with mock frustration. "How could I possibly forget? You haven't stopped talking about it."

"Being in state honors choir is, like, a big deal, Mom."

"I know it is, and I'm proud of you."

Gillian studied her daughter, who had been taking voice lessons since she was seven and had a voice to prove it. Crystal had long, blonde hair and the most beautiful blue eyes Gillian had ever seen— both traits handed down from her father. *But her artistic side comes from me*, Gillian reminded herself with some pride.

Gillian had inherited her own talent from her mother, Rose, who had been painting book cover art for Cherish Press, a successful Christian publisher near Cleveland, for more than thirty years. "Real art," her mother called it, though Gillian wouldn't necessarily call prairie romance covers "real art." But in all fairness, her mother's artistry *was* amazing, and it often made Gillian feel jealous when she saw her mom's most recent offering. During those moments, Gillian found herself questioning her own work. Was calligraphy *real* art? She'd tried painting when she was younger, starting with landscapes, but her paintings had never rung true. For whatever reason—providence, she guessed—calligraphy had emerged as her area of true skill.

At night, Crystal had been designing Web sites—"a sensitive blend of art and electronics," in Gillian's words—for several clients. The demand for her work had been escalating over the past few months, but Crystal would not give up choir to meet the demand.

"So you'll pick me up from practice?" Crystal asked.

"I'll be there. Four o'clock, right?"

"Right. Is Dad gone already? I didn't hear him leave this morning."

"Yep. He's got an important meeting at nine. A church discipline situation that could turn ugly. Pray for him."

Before beginning her day's projects, Gillian had joined Marc for a quick breakfast of hard-boiled eggs, fruit, and bagels. They had talked about their plans for the fall, about Crystal's upcoming weekend at a youth retreat, and about a possible weekend getaway to Door County, a favorite tourist spot northeast of Green Bay, Wisconsin, while she was gone. Gillian had warmed to the possibility, but Marc had seemed reluctant, pressured by the responsibilities he would be leaving behind.

Being one of six pastors at one of the largest Bible-believing churches in the Chicagoland area had heaped more stress and commitments on Marc than Gillian cared to consider. Almost every evening seemed jam-packed with something: visitation, the Bible institute, prayer meetings, the prison ministry. The list never ended, and neither did her frustration of late.

Crystal's eyes clouded with concern. "He'll be home tonight, won't he?"

Gillian glanced at the wall calendar. "Nope, it's Monday. He's got prison ministry tonight, remember? He'll grab a quick bite to eat and be out the door again."

Crystal sighed. "Mom, he's never home anymore. When do I ever get to see him?"

Gillian locked her heart and hid the key, knowing that if she agreed with her daughter and started talking, Crystal would hear things no daughter ought to hear from her own mother. Gillian ignored Crystal's question.

From the driveway came the sound of a car's horn.

"Lauren's here," Gillian said. "You better go. You're going to be late."

Crystal kissed her mom again and paused to peer into her eyes. Gillian could tell she was probing, wondering if she was okay, uneasy to leave her alone. Last night after church, while Marc had an emergency counseling session, she and Crystal had watched a made-for-TV drama about parents whose son died in a horrific car accident. During a commercial break, Gillian had fled to the bathroom and pressed her face into a towel to muffle her sobs.

"Get going, sweetie," Gillian said. "You're going to be late."

Gillian could tell that Crystal wanted to stay home and comfort her and try to help her with something she could never hope to understand. The role reversal was uncanny. Gillian was now the weepy child in need of a parent's strong arms and tender words.

Crystal lingered.

"Crystal, I'll be fine. Now *go*."

Reluctantly, she moved toward the door and glanced back. "Okay, Mom, I'm leaving. But give me a call if you need to talk. Promise?"

Gillian nodded, though she had no intention of weighing her daughter down with her burdens. She blew a kiss, and Crystal was gone, the front door closing behind her with a gentle click. Then came silence—always silence, Gillian's constant enemy. As if on cue, dark thoughts assailed her.

She turned on the CD player, and relaxing piano music created a tranquil ambiance. The music took the edge off her loneliness, yet she longed for someone to be around—a physical presence. Pressing her lips together, her gaze straying out the window in a moment's hesitation, she reached for the right desk drawer and slid it open. Concealed under a pile of parchment lay a thin, silky sheet of paper.

The image on the paper resembled a photo negative: confusing blotches of white appeared spray-painted against a black background, bordered by white block lettering—her name and a date and time—along with other combinations of letters and numbers that might as well have been Chinese. Inside the border, small white ridges and lines circled and met, outlining what the untrained eye might have assumed were the rugged contours of valleys and mountains.

In the center of this assumed landscape, her eyes rested on what looked to be a strand of pearls. A perfect baby's spine.

The dryer buzzer made Gillian jump. Wiping her eyes, she glanced at the clock, dismayed by how much time had passed. She had too much to do to be getting sidetracked.

Getting up, she headed to the mudroom, mechanically taking the clothes out of the dryer and piling them in a basket. Beside the dryer hung two of Marc's suits, which she intended to take to the dry cleaner later that morning if she could still find the time.

A couple of years ago, Marc's olive suit, his favorite, had been destroyed when he'd left a pen in one of its pockets. Since then, she'd become religious about checking his pockets. Now, as she ran her fingers down into the inside pocket of his navy, double-breasted jacket, she felt something smooth against her fingers.

"I'm glad I checked," she muttered to herself as she pulled out a small square of what appeared to be purple stationery, neatly folded into fourths. A feminine fragrance drifted up to her nose, and a cold streak ran down her neck.

Sometimes, when she was feeling romantic, she'd write a Shakespearean sonnet on a scrap of parchment and leave it in Marc's sock drawer. Or she'd fancy up a quote that she knew would make him smile. Dr. Seuss or *Calvin and Hobbes*. But this note was nothing she'd written.

She felt the blood drain from her face as she began to read. The letter slipped from her fingers and fluttered to the floor like a wounded bird, and she leaned against the dryer for support.

It was a love letter.

To her husband.

From another woman.

CHAPTER 2

DRUMMING HIS FINGERS ON the conference table, waiting for the dreaded meeting to begin, Pastor Marc Thayer peered out the window at the radiant, sun-drenched morning. The sun slanting down on the well-manicured grounds of Heritage Bible Church confirmed in his mind that he'd rather be anywhere else than here right now.

Across the street, children were playing basketball in a cracked, forsaken parking lot. He imagined the rhythm of the basketball in his hand and pictured himself going in for a layup. Shaking his head, he wondered if his craving for the game was anything like the craving of a smoker.

Except they don't make a patch for basketball addicts.

He turned his thoughts toward home and pictured Gillian working on her calligraphy, head bent over a piece of parchment paper, red hair draped across her pretty face like a shimmering veil. She'd been so depressed lately, so lost in her private world.

When will she ever get over her grief? It's been six months.

He wondered what he could do to cheer her up. A box of candies? No, most of them had chocolate, and she was allergic to chocolate. Flowers might be a good idea, except she already had a garden full of them.

God, please heal her heart and show me what I can do to help her. Sometimes she's so closed off to the world and to me. I'm just not sure how to reach her anymore.

The door opened, and Dave Ritchie, the church's youth pastor and Marc's best friend, lumbered in. Sporting a military-style haircut, with a square jaw and confident bearing, he carried his black leather

Bible and a tall, steaming cup of coffee—most likely Gevalia, and no doubt strong and black. He gave Marc a reassuring nod, set his items down, and grabbed the nearest chair.

"Hey, Shorty. You ready?"

Marc smiled at the ironic nickname; he was six feet, five inches tall. "Ready as I'll ever be."

Once a weightlifting fanatic, Dave had let himself go soft, though some muscle remained. Rarely did a sport coat fit him correctly, unless it was tailored. The khaki number he had on this morning was strictly off-the-rack, and where his biceps bulged, the tight fabric appeared ready to rip at the seams. Marc had recommended that Dave cut back on the carbs and try running, but Dave insisted he had bad knees and couldn't curb his appetite for junk food.

Marc was glad that Dave was there to satisfy the conditions of Matthew 18—"that 'by the mouth of two or three witnesses every word may be established'"—and to provide moral support. Church discipline wasn't fun for anyone, and the meeting they were about to have was bound to turn ugly.

Of all his counselees, Stacey James had been the most challenging—and disturbing. She seemed to have a conflict with everyone: her absent, unfaithful husband; her domineering mother; her competitive siblings; even the garbage man.

In fact, it seemed the only person she got along with—carried a torch for might be more accurate—was him. Her desire for a man's attention, no doubt fueled by her husband Jake's rejection, and by the father who had abandoned her long ago, had forced Marc to end his counseling sessions with her two months ago. Her flirtations had become more than he could stomach, and his secretary, Liz Simons, also a trained biblical counselor, had continued where he'd left off.

It was just as well. He wanted to help Stacey deal with her problems, and he wanted to see her grow in her faith since she'd recently trusted Jesus Christ as her personal Savior, but sooner or later he knew she was going to put him in a compromising situation. She'd already made it quite clear that she was interested in more than his biblical advice. Putting the brakes on their counseling times was the best thing he could have done. But now, because of recent events, he'd been forced to get involved again. But things were different now. He'd traded his counselor's cap for that of a referee.

"Wanna play 'Lunch Bunch' today?" Dave's nasal tenor intruded into Marc's thoughts. "Lunch Bunch" was the name of a group of pastors and staffers who regularly played hoops after a quick lunch. The group was known more for their many injuries than for their competitive edge.

"I don't think so."

"Why not?" Dave caught Marc's gaze and held it.

Marc sighed. "I thought I explained it to you. Competition brings out a side of me that can turn pretty ugly. You know what I'm talking about. You've seen it."

Dave chuckled, his brown eyes crinkling in amusement. "Oh, yeah. Dr. Jekyll and Mr. Hyde."

The last time Marc had played hoops with the Lunch Bunch, he'd lost his cool and nearly taken a poke at one of the other guys. Later, he had asked for forgiveness, but he'd also decided to avoid the sport altogether, at least for a while. At least until he could learn to control his temper a little better.

"Look, before I met God, basketball *was* my god. On the court, I was driven by one goal: personal glory. So whenever I get back on the court, I'm tempted to slide back into that old way of thinking. It's just not a good idea for me right now."

A drop of sweat trickled down Dave's cheek. He absently wiped it away. "But you're so gifted, Marc. You shouldn't give up basketball altogether. You could reach lots of kids with a tool like that. Imagine doing basketball clinics in local schools. You'd have a platform for ministry that most of us could only dream of. I've told you that before."

Marc glanced at the kids across the street, still engaged in an aggressive game. He shrugged. "Maybe someday. But I think God needs to change me a lot first." Nearby, a door closed. Someone was coming down the hallway toward them.

Marc wished he'd spent more time praying for this meeting. He felt unprepared for what needed to be said, and anxious about how Stacey would respond. A familiar verse in 2 Corinthians 12 ran through his mind: *For when I am weak, then I am strong.*

✳   ✳   ✳

Tossing her bleached-blonde hair, Stacey James breezed into the room and perched on a chair at the cherry conference table across from Marc and Dave. She was all smiles and carefree charm, apparently oblivious to what had precipitated this meeting.

"Howdy, Marc! What are *you* doin' here?" Her smile faded as she glanced around the room in confusion. "Where's Liz? I thought I was meetin' with her today."

"Liz wishes she could be here," Marc said, "but she has the flu. You'll be meeting with me and Pastor Ritchie today. You've met Pastor Ritchie, right?"

"Oh yes, we've met." Stacey glanced away shyly, as if smitten, a look Marc had seen countless times before. Abruptly, she changed the subject and her blue eyes met Marc's. "Did you know, honey,"— she called everyone "honey" in that manufactured southern drawl of hers—"that the wind out there is really causin' a ruckus. I must look a frightful mess!"

Marc remained silent. Saying what he really thought wouldn't have been productive. As usual, Stacey looked like a hooker. Overdone makeup reddened her cheeks and bruised her eyes. Her tight, low-cut pink blouse hugged her torso, and the black leather miniskirt she had on looked to Marc like someone had wrapped electrical tape around her waist and hips.

The thick cloud of perfume that drifted around Stacey wherever she went made Marc's nose burn. If she intended the scent to be alluring, she had no clue as to its opposite effect.

After opening the meeting in prayer, Marc said, "Stacey, we're here today because of a serious matter that has come to my attention. Last spring, you made a profession of faith in Jesus Christ at the ladies' retreat, right?"

"That's right." She eyed him and Dave warily as if realizing the meeting was more than a counseling session.

"Liz has been counseling you for several months about sexual purity, but I recently learned that you've been . . . um, involved with a man who's not your husband. Is that correct?"

The layers of makeup couldn't hide the ugly look that came over her face. She stared at Marc in disbelief. "Who told you that? That's a pack of lies!"

A week ago, Liz had confronted Stacey about the reported adultery, but she'd denied the affair—had, in fact, joked about it. Marc had called the new boyfriend for the facts. The boyfriend hadn't minced words.

Liz had told Marc that Stacey was committed to mending her marriage, but apparently she'd decided to find a boyfriend instead. Marc had been praying for her and Jake to reconcile, but now he didn't see that happening unless Stacey became faithful and the Lord saved Jake's soul. It was a long shot, but Marc wasn't giving up hope. God could do anything. Marc had seen miracles happen before.

He cleared his throat. "Stacey, I've talked to Scott. I know the two of you are having an affair. Now are you going to be honest with us?"

Stacey didn't answer. She kept her lips pressed tightly together, her jaw muscles flexing.

Marc hated what needed to be said next. He'd been there when Stacey had burst into tears and confessed thoughts of suicide. He couldn't understand why she wore so much mascara when she knew it would just streak down her face like water gushing toward a storm drain.

"We're not here today to hurt you, but to help you," he continued. "As a child of God, you know you're not living the way God wants you to. We're here to remind you of what God says in His Word so you can repent of your sin and get help."

Stacey's well-manicured hands, clutching an expensive alligator purse, were trembling. When she spoke, her icy words drilled into Marc, her voice barely a whisper. "I hate you."

"I'm sorry to hear that, Stacey, but you know what? I don't hate you. Neither does Pastor Ritchie here. In fact, the whole reason we're talking to you today is because we care for you as a sister in Christ— because we want you to do the right thing, the biblical thing. God doesn't want this kind of lifestyle to continue, and neither do we. Thankfully, God is ready to forgive you if you're willing to let Him. So what do you say?"

No response. Her eyes were like bullets, lacking only a gun. Marc leaned back in his chair and took a slow, deliberate breath. He'd had difficult talks with Stacey before, talks that hadn't always ended happily. He knew how she was prone to hold things in until an explosion was imminent.

As if sensing the increasing tension in the room, Dave gave Stacey a placating smile and leaned forward, his bulging sleeves resting on the tabletop. "Stacey, we're here today to confront you about your sin, based on the instructions in Matthew 18. Liz spoke to you about this last week, but apparently you weren't ready to repent. So today Marc is confronting you, with me here as a witness. If you still choose not to repent, I'm afraid we'll have to take the matter before the church."

She certainly knew what that meant. After the next Lord's Supper, Pastor Bruce Wellers would announce her adultery to the church and implore everyone to pray for her and confront her. If she didn't repent after that, they would vote her out of church membership.

"I hate you," Stacey said, her voice rising. "I hate both of you!"

Stumbling to her feet, she skirted the edge of the table and lunged at Marc, fists raised.

CHAPTER 3

GILLIAN SAT RAMROD STRAIGHT at the kitchen table, the unfolded letter spread on the tabletop before her. The letter reeked of perfume, an aroma both seductive and repulsive. Each time her gaze drifted back to the feminine cursive and the playful shape of the letters, she wanted to tear the letter into tiny pieces.

Wanted to burn it.

Wanted to slap Marc across the face.

Fear not, for I am with you; be not dismayed, for I am your God . . .

She kept repeating Isaiah 41:10 to herself, hoping it would soothe her fury. But so far, she felt no relief. Closing her eyes, she gripped the edges of the table until her fingers ached, her knuckles white. She cast a wadded-up tissue, sodden from her tears, onto the table beside the letter and reached for another one.

Rolling her head from shoulder to shoulder, she tried to loosen the tightness in her shoulders and neck. Right now, she felt every one of her forty-two years and sensed herself aging in just a few seconds.

God, how can this be happening?

Opening her eyes, she stared at the letter that had turned to molten lead in her hand when she realized what it was.

Fear not, for I am with you; be not dismayed, for I am your God. I will strengthen you . . .

She rubbed her forehead, trying to massage the dull ache away, but it was no use. Each time she cried this way—and she'd cried a lot over the last six months—the headaches returned. Sometimes they flattened her on the couch, unable to move, every noise a serrated edge scraping across her nerves.

Rising, she turned her back to the table and faced the glass patio door. She folded her arms across her chest, her eyes sweeping across the plush lawn to her flower garden, the oasis to which she sometimes fled for private, unbidden tears.

She considered her options. Should she call her mother? Should she drive to Marc's office and confront him? At the moment, she doubted she had the presence of mind for either option. She felt beaten, downtrodden, smeared on the floor like the spider Marc had squashed a couple of weeks ago.

Marc, what on earth have you done?

Just a month ago, they had celebrated eighteen years of marriage by enjoying a romantic, candlelit dinner and a downtown performance of *Fiddler on the Roof.* Eighteen happy years—at least, that's how she had felt. So what had happened? Had she failed Marc somehow? Did he no longer find her attractive?

Combing her fingers through her wavy, shoulder-length hair, she wondered if a perm might be in order. True, she hadn't been herself lately—well, for months actually. Normally an early riser, her hair curled and makeup in place by the time Marc left for work, she'd succumbed to a routine of bumming around the house in T-shirts and jeans with little regard for her appearance. *But still, I'm a good wife. Marc knows I have stuff I'm dealing with, and he promised to be patient. So how could he do this?*

Recalling her parents' turbulent marriage, Gillian pictured her father sitting in a casino in Vegas and gambling away thirty years' worth of savings. Memories of slammed doors, voices raised, and words best unsaid skittered across her mind. Then God had reached His omnipotent fingers into her father's soul, answering thirty years' worth of prayers. Though essentially penniless, he was now a believer; but each day he lived with the regret over what he had done. Rarely at family reunions could he look her in the eye, though she always went out of her way to hug him and to tell him how much she loved him. And that she'd forgiven him.

Sometimes men struggle with secret sins. Is Marc so different?

Deep inside, she knew that Marc's willingness to counsel women had always been a problem for her. "Let a pastor's wife do it," she'd insisted. "Let someone who understands what a woman needs, how a woman's mind works." But he hadn't listened, assuring her that things would be fine, that his secretary would attend the sessions to keep things above reproach.

Above reproach.

The words rose like bile in her throat. Where were his noble goals now? She turned back to the table, her eyes drawn to the letter in spite of herself. Her hand trembled as she picked it up again.

Dearest Marc,

I love you! Are you surprised that I've written those words? Don't be. It's time that the truth came out, honey, though I think you've known the truth for quite some time, haven't you? I've always dreamed of loving a man like you. A strong man. Not someone weak, like Jake, who never cared for me as much as he cared for his precious horses. You are a beautiful man, and your words fill me with longing. I hear the tenderness in your voice, and I see the strength in your hands. And when you look into my eyes, I long to feel your arms around me again . . .

Unable to read another word, Gillian turned her face away, a throbbing ache lodged in her throat. It was bad enough that the letter continued with provocative language that escalated in a way that would have made anyone blush. More disturbing was the one word that seemed to leap above the rest.

Again.

Marc had held her in his arms *before*?

God, no. How could it be?

Then she studied the name scribbled brazenly at the bottom of the letter and understood.

Stacey James.

She had met Stacey at a women's Bible study last spring, and the woman was a real piece of work. Even at a Thursday morning study, she'd dressed like a lady of the night. Any wife with sense would have been uneasy about her husband counseling such a woman on a weekly basis. Thankfully, two months ago, Marc had delegated the counseling responsibilities to his secretary, Liz. But that gesture must not have created enough distance.

Fear not, for I am with you; be not dismayed, for I am your God. I will strengthen you, Yes, I will help you . . .

Gillian couldn't breathe; her ears filled with a white noise that made her deaf to everything else. She fumbled with the clasp to the patio door, forced the slider open, and stumbled across the patio and down the steps to the backyard. For a while, she wandered aimlessly down the path that wound through her flower garden, feeling the cool grass beneath her bare feet.

It was a beautiful fall day, and the leaves on the maple tree were slowly blushing toward crimson. Usually, the sight of her red dahlias, gladiolas, and blue hydrangeas lifted her spirits, but not today. Today, she felt nothing, as if a candle had been snuffed out deep in her soul.

Soon the cool winds of autumn would sweep in for their annual visit, bringing down leaves by the barrelful. Some people enjoyed autumn, but not her. The falling leaves reminded her of death, and death reminded her of the cemetery. And the cemetery reminded her of two little graves she hadn't visited in days.

The cemetery had become a getaway for her, a place where tears were appreciated, even expected. At least there, people understood. Marc didn't understand, and she wondered if he ever would.

My dearest children, what am I supposed to do? Does your father even love me anymore?

Gillian strolled among the flowers, spotting weeds and snatching them from the earth with satisfaction at finding something she could conquer. She didn't know where she was going, nor did she care . . . until she heard the phone ringing.

Hurrying back to the house, smearing tears away with her fingertips, she reached the phone in time. It was Crystal.

"Oh, hi, sweetie." She hoped the tears weren't evident in her voice.

She could barely concentrate on what her daughter was saying. Part of her wanted to share her discovery. After all, she needed to talk to someone—but no. Not Crystal. Her daughter adored her father and would be crushed by the weight of news like this. Gillian wondered if Marc even loved her, wondered how their marriage could survive. Divorce had become so common among friends and acquaintances. *Could it happen to us?*

Somehow, she kept her emotions in check and heard what Crystal said about the choir rehearsal, though her mind could barely function. "Okay, the practice is still on, but delayed. Got it. I'll be there to pick you up."

"Hey, you okay?"

She hooked her hair behind her ear with her free hand. "Of course, I'm fine."

"You sound kind of funny."

"I—um." Gillian tried to swallow the choking ache lodged in her throat. "I've got one of those stupid headaches again. Don't worry about me. You'd better get going. I'll see you at five thirty."

Hanging up, she went upstairs and passed the quiet, empty nursery she'd painstakingly decorated in a Peter Rabbit theme. She retreated to the master bedroom and crawled atop the dusty rose comforter, lying facedown, unable to move. She felt too numb, too exhausted, to cry.

I have to be strong. I have to confront Marc tonight.

Something like this couldn't wait. Marc had a lot to answer for, and she wasn't going to let him off easily.

CHAPTER 4

DAVE RITCHIE PLACED HIMSELF between Marc and Stacey. Grabbing Stacey's wrists, he kept her from slamming her fists into Marc's face.

"I'll kill you!" she yelled, and then added a vile string of curses. "You haven't seen the last of me!"

Marc rose from his chair and watched her tantrum, overcome by a strange peace. He'd done everything he could. God would have to deal with Stacey now.

After escorting Stacey to her car, Dave returned and looked at Marc in amazement. "Wow," he said. "She's gone, but do you want me to call the police?"

Marc scrubbed a hand across his face. "What good would that do? She already has a rap sheet a mile long." He wasn't worried about her threats. She'd been angry before, but had never been violent. When she cooled off, she'd probably call him with a tearful apology.

✳   ✳   ✳

At the end of the day, Marc grabbed his briefcase and crossed the parking lot to his navy Saturn. A burning ache in his right knee reminded him of a car accident years ago and of injuries that refused to heal . . . at least, not completely. *I've been sitting too much today.*

He'd decided to leave a half hour early, knowing he wouldn't get more work done today, not with Stacey on his mind. He'd delegated his prison ministry responsibilities so he could spend a quiet evening at home with Gillian and Crystal.

Realizing that he was hunching again, he stood up straight and pushed his shoulders back. His chiropractor had warned him of worse back pain if he didn't improve his posture. He was almost to his car when his cell phone blurted out an electronic rendition of "Ghost Riders in the Sky," one of his favorite classic cowboy songs.

"Hey, got your message." It was Liz Simons, no doubt wanting to know how the meeting had gone.

"How are you feeling? Any better?" He unlocked the car and tossed his briefcase onto the backseat.

"Some, but now my kids are getting it. So the meeting was a total disaster, huh?"

"You could say that." He gave her a play-by-play recap while strolling around the parking lot, following a crack as big as the San Andreas Fault that meandered through the aging asphalt.

"Heavens! I'm glad I wasn't there."

"Believe me, you were better off at home with the flu."

"That bad, huh?" Children squealed in the background, and Liz apologized to Marc as she shushed her kids. "I was praying for you guys. I knew Stacey wouldn't like what you had to say."

"That's the understatement of the year."

"Nothing like taking two steps forward, three steps back, huh?" She sighed. "Marc, I don't know what to say. During my meetings with Stacey, she's seemed sincere—like she really wants to do the right thing. I've probed her faith, and she appears to be connecting the dots."

"But that's the tragedy—Stacey *knows* what's right. She just doesn't want to do it. Remember, she grew up in a solid church where she heard the truth all the time. Her dad was the pastor, for goodness sakes."

"I bet if I'd been the one to confront her at the meeting, things might have gone differently."

"I'm not sure I'm following you."

Liz paused as if weighing her words. "I know this sounds weird, but I think maybe you remind Stacey of her dad. That could be the dynamic going on here."

"Uh-oh. You aren't going to go all psychobabble on me, are you?"

She chuckled. "Remember, we talked about this. We were trying to nail down what it is about you that makes Stacey go particularly gaga."

You mean my drop-dead good looks aren't enough? He shook his head at the silly thought. "But what about Scott? She's having an *affair* with *him*."

"Not to belittle Stacey's adultery, but I think her thing with Scott may have been a ploy to try to make you jealous. It's like how Stacey dresses. She's like a child who acts out to get attention. You bet she knows how to dress appropriately. And take her silly southern accent. Marc, you know she grew up in Indiana."

"Interesting. Just when I thought I finally had her figured out, you throw me a curveball." He sighed. "Okay, so let's go back to your theory. Last time we talked about this, you said maybe I remind Stacey of her dad in happier times."

"The daddy she idolized when she was a little girl. The caring counselor who had the spiritual answers to her problems. Definitely not the pastor who abandoned his family and ran off with another woman."

"Then she'd probably hate my guts, right?"

"Absolutely."

Marc mentally reviewed Stacey's sordid background. After her father's fall from grace, she had taken off on her own, determined to get a taste of the world her parents had sheltered her from. And taste the world she had. Marc had lost count of how many men had passed through the revolving door of her life. Apparently on a mission, she'd never found what she was looking for. A year or so ago, she'd begun attending church again, and God had appeared to be doing a work in her life. But then came her fixation on him.

Liz said, "There *are* similarities between you and her dad. He was a pastor. You're a pastor. I've never met him, of course, but I've seen pictures, and there's even a slight resemblance."

"Fascinating. I think I'm beginning to see why my rebuke might have set her off. It was like experiencing her dad's rejection all over again."

"Bingo! So now what?"

"Now we sit tight and hope she comes around. She knows what's broken, and she knows how to fix it. It's up to her to do the right thing, take responsibility for her actions, and not play the victim card."

"Well, I need to go. I'll keep praying."

"Why don't we pray right now?" After the prayer, Marc said good-bye and clicked off. He turned his face toward the sun. *God, please help Stacey to repent. She can still come back to You and do the right thing.*

Movement blurred at the edge of his vision.

Marc swung around, but nobody was there. It was just his overactive imagination, he decided. He had to admit that Stacey's threat had rattled him. He'd seen her upset before, but he'd never seen her attempt physical violence.

Getting into his car, Marc reached for the automatic door locks and scanned the parking lot through his mirrors. Feeling foolish, he started the engine, steered the car out of the parking lot, and headed toward the expressway while the Sons of the Pioneers sang "Red River Valley."

CHAPTER 5

IN CINCINNATI, THEY FOUND the body in a patch of woods—two boys who were looking for their lost dog and reportedly didn't realize what they were seeing. Repulsed by the terrible smell, they hadn't lingered long enough to get a good look and engrave the image of the strangled girl in their minds forever.

Mercifully, they had run. Fast. One of the boy's mothers had called the police, and that's why Chuck Riley's going-away party had been interrupted.

It was supposed to have been a happy occasion, his retirement after serving the Cincinnati Police Department as a homicide detective for more than thirty years. Jerry, Greg, and his other buddies had thrown the party for him, complete with cake, junk food, and sparkling grape juice.

Riley was impressed that they'd honored his Christian beliefs and hadn't brought a keg or two. For years, he'd been trying to be a witness on the job—not always as successfully as he would have liked. *But God blesses in spite of our meager efforts.*

Jerry O'Hearn—a divorced, stock car racing fanatic with loneliness staring him square in the face—had been the first to drop to his knees and trust Jesus Christ as his personal Savior. As Riley's best friend and partner, O'Hearn was taking Riley's retirement harder than anybody, even harder than Riley himself.

As far as the other guys, Riley planned to keep their names in his little black notepad where he jotted down prayer requests, among other things, throughout the day. And he always made good on those prayer requests, too—at least a half hour each morning.

Some of the guys called him "Preacher." Well, that was fine by him. Retirement or not, he'd be praying for those guys faithfully for a long time—and not just for their souls. He knew what it was like being a homicide detective in a crime-infested city like Cincinnati, with a murder rate more than four times the national average.

In the middle of the party, right after they'd cut the cake, the telephone jangled and it was time to get back to work.

"No fair!" O'Hearn's right hand held a piece of cake while his left clapped Riley on the shoulder. "This is your last day on the job. This is your party. You can't go out now."

Riley hung up the phone. He had been inclined to agree, but he'd taken the call himself.

"Riley, you okay?" asked Mario, a Hispanic officer and the father of five. "You don't look so good."

All eyes were on the retiring officer. Riley rubbed his lower lip with the ball of his thumb. "Sorry, guys, the party's over. They just found a dump site on the south side. It looks like another strangling."

CHAPTER 6

MARC FOUND A NOTE from Gillian taped to the front door. "Picking Crystal up from choir practice. Chili's in fridge. Gillian."

He studied the note, struck by Gillian's abrupt, matter-of-fact tone. So things had come to this. Whatever happened to the playful love notes, written in calligraphy, she used to leave in his sock drawer? Why no Shakespeare sonnets or excerpts from Browning? Gillian scripted love poems in calligraphy for clients every day; she couldn't help knowing them by heart.

But do I know her by heart? God, whatever happened to the woman I married?

Groaning in his spirit, Marc entered the spacious, two-story Victorian. Usually, Max, the Thayers' seven-year-old black Lab, greeted him at the front door with a spirited tongue-licking and tail-lashing. But the dog was nowhere in sight.

Stepping into the living room, Marc cast his suit coat over a nearby antique rocker and whistled for the dog. Gillian rarely took Max with her in the Tahoe, because she hated how his black hair stuck to the tan seats. And if she *had* taken Max, certainly she would have said so in her note.

"Max?" Marc called. "Here, boy!"

Silence.

Something was wrong.

Glancing around warily, Marc crept to the mudroom, where Max's food and water containers were kept. As he entered the small room, fine hairs rose on the back of his neck.

Max was sprawled on his side across the hardwood floor.

He didn't move. His brown, sightless eyes stared vacantly. His tongue, swollen and gray, protruded from his open mouth.

His senses on high alert, Marc crouched beside the dog and felt his side. Max wasn't breathing. Marc noticed a rawhide bone he didn't recognize. The bone had been dipped in something foul. The acrid smell made his stomach heave.

Repulsed, Marc rose and backed out of the room and into the kitchen, his legs weak. Someone had poisoned the dog, and that someone could still be lurking somewhere inside the house. He decided to call the police from the safety of a neighbor's house. That is, if he could get out the—

A loud, shattering sound made Marc's heart seize in his chest. The sound had come from upstairs. He imagined the large bathroom mirrors shattering into a thousand pieces and remembered Stacey's fury that morning. Had she broken into his house and waited for him to come home? She *had* spent time in jail for breaking and entering, so he couldn't put it past her.

Okay, Thayer, get a grip. You had a bad experience today. You're still shaken up. Think clearly. Stacey's a seductress, but she's no stalker or vandal.

Still, her parting words echoed in his mind. *I'll kill you!*

He hadn't taken her threat seriously. Had that been a mistake?

More glass shattered upstairs.

Marc grabbed the phone. As he punched 9-1-1, he felt a draft, saw the shifting curtains, and noticed the shattered patio door. His pulse spiked.

A woman picked up on the first ring. "Streamwood 9-1-1. What's your emergency?"

Marc's breath came in short, quick gasps. Trying to calm himself, he loosened his tie. "Someone killed my dog, and I think they're still upstairs in my house. Three twenty-three Green Meadows Boulevard. Send the police. Hurry!"

Marc dropped the cordless phone on the counter and rifled through the kitchen drawers, searching for something he might use as a weapon. Sweat dripped down his forehead and stung his eyes as he debated what to do. His 9mm Glock, which he'd purchased for such a time as this, was upstairs under the bed.

Should he go upstairs or wait for the police?

Something else shattered. It sounded like a demolition team from one of those home improvement shows was taking out the entire second floor. He imagined Gillian's antique Tiffany lamp being pulverized and felt angrier by the second. He knew he needed to watch his temper, but how could he ignore what was happening?

Grabbing the biggest kitchen knife he could find, he headed for the stairs. When he reached the top, he turned left and followed the hallway toward the master bedroom, the source of all the racket.

His back pressed to the wall, he held the knife in front of him and took one measured step at a time. He bumped into a wall hanging, but stopped and righted it before it could fall.

After a few more cautious steps, he reached the doorway to the master bedroom. The door was open, and the noise had ceased. Steeling his nerves, he peered inside.

The room looked like a fallout zone. The bedding and mattress were torn to shreds. The doors of the cherry armoire hung on twisted hinges. The beautiful mirror he'd given Gillian on their tenth anniversary had been smashed, its wood frame splintered. As he'd expected, the Tiffany lamp was history. But where was the intruder?

Marc scanned every corner and glanced into every conceivable hiding place, but there was no one to be found. And not even a sound, except the minuscule *tick tick tick* of the anniversary clock on the bedside table. Amazingly, the clock and table were still intact.

Setting the knife aside, he knelt beside the bed and reached underneath. His fingers fumbled with the clasps on the gun case, and he grasped at the pistol's cool, polymer stock. He checked the magazine. *Empty!* Where had he put the bullets? Gillian often teased him about his forgetfulness, but right now, it wasn't funny. Brushing a sleeve across his forehead, he realized his shirt was soaked in sweat.

Casting the gun aside in frustration, he retrieved the knife and rose to his feet. He knew the intruder must still be somewhere in the room. Only two hiding places remained—the closet, which was right beside him, or the master bath. He eyed the closet and shook his head. *No, too much junk stored in there.*

Inching toward the master bath, wincing as his shoes crunched on broken glass, he peered through the dark doorway and reached in for the light switch.

The marquee-style lights over the vanity came on in a blaze.

Standing rigid beside the bathtub, Stacey James held a gun with both hands at arm's length, elbows locked.

The barrel did a little dance in her shaking hands. She was aiming the gun at him.

Mascara had streaked down her rage-twisted face. Her cheek twitched. A wounded, keening sound escaped her lips.

"I told you I'd kill you," she said between clenched teeth. Then she pulled the trigger.

CHAPTER 7

THE SUN SMEARED A crimson band across the thick, cumulus clouds that scudded across an otherwise perfectly blue sky. Where the Tahoe's visor couldn't reach, Gillian raised a hand to ward off the sun's blinding glare and did a quick head check before flicking on her directional and changing lanes.

Slouching in the front passenger seat, Crystal was strangely quiet, her gaze directed somewhere out the window. She was wearing her new wire rim glasses, which Gillian thought gave her an appealing, scholarly look. Crystal had openly declared that she couldn't stand them, but at least now her headaches were going away.

Her tapping hand on the armrest was apparently keeping time with a tune in her head, since the radio and CD player were off, and the car was silent. Today she wore a sensible, short-sleeved lime T-shirt, a jean skirt, and sandals. A strand of wavy, blonde hair came loose from where she'd tucked it behind her ear and spilled across her tan face. She impatiently brushed the hair aside, fingernails polished and glistening.

Seeing her daughter's radiant but innocent beauty reminded Gillian why she was an overprotective mom and was especially suspicious of attentive young men. Which meant Crystal resented her on occasion, because she happened to like attentive young men.

Lost in her thoughts, Crystal didn't seem to notice Gillian's puffy eyes or pinched face, to which Gillian had applied extra makeup. Gillian hoped her daughter wouldn't notice her voice, which resounded in a lower register, as if she were fighting a cold.

After merging onto the highway, Gillian asked, "Okay, are you going to tell me what's up? You're awfully quiet."

"I don't want to talk about it."

"Did one of your friends do something to make you mad?"

"Mom, *please.*"

"Is it boy trouble?" The lengthening silence confirmed that she'd hit the mark.

"Maybe."

"Why don't you tell me?"

Crystal sighed. "Okay, Christy Nichols was flirting with Ryan at choir practice today. It just ticked me off. That's all."

Lately, Crystal had been smitten with Ryan Brodski, a guy in her church youth group. A black belt in karate, he was from an upstanding, respectable family and at the top of the short list when it came to decent, God-loving guys Crystal's age. Gillian thought they made a cute couple and hated to think that something had come between them. "Got some competition, huh?"

"If you want to call it that."

"Well, if Ryan is committed to your relationship, then you don't have anything to worry about, right?" *Just listen to yourself. You find a love letter to your husband and automatically assume he's been having an affair. What a hypocrite!*

Crystal shrugged. "I guess not. It just bothered me. That's all."

Competition should *bother you. I know how you feel.*

Anger flared like an unquenchable fire as Gillian remembered the letter she'd found that morning. Throughout the afternoon and during the half-hour drive to pick up her daughter, potential scenarios had run through her mind. Reasons for a committed husband and loving father like Marc to cheat on her. After pushing her feelings aside and thinking rationally (a step often late in coming), Gillian couldn't ignore another possibility.

Perhaps Stacey's letter was a lie. Perhaps her anger toward Marc was exactly what Stacey had intended. Maybe Stacey had fabricated the letter and planted it in an obvious place, knowing Gillian would find it and take Marc to task.

Or what if an affair *had* been going on, and Stacey, tired of the hypocrisy, had wanted Gillian to know the truth? That possibility made the hussy seem a tad less offensive, though it made Gillian's anger at Marc more acute.

Familiar words from Shakespeare's *Much Ado About Nothing* wafted through her brain. "Sigh no more ladies, sigh no more. Men were deceivers ever."

Deceivers. That's for sure! Gillian's hands tightened around the steering wheel, her gaze lingering on an overpass that stretched starkly across the horizon.

Marc had told her that he'd discontinued his counseling sessions with Stacey due to her obvious desire for more than a counseling relationship. Perhaps Stacey had felt rejected and had sought revenge. The possibility took the edge off Gillian's anger and made her feel foolish for crying herself to sleep earlier that afternoon.

Perhaps, as usual, I've jumped to conclusions and thought the worst of Marc before giving him the benefit of the doubt. She bit the inside of her cheek. *God, I'm so clueless. Please change me.*

As the road unraveled before her, she realized she'd never know the truth until she confronted Marc, hard as that might be. But even with the possibility of Stacey's deception, she couldn't shake the gut-wrenching suspicion that Marc was still somehow to blame.

The sky was darkening, the sunset only a memory, when they exited the highway and turned onto a familiar street. A remnant of the old, historical district, their neighborhood was lined with perfectly manicured yards and pristine Victorian homes, not the ranches and frame houses so typical throughout the western suburbs. The fact that they lived here—on a modest pastor's salary—still amazed Gillian.

When the Victorian went on the market eight years ago, she and Marc had taken a tour on a whim, well knowing they could never afford such a palatial place. But the stooped, white-haired owner had perked up when Marc told him he was a pastor. Something had sparked in the old man's heart, and a twinkle had come to his eyes.

"My father was a pastor," he'd said, his eyes misting. "He would have been happy for someone like you to come along. Guess what? I'm feeling generous today." He'd then proceeded to offer them a deal no one in his right mind could have refused.

Now, cruising down their street, just a block from the house,

Gillian touched the brakes when she saw flashing blue and red lights ahead. "Somebody must have been speeding," she said. The police were particularly attentive to the speed limit in their neighborhood.

The twirling lights kaleidoscoped into the trees, bathing them in a surreal glow. Then Gillian realized that what she was seeing went far beyond a speeding violation. So many police cruisers jammed the street, their roof-rack beacons flashing, that she wasn't sure she could get through.

Crystal clutched her arm, her fingers like talons. "Mom, they're parked in front of our house."

The planet tilted, and Gillian struggled to maintain her equilibrium. With heart-sickening certainty, she realized their driveway was cordoned off. Not knowing where to park, she pulled alongside the curb in the only remaining spot and put the Tahoe into park.

For a moment, she sat and blinked, debating what to do. Policemen and other people she didn't recognize were milling around in their driveway and tromping across their yard.

An impatient-looking policeman strolled toward the Tahoe and tapped Gillian's window. He favored her with weary, brown eyes and a meaty face, his fingers as fat as sausages.

Gillian realized her hands were shaking as she reached for the switch. The window slid down noiselessly.

"Ma'am, you need to keep moving down the street."

"But I live here. This is my house."

He paused to take this in. "You're Gillian Thayer?"

"Yes."

A wary look flickered in his eyes. He knew something, but wasn't saying it, at least not yet. He jerked his thumb. "Mrs. Thayer, please come with me."

Gillian turned off the engine, got out, and followed him, Crystal at her side. "What's happened?"

The policeman ignored her question and turned to address Crystal. "Who are you?"

"This is my daughter," Gillian said more curtly than she'd intended. "Now would you mind telling me what's going on? This is my house. I want to know."

Hesitating, he studied Crystal's face. He was mostly bald, and what was left of his thinning, brown hair was laced with gray. He probably had a wife and kids and had seen enough of life to know how painful, how merciless, it could be. He glanced back at the house—Gillian's house—drawing conclusions, making decisions.

Finally, he motioned them toward a police car. "Follow me, please."

Gillian wondered why they couldn't just sit in her living room and talk. *Because the house is a crime scene,* she realized with disturbing, jolting clarity.

Once they were seated in the car, which reeked of secondhand cigarette smoke that made Gillian's nose burn, the policeman's words confirmed her worst fears. "Your husband was shot by an intruder. I'm afraid your dog's dead, too. Probably poisoned. A neighbor heard a gunshot and called us." His tone was matter-of-fact, as if he were telling his buddies what he'd eaten for lunch.

A clammy coldness crawled across Gillian's skin, as if someone had turned off the heat and the whole world had gone frigid. She grabbed Crystal's hand, hoping for warmth, but her daughter's fingers were just as icy as hers.

Gillian brought a hand to her mouth. "Is Marc okay?"

"He was alive, but barely, when the paramedics got here. They rushed him to the hospital for emergency surgery. Sorry, I don't know anything about his status."

Gillian squeezed her eyes closed. All day, she'd felt furious toward Marc and had wanted to slap him hard across the face. Now, she felt the gravity of her thoughts, and guilt struck her like a hammer. Bent forward, face in her hands, Gillian heard a distant sobbing and realized it was her own. An arm was around her. Crystal's arm.

Raising her head, arms braced against her knees, she could see the police officer through her tears, the innocent bearer of terrible news. He was crouched beside the open door, glancing off into the street, the awkwardness palpable. Inside the car, the radio crackled. Disembodied voices announced police codes and street names of people and problems she knew nothing about.

So much cruelty and evil in the world. God, where are You in all this? Gillian sat up and wiped her face. "I want to see my husband."

The policeman nodded and stood. "I'll drive you to the hospital, but first I'd like to ask you some questions. Your neighbor said he saw a woman fleeing the scene, but we haven't yet been able to make a positive ID. I was hoping you might have an idea who she is."

CHAPTER 8

SHINING HIS FLASHLIGHT ALONG a dark alley in Elmwood Place, Chuck Riley followed O'Hearn toward another reminder of grim mortality. It was near midnight on a sticky, humid evening, and most of Cincinnati was asleep.

Emily was probably in bed right now, wondering where he was. He had told her he'd be late, celebrating his retirement with the guys. He realized now that he'd be a lot later than expected, and he hoped she wouldn't worry.

He braced himself for what lay ahead. So far, the perp had been organized, almost staged, in how he'd left the bodies. What kind of man was he? Was he purely evil or perhaps just a man driven by his own lusts, by pure rage?

Riley couldn't help considering the spiritual implications, reminding himself that the man responsible for the crime was a sinner just like him—was, in fact, just another sinner Jesus had died to save. If only the sinner could come to the end of himself, could call out for mercy. Jesus could forgive him, because Jesus could forgive anyone.

Riley reflected on his life and on the years of emotional abuse he'd inflicted on his wife and daughter long before he met Christ. God had been merciful and had given him a new life and a second chance. If God hadn't intervened, Riley wondered where he'd be now. Certainly divorced. Probably pickling his brain in a bar somewhere.

He knew where evil could lead, and the picture wasn't pretty.

The alley grew brighter. Ahead glowed an amalgamation of blue and red lights from several unmarked police units. Nearby stood an EMS truck and an ambulance. As usual, a crowd of bystanders had swarmed to the spot, their eyes anxious, their voices troubled. Why weren't these people at home in bed?

Riley and O'Hearn angled their way through the crowd and approached the grassy edge of a cracked parking lot. Even after so many years of seeing the evidence of violent crime, Riley still felt a small, tight place in his stomach. Some things you just never get used to. *Thank You, Jesus, for keeping me sensitive.*

Beyond the parking lot stretched a small, densely wooded area choked by creepers and briar bushes. Ten feet into the trees, beyond the yellow crime-scene tape, a couple of investigators were conferring about something on the ground. Riley was glad the group was small. Too many investigators threatened a scene with contamination.

He reached into his pocket for a stick of Wrigley's Juicy Fruit gum. Unwrapping it, he folded it into his mouth, the sweetness always triggering an uncanny alertness. It was an unusual habit, and O'Hearn often teased him about it. But the gum always seemed to help him somehow. Why stop a good thing?

A step ahead, O'Hearn lifted the tape to let Riley duck under. A familiar officer, whose name Riley couldn't remember, was guarding the perimeter and the entrance to the crime scene. He checked their names on a crime scene attendance list and stepped aside. That's when Riley saw her.

Small. Young. Blonde haired. What was she doing out here alone? She should have been home with her parents, safe in bed. The wad of gum sat on Riley's tongue like a rock.

Numbered cards were stationed on the ground around the body, indicating possible evidence. He noticed the rope around her neck and studied the knots. He was certain he'd seen this ligature before, but he didn't want to make premature assumptions.

Cliff Henry, the forensic pathologist, clad in protective coveralls and gloves, was taking soil samples that could later be compared to soil found on a suspect's shoes. Bending over the body, an ID officer was coating various surfaces with dusting powder, searching for latent fingerprints, those not visible to the naked eye. Another SOCO—a scene of crime officer—was videotaping the scene from various angles. And as if video wasn't good enough, a crime scene photographer was shooting stills, his flash igniting the woods, making Riley's eyes ache.

Someone moved close to Riley's side. It was Brent Jenkins, a young cop who had assisted Riley on countless cases. Husky but not from lifting weights, Jenkins was in a perpetual pant, even when he wasn't in a hurry. Today he was breathing harder than ever. "Looks like . . . she's been here . . . a couple days at least."

Riley nodded. The stench of decomposing flesh had already confirmed that fact.

"Any identification?" O'Hearn grasped wattles of skin at his neck.

Jenkins studied his notepad. "We did a fingertip search . . . and found her glasses and purse. Her name's Amanda Forbes. A high school student."

Using low-tack adhesive tape, a SOCO in gloves and coveralls was lifting prints off Amanda's purse and mounting them on an acetate sheet for further study.

Riley nodded. "Parents been notified?"

"I believe someone is . . . calling them now," Jenkins said.

Riley stared off into space. Somewhere, a parent was hearing the words no parent should ever hear. *Your daughter has been strangled.* Of course, he couldn't be positive about cause of death until the medical examiner conducted the autopsy. But he'd seen this signature before—or had he?

As much as he hated it, Riley knew he needed a closer look. Fishing latex gloves and a face mask out of his pocket, he pulled them on—first blowing into the gloves to expand the fingers—and stepped closer.

He knew better than to touch the body—that was the medical examiner's job—but he'd been on the trail of this perp for too long not to take a look for himself. That way, if vital clues were missed, he had no one to blame but himself. Lyrics from a familiar hymn tickled his memory. *Open my eyes, that I may see / Glimpses of truth Thou hast for me.*

Crouching, he tried to examine the details objectively and not to think about his own little girl, Samantha, now a grown woman with a husband and twin daughters.

Lying on her back in a burgundy shirt and navy capris, Amanda Forbes looked as if she were asleep, her head angled to one side. Long, blonde hair, styled in a layered cut, fell past the collar of her shirt. Cheap, silver stars gleamed from thin, almost translucent earlobes. She looked stylish really—until one saw her face, which was an unnatural shade of blue and purple due to the unmercifully tight cord around her neck.

She was stiff from rigor mortis—which meant she'd been killed at least twelve hours ago; the medical examiner would pinpoint the time of death more precisely. Someone had already bagged her hands, secured at the wrists by rubber bands. Later, the medical examiner would check under her fingernails for hair, skin, and other sources of the killer's DNA.

Then he noticed it—the detail he might have missed without closer inspection.

Amanda Forbes's eyes were closed.

Rising, his knees creaking, Riley turned to Jenkins. "This the way you found her?"

"Absolutely. Nobody's laid a finger on her . . . since we got here."

A childhood memory skittered across Riley's mind. A dead deer with staring eyes was enough to scare a child spitless. No, the boys who found the body hadn't closed Amanda's eyes—he was sure about that.

But if the boys hadn't done it, who had? The perp? If so, why? Might the cold-blooded killer be not so cold-blooded after all? Could he have acted out of a blind rage, only to awaken seconds later, remorseful about what he had done?

Riley's partnership with the FBI on several investigations had taught him a thing or two about behavioral profiling. The killer here had concealed Amanda's body in the brush and had closed her eyes, clear signs of remorse and reverence for the dead. This wasn't a killing he was proud of. But why?

Riley recalled the other strangling victims. Had their eyes been closed, too? He would have to check the case files again and compare the details. Then again, wasn't he retiring? In fact, wasn't this his last night on the streets?

"Did you see the rope?" O'Hearn asked.

Riley nodded. "It's the same signature. Even the knots match."

"So we're pretty certain then?" Jenkins asked.

The hole in Riley's stomach plummeted to China.

Over the last four years, Cincinnati had been terrorized by a string of serial killings. All victims were white females in their late teens and early twenties; all with blue eyes; long, blonde hair; and wire rim glasses. All were considered low risk, which meant their lifestyle hadn't particularly placed them in harm's way. High-risk victims would have included prostitutes, strippers, and battered women, but these were mostly high school girls or young women with normal jobs and loving families.

Each victim—this was the fourth—had been strangled with a trick rope, the type magicians use to entertain children with simple knot tricks. Riley felt ill when he considered how an object of entertainment had been used to end someone's life in such a gruesome manner. The unique nature of the rope was a detail that law enforcement officials had withheld from the media, for the purpose of identifying the killer if and when he was caught.

ViCAP, the Violent Criminal Apprehension Program database, hadn't identified any murders using a similar rope anywhere else in the country. Therefore, they knew the strangler had thus far confined himself to Cincinnati. Unfortunately, an analysis of the rope had confirmed that it was a typical magician's trick rope, sold by several manufacturers and used by thousands of magicians worldwide.

The first murder had occurred almost exactly four years ago. A young girl had witnessed her babysitter being pulled into a car before the driver sped away. Unfortunately, the witness was too young to provide a usable description of the abductor or his car.

The second murder, about nine months later, had been similar to the first. A girl walking home from a party in a suburban neighborhood had been picked up by an unknown assailant, strangled, and later dumped at a secondary location.

The third strangling, which involved a risky abduction in the parking lot of a busy mall, had been more than a year ago.

At first, Riley had vowed not to retire until the Magician Murderer was caught. But when the trail went cold, and with the pressure at home from Emily, he had finally realized it was time. He had no choice. He couldn't stay on the force forever. And even now, with a fresh victim and a fresh set of clues, he couldn't delay his retirement a day longer.

If he went home now and told Emily he was staying on, she would either kill him or leave him. She wasn't about to postpone their retirement plans. Not after all the neglect she'd suffered due to his inhumane schedule. Not after all the nights when she'd feared he wouldn't come home. Still, he hated to leave things undone. It wasn't a language he spoke.

On the way back to headquarters, Riley spotted a phone booth and asked O'Hearn to pull over. His partner glanced at him with questioning eyes. "You okay?"

"I'm fine. Just need to make a call, that's all."

"That's what your cell phone's for, buddy."

"A private call, okay? I want to use the pay phone." He'd never gotten used to the cell phone anyhow.

"Okay, okay. Don't get all uptight."

After O'Hearn pulled over, Riley put his change into the pay phone and spat out his gum. When he heard the familiar voice at the other end, he felt foolish.

"Dad, is that you?"

He imagined wide, brown eyes. A whimsical smile. Hair pulled back in a wispy French braid. "Hey, Samantha. How are you doing, pumpkin?"

"I'm okay, Dad. It's awfully late. What's wrong? Is Mom okay?"

"Your mother's fine. I just—I just wanted to call to make sure you're okay."

"Of course, I'm okay. Why wouldn't I be?"

Riley felt his face burn. *Stupid idea.* "I just had the sudden impulse that I needed to call you. That's all."

"Well, I'm fine. The twins are fine. Darrell's fine. Are you sure you're okay?"

No, I'm not okay. Thank God, I'm getting out of this city, and I'm never coming back. "I just saw something tonight that, uh . . . made me think of you."

"Dad, I'm so glad you're retiring. It'll do wonders for you and Mom."

Wonders. That's what Emily hoped. He had to admit their marriage hadn't been the greatest over the last decade; and the fault, he knew, lay entirely at his feet. He had let his job, the morbid work he did, skew his priorities and push him away from the woman who loved him more than life itself. He knew it was true and knew he didn't deserve any of her love.

Back in the car, with O'Hearn's lead foot on the accelerator, Riley felt foolish. Samantha was right. It was good that he was retiring. This wasn't his line of work anymore. Besides, he was pushing seventy. He was too old, too spent. He had lost his edge a long time ago, and everybody, including O'Hearn, knew it. He needed to get far away from the city and from the murders.

Emily's plans included a condo in Florida overlooking the ocean. They would spend their days strolling the beach and their evenings watching the sunset. Peace would pervade their lives, and he would never need to investigate another gruesome murder case again.

CHAPTER 9

"IT'S ONLY FOR ONE night, honey. I'll be leavin' tomorrow mornin'."

"Well, I guess it should be okay." Maralee Pochek stood on her front porch, hands tucked into the pockets of her roomy shorts, her flowery blouse bright enough to make Stacey's eyes hurt, even in the semidarkness of the porch light. Maralee glanced at the street, forehead furrowed, and peered down at Stacey. "Where's your car?"

"I walked."

"You walked." Maralee shook her head, black curls brushing the tops of her shoulders. "So what's this all about?"

Stacey recognized Maralee's tone and hoped she wouldn't give her a hard time. "Don't even ask. I'm sorry for comin' unannounced like this."

Maralee perched her hands on her hips. "I'd feel better if you told me what's going on."

Stacey mounted the steps until they were at eye level. "We've been friends how long—fifteen years? Have I ever asked you to do a favor like this before?"

"No—"

"Remember the times you needed cash. Did I demand an explanation? No. That's what good friends do—they're willin' to help each other out. No questions asked."

Stacey didn't want to linger on the porch; somebody might drive by and see her, and remember her face. Neighbors might wonder who she was and ask too many questions.

Brushing past her friend, Stacey entered the tiny living room, which reeked of cigarette smoke, and glimpsed the corner piano where

Maralee taught children how to play "Mary Had a Little Lamb" to help make ends meet. She was just another woman in a long line of single moms trying to raise a family without a husband's support. Two unimaginative end-table lamps provided enough light so that Stacey didn't trip on the toys and break her neck.

"But why can't you just go home?" Maralee followed Stacey inside and closed the door. "You got a nicer place than I do. Did you and Jake have another fight? Is that what this is all about?"

You can't have a fight with somebody who doesn't even talk to you. Stacey faced her friend, trying to hide her desperation. "Ask me no questions, and I'll tell you no lies."

"Stacey, c'mon. What gives? You've been crying." Maralee touched her arm, her dark eyes widening. "Hey, you're shaking, too. What's happened?"

Stacey pulled away, her defenses beginning to crumble. "Please— just—don't ask, okay? You're better off not knowin'."

Maralee looked her in the eye, her pretty, oval face begging the question of why any man would turn his back on such a face. "But I have to ask. I've got kids, remember? I don't want you bringing trouble into my house."

Stacey lifted her hands, palms out. "This doesn't have nothin' to do with harmin' you or your kids. I promise. I just—I just can't go home right now, okay? In fact, I just want to go to bed." She headed for the guest bedroom, hoping Maralee would get the hint. A tune from a music box—"Twinkle, Twinkle Little Star"—drifted down the hall.

"Where's your suitcase?" Maralee called, as if forgetting she'd just put her girls to bed. "Didn't you even bring a toothbrush?"

Deciding that silence was best, Stacey entered the tiny bedroom and closed the door. She flicked on the bedside lamp and perched on the edge of the bed as the tears came—a torrent of unexpected emotion flooding over her.

Sure, she'd done a lot of things she wasn't proud of, but she'd never killed somebody before.

Maralee's half whisper penetrated the door, betraying a tinge of hurt. "Stacey, this isn't fair. You need to tell me what's going on. Friends don't keep secrets like this."

Stacey somehow found her voice. "I can't talk now."

Maralee's voice softened. "This isn't like you. Something really bad must have happened. You sure you're okay?"

"I'll tell you all about it in the mornin'. I promise."

Uncertainty edged Maralee's voice. "Okay, but if there's anything you need, you just let me know, okay? Good night."

Tears clogged Stacey's throat, making a reply impossible.

Maralee's feet padded away.

Stacey pulled herself into a fetal position on the bed and let herself cry.

So tired. So confused. What was she going to do?

When she closed her eyes, a video clip played in a maddening, endless loop. Marc peering stupidly at the dime-size hole in his dress shirt as the seeping blood spread across his chest. His right hand reaching toward the wound as if his mind were incapable of processing what she'd just done. Then, in slow motion, his body crumpling to the floor—and the sound! A dull, clumsy thud that reverberated endlessly in her mind.

She'd killed him. The only man she truly loved.

Why had he said those mean things to her? Threatening her like that when he was the one man whose opinion truly mattered? She'd tried so hard to win his heart, but he'd made his decision. His rejection had left her only one choice. Given a second chance, she was certain she wouldn't have changed a thing.

He was dead, and that's just the way things were.

But now she had no idea what to do, where to go. She couldn't go back to the beautiful, two-story colonial she shared with Jake, or to the valuable doll collection she'd maintained since childhood. She had always wanted to be like one of those dolls—perfect and unchanging. Without anything to worry about. Without feelings.

Feelings are exactly what caused this mess.

Tears pooled in her eyes again, causing her recently reapplied mascara to run in dirty black streaks. She rose, opened the door, and crossed the hall to Maralee's bathroom. Peering into the mirror, she cringed.

She'd watched enough crime shows to realize she was covered

in crime scene evidence invisible to the naked eye. Had firing the gun left gunpowder residue on her hands, on her clothes? If the cops showed up now, that evidence alone would be enough to send her to prison. At least she'd hidden the gun in a safe place; they'd never find it and she could retrieve it later.

Grabbing a bar of soap, she scrubbed her hands under scalding hot water until her skin was raw. She studied her clothes and considered her options. Perhaps in the morning she could leave the clothes here and ask Maralee for something to borrow. Better yet, she'd take them with her and burn them.

Peering into her red-rimmed eyes, she realized her biggest problem was still unresolved. Where could she go? She couldn't go home; the police would look there first, and Jake would never let her in anyhow, especially once he knew about the shooting. Scott had recently dumped her—there was no hope of going back to him, not that he meant anything to her anyhow.

Where else would the police look? They were probably knocking on her mom's door right now. What would her mom say when she heard the news? How would she feel? Stacey had given up trying to meet her mom's high expectations long ago, and what she'd done only hours ago certainly wouldn't help matters.

Staying here seemed like the best option. As long as Maralee remained blissfully ignorant, she couldn't get into trouble for harboring her. But Maralee wanted answers, and Stacey couldn't hide the truth forever. She'd promised to tell Maralee in the morning. Why had she done that? Biting her lip, she wracked her brain for a solution.

An insistent knock on the bathroom door broke into her thoughts. She heard Maralee's shaky voice. "Stacey, you need to come see this."

Stacey bolted out of the bathroom and dashed to the living room. A newscast was in progress on the TV.

Maralee lingered at her side, breathing hard. "Somebody shot that pastor friend of yours."

Stacey shushed her friend as a Ward Cleaver look-alike peered off camera, presumably at a reporter, and talked excitedly into a black microphone. "Yeah, I heard something that sounded like a gunshot coming from the Thayers' house. Then a minute or two later, I see this woman run out of the house with a gun in her hand. She yelled something about a man trying to rape her and took off down the sidewalk."

Stacey smiled to herself. The rape accusation had been a nice touch.

The man continued. "Something was obviously wrong, so I called the police. The Thayers are nice people and have never caused trouble in our neighborhood as far as I can remember."

The video feed switched to the newsroom. An immaculately dressed man with model good looks and a radio-quality voice read the teleprompter with panache. "Again, authorities have not yet identified the shooter, who is still at large. Residents are encouraged to exercise extreme caution. The assailant is considered armed and dangerous."

Maralee stared at Stacey, her eyes widening. "No way! It was you, wasn't it?"

When Stacey didn't reply, Maralee backed away. "You said you weren't bringing trouble here. He says you got a gun."

"I don't have it with me. Did you think I'd bring a gun into your house?"

"What am I supposed to think?" Maralee's voice rose an octave. "You shot somebody. I can't believe this." Hands shaking, she somehow managed to light a cigarette.

Stacey tried to tune her out and focus on the announcer.

"Anyone with information related to the shooting, please call the number listed at the bottom of your screen. Meanwhile, Thayer remains in serious condition at Stroger Hospital."

Stacey's heart somersaulted. *Marc is still alive!* A flood of disappointment and relief warred inside her like opposing armies.

Fool! She should have emptied the gun into him. Just to be sure.

Crossing the room, Maralee grabbed the cordless telephone and thrust it toward Stacey's face, her lips a tight seam, her eyes livid. "You got exactly five minutes to get out of here before I call the police."

CHAPTER 10

WHILE MARIA FROM *West Side Story* serenaded him from the CD player, Haydon Owens pressed the accelerator of his brown Chevy sedan and watched Cincinnati disappear in his rearview mirror. It was barely dawn on Tuesday morning, and he was making his getaway while the city was still asleep.

Last night, his final performance with Rent-a-Magician had been bittersweet. The school gym had been crammed with cheering children who had been eager to watch him make Sandy disappear in his massive trunk. As usual, he'd felt invincible in his traditional black suit, red-velvet-lined cape, and top hat. He'd performed the illusions flawlessly, his only slipup occurring when he saw a girl on the front row who looked vaguely familiar.

Blonde hair. Blue eyes. Wire rim glasses.

Palms moist, he tried to focus on his driving and on his destination. He remembered Michigan from his boyhood as a land of lakes and woods. He never dreamed he'd be heading to the North Woods to live, but first he had another destination in mind.

The sun hadn't yet risen, but the sky's meager light had been sufficient for packing the sedan and his trailer of Houdini memorabilia and magician equipment. After one last, quick pass to wipe down doorknobs, light switches, and countertops, he had slipped quietly out of the apartment complex forever.

Cincinnati had never been home to him, so he felt nothing akin to sadness. What he did feel was a sense of exhilaration at the thought of making a clean break, of leaving his darkest demons behind. Starting over had a cleansing feel, a purifying effect. He felt a heavy burden lifted at the thought of putting distance between himself and the city of his darkest days on planet Earth.

Exhilaration wasn't all he felt. He'd followed the breaking stories on the news and knew the cops had never even come close to catching him. Understanding why was simple enough. He was so clever, and this realization made him feel invincible, almost giddy, with the morning wind whipping his black, curly hair.

Then again, he'd known for a while that it was time to move on. Sooner or later, the cops would have come knocking at his door. Especially after a couple nights ago, after picking up that pretty, blonde-haired girl with the star earrings. When he tightened the rope around her neck, she'd stared at him in confusion, as if to say, "You've got the wrong girl."

His cell phone chirped. He snatched it up.

"Mr. Owens, I believe I have the information you requested," said a woman's businesslike voice.

"I'm listening."

"You expressed interest in renting a piece of real estate."

"That's right."

"Could you confirm the address?"

Since he had the address memorized, he didn't need to look it up. Waiting, he listened to her fingernails clicking on the keyboard and imagined what she looked like.

Blonde hair. Blue eyes. Wire rim glasses.

"Yes, I have it right here. The property is still available."

"Wonderful. I'll be by in a couple of days to sign the paperwork."

"Very good, sir."

Hanging up, he smiled to himself. The cabin he remembered from childhood was hidden away on several acres of deep woods on a private lake. It was the perfect place for getting away from the world, for hiding from those who would lock him away forever.

The cops would never find him once he'd settled in the Upper Peninsula. In fact, now that he'd crossed state lines, they'd have to call the FBI to find him. He smiled at the thought, imagining a massive manhunt. *All because of me.* But they would have no hope of finding him once he had a new identity, a new name, a new life.

It was so simple. He would simply fade into the wilderness of the North Woods and become a law-abiding citizen with cable TV and a dog. He might even cheer at local high school football games.

He felt confident in his plan—and why not? The past was behind him, as were the bodies of four young women he'd left in Cincinnati. The police knew their names by now, but what they didn't know was what made them all, beyond their looks, so much alike. Only he knew that.

Now he would simply vanish and take the secret with him. Maybe even take it to his grave.

"They'll never find me now." He said the words aloud. "They'll never find me, because I'll disappear. I'll vanish like Houdini."

CHAPTER 11

TURNING HER FACE TOWARD the morning sun, Gillian peered out the hospital window and studied the pigeons perched on a nearby telephone wire. Below, the Chicago streets teemed with life. Cars, buses, and trucks were crammed bumper to bumper in the morning rush hour. *Somebody's going to be late for work.*

Just a month ago, she and Marc had taken Crystal downtown to visit the Shedd Aquarium and have supper at Ed Debevic's, a fifties-style restaurant where the waiters are rude on purpose. She'd had no idea that a month later Marc would be lying in ICU, fortunate to be alive.

Turning toward the bed, watching Marc sleep, she seethed, still furious at him because of Stacey's letter. At the same time, she felt relieved that he was still alive, that they would have an opportunity to mend their marriage.

That is, if it isn't too late.

Last night, while waiting for news about Marc, she'd shed more tears than she thought were humanly possible. At first, none of the details had seemed real. She'd felt as if she were watching a TV drama, as if observing someone else's sob story unfold in sixty minutes. Except when the sixty minutes were up, her nightmare had continued.

But hope had finally arrived with a surgical nurse's report around midnight. Marc's vital signs were stable. One lung was punctured but not beyond repair. He'd lost a lot of blood, but he wasn't going to die.

Praise God! He's going to be okay!

She still felt shaken to see him lying there, his handsome face pale and stubbly. At forty-six, he looked so weak, so vulnerable, not at all

like the six-foot-five athlete who could slam-dunk a basketball like the
best of them.

"Your hubby's a tall man," one of the nurses had told her an hour
ago. "He didn't happen to play professional basketball once, did he?"

"Actually, he did," Gillian had replied with surprise. Marc had
been playing point guard on a junior college team when a scout approached him with promises of fame and fortune. Marc's life had
changed overnight when he signed a contract that would have made
him a wealthy superstar.

"Holy Toledo, that's what I thought!" Tessa—that's what her name
tag said—had leaned against the doorjamb, a fist on one ample hip,
her teeth pearly white against ebony skin. "See, I follow professional
basketball like a crazy woman and never forget a face." She paused,
studying Marc's face intently. "Our beloved Chicago Bulls, right?"

Gillian had nodded, impressed. "They drafted him about twenty-
five years ago, but he didn't play more than half a season."

Concern had clouded Tessa's eyes. "What on earth happened? He
must have been pretty good. The Bulls don't draft just anybody."

"He was in a serious car accident and tore up his knee pretty bad.
The team doctors said he couldn't play after that." A line from a poem
by Algernon Charles Swinburne sprang to Gillian's memory: *Dead
dreams of days forsaken.*

Now, Marc's lean, tall body, clad in a typical paper-thin gown, was
hooked to a confusing tangle of tubes and monitors, and a machine
on a wheeled cart monitored his heart. Gillian watched the steady blip
of his heartbeat, drawing comfort in the fact that it was strong, that
she wasn't going to be a widow after all.

She glanced around the room, her eyes resting on the untouched
breakfast tray that Tessa had kindly brought her. Hospitals gave her
the creeps, because she'd seen her share of them—and doctors—during some expensive and painful fertility therapy. That period of her
life was one she had determined to forget, but unbidden memories
seemed impossible to suppress.

She'd always wanted to give Marc a son, to whom he could pass on
the basketball tradition. But God seemed to have other plans—plans
that hadn't always been easy for her to accept. Her eyes still filled

with tears at the sight of a newborn baby boy in a mother's arms. The fact that another woman could have what she had always wanted and lacked—well, it was still a hard pill for her to swallow.

She turned her gaze back to the window, her right index finger absently drawing calligraphy letters on the glass. *God, You are good. You make no mistakes. I have no reason to be discontented.*

But she *was* discontented. She had the unfinished business of Stacey's letter that now had to be delayed, in spite of the unquenchable anger flaring deep inside her. Last night, she'd planned to confront Marc with every word rehearsed, every response premeditated so he would have stood naked before her, his sin exposed.

My dearest children, what am I supposed to do? Your father is alive, but am I alive? I feel so dead inside.

To make matters worse, the police had said that their neighbor, Dr. Atkinson, had been out getting his mail when he heard a gunshot. Moments later, he'd seen a woman running out of their house and yelling something about someone trying to rape her.

God, what is going on?

The allegation, of course, was absurd. Marc would never have hurt anyone. But who was the woman, and why would she shoot Marc and then make a crazy accusation like that? Dave Ritchie had dropped by to see her last night, and had told her about Stacey James's rage during the church discipline meeting. Clearly, he thought Stacey was responsible and had told the police as much.

Stacey James.

First, the discovery of her love letter to Marc. And then the shooting. Was it too coincidental that both events had occurred on the same day? No, she knew too much about God's ways by now to believe in coincidence. Perhaps the puzzle pieces were beginning to fit together after all. But the puzzle itself still wasn't making sense, and she couldn't help thinking the worst.

Stacey's letter had indicated a possible affair. Then, if Dave's suspicion was correct, Stacey had been alone in the house with Marc. *What was she doing in our house?*

Gillian felt something hot coil in her belly. Taking a deep breath, she tried to calm down, tried to pray. But she couldn't focus.

Crystal sat in a chair on the other side of the room, as if too afraid to see her father up close. Wearing her new glasses, she was flipping absently through *Good Housekeeping*. "When do you think he'll wake up?" she asked.

Gillian heard a low moan and turned to Marc in surprise. His eyelashes fluttered, opening to slits. Returning to her chair, she reached for his hand. His fingers fumbled and didn't seem to have the strength to grasp hers.

Pretend everything's okay. Don't make hasty judgments. Wait until you have facts. "It's okay, Marc. I'm here. Are you okay?"

It took him a moment to respond, his words slow and lazy. "Never better." He worked his lips. "Mouth's dry."

Crystal brought Marc a cup of water, which he drank slowly, as if taking strength from each swallow. When he was finished, he smiled at Gillian weakly. "I love you," he whispered.

"I love you, too." Gillian brushed gray-flecked blond hair away from his forehead. For a moment, her simmering anger toward him was cooled by the fact that he was alive. "The doctor says you're going to be okay. How are you feeling?"

"The truth?" His weak smile grew fainter. "Absolutely terrible."

"That's only to be expected, Dad." Crystal took a seat on the other side of the bed. "You lost a lot of blood. The doctor says he lost you once on the operating table but was able to bring you back."

Gillian pressed her eyes shut tight. That was classic Crystal: so blunt, so matter-of-fact. Gillian didn't want to hear a recap of the most terrifying night of her life, about waiting wide-eyed to see whether Marc would live or die. He had come so close to dying last night. She'd been so afraid, had prayed like she'd never prayed before. How many times had she counseled wives in similar circumstances, exhorting them to find their strength in Christ? Her lack of faith made her feel like such a hypocrite.

Marc turned his head slowly, as if any quick movement was painful. He gave her his eyes. "You look terrific."

"Sorry I can't say the same for you. But in a few weeks, if you pass all your tests, you should be able to come home. At least, that's what the doctor said."

He groaned. "A few weeks?"

Gillian brushed hair behind her ear. "Maybe earlier. We'll have to wait and see."

Crystal announced that she needed to use the restroom and left. Gillian was glad for a few moments alone with Marc. Was this a good time to ask him about Stacey? Just then, Tessa strolled in, and Gillian decided to wait.

Ignoring the nurse, who began taking his blood pressure, Marc studied Gillian. "How are *you* doing?"

Gillian's eyes avoided his for only an instant, but it was enough. Nothing ever got past him, even when he was laid out in a hospital bed.

"Hey, what's wrong? You okay?"

What a question! I almost lost you to death, and I'm almost certain I've lost you to another woman. "No, I'm not okay. You almost died, remember? Do you have any idea what the last twelve hours have been like for me?"

He looked sheepish. "I didn't mean to sound so heartless, but I don't really remember anything after she pulled the trigger."

She. "Marc, who did this to you?"

"Stacey James."

Gillian felt a heaviness in her chest. So it was true.

"I've never seen her so ticked. At first, I couldn't believe it was real." Marc studied the IV hooked to his arm with a bemused expression as Gillian scrutinized his face. Did he look guilty? Did he have any idea how angry she felt toward him right now?

Gillian felt her patience slipping, but tried to keep her tone measured. "What was she doing in our house?"

Surprise registered in Marc's eyes. "Gill, she was there when I got home. It's not like I invited her in." He described Stacey's rage at the church discipline meeting. "I figured she just needed time to cool off. I had no idea she'd be waiting for me in our house with a gun." He hesitated. "I don't know what the police have told you, but shooting me was only part of what happened. She practically destroyed the master bedroom and bath."

Gillian closed her eyes, allowing some relief to seep in. Who cared about the master bedroom and bathroom? The police had mentioned vandalism, but that was the least of her concerns.

"And Max is dead. Stacey must have poisoned him to get him out of the way."

"I know."

"What happened to Stacey? I don't remember anything after the shooting."

Opening her eyes, Gillian wondered why he would care about Stacey at a time like this. She'd almost killed him, for crying out loud. But in a sense, that fact heightened her relief. The shooting cast doubts on the possible affair.

She sucked in some air. "Nobody knows where Stacey is. The police have been looking all over, but they haven't been able to find her yet. Look, there's something you need to know about her."

Gillian tried to swallow the tightness in her throat. It was difficult even speaking the words. She waited until Tessa had left, the door swinging shut behind her, before she told Marc about what Dr. Atkinson had heard.

Irritation flashed across Marc's face. "Stacey said I tried to rape her? That's ridiculous! As if shooting me wasn't bad enough."

"Ridiculous or not, the media got wind of her story, and now we've got a real circus on our hands. Don't even look out the window. Your mug would probably end up on the six o'clock news."

Marc rolled his eyes.

"Several reporters have been begging to interview you, but the doctors told them no. I'm afraid before all this is over, there's going to be a lot of publicity and a lot of fingers pointing at you. People are already speculating that Stacey shot you in self-defense."

"Oh, brother! I think a coma would have been preferable to this." Seeing Gillian flinch, he added, "Just kidding."

"It's nothing to joke about." She rose and headed toward the door.

"Where you going?"

"I'll be right back. The police don't even know for sure who they're looking for. The sooner they catch Stacey and put this silly allegation to rest, the better."

CHAPTER 12

WITHOUT WARNING, THE TRAFFIC grew thick, making Haydon feel boxed inside the mass of humanity that rushed forward at a clip far exceeding the speed limit. To pause and try to look at a map now would only court disaster. Thankfully, he had the directions memorized, so he had no reason to stop.

As night draped its black shawl over New York City, he crossed the bridge from Staten Island to Brooklyn, following Highway 278 north to Queens. There, near the Brooklyn border, he exited the freeway.

All in all, he was surprised by how easily he'd found the place, having not been there before. But that was another thing his mother had always commented on: his keen sense of direction.

Why, Donny, you could find a place with your eyes blindfolded. Though his parents had named him Haydon, she'd always preferred to call him Donny after a favorite uncle.

As he cruised the quiet streets, surprised by the absence of traffic, the strains of Lerner and Loewe's *Brigadoon* drifted from his CD player. The familiar measures of "It's Almost Like Being in Love" brought a smile to his lips, and he couldn't help humming along.

His trip had been fueled by an obsession he'd known since childhood. In many ways, it was like being in love as he anticipated meeting someone for the first time—someone, in fact, he'd idolized all his life.

Away from the busy traffic that had made his fingers tighten around the steering wheel, he drove slowly, passing well-lit older homes and well-tended parks. It was an upscale neighborhood, not the type he'd known as a child.

He studied the street signs that seemed purposely hidden from out-siders and thought he'd found his destination easily—almost too easily. Taking a deep breath, his palms moist with anticipation, he followed the building numbers. Finding the one he was seeking, he parked along the curb. Getting out, he slammed the door shut behind him and breathed in the evening air, which was typically cool for October.

He'd dreamed of this moment . . .

Before him rose a tall, stone building separated from him by only a black, wrought-iron fence. A small, well-maintained sidewalk led from the street to the building's large front door, but the fence gate was padlocked. This fact, however, didn't deter him. He'd known all along that the gate would be locked, that the place would be off limits. Only living relatives and groups with special permission were allowed inside. But prohibited entry only made the experience more titillating.

He hesitated, thinking of his mother, who would have shaken her head with disappointment to see him trespassing like this. *Donny, you naughty boy!* He could hear her husky voice echoing in his mind and pushed the memory aside, determined not to let thoughts of her spoil his evening.

Somewhere nearby, a dog barked. Glancing around, he realized he was alone, the street vacant of traffic. He climbed the fence and dropped easily to the other side. Scurrying into the building's shad-ows, he waited for any indication that his presence had been observed.

Nothing stirred.

He scanned his surroundings and listened. Moments ago, he'd been surrounded by speeding, honking traffic. It seemed strange now to be cloaked in watchful silence.

Turning toward the building, he strode along its perimeter and followed a grassy lane that led toward the rear. Glancing up, he noted the tall, dark windows. The place seemed deserted, but he cared little for the building or for its daytime occupants. He was more interested in what lay beyond.

Seconds later, his hand touched the rough texture of the nearest headstone in Machpelah Cemetery. He had done his homework well. It was surprising what he'd learned simply by surfing the Internet.

The private Jewish cemetery stretched several acres, but he couldn't see that far, not in the dark, and he dared not use the flashlight in his jacket pocket unless he had to. The sky was clear with no trace of clouds, and the moon smiled down with all the light he needed.

Strolling among the headstones, he paused to study the names. Stein. Goldberg. Singer. Perlman. These were not the graves of common people like him. They entombed the pampered bodies of the privileged class of another time, another era.

His eyes strained into the distance as far as the moonlight would allow. It wouldn't be a small stone he was looking for. He remembered photos on the Internet and tried to find something matching their description. The search took only five minutes but felt more like an eternity.

Startled by his discovery, his knees weak, he knelt on the grass as if the stone monument rising before him were an altar. Just to be sure, he pulled out his flashlight and pointed its beam with a trembling hand.

Yes, this is it.

At the top of the monument's three small steps knelt a stone woman in mourning, her body shrouded in a gown flowing past her feet. To the immediate right of her unseeing eyes was engraved a word that confirmed he'd found the right grave.

WEISS.

Inset above that was a second name that made his heart pound like a jackhammer.

HOUDINI.

He had found the resting place of the man he revered more than anyone on earth. The cemetery was so exclusive that even Houdini's wife, Bess, a Gentile, hadn't been permitted to be buried beside her husband. The realization that the famous magician's remains lay only feet away made Haydon tremble. How could such a man be dead, killed from peritonitis caused by a ruptured appendix?

Engraved in stone at his feet was a repetition of Houdini's name and the dates of his life: 1874–1926. Haydon didn't care that Houdini had been dead more than fifty years before he was born. Call him crazy.

If only you were alive. Together, the two of us could have astounded the world, could have gone down as the greatest magic duo in history.

Inset above the word *HOUDINI* was a bronze-colored crest that Haydon recognized. It was the crest of the Society of American Magicians, the same crest Haydon coveted on his grave someday. But such an honor didn't come lightly, and he had so much work to do to impress the Society.

First, he needed to begin practicing magic again. Then he needed to learn and perform tricks even more astounding than those popularized by the man buried at his feet. But, his heart sinking, he realized he couldn't go back to magic. At least, not yet. He needed to put the murders behind him before he could redirect his focus on his destiny—on becoming the most famous magician since Houdini. He heard his mother's counsel ringing in his ears.

When you've got a job to do, Donny, you do it.

Yes, Mother, I will.

Yet his shoulders felt heavy, overwhelmed by the immensity of the task. His hopes of achieving such success seemed as dead and buried as the great man who lay entombed at his feet. But still . . .

I have to try, I can't give up, and I must succeed.

The words burned in his brain as if stamped by a fiery brand. He rose, eyeing the stone woman in mourning and the crest. What a nice addition they would make to his collection. Dare he?

Nearby, an owl hooted. It was time to go, and he had so much work to do. He could never return to magic until he took the necessary steps to change his identity so the police wouldn't be able to track him down. That meant hiding away in the North Woods until he was ready to present himself to the public again—new and transformed. He also needed to give himself a new name, a name that would go down in the history books as Houdini's name had.

Then there was the *Masters of Illusion* TV show, which was taped in Las Vegas. He'd mailed video of several of his magic acts to the producers, and their reply had sounded promising. They wanted to see more of his work before deciding whether to invite him to appear on their program. If he appeared on the nationally televised show and wowed TV audiences with a spectacle unlike anything they'd seen before, his future as a famous illusionist would be guaranteed. More dreams to record in his diary.

Move over, David Copperfield. Here I come.

Of course, his dream would require so much planning and hard work. Suddenly, he felt guilty to be making selfish plans before the grave of the man who had inspired them all. He owed so much to this man, and overwhelming feelings of gratitude made his throat tighten.

"If only you were here to help me," he said aloud. "Just imagine what the two of us could have done together."

CHAPTER 13

STRETCHED OUT ON THE king-size adjustable bed, Stacey decided she'd take Jared's condo over Maralee's tiny ranch-style any day. Actually, she didn't even know Jared, but Maralee had described his posh bachelor pad after house-sitting for him. She'd even joked about how brainless he was to hide his condo key in the most obvious place imaginable: under his welcome mat—and no security system! Perhaps the size of the guy's investment portfolio made up for the size of his brain.

It was Friday morning, almost two weeks after the shooting. Trekking miles across town in the dead of night after leaving Maralee's house, paranoid that someone would recognize her, Stacey had reached the condo and found the key exactly where Maralee had said it would be. The young executive was definitely loaded, and Stacey relished the condo's amenities—granite kitchen countertops, stainless steel appliances, hardwood floors, even a heated bathroom floor. She especially enjoyed the Jacuzzi, which was bigger than Maralee's entire bathroom.

Maralee had unwittingly mentioned that Jared was on a five-week business trip to Europe. Therefore, she had the place to herself, and she made herself right at home.

Shivering as she got out of bed, Stacey pulled on one of Jared's masculine housecoats and padded into the living room. She flipped on the gas fireplace before turning on the wall-mounted big-screen TV to catch the news at the top of the hour.

She was enjoying her instant celebrity. Her declaration of rape had turned the shooting, a story that might otherwise have slipped under the radar, into an overnight media sensation. Now everyone was speculating about who she was and why she'd shot her pastor and biblical counselor. Had her acquaintance with Marc Thayer tempted him to take liberties?

Thanks to Jim Bakker and Jimmy Swaggart, a sex scandal involving a church or religious organization promised plenty of media attention. Now Chicago had the story of the year in its own backyard, and everybody wanted a piece of the action.

Being a celebrity, however, made the condo feel like a prison. If she stepped outside, someone might recognize her and notify the news media or the police. To avoid that chance, she took out the trash in the middle of the night.

Thankfully, Jared fit the bachelor stereotype and, though neat and meticulous, was apparently challenged in all things culinary. His freezer and cupboards were crammed with enough TV dinners and canned goods to feed a small army. She wouldn't go hungry, but the unimaginative menu was getting monotonous. Forget anything fresh. How she longed for a banana or a glass of milk, both of which she'd taken for granted for far too long.

Opening yet another can of mandarin oranges, she perched on the leather settee to watch the news. The big headline was that Marc Thayer was being released from the hospital today, and she wanted to see him.

She sat up straight, fork in midair, as the camera zoomed in on Marc. He approached a lectern in a conference room crammed with reporters. Dressed in his best navy Sunday suit with that crimson diamond tie she always adored, he looked paler and thinner than she remembered. Something sucked at her heart.

When Marc reached the microphone, the barrage of camera flashes must have been unnerving. But he looked unruffled. Unfolding a piece of paper, he cleared his throat, then looked up, making eye contact with his audience before reading his prepared speech. Marc had always been at ease in front of a crowd, and today was no different. If anything, he looked mildly irritated by the attention and more than ready to put the shooting behind him.

"I would like to publicly thank the staff of Stroger Hospital for saving my life and for making my stay here as comfortable as possible," he said in his crisp, well-modulated baritone. "I'd also like to thank the paramedics who were first at the scene. If not for their skillful and immediate care, I probably wouldn't have survived the trip to the hospital." He swallowed hard, the first sign of weakness.

Stacey squeezed the can hard. For an instant, she was back in Marc's house and remembered . . . the stunned look in his eyes when he saw her in the bathroom . . . the unexpected kickback of the gun . . . the jolt of Marc's body as the bullet found its mark . . . the sound of his limp frame hitting the floor.

Marc glanced up from his speech to ad lib. "God has a reason for certain events I can't explain. I certainly didn't ask for this event to happen, but God in His goodness chose this path for my life, so I thank Him for it. What I know is that no matter what happens, He is always good."

Marc looked down, reading his speech again. "I would like to put to rest certain inaccuracies that have been reported nonstop through various media outlets for the past two weeks. First, I did *not* try to rape Stacey James. In fact, Stacey and I had only a professional and proper counseling relationship in the context of Heritage Bible Church, where I have served on the pastoral staff for the past ten years. Stacey was a friend and a church member whom I was merely seeking to help; the details of her counseling are not for public record and are protected by pastoral confidentiality. Simply put, an improper relationship between Stacey James and me never took place."

Marc glanced up, his eyes flaring as if to underline this last statement. "Stacey did not shoot me in self-defense. Due to a church matter, about which Stacey and I disagreed, she vandalized my house, killed my dog, and waited in my house for me to come home. Hearing the sounds of vandalism in progress, I went to investigate and found her upstairs. She then shot me at point-blank range with an eight millimeter handgun, which the police have not yet been able to locate.

"So why did Stacey run from my house, yelling that someone had tried to rape her? Let me tell you why. She was merely seeking to deflect scrutiny of her own behavior and to create a defense for her role in the shooting. The sheriff's office believes that Stacey's actions were part of a deliberate plan to kill me. Forensic evidence shows that Stacey broke into my house, poisoned my dog, and vandalized the master bedroom and bathroom *before* the shooting occurred. How else could my blood be found *on top of* broken glass littering my bathroom floor? These actions were clearly premeditated, and not the result of someone defending herself from a sexual assault. The evidence speaks for itself.

"People have asked me, 'Do you hate Stacey James?' No, I do not hate Stacey, and I forgive her for what she has done, as God has commanded me to. In fact, I love her as a sister in Christ, according to the love taught in the Bible and illustrated through the sacrificial death and resurrection of Jesus Christ, who gave His life to save us all. I am saddened that Stacey has chosen this violent path, and I pray for her every day. I am also praying that law enforcement will apprehend her soon and that the district attorney will take whatever legal action he deems necessary to keep her from hurting anyone else. That's all I have to say. Thank you."

The can of mandarin oranges crashed into the wall beside the TV, its remaining contents spewing onto the hardwood floor. Stacey got up and flicked off the TV before burying her face in her hands. Marc's public rebuke was more than she could bear. He could have smeared her for all the world to see. Instead he'd forgiven her—in fact, he had said he *loved* her.

Loved *her.*

She'd never heard him say those words before. Those words changed everything.

They meant he cared after all—perhaps even more than he'd said. *What have I done?*

Closing her eyes, she pictured Marc's gray-blond hair, his blue eyes, and the delicate lines around the corners of his mouth. And then she remembered how he could speak so forcefully, yet so gently, his eyes melting into hers, the gentle turning of his eyes, the conviction that he cared. Cared deeply. No matter that he'd distanced himself and declared that he had no romantic feelings for her.

She didn't care what he'd said. She knew he loved her; he hadn't been able to hide that fact from her, though he'd been able to hide it

from everyone else, including his own wife, that plump redhead with
the big lips.

Stacey had loathed Gillian Thayer at first sight. Marc deserved better than that. He deserved a sensitive woman who knew what a man
needed. Stacey believed she was that woman, believed it with all her
heart. Had always believed it, in fact.

In the back of her mind, a tremulous voice of uncertainty whispered. But the vandalism, the poisoning of the dog, the shooting—
they had all been honest mistakes. She'd had a bad day and hadn't
been thinking rationally. The church discipline threat had pushed her
over the edge, but she was fine now. Bygones were bygones.

Of course, Marc would accept her apology and move on, wouldn't
he?

She felt excited by the realization that she had to see him again.
That she had to explain.

But how? The police were looking for her. They would be waiting.
No, not yet. Be patient.

She just needed to wait until the right opportunity presented itself.
Then when the time was right, she'd be ready.

CHAPTER 14

"WELL, MOM, I GUESS I'm off."

Standing on the Victorian's grassy front yard on Friday afternoon, Gillian kissed Crystal on the cheek and hugged her tightly. At the curb idled a green minivan crammed with teens, their boisterous chatter and laughter drifting out of the open windows.

Peering past the church van, Gillian glimpsed the white news van of the local NBC affiliate parked across the street. Standing nearby, a blonde female reporter in a too-tight, purple business suit spoke with animated frustration to her cameraman, who leveled an undisguised scowl at Gillian. Moments ago, when the woman had thrust a microphone in Crystal's face, Gillian had cut the interview short.

"I know you folks are only looking for a story," she'd said, "but please don't harass my daughter."

The media had been a constant frustration over the last couple of weeks since the story of Marc's shooting and the rape allegation gained national attention. Upon returning home from the hospital after the shooting, Gillian had been shocked to find reporters and camera crews waiting to pounce on her as soon as she stepped out of the Tahoe. Newspaper columns and television reports had portrayed Stacey as a helpless victim and cast suspicions on Marc, as if certain he was somehow to blame for the shooting that had nearly cost him his life.

After watching the latest news opinion piece about the rise of sexual scandals among religious organizations, Gillian felt like screaming. Stacey James had tried to kill her husband—*that* was the story. Why was everyone missing it? If not for the quick work of the paramedics,

Marc wouldn't be alive today. Hopefully, the police would track Stacey down soon and put her behind bars, where she would be unable to hurt anyone else.

And out of our lives, where she can stay.

Now, watching Crystal leave for her weekend retreat, Gillian felt a tugging at her heart and recalled words from Emily Dickinson: "Parting is all we know of heaven."

"Bye, Mom."

"Call me as soon as you get there. I need to know that you made it safely."

Crystal turned mid-stride and shook her head. "Good grief, Mom. It's only for the weekend." When Gillian didn't respond, she added, "Okay, fine. I'll call as soon as we get there."

"Did you say good-bye to your father?"

"Yep."

"You didn't forget your toothbrush, did you?"

Crystal rolled her eyes. "No, Mom. Good-bye." She practically dove into the van before Gillian could ask more embarrassing questions in front of her friends.

Gillian bit her lip. *Great. Now she's annoyed with me. She's relieved to get away from her overprotective mother. Well, can I blame her?*

"I think she's got the kitchen sink in here, Mrs. Thayer." This complaint came from a lanky, black-haired young man who was loading Crystal's suitcases into the already crammed trailer.

"Thanks for taking her bags, Ryan," Gillian said. "You're a true gentleman."

Actually he was more than a gentleman. The way Crystal talked about Ryan Brodski, Gillian wondered if something serious was going on between them. But Crystal, of course, was too young for anything serious.

She knows that, I'm sure. Gillian stopped herself. *Or does she?*

As the van pulled away, Gillian waved at her daughter, uncertain whether Crystal was waving back. She watched the van veer around a corner and disappear before she turned back to the house, still wrestling with her emotions. In a couple of years, Crystal would be heading off to college.

Saying good-bye will never get any easier. I need to get used to this, whether I like it or not.

The blonde reporter sprinted across the street with her cameraman in tow. "Gillian Thayer! Could we get your comment on the shooting and the rape allegation?"

Smoothing strands of hair behind her ear, Gillian faced the reporter with a pasted-on smile. "My husband gave you a formal statement at the press conference. Sorry, but we have nothing more to say."

Returning to the house, where construction workers were banging away on the master bedroom and bathroom renovations, Gillian paused in the front hallway and glanced around. She had the distinct impression that something was missing. Then she realized it was Max, their dear departed pet, whose loss Crystal had taken hardest. Gillian couldn't get used to the mailman showing up without her being alerted to his presence by Max's boisterous barking.

In the living room, Marc was ensconced in his favorite recliner, a pile of books at his elbow. Wearing black sweats and a red T-shirt, he was watching the headlines on Fox News.

After arriving home from the hospital and running the gauntlet of news organizations on the front lawn, he would be taking it easy for the rest of the weekend before returning to work on Monday. The TV remote, a tall glass of sweetened iced tea, his reading glasses, the newspaper—everything was within easy reach so he wouldn't need to get up unless he needed to use the bathroom.

Sitting on the couch beside Marc's recliner, Gillian pulled the well-worn piece of purple stationery from her pocket. As she unfolded it, a remaining wisp of the letter's fragrance drifted up. She could smell it and wondered if Marc could, too.

"I want you to read this."

Marc tore his gaze away from the TV and gave the letter a cursory glance before accepting it. "What is it?"

"You'll see."

Marc met her gaze with a skeptical look, as if trying to discern whether this was a joke. Seeing her serious expression, he muted the TV and began to read. Gillian watched him closely, looking for any trace of recognition. Either he had a good poker face, or he'd never seen the letter before. In her stomach, a tight fist squeezed even tighter.

Marc lifted his gaze to hers in surprise, his face ashen. "Where— where did this come from?" His voice was strained. He barely sounded like himself.

"From one of your suits. I found it the morning of the shooting," she said calmly, hearing how steady her voice could be. "I wanted to show it to you at the hospital, but it never seemed like the right time, not with attorneys, cops, and friends dropping by at all hours."

He stared at the letter in bewilderment. "I've never seen this before."

"So I guess Stacey must have slipped it into your suit coat thinking you'd find it later. But she never counting on *me* finding it, did she?" *Unless she actually intended for me to find it.*

"Gill, I've never seen this before. This doesn't mean anything."

"Don't even!" She glared at him. "It means everything, and you know it!"

He reached out to touch her arm, but she jerked away. Now she could hear the quaver in her voice. "I want to know why—"

"Please, Gill—"

"—why Stacey wrote a letter like that to you."

"You don't think—"

"What am I supposed to think? Were you having an affair with her?" The words tumbled out, startling her even as she spoke them.

His blue eyes flashed. "I never touched her, Gill! Never. You have to believe me." She saw shock register in his eyes and something else. Hurt? Anger? "How could you ask me such a thing? You know how much I love you."

Rising, she walked to the window, turning her back to him. Crossing her arms across her chest, she peered out at her flower garden, at the crimson leaves falling from the maple. If only everything in life could be so beautiful. "What else was I supposed to think? Read what she wrote to you. Just read it."

She rounded on him to see his reaction, but he appeared too physically ill to read the letter again. He cast it onto the coffee table as if it were a brand too hot to hold.

His blue eyes were pleading. "Nothing happened between me and

Stacey. But you remember—her husband couldn't have cared less. She was hungry for attention from a man—any man—who would give it to her, so she flirted. For a time, she was fixated on me like a teenager with a silly crush. That's why I stopped counseling her, if you recall. But Stacey still sent me silly e-mails and occasional letters."

"So why didn't you tell me about all this? Why the secrecy? Why did I have to find out this way?"

He shrugged. "I knew the letters would only upset you, so I threw them all away, afraid you would find one and misunderstand. Which is exactly what happened—though I don't recall ever seeing this particular letter before. Gill, I kept away from Stacey. I really did."

Gillian crossed to the coffee table and snatched up the letter. "You obviously didn't stay far enough away. Just look"—she thrust the letter toward his face—"She says right here that you put your arms around her. Why would she say something like that?"

"You don't know Stacey like I do. Stacey lives in a fantasy world. She likes to make things up, even inappropriate things. Maybe she believes those things happened—I don't know." He hesitated. "Okay, there was one time—last January, I think. I was walking across the church parking lot to my car, and we were talking. She slipped on the ice. I grabbed her by the arm to keep her from falling, and she held onto me. But that's all I did. I guess she must have misunderstood."

Gillian saw how Stacey could have misunderstood, but again she wondered why Marc hadn't told her this before.

"I did the best I could to help her, but . . . well, I guess we're better off now that she's out of our lives."

"Yes, how convenient! Let's just forget the whole thing happened."

"But nothing happened, Gill. I never touched her."

She stared at him. *Just because you didn't touch her doesn't mean nothing happened. Why can't you see that?*

Words were flowing out of her now, words best left unsaid. She felt as if a dam had burst, as if a torrent of rushing water were sweeping her away. "Marc, think about all those women you've counseled over the years. Didn't you ever wonder how it must have made me feel when you always had time for them but never for me?" Tears pooled in her eyes, blurring her vision. "I hated them—every single one of them—and the way they stole you away from me!"

Marc spread his hands, frustration in his eyes. "Gill, how can you say that? I've always made time for you. But if you haven't noticed, helping people is what I do. It takes time, and people can be difficult. I thought you understood that."

She folded her arms across her chest again. "That's right, Marc. Help everybody else and ignore your own family. Ignore the fact that I'm here alone, every day, trying to live with my grief—" A sob stole her breath away. She tried to speak over the tightness in her throat. "And you never . . . even ask sometimes . . . how I'm doing."

Head bowed, she pressed her face into her hands. Suddenly, he stood tall before her, arms outstretched, the faint scent of his woodsy aftershave mingling in the air between them.

"Come here," he said.

She shook her head, not wanting him to touch her. She wanted him to experience just a sliver of the pain she was feeling right now. How dare he try to explain all this away! Did he think she was a complete fool?

"Gillian, come here."

Grudgingly, she stepped toward him and felt his arms enfold her. This time, feeling too numb to resist, she succumbed. His hug would have felt welcome on any other occasion. But right now, it seemed obvious he was just trying to dig himself out of the hole he was in. Wasn't it just like a man to use gentle caresses to get his way? Had he held Stacey the same way and whispered sweet nothings in her ear?

Her scalp tingled as he breathed against her hair. "I'm so sorry. I didn't realize you were feeling neglected. I know you've been through a tough time. I promise things will change; I'll make more time for you from now on. But please believe me. Nothing inappropriate ever happened—"

Enough!

Jerking away from him, she rushed toward the door, longing to be away. She heard him calling her name, but she pretended she didn't hear him, driven by the need to escape. Within seconds, she was out the back door and racing across the lawn toward her flower garden.

Stuffing the crumpled love letter into her pocket, she reached the bed of red dahlias as tears spilled down her cheeks.

"Meredith, Blaine, my dearest children," she whispered. "If only you were here right now."

CHAPTER 15

LYING ON THE COUCH, Marc counted the gongs as the antique clock struck midnight. Sitting up, he wiped a hand across his face and peered out the window. The yard was draped in moonlight, and nothing—not even the trees—stirred. The whole world seemed to be holding its collective breath, waiting for Gillian to come home.

That afternoon, she had stormed out of the house and spent an hour or two in her garden. She had returned to the house just long enough to grab her purse and keys, and then had driven away in a squeal of tires.

Supper time had come and gone, but still no Gillian.

He'd fixed a bowl of soup and waited up, worried sick that something bad had happened to her. Then he realized she was probably at the cemetery cooling off. Apart from her flower garden and the upstairs bedroom they had decorated as a nursery, that was her third favorite refuge when she needed a good cry. And, boy, how she'd cried lately! Would the tears never end?

He'd read some verses in Psalms, his favorite book of the Bible, and spent several hours praying for her and for himself—praying that God would show him what to do. *Lord, please mend whatever has gone wrong in our marriage. Please show me how I can help her.*

After finding letters that Gillian had written to Meredith and Blaine, their dead twins, Marc had encouraged her to seek counseling, but she'd laughed off his suggestion. He had heard of women who'd had an abortion writing letters to their unborn children as therapy to ease their guilt, but what did Gillian have to feel guilty about? It wasn't her fault the twins had been stillborn.

He regretted that he hadn't had much time lately for Gillian or for Crystal. Church commitments had dominated his summer and fall, making discretionary family time a feeble attempt at best. The nature of the ministry was that more shoes needed filling than the church had feet to fill them. He was stumped as to how to solve that problem, other than to request that his responsibilities be cut back so he could have more time at home. But every pastor at the church faced the same dilemma, and he didn't want one of the other guys to have to pick up the slack for him.

Another accusation had also rung true. He hadn't worked hard enough to distance himself from Stacey James. At the first sign of inappropriate affection, he had terminated the counseling sessions and passed her over to Liz. When he'd heard from Liz that Stacey was clamming up and skipping sessions, however, he'd feared she would never get help for her problems if he didn't maintain some contact. So he had unwisely accepted her phone calls and e-mails, both of which had become excessive.

Perhaps, he reflected, that was one of his biggest faults as a counselor—being so burdened for people and their problems that he sometimes neglected his family and put himself at risk. Maybe he fancied he could fix problems in people's lives. How foolish! Only God was the Problem Solver. Not him. He was just a channel—a frail human channel, at that—who could be tempted just like any other man.

Marc glanced at the clock again. He'd made himself comfortable on the couch, knowing they wouldn't be sharing a bed tonight—certainly not with their differences unresolved.

He must have dozed, because he was suddenly awake, startled by the creak of the screen door. A silhouette loomed in the doorway.

Gillian didn't move. She just stood there, peering in as if debating whether to enter. Marc almost rose, wanting to hold her and comfort her, but he remembered she didn't want to be touched, at least not by him. At least not yet.

"Are you okay?" he asked.

A long pause. "No, I'm not okay; but maybe I will be someday."

She didn't sound angry anymore, just exhausted; that was an improvement, at least. He wondered if she'd spent the last few hours as he had—pleading with God for an answer. "Gill, please believe me. I didn't—"

"I know, Marc. I was there, remember? I heard you. You said you didn't touch Stacey. There's nothing more to say." Her tone wasn't unkind, just matter-of-fact. "Look, I don't want to talk about it anymore, all right?"

"But we need to talk about it. I don't want you going to bed angry with me."

She sighed. "I'm not angry with you. I'm just . . . I don't know. I'm not sure how I am anymore."

"I want to help you, but I don't—"

"I know, I know." She draped her arms across the screen, as if she were a moth wanting so desperately to come in out of the night. "You want to help me just like you help everybody else with their problems. You want to put me under a microscope and probe every defect. Then you'll give me your prescription: exercise, eat right, get some sleep, take a pill, read my Bible, memorize Scripture, pray."

She chuckled, shaking her head. "Sometimes, Marc, it isn't that easy. Sometimes hurts take time. Even then they don't make sense, and nothing makes them any easier."

Nothing? "God can make them easier."

"Really?" She paused. "I'm not so sure anymore."

He stared at her. "Do you realize what you're saying?"

"Yes."

"You're scaring me."

"Not nearly as much as I'm scaring myself. Look, sometimes I'm just not sure what I believe anymore, okay? If only life made more sense . . ."

"I know."

"Do you?"

"Of course I do. What kind of question is that?"

"Do you even care that our twins are dead?"

A kick to the gut couldn't have jolted him more. "Of course I care."

"You don't show it."

"I grieve for them every day—just like you do. I just don't show it the same way." He sighed, not wanting to argue, yet wondering how the twins' deaths factored into this tension between them. "Gill, I want to help you. Just—just tell me what I can do."

"I don't know that there's anything you *can* do. I just—I guess I just need some time and—and a lot of prayer—and some space, okay?"

In other words, he would be sleeping on the couch until further notice. *Thank You, Lord. At least that's something.* "That's fine. Take as long as you need. Maybe when you're feeling better, we can talk about this again."

"When I'm feeling better?" Her shoulders shook, and he realized she was laughing. "When in the last six months have I felt better?"

Before he could reply, Gillian darted into the house, bounded up the stairs, and slipped out of sight, obviously not wishing to discuss the subject further.

Six months. Ever since the funeral. He couldn't suppress the sudden mental image of those two tiny, white coffins. A rainy spring day. He was holding an umbrella for Gillian, but what difference did it make? Even the heavens were crying. The heart-wrenching grief had festered in her soul like a sore that refused to heal.

Sometimes he wondered if she considered what he was going through. Hardly a day went by that he didn't think about the son and daughter who might have been. Or he caught himself daydreaming about a one-on-one game of basketball with Blaine. He imagined the hours he would have spent teaching his son the fundamentals and sharing his love for the game—just the two of them. Father and son. Just the way it was meant to be.

Meant to be. Not would be.

He sat quietly in the dark, waiting, wondering if she might come back.

She didn't.

Upstairs, water sloshed into the bathroom sink. She would be brushing her teeth before sleeping in Crystal's bedroom due to the renovations. Finally, he lay down, drawing the old quilt up to his chin like a small child seeking security during a storm. His long legs hung off the end of the couch, but he hardly cared.

At least she's talking to me, Lord. Please show me how to win her back.

CHAPTER 16

"HOW ARE YOU DOING, honey? I haven't heard from you in weeks."

Gillian listened to her mother's distinctive alto emanating from the other end of the phone and bit her lip, wondering what she could say. She'd never kept secrets from her mom before, but some things—her marriage problems, for example—were just too private to share, even with her mother.

It was Monday morning, Marc's first day back at work. He had just left for the church, and Gillian was beginning her day's projects. Actually, she'd put off her first project and decided to write a letter to her babies instead. It was a bad time for an extended call, but sometimes her mom called at unpredictable times, which usually meant something was on her mind.

"I'm okay, Mom."

"Just okay?"

"I can't complain. How are you?"

"Oh, fair to middling. I need your advice. I've been struggling with a new book cover, so I thought I'd take a break and call you. My art director keeps telling me to go lower on the heroine's neckline and show some cleavage, but I'm determined to stick to my principles."

"Don't budge an inch, Mom."

"I don't intend to. What are things coming to when even the art director at a respectable Christian publishing house is telling me to show more skin? Good heavens, it's downright appalling."

"It's the 'undressing of America,' as Marc calls it. It *is* sad. We need to pray for our country."

"And for Christianity." Her mom snorted. "I absolutely refuse to show cleavage. I told Alex that, but I could hear in his voice that he wasn't happy with me. Of course, it doesn't help that I'm a week late on this project, but that's his fault. He's the one who keeps changing his mind. Well, anyhow, I didn't call to bother you with my troubles."

Oh, yes you did. At least be honest about it.

Gillian knew her mom's marriage had its own share of bumps in the road. A year ago, Gillian's dad had begun inquiring into every work-at-home-and-get-rich scheme he could find. As a result of his fixation, he attended a seminar almost every evening of the week, leaving Gillian's mom at home alone. Sometimes she just needed someone to talk to.

Gillian prayed for her dad every day, anxious about his drive for riches. The Bible was clear about where the love of money could take him.

"The last time we talked," her mom said, "I recommended you get some counseling. You agreed that maybe it's a good idea. So have you given it more thought?"

"Yes, I've thought about it."

"And?"

"I'm just not comfortable with the idea."

"So you just want to stay miserable, huh?"

"I'm not *miserable.*"

"Yes, you are. I know you."

"Well, okay. Things could be better, but I just don't see how talking about my problems with some counselor is going to solve anything."

"I know you, Gillian. You're just like your father. You hold things inside and don't deal with them. If you talked to someone about how you're feeling, at least you could communicate your grief instead of bottling it up inside. You could get the comfort you need right now. Good heavens, having one stillborn baby is bad enough. But you had stillborn twins. I don't care who you are. Any woman who's gone through that experience needs some pretty vigorous therapy."

Gillian closed her eyes. "I don't need therapy, Mom. I'm fine."

"You say you're fine, but tell me the truth. Have you cried today?"

"Yes."

"And yesterday?"

"Yes."

"And the day before?"

Gillian opened her eyes. She knew where her mom was going with this. "Mom, there's nothing wrong with crying. From what I understand, crying is the best form of therapy there is. Even the Bible talks about the right time for tears."

"Yes, but you're not crying on someone's shoulder. You're crying all by yourself, and that's not healthy. You know how much I want to be there for you. I'd love to visit, but I just can't get away with all these projects on my plate."

It doesn't help that you're a workaholic who doesn't know how to take a day off.

"I know, Mom. I know you'd be here in a heartbeat if you could. That means a lot. Look, I need to go."

"You're tired of hearing me talk."

"No, that's not it. I really need to go. I have work to do, and you do, too."

"I love you."

"I love you, too. And, Mom, don't budge on the neckline."

CHAPTER 17

STEERING THE SATURN ONTO the expressway, Marc felt eager to return to work. He reflected on the last few eventful weeks and breathed a prayer of thanks to God for His continued grace. Though he didn't feel quite like his old self, sitting at a desk was hardly physically demanding. Besides, if he wasn't sitting at work, he would be sitting around at home, staring at the walls and watching reruns of *Gunsmoke*, his favorite TV show of all time.

As the red brick, colonial facade of Heritage Bible Church swung into view, he felt eager to get his life back into a routine and to return to the work he loved best. At the same time, he hated leaving Gillian at home alone.

He'd never seen her so depressed, but he wondered how much of her depression had been caused by Stacey's letter. Deeper issues were in conflict. *God, what should I say? What should I do?* He wondered if he should ask Bruce about marriage counseling.

Pulling into his usual spot, Marc grabbed his briefcase and headed for his office. On the way, several coworkers greeted him and told him how pleased they were to see him returning to work. Many had visited him in the hospital, and their thoughtful cards and words of encouragement had touched him deeply.

Liz Simons seemed especially glad to see him. After Marc got settled at his desk, she sat down across from him, her expressive hands seemingly tied in a knot. Something was obviously on her mind.

Marc was happy to see her again. Liz reminded him so much of his sister, Amber, who lived near Detroit with her husband and six kids. Liz had the same way of curling her hair, of tilting her head to one side when she was listening. Even the way Liz spoke sometimes made him do a double take. And, of course, there were those expressive, bejeweled hands. They reminded him of caged birds wanting to be set free.

"I feel terrible, just terrible, about what happened, Marc," she said. "I knew Stacey was unstable. I could have warned you."

"Don't blame yourself. There's no way you could have known that Stacey would try to kill me. Honestly, if anybody should feel guilty, it should be me. I knew how dangerous she could be. I should have seen it coming."

"I can't tell you how happy I am to see that you're okay." Her voice turned businesslike as she gestured to his desk. "As you can see, a lot of stuff piled up while you were away. It's probably going to take you a few days just to sort through your mail. Just let me know what you want me to do first."

She rose and turned to leave. Then, as if remembering, she glanced back. "Really, you know, it's a miracle you're even alive."

After she left, Marc leaned back in his chair to the familiar hum of his computer's hard drive booting up. He scanned his office, taking in the Western motif that made him envision relaxing days of herding cattle on the open range. Framed photos of singing cowboy legends Roy Rogers and Gene Autry adorned his walls.

Reflecting on his life, he tried to recall something he could honestly peg as a miracle. Perhaps surviving the car wreck that had sidelined his dream of playing professional basketball, his lifelong dream. Yes, perhaps that had been a miracle.

While lying on his back at the hospital, with his leg in a cast and his body aching all over, Marc had heard someone talk about Jesus Christ without using His name as a swear word. That had been the turning point for him: being at rock bottom and knowing that only God could pick him up and make something useful out of his broken life. Through the dedicated testimony of a Christian nurse, God had opened Marc's eyes to the truth of His Word and to the reality of where his life was headed without Christ. That had been a miracle, too—God's saving him and putting him in the ministry.

But sometimes he looked back at his days in professional basketball and wondered what his life would have been like had the accident never occurred. What would life have been like with the world by the tail and a big bank account? Then again, apart from the accident, he wouldn't have trusted Christ. Wouldn't have gone to Bible college. Wouldn't have met Gillian. Wouldn't—

The ringing of the telephone snapped him back to the present. Pastor Bruce Wellers, Marc's boss, wanted to see him in his office right away. Just by the tone of Bruce's voice, Marc knew something was wrong.

*   *   *

"I am glad to see that you've recovered so well," Bruce said as Marc took a seat on the other side of the senior pastor's expansive mahogany desk. Bruce's bald head made the wrinkles around his eyes seem more pronounced. "I'm sure you are eager to see your life return to some sort of normalcy."

"Very much so."

Bruce took a deep breath and let it out slowly, his usual mannerism when something difficult needed to be said. Marc tried to relax. He'd been back in his office barely half an hour—hardly enough time to get into trouble. Not that he'd ever gotten into serious trouble in the past. He had, however, pulled a few practical jokes that hadn't been appreciated by everyone, namely Bruce, who seemed to lack a sense of humor.

Marc supposed that Bruce's losing his first wife to cancer had something to do with his reluctance to laugh at a good joke. But the situation was more than that. Bruce had a weathered side to his personality, a side to him that had stared grim reality in the eye, that always made Marc feel inexperienced and not quite up to snuff. As if Bruce were on a spiritual plane that Marc could never hope to attain.

"Marc, the pastoral staff and I have discussed everything that has happened to you and to this ministry over the last few weeks. As much as we would like to see you return to your place in this ministry, we feel that—um—in the church's best interests, it would be best for everyone if you would just hang low for a while."

Hang low? "I'm not sure I understand."

Bruce waved his hand as if swatting a fly. "A sabbatical somewhere out of the area, Marc. We need time to let things cool off in the public's perception. As you know, the media have gone crazy over Stacey James's accusation that you tried to rape her. Even if the police track her down, no prosecutor worth his salt is going to take her flimsy story to court apart from physical evidence, which we both know they will not find. One need only take a look at the inside of your house and at your X-rays to understand what really happened. Stacey obviously went after you."

Marc nodded. *So far so good.*

"But I'm afraid most people are not interested in the truth. You know why we had to hire another part-time secretary, don't you? The phone has been ringing off the hook. Why? Gossip. That is all people seem to care about these days, and some of the news networks are just as bad. They just fan the flames." Bruce wrinkled his nose. "It's disgusting."

"I'm sorry." It was all Marc could think to say.

"It is not your fault, Marc. But you weren't the only one on the six o'clock news for the last few weeks. So was this church. And I have to be frank, this ministry has suffered because of it. Of course, no one is blaming you. You had no idea Stacey would pull the trigger and make that silly accusation, but there it is. We cannot just ignore what happened. I don't think I need to remind you of how much of the public has sided with Stacey; they think she shot you in self-defense."

"But that's not how it happened."

"Of course not. But like I said, people do not care about the truth. They just want a sensational story." Bruce spread his hands and shrugged. "People believe what they want to believe. And as long as the public keeps buzzing about a sex scandal, we have a problem on our hands."

Bruce peered at Marc over steepled fingers. "If the media would just let this story go, then I would see no reason for this conversation. But since they seem dead set on smearing your character and casting suspicions on this ministry, there appears to be no other choice."

Marc could hardly believe what he was hearing. Regardless of his guilt or innocence, he was a liability to the ministry now, an embarrassment that needed to be swept under a rug. Because the public thought he was guilty, Bruce expected him to run away like a guilty man. Marc didn't agree with the decision—not at all—but he realized he wasn't going to change any minds at this point.

Marc sucked in some air. "How long is this sabbatical supposed to last?"

Bruce was all business and obviously prepared. "A few months, at least. Perhaps until Christmas. Later, after all of this—this fervor—dies down, there will be a place for you here."

At least he isn't asking for my resignation, and he is inviting me back. A hundred questions raced through Marc's mind. What was he supposed to tell Gillian and Crystal?

"You said a sabbatical far away from here." Marc managed to keep his voice steady. "Okay, so my family and I go away for a while. What happens to our house in the meantime?"

Bruce had anticipated Marc's question. "Plenty of singles in our church would be more than happy to house-sit for a few months."

"But where are we supposed to go? What am I supposed to do?"

Getting up, Bruce sat on the edge of his desk, a common practice when he was trying to appear less formal—an impossibility for Bruce. "Relax, Marc. Think of it as an extended vacation. Besides, this will be good for Gillian, I think. I know she has been struggling with depression since her infertility and then the death of your twin babies."

Marc flushed in response to Bruce's bluntness. Perhaps getting away from the city—in particular, from the two headstones in the cemetery—*would* do her good.

"There is something else to consider." Bruce regarded Marc with a discerning eye. "There have been suspicions about you and Stacey James."

Marc's chest turned to ice. "Suspicions?"

"It's nothing for you to worry about. The matter has been kept completely confidential, but I feel that I need to make you aware of it."

"I don't know what you're referring to. As you know, Stacey has displayed some obsessive tendencies toward me. So a few months ago, I distanced myself from her and asked Liz—"

"Yes, yes." Bruce held up a hand. "I know about all that. This is something else. Last January, a staff member said she saw you and Stacey James hugging in the church parking lot."

Marc felt annoyed that the staff member hadn't come to him before going to Bruce. He repeated the story of how he'd kept Stacey from falling when she slipped on the ice. "I can see how the incident may have looked to someone else, but that's honestly all that happened."

Bruce shrugged. "I honestly did not give the story much credence when I heard it last winter; otherwise I would have come to you. Honestly, if something were going on between you and Stacey—which I do not believe for one second—I doubt the church parking lot would have been the most logical choice to be so demonstrative. Nothing gets past our secretaries."

He cleared his throat. "I bring up the report now only because of recent events. The media would just love a juicy tidbit like that, but do not worry. The story is not going past these walls."

Marc thought about the many notes and e-mails Stacey had sent him over the past six months. Though certain he'd thrown the notes away and deleted the e-mails, he recalled seeing something on TV about deleted computer files not really being deleted after all. Could someone still retrieve those e-mails? Perhaps some computer cleaning was in order.

"Look, Marc, I am not saying you did anything improper. We all know Stacey has issues. It is a tragic story. I knew her father when he was still in the pastorate years ago. It was a real shocker when he walked away from everything for a woman. Anyhow, for all concerned, I think some time away would be best—especially for Gillian. She has been through the ringer, Marc. First, she loses her babies, then she almost loses you."

Marc nodded. She *had* been through a lot—perhaps more than he realized.

"As far as finances," Bruce went on, "don't worry. If we ask you to go on a sabbatical, we will certainly take care of you."

Marc supposed several members of the pastoral staff would have gladly traded places with him, if given the opportunity. He knew he should be thankful, but something about the sabbatical didn't sit right.

"That takes a lot off my mind, but you still haven't told me where I'm going and what I'm going to do while I'm there."

Bruce looked at Marc for a long moment before responding. "I don't know, at least not yet. I'll start making inquiries right away."

CHAPTER 18

THE DROOPING LEAVES ON Gillian's dahlias mirrored how she'd been feeling lately. Sapped of strength. Wondering when her joy would return from wherever it was hiding.

She turned on the hose and gave her dahlias a good dousing. While turning off the hose, her eyes alighted on the pink hydrangea Marc had given to her on Mother's Day. He knew she liked hydrangeas; and though she had several blue ones, she'd never had a pink one before. Until that day.

Sometimes Marc could be the most thoughtful man on the planet. Contemplating his giving nature, she tried to ignore the pricking of her conscience when she recalled how cold she'd been to him lately. If only she hadn't found Stacey's letter . . .

She heard Marc's car pull into the driveway. Moments later, he strolled across the lawn toward her, suit coat removed and folded over one arm, a grave look on his face. Then he gave her news she never expected to hear.

Standing amid flowers—weeds in one hand, a trowel in the other—Gillian stared at him, barely comprehending what he was saying. Then she whirled away from him, casting the weeds and trowel to the ground and yanking the gardening gloves off her hands in quick, jerky movements. "He asked you to take a sabbatical? You've gotta be kidding me!"

"I'm sorry, Gill," he said to her back. "I'm just as surprised as you are. Bruce just wants us to take some time off somewhere else."

She heard her voice turn brittle with anger as she wheeled toward him. "Yeah, right. He expects us just to pack our bags and move away.

Sure, no problem. It doesn't matter that our whole life is here. Do you have any idea how hard this news is going to be for Crystal?"

"It's only for a few months," he said in a contrite voice. "Maybe only until Christmas."

"So where are we supposed to go?"

"Bruce doesn't know yet. He's going to start making inquiries right away. He'll let us know."

She searched his face. "But why? I just don't get it."

"I already explained it to you." His voice betrayed an edge of impatience. "Stacey's rape allegations have made the church look bad in the public perception. Just the whisper of an accusation is enough to send any ministry into a tailspin. Bruce thinks we should move away until things settle down here."

Hands on hips, she flicked her gaze from one flower to another. *Who will take care of my flowers? If someone doesn't take care of them, the weeds will flourish and choke them out.* "All the idle weeds that grow," Shakespeare had written in *King Lear.* Then something worse than her untended garden dawned on her. Meredith and Blaine. Who would tend their graves?

God, please don't make me leave my babies.

Lyrics from a familiar hymn, words she'd scripted for a recent project, ran through her mind. *I'll go where you want me to go, dear Lord. O'er mountain, or plain, or sea.*

She sensed the Holy Spirit gently prodding her heart. Sure, she'd sung that song at countless missions conferences, always attributing its message to missionaries off to save starving children in Africa. She had never considered the song's message in light of her own circumstances. Until now. And now her mind rebelled at the prospect of being plucked out of her safety zone.

Marc said, "Did you hear what I said?"

She nodded. It was all she could do. Words were trapped somewhere in her heart, lodged in her throat, unable to reach her lips. Then something gave—was it her will?—like the crumbling of a wall. "How long before we have to leave?"

"A few weeks at least."

A few weeks? Despair wrung her soul dry as she thought of the house, of all the things that would need to be packed. Balling her hands into fists, she marched toward the house, not looking at Marc.

"Gill, please don't walk away mad at me. Running away from your problems isn't going to solve anything. We need to talk."

She stopped and glared at him. "What else is there to say? Bruce obviously thinks you had an affair with Stacey and wants you to leave. You call this a 'sabbatical.' But it sounds to me like he's putting you out to pasture."

Marc shook his head. "Bruce thinks no such thing. The media have jumped all over this story and are determined to make the church look bad and make the community think I'm guilty."

She held his gaze. "Well, *are* you guilty?"

"I've already told you I'm innocent. Why won't you believe me?" He threw up his hands. "Gill, this has to stop. I've asked God to change your heart, because you have no idea how it hurts to know you don't believe me. Look, what does 1 Corinthians 13 say? Real love means we think the best of each other. Couldn't you just *try* to give me the benefit of the doubt?"

God, can I believe him? Is he really telling me the truth?

Seeing the hurt in his eyes, Gillian felt her rage dwindling. In her heart flickered a sincere desire for reconciliation, but her mind doubted such restoration could take place. "Marc, I'm prepared to forgive you, but please—just be honest with me about Stacey. I can accept that, we can move on, and I'll never bring it up again. I promise."

Marc's jaw muscles bunched. "Gillian, Stacey and I never, *ever,* had an affair—got it? I can't believe you'd take Stacey's word over mine. If you can't trust me on this, then I have nothing else to say. But think long and hard about what you're doing to us, to our marriage." He hesitated, as if debating whether to go on. "You're distrusting me just like . . . just like you distrust your dad. Just because he gambled away your inheritance in Vegas and practically put your mom in the poorhouse, you're convinced no other man can be trusted."

Gillian shook her head, fuming that he would drag her father into this discussion. But before reacting, she chewed her lower lip and considered. This news had to be hard on Marc, too; he deserved some compassion. And suppose he *was* right after all. Suppose she *had* been behaving foolishly, distrusting him when he had been innocent all along. He had never lied to her before, so why did she have such a hard time believing him now?

Perhaps it *was* because of her father. Ever since his betrayal, trust didn't come easily to her, especially with men. Secrecy was something else that bothered her. Why had Marc kept Stacey's love letters and e-mails a secret? His secrecy made her wonder if he was hiding something else. Something far worse than Stacey's apparently baseless allegation.

Marc stepped toward her. "There's something else you need to consider. Suppose Stacey fabricated that letter and meant for you to find it. Have you considered that the letter could have been part of her plan to stir things up between us?"

"Yes, I've thought of that, too," she said quietly.

"Then I could be innocent. You have to admit the possibility."

She felt an ache at his words and realized she'd hurt him. Hurt him deeply. But still, Stacey's letter made his words so hard to believe. Could Stacey have been so disillusioned as to have manufactured an affair in her mind? Her gaze drifted to the pink hydrangea, a symbol of Marc's love. He deserved her love in return.

She pressed her eyes closed and prayed for grace, for the right words. Regardless of her feelings of betrayal, she realized Marc was right, that she needed to give him the benefit of the doubt. She swallowed hard. "I'm sorry, Marc. You're right. I'm sorry for not believing you and for hurting you."

Disbelief glinted in his eyes. "Really?"

"Yes, I was being stupid." She felt herself tearing up. "Of course, I believe you. I was just feeling emotional about leaving this place." *And about leaving my babies. And about finding Stacey's letter, which still seems so hard to dismiss.* "Will you forgive me?"

He smiled, clearly relieved. "Of course, I forgive you. I'm sorry for not telling you about the letters before. And I'm so sorry about the sabbatical, Gill. I really am. I can only imagine the pressure this puts on you."

She wiped her eyes. "No, I'm okay with it. Really, I am. But it's just so sudden, and there's so much to do. Two weeks isn't very long to put things in order." *And surely he understands how I like things in order. The garden rows are straight for a reason.*

"I know, but a change of scenery might be good for all of us, don't you think?"

She peered down at her flowers and shook her head slowly as she mentally checked off her recent calligraphy projects. She wondered how her business would survive if she moved farther away from her clients.

She wondered if Christine at the frame shop would be willing to take orders for her. *If so, that could probably work.* Besides, most of her customers had worked with her before and would trust her work, even if she wasn't local for a while. As long as she had the U.S. Postal Service, she could work from anywhere in the country.

She felt Marc's arms around her, pulling her close in a way he hadn't held her since the shooting two weeks ago. With a start, she realized how intensely she'd longed for his embrace. Resting the side of her face against his chest, she marveled that she could ever have been angry with him.

They pulled apart, and he peered down into her eyes. "I'm surprised by how well you're taking this."

I guess I'm surprising myself. She shrugged. "God's in control. Do I want to leave? No. But, whether I like it or not, God must have a plan in all of this. What's the point in fighting?"

"I love you, Gill." He bent down and kissed her, his hands cupping her face. "It's so nice to have you back."

"It's nice to *be* back."

But even as he embraced her again, doubts nagged at the back of her mind. She mentally locked them away, determined not to speak of them again.

CHAPTER 19

"CHUCK, PUT ME DOWN! I don't want to be carried. Have you taken leave of your senses?"

While Emily giggled like a little girl, Chuck Riley carried her across the threshold and set her down among the boxes in their condo in Cocoa Beach, Florida. It felt good to flex his arms, not that she was any burden; Emily had always been a featherweight. *Thank the Lord for that!* he thought, remembering his sensitive knees and back.

Together they surveyed the summation of their lives in the pile of boxes cluttering the middle of the condo floor. Riley sensed weariness in the way Emily stood, hands on hips, arthritic fingers knobby and bent. He knew the long drive from Cincinnati to Florida in the U-Haul had been an ordeal for her, though she wasn't the type to complain.

Suddenly, he knew what he would do. He would lead her to her favorite chair—at least *that* wasn't packed away—and make her a steaming cup of chamomile tea, her favorite. He would face the chair to the window so she could admire the ocean while he tidied the place up a bit. He looked forward to getting some exercise after sitting in the truck for all those hours. But first . . .

He wrapped his arms around her and held her tight, her curly gray hair smelling faintly of raspberries and cinnamon. She turned and smiled at him, the light in her eyes the same as it had been forty-six years ago on their wedding day. For many years, they had dreamed of this moment. It was a special treat to hold each other and to realize their dream had come true.

"Someday when we're rich, we'll buy a condo on the ocean," they had joked. Neither had taken the words seriously until an unexpected inheritance from an obscure cousin had come Emily's way. Now they could spend the rest of their lives admiring the view of the ocean below.

He hated it already. *What am I going to do with my days?*

How could he spend each day staring at the ocean? There was no mystery here, nothing to keep his inquisitive mind active. He supposed that was why many of his friends had wasted away after retirement—something he had determined would never happen to him. It was a change without excitement, and he wasn't sure he liked it. At least, not yet.

"Pinch me, Chuck," Emily said. "We've dreamed of this day for so long. I can't believe it's finally here."

He almost did pinch her, but he swallowed his fears instead. It would take some getting used to, but he would be fine once he learned how to be idle and how to count the waves on the ocean.

He didn't intend to be bored. He and Emily had found a small, vibrant church where they could serve in the senior citizens' ministry. He also had his speedboat, his old-time radio programs, and his library of Perry Mason novels. And if he felt daring, he might even take a dip in the ocean with Emily. He knew she would be swimming out there every chance she got. Years ago, as a young slip of a girl, she had won an Olympic bronze medal, and swimming had remained a lifelong pursuit of hers. Her medal had always enjoyed a prominent display over the fireplace, along with the many portraits of their daughter, her husband, and their granddaughters.

Maybe retirement wouldn't be so bad after all.

Later, they stood on the dock and watched the way the waves sent the sunbeams dancing. Seagulls circled overhead, their cries reminding Riley of violent crime scenes that sometimes flashed in his mind like a macabre slide show.

"This is paradise." Emily squeezed his hand. "I don't think there's another soul out today."

Now that they were nearing the end of October, the majority of vacationers had flown north, and most people were back to work. He felt like a child abandoned by an absentminded parent in a large supermarket.

Emily rubbed his back as if sensing his uneasiness. "You'll like it. Give it a chance."

Riley waved his hand, a characteristic gesture he reserved for whenever she nagged. "I *am* giving it a chance. It's just a big change for you and me."

"And don't I know it." She looked him square in the eye. "Now we'll be seeing each other more often than at breakfast and bedtime."

"It'll just take some adjusting—that's all I'm saying. A couple weeks ago, I was chasing murderers one-third my age. Now I'm just supposed to sit in a lawn chair all day?"

"Or just for a few hours. That's the fun of it. You can do whatever you want. Read a book. Watch TV."

Not solve murders. I can't do that. "It'll just take some adjusting," he repeated.

And then there was that other matter he had conveniently forgotten about until now. The Magician Murders. Somewhere, because of his careless investigation, a man who had strangled four women still walked free.

Okay, I'm blaming myself, but what else am I supposed to do? I suppose the guilt will nag me until either the killer is caught or I'm in the grave—whichever comes first. He thought about the many grieving parents who had so graciously cooperated with his investigation, never to receive answers to their questions. Never to experience closure.

Four years of endless interviews, dead-end leads, and fruitless background checks had ended in whimpering futility. He'd come up with nothing. Just four women buried in a cemetery. Four women who had looked into the eyes of a demon.

Shaking his head, Riley scanned the horizon. On the beach below, a seagull pecked at a dead fish.

Even hundreds of miles from where the crimes had been committed, he had a hard time letting go. In fact, he *couldn't* let go. He could hope, and he could pray. And maybe somehow in the sphere of God's mercy, there was something more he could do.

If only God would show him the way.

Part 2

CASTLE IN THE MIDDLE OF NOWHERE

The Past is such a curious Creature
To look her in the Face
A Transport may reward us
Or a Disgrace—

Unarmed if any meet her
I charge him fly
Her rusty Ammunition
Might yet reply.

—Emily Dickinson, "The Past Is Such
a Curious Creature"

CHAPTER 20

GRIPPING THE TAHOE'S STEERING wheel with both hands, Gillian fastened heavy eyes on the back of the U-Haul truck that rumbled down the highway ahead of her. Everything they would need for the next two months was meticulously packed inside that truck. The rest of their belongings, along with the Saturn, would remain in Chicago under the watchful eye of a house sitter.

We couldn't have picked nicer weather for our move, she thought. The November sky was pristine, with what Milton would have called "fleecy clouds" congregating to the west. Fighting a losing battle with drowsiness, she was contemplating asking Marc to pull over at the next rest stop. A cup of coffee had done its duty after a quick lunch near the Wisconsin-Michigan border. But now, bug-eyed and listless, she wondered if toothpicks could help keep her eyes open.

"This is ridiculous!" Crystal cried from the passenger seat. "We should have been there a half hour ago."

"We've gotta be pretty close, sweetie. I bet it won't be long now."

Brow furrowed in concentration, Crystal was bent over a map of Michigan that was stretched across the lap of her blue jeans. Tracing their route with her index finger, she frowned out the window at rural roads and dilapidated farmhouses that flashed by, as if she would be able to pinpoint their location simply by studying their surroundings.

Two hours after heading north on Highway 117 from Highway 2, they had passed plenty of tiny towns, ramshackle motels, and shops specializing in smoked fish and live bait. A half hour ago, they had passed through the small town of Newberry, Michigan, which meant they were close. But they hadn't seen anything matching the description of their temporary home.

Gillian reflected on the events of the past few weeks. Crystal had taken the news of their move hardest—first weeping, and then sulking, until Marc had sat her down for a heart-to-heart chat about submitting to God's will. Later, she had seemed to come to terms with their situation. But "coming to terms," Gillian knew, was as far as it went. Crystal wasn't happy about the move. Not one bit. After all, she had left all of her friends behind, not the least of whom was Ryan Brodski.

In some ways, Gillian and Marc saw the move as an answer to prayer; Crystal was too young to be getting serious. Besides, the distance between Crystal and Ryan would test the relationship and prove whether anything lasting would endure.

Crystal wasn't the only one feeling less than enthusiastic about the sudden move. Working at a historic lighthouse on Lake Superior in Michigan's Upper Peninsula was hardly on Gillian's list of top ten ways to spend the fall. But how the details had fallen into place had convinced Marc and her that it was God's leading.

First, Bruce Wellers's aunt and uncle, the Hendersons, were caretakers at Whistler's Point. Second, Mrs. Henderson had promptly replied to Bruce's e-mail inquiry with great interest. *Yes, we could certainly use more help. It would be wonderful to have a nice Christian couple assisting us this fall.*

Crystal grabbed the cell phone and hit redial. "Hey, Dad. Still awake?"

Marc's bored voice emanated through the phone's tiny speaker. "Holding my own, munchkin."

"That guy at the gas station didn't know what he was talking about. According to his directions, we should have found Whistler's Point a half hour ago. I think maybe—"

"Crystal."

"Yeah?"

"Look out your right window."

Crystal turned her head and stared. "Mom, I think we found it."

Glancing past Crystal, Gillian struggled to stay in her lane. On a distant hill, rising against the cobalt blue of Lake Superior, stood a beautiful, red brick structure that resembled a mansion. Attached to the mansion was a stark white lighthouse tower that rose into the sky.

Gillian sucked in a quick breath, surprised by the lift in her emotions. She hadn't expected anything this grand. Resembling something between Thomas Jefferson's Monticello and the colonial houses popular in Williamsburg, Virginia, the lighthouse looked strangely out of place against the rugged pines and rolling hills of the North Woods—like a castle in the middle of nowhere.

Marc's voice crackled with excitement. "This must be the place. Wow! It looks pretty impressive to me."

After heading north from Milwaukee, the sight of sprawling farmlands and dense forests had washed over Gillian like a dream from her childhood days on a Michigan farm. She eagerly anticipated plopping down on their bed tonight and listening to the crickets.

Of course, going to bed is way down on our priority list. First, we have to move in.

She doubted that seven sturdy fellows were awaiting them at Whistler's Point as they had been at their Chicago home early that morning. In fact, she wasn't sure what to expect. Again, the uneasiness that had been gnawing at the edges of her mind over the past few weeks loomed afresh in her thoughts. Was it such a good idea leaving the Windy City for this exile in the wilderness?

Gillian followed the U-Haul through massive wrought-iron gates and onto a paved driveway that wound up a steep incline. As they crested the hill, the enormous lighthouse rose into view again, even larger and more spectacular than before. The red brick walls of the mansion towered three stories high before concluding in a black-shingled roof, punctuated by regal, white gables. Tall, narrow windows of a bygone era winked in the afternoon sun.

At the top of the attached white tower stood a hexagonal, glass-paneled room encircled by a black catwalk and crowned by a golden top that reminded Gillian of the knobbed lid on a teapot. She wondered how many steps she would need to climb to reach the top.

The driveway continued past the lighthouse, and they followed it another fifty yards, passing the Great Lakes Shipwreck Museum and a couple of other buildings that Gillian couldn't identify, before parking in front of a white two-story house with a black roof and a charming wraparound front porch. She assumed this was the caretaker's house, where they'd be staying until Christmas.

Getting out of the truck, Gillian saw that Marc was greeting a silver-haired couple she presumed were Henry and Clara Henderson, Bruce Wellers's aunt and uncle and caretakers of Whistler's Point.

"My, you're a tall fella." Henry was shaking Marc's hand. "What do they feed you folks down in Chicago?"

"This is my wife, Gillian, and my daughter, Crystal," Marc said as Crystal and Gillian approached.

Gillian extended her hand to the grandmotherly woman with the wrinkled face and the sparkling gray eyes. Clara's grip was surprisingly firm, her smile warm and disarming. But behind her welcoming smile, Gillian sensed a weariness that spoke of many years of hard, painstaking labor.

Keeping up a national historic site like Whistler's Point must be no small task.

"How are yous?" Clara asked. "We're so glad to have you here. You must be bone tired after your journey."

Gillian had never heard anyone say "yous" before; perhaps it was part of the Upper Peninsula dialect. Hooking a lock of hair behind her ear, she said, "It sure was a pretty drive, but I don't think I've ever been this far north before. I didn't really know what to expect. Maybe I was thinking of Eskimos."

"They aren't here yet," Clara said with a straight face, "but they should be here any day now. Here the winters come early and stay late."

"But, of course, if you love snow like I do," Henry said with a wink, "winter can't come any sooner."

Amazed that anyone could love cold weather, Gillian shook Henry's large, well-muscled hand, which had grown calloused over the years. In spite of his years—he had to be in his seventies—Henry showed no trace of the stooped back so common among men his age. If anything, he looked athletic. A full head of thick, white hair added to his seeming youthfulness. The only distraction to his confident image was a facial tic; his right eye blinked nonstop.

"I was exaggerating a little bit," Clara said with an amused expression. "We should have another month before the snow flies, though sometimes we have a white Thanksgiving."

"So you folks decided to join us Yoopers, eh?" Henry asked Marc with a twinkle in his eye.

"Yoopers?" Gillian glanced at Marc. "What's that?"

Clara laughed. "That's what people who live in Michigan's Upper Peninsula are called. Get it? U.P.—Yooper."

While the Hendersons greeted Crystal, Gillian realized that she had almost missed seeing a thin wisp of a woman who seemed to have materialized out of nowhere. Possibly in her late thirties, she was dressed in a long, old-fashioned dress, her features dark against white, buttermilk skin. Gillian was struck by the sharp contrast the woman painted to the gray-haired Hendersons. Looking closer, she wondered if the woman was possibly related to Liza Minnelli, actress-daughter of Judy Garland. Her luminous, black eyes and cropped, raven hair were features one did not quickly forget.

"I'm Nicole Wood." The woman offered a limp hand to Gillian. "I'm the Whistler's Point tour guide."

Gillian remembered reading the Whistler's Point brochures that Clara had mailed to them. It hadn't occurred to her until now that someone must guide the public tours. That explained Nicole's old-fashioned dress.

Before she could ask Nicole if she ever grew tired of saying her lines, Henry swiped Marc's keys and promised to unload the trailer, with the help of three of his assistant groundskeepers, while Nicole gave the Thayers a tour of the lighthouse.

Henry unlocked the front door of the caretaker's house and turned to them with a smile. "This is where you'll be living. It's almost as old as the lighthouse. I hope it'll be suitable."

"It's beautiful," Gillian said, and meant it. "I'm sure it will be more than suitable."

"You go on ahead." Clara patted her arm. "You will join us for supper, won't you? We live just a couple of miles down the road. Henry will give you directions."

Gillian felt surprised by her off-handed invitation, but wasn't about to argue. Preparing a meal was one thing she didn't want to contend with after the long drive. Besides, in the mess that would need arranging, she wasn't even sure where the food was.

"That sounds wonderful," Marc said.

"The steaks have been soaking in my secret marinade all day," Clara said with a wink. "And you'll have to try a traditional U.P. pasty."

Gillian had heard of, but never tasted, the meat-and-vegetable-stuffed pies common in the region. Pasties had provided the ideal lunch for workers drilling for iron ore in the many mines scattered across the Upper Peninsula at the turn of the twentieth century.

"We'll see you at six then," Clara said.

"If you'd like to step this way." Nicole beckoned them down a flagstone pathway that wound around the perimeter of the lighthouse. Gillian marveled at the size and grandeur of the place. Inside, she was amazed by the high ceilings, varnished woodwork, and priceless antique furniture. She had the distinct impression of stepping back in time.

After ninety-six calf-straining steps up a circular staircase, they reached the top of the tower, out of breath. Standing in the octagonal lantern room, Gillian peered out the tall windows at the distant horizon. Lake Superior stretched as far as the eye could see. Beyond the sandy shoreline, the blue water sparkled in the sunlight. In the distance, a freighter inched across the shimmering expanse.

God, You are so good. Gillian felt Marc take her hand and squeeze it. Instantly, she felt foolish to have had reservations about Whistler's Point. Marc was always so sure of himself, so talented at seeing the sunny side of life.

When they first met at Bible college, she'd been amazed at his incessant activity and tenacity. Once she got to know him, she wasn't surprised when he went on to cram three years of seminary into two. She recalled their first church, a struggling congregation of thirty-five. Marc had hit the streets of the neighborhood with enthusiasm, determined to see the ministry grow.

After about six years, the membership had tripled in size, but Marc was restless; the administrative responsibilities weren't what he'd expected. His greatest desire was to counsel people in God's Word, preferably one-on-one. He was ready for a new challenge, and that's when the Lord had led them to Heritage Bible Church in Chicago.

But it's all gone now, she realized with a start, then corrected herself. *Don't be silly. This is only temporary. We're here for only a few months. We'll be back in Chicago in no time.*

But a little voice at the back of her mind told her to stop believing such lies.

CHAPTER 21

BROWN PLASTIC-FRAME GLASSES dangled on a silver chain around the skinny neck of the head librarian at the Tahquamenon Area Public Library. Her name tag read "Marjorie Stevens," an old-fashioned name, and she looked older than her thirty-two years.

"It isn't a very demanding job." Peering at the young man sitting across from her, she leaned on her elbows over the cluttered top of her old, varnished desk. "But we need someone who's reliable, someone who doesn't mind working behind the scenes."

Marjorie wondered if she should reconsider the Mary Kay makeover her sister had offered yesterday. Perhaps the handsome young man sitting across from her might find her more attractive. Was he married? The way he kept his hands knotted in his lap, she couldn't tell.

"Actually, that's the type of work I prefer," he said. "Stacking books is fine with me."

"Of course, there will be other duties, too. But for a small town, you'd be surprised by how many books are checked out each week. There are a lot of books that need to be sorted and put back on the shelves." She stressed this point to ensure he understood the immense responsibility that would be facing him. His serious expression showed that her words had registered.

"Once the snow flies and it's too cold to be outdoors," she went on, "I guess people just stay indoors and read books. I suppose there are worse things they could be doing with their time."

He seemed sincere enough with those conservative black-frame glasses; serious, black eyes; and curly, blond hair, which he'd obviously bleached. On the other hand, she didn't care for his sparse blond goatee, and she found his fingernails rather disgusting. She wondered why he wore them so long. Perhaps he played the guitar.

"Frankly"—she perched her glasses on her nose to glance at his résumé—"there's not much else to do up here during the winter months, unless you like snowmobiling. But you don't exactly look like the snowmobiling type."

"No, I'm not," he said in a radio-quality voice that she found mesmerizing. "But I'm quite a reader myself, and I love music. In fact, I couldn't help noticing that you have quite a collection of recordings here. I especially love Broadway musicals. If there's ever anything you need to know about, say, Rodgers and Hammerstein, Alan Jay Lerner and Frederick Loewe, or Andrew Lloyd Webber, just let me know. I know all their songs and lyrics by heart."

She peered at him, fascinated, over the rim of her glasses. "Really. Well, I must say that you should be quite an asset here. Very good." She glanced at his résumé and frowned. "I see that you have absolutely no library experience—in fact, very little work history at all."

"I'm a good, hard worker. You'll see that right away if you just give me a chance. I'll be on time every morning. I'll even work evenings and weekends if you need me to."

Did she hear desperation in his voice? "Do you mind telling me why you need the job so badly?"

"I just moved to the area and need to pay my rent. Gotta make a living, if you know what I mean."

"Oh, yes. I do, indeed." Marjorie Stevens thought of her own dear father, who had once worked three jobs just to keep food on the table for her and her three sisters.

"If you aren't sure, you could hire me for thirty days, kind of like on probation. If at the end of the thirty days you don't like what you see, I'll pack my bags."

Marjorie doubted she would ever dislike what she saw in the young man sitting across from her. In fact, she was amazed to discover he had brains as well as good looks. She pursed her lips, tapping her scarlet fingernails against her cheek.

"Well, we are rather in a pinch right now. See, the lady who vacated her position just found out she has terminal cancer." She paused for effect. "Yes, I know. It's a terribly depressing story. Anyhow, she called and said she couldn't come in anymore—rather sudden, to be sure. So that was that, and so here we are."

He didn't answer. He just stared at her with those magical, black eyes. He reminded her of someone, but she couldn't quite put her finger on whom. Then it hit her. His eyes reminded her of Cary Grant's—the late movie star's. He was thinner than Cary Grant, but those eyes—well, they made up for the deficiency. She wouldn't mind seeing those eyes every day of her life.

Realizing that she was staring at him, she steered her gaze back to his résumé. "Well, I don't see why not." She looked up, meeting his eyes again. "You seem nice enough, and I'm sure you'll work out just fine. How does tomorrow sound?"

He seemed pleased. "Tomorrow would be perfect."

She handed him her gold cross pen so he could fill out the paperwork. When he was finished, what happened next was something she would later tell the police. He waved his hands before her face, and the pen disappeared. She gasped.

"Oh my!" he said in a singsong voice. "Where did the pen go?" He grinned and waved his hands theatrically, showing they were empty. Then—*voila!*—the pen was back in his hands. He handed it back to her.

She struggled to breathe. "My goodness, that was . . . um, amazing."

He winked at her and stood. "Just something I picked up." He headed for the door and glanced back. "See you tomorrow, bright and early."

CHAPTER 22

My dearest children,

How I miss visiting your graves and singing to you. Life here is very different from what I'd expected. Already a week has passed since our arrival at Whistler's Point, and I'm not exactly sure how I fit in. At least not yet.

So what is the Whistler's Point lighthouse like? Well, it's like a castle. I can't imagine how Clara even begins to keep all those rooms clean. And the rooms are filled with antiques that belong in a museum, in my opinion.

This is what Nicole—she's the tour guide—told me about Whistler's Point. It was built in 1883 by a crotchety old man named George Whistler. Wealthy from his gold strike in Alaska, he decided to build a mansion on Upper Michigan's Lake Superior. A friend had assured him that building a mansion on Lake Superior was comparable to building one on the Atlantic Ocean. That friend obviously knew nothing about the rough weather so common on the Great Lakes coast. In fact, George Whistler's first winter was one of the severest in decades. In March, when the snow still hadn't melted, Harriet, his wife, packed her bags and left, vowing never to return. According to records, she never did.

But Captain Whistler—that's what he called himself after that—was determined to stick it out with his two sons, Fred and Christian, and his daughter, Emily. He decided to spend his time profitably by assuming the rugged life of a lighthouse keeper. He built a lighthouse tower onto the mansion. Back when the lighthouse was staffed with a keeper and full-time workers, the revolving light had to be frequently rewound, cleaned, and carefully monitored. Though some jeered at Captain Whistler's

*enterprise, his service paid off. At least fifty ships, lost in the fog, were
saved from disaster due to the Whistler's Point lighthouse.*

*Later, his older son, Christian, inherited the mansion, and Christian's
son, Edward, gave it to the state in 1990. Today, the United States Coast
Guard inspects the lighthouse regularly to ensure it remains in proper
working order.*

*Well, enough history. What do I do with my time? I still have my cal-
ligraphy. Of course, that's after homeschooling Crystal, which isn't at all
what I expected. It's much more demanding and time consuming.*

*Your father seems to be fitting in here just fine. Crystal and I set up an
upstairs office for him so he could continue his studies. During the week-
days, he helps Henry with landscaping. Your father grew up helping his
dad with his landscaping business, so this is nothing new to him.*

*Your sister, Crystal, hates it here. She complains that she doesn't have
any friends her own age. The local teen theater group is doing* The Sound
of Music *at the high school auditorium the weekend before Thanksgiving.
I encouraged Crystal to try out for a part, but it's too late. The cast has
been rehearsing since September, and all the parts are taken. But at least
Crystal can serve on the stage crew.*

*The Hendersons invited us to their small Baptist church, which will
do for now. It's much smaller than what we're used to, but the people are
friendly, and the teaching seems solid. The pastor asked your father if he'd
be willing to teach the adult Sunday school class. That should be a big
encouragement to him, I think.*

*Whistler's Point doesn't really fit into any of our hopes and dreams.
Now I understand better how Abraham must have felt when God told
him to leave his home and move to Canaan. I can tell that your father misses his ministry in Chicago very much. Well, I must go and start
supper.*

I think of you often. I love you.

Your loving Mother

CHAPTER 23

As Gillian stacked the evening's dirty supper plates in the sink, Marc offered to wash the dishes.

"No, you've had a hard day." She patted his arm, knowing that his sore muscles hadn't yet adapted to the landscaping routine. "Why don't you go take a shower and relax."

Marc dragged his feet toward the bathroom, then stood up straight, pushing his shoulders back. "I don't think I've ever been this sore in all my life."

"When you're done," she called, suppressing a smirk, "I think I'll take a bath and read in bed for a while. I'm beat."

"I get the bathtub after you," Crystal said. "That is if you guys leave me any hot water."

Crystal had slumped on the living room couch, arms folded across her chest. Leaving the dishes to soak, Gillian sank into the hunter green wingback chair across from her daughter and reached forward to pat her knee. "Hey, you can't expect to waltz right in and take the lead role in a musical when folks have been practicing since September. It wouldn't be fair."

Crystal shrugged. "I know, but being on stage crew isn't quite what I had in mind. I told Mrs. Jamison I've been in *The Sound of Music* before. I've even sung Maria's part."

"Crystal, you can't expect her just to take the part of Maria away from Tanya Wright and give it to you. C'mon, you know that wouldn't be right. Besides, Mrs. Jamison must have thought Tanya would do a good job as Maria. Otherwise, she wouldn't have chosen her."

Crystal glared at the floor as if it were somehow to blame. "Yeah, well, she must be deaf. You should hear how Tanya slurs and scoops her notes."

Gillian peered into Crystal's eyes, knowing her daughter should know the look. *Be kind.*

Crystal squirmed. "Well, okay, Tanya's got a decent voice, but she doesn't support any of her high notes properly."

"Well, maybe she hasn't had voice lessons like you have. Even if you had tried out, Mrs. Jamison may not have been looking for someone with a lot of vocal training anyhow. Maybe you're overqualified."

Crystal's mouth twisted to one side as if she hadn't considered that possibility. "Maybe you're right."

"Be careful you don't look down on her, okay? Maybe you'll have a chance to help her."

Crystal nodded. "You never know."

Silently, Gillian prayed that God would help Crystal keep the right attitude about her singing. She had always told Crystal that if she sang for God's glory and not for men's applause, He would bless her abilities and take her to the moon if that's what He wanted. "You and Tanya are going to be working together. Maybe she doesn't know Jesus. Maybe she doesn't have a new song to sing like you do."

Crystal sighed and nodded. "You're right, Mom. Thanks for the attitude check."

After a quick hug, Gillian watched Crystal head upstairs to her room. Now that Crystal's computer and Internet were working, she had plenty of Web site projects for clients back in Chicago. But with homeschooling and twice-weekly play practices that demanded the stage crew's participation, Gillian wondered how her daughter was going to keep up.

After his shower, Marc ambled into the room and glanced at his boxes of Bible commentaries and biblical counseling books that had been piled in one corner. They were among the last few boxes waiting for someone to give them a proper home. Gillian hated clutter, but she'd promised herself not to nag. Whenever Marc got around to the books was fine.

After her bath, she returned to the living room and noticed that Marc and the boxes had disappeared. Glancing into the study, she expected to find Marc, but the room was empty. She searched the house but couldn't find him anywhere. What she *did* find were his boxes of books stacked neatly in a dark corner of the cobwebbed basement.

Biting her lip, she went upstairs and asked Crystal if she'd seen Marc.

"I think I might have seen him heading down to the shoreline," Crystal replied.

The sun hung low in the sky, which was a vibrant shade of pink and azure, when Gillian pulled on her jacket and headed down to the sandy path. On her first trip to the shore, she'd been stunned by the brisk breeze.

Winter will be here soon. Then I'll discover what cold in the North Woods really means.

In spite of the bracing chill of the wind, she admired the beauty around her. Just beyond the lighthouse, a ridge of rugged rock jutted above the sandy shoreline. Henry called it the "diving rock" and said it was a great place for jumping into the lake on a hot summer day. She shook her head, unable to comprehend jumping into the frigid water from that height. It had to be at least a thirty-foot drop!

Waves lapped the rocky shoreline, leaving a trail of pebbles and tiny pieces of driftwood along the beach. It was a beautiful place, almost like a paradise. Shortly before her untimely death during World War II, a young Jewish girl named Anne Frank had written in her diary, "Think of all the beauty still left around you and be happy." Gillian meditated on those words.

Spotting Marc's red windbreaker in the distance, she set off at a brisk pace. The fresh, frigid air cleared her head and made her feel glad for the stroll. Marc stood facing the water, arms folded across his chest. His blond-gray hair, still wet from his shower, blew in the breeze, his red jacket ballooning at his back. She wondered what he was thinking about as he stood there so thoughtfully.

"Crystal told me I'd find you here."

Reaching an arm around Gillian, he pulled her close, and she detected the faint aroma of soap and aftershave. "This eighty-mile stretch is called 'the shipwreck coast of Lake Superior,'" he said. "There are more than five-hundred-fifty known shipwrecks in this lake. The most recent one was the *Edmund Fitzgerald* in 1975. Interesting, huh?"

Gillian nodded and decided that the direct approach was best. "Why did you put your books in the basement?"

He fixed his eyes on a point somewhere in the distance, a sure sign he didn't want to be open with her. "If you're concerned about mold, I'll put them somewhere else. But I don't know that I'll ever use those books up here. Why clutter up the house with something we don't need right now?"

"What do you mean? You plan to keep up your studies while we're here, don't you?"

"Maybe. I don't know." Removing his arm from around her, he aimed a rock at the water and released it obliquely. It skipped once, twice, then disappeared.

Gillian rephrased the question, wondering if he'd misunderstood her. "You'll want to keep up your studies for when we return to Chicago for Christmas, right?"

He arched an eyebrow. "You think we'll be back by Christmas?"

"Well, isn't that what Bruce said?"

"Bruce never really said anything concrete. You know how he is. He likes to speak wishfully about things that rarely take place. Remember all that talk about building a Christian retirement center? We never got past preliminary blueprints." He glanced at her with a look of cynicism that was so unlike him. "We could be here longer than this fall. I'm sorry I didn't tell you earlier."

Gillian stuffed her hands into her pockets, unsettled by this news. "But we'll get back to Chicago eventually, even if it's longer than we thought. You'll want to be ready to continue your ministry when we return, right?"

"I don't know, Gill. I've been giving this a lot of thought and prayer. Maybe God doesn't want me to return to counseling."

She stared at him. "But of course He does. That's the whole reason we moved to Chicago in the first place, remember?"

Marc overturned some pebbles with his foot and dug a furrow in the ground. "Yeah, I know, but . . . well, things change, Gill. And they changed a whole lot for me when Stacey pulled the trigger and I nearly died."

"But, Marc—"

"No, hear me out." He faced her, his jaw muscles bunching. "Lying on my back in the hospital, I began to see my life in a whole new way. I evaluated where my life was heading, especially after what happened with Stacey. And, frankly, I didn't like what I saw."

He shrugged. "I tried to help Stacey—I truly did. I gave it my best shot, and look what good it did her. Good grief! She almost killed me." He shook his head. "I'm not any good as a counselor. The sooner we both accept that fact, the better."

His words made her feel more afraid than she'd felt in a long time. It was so unlike Marc to give up, to turn his back on something for which he'd worked so long.

She shook her head. "You're wrong. You're a wonderful counselor. Think about all the people you've helped over the years. Think about Tim Rooney, on the point of suicide before he met you. Now he's in seminary, planning to go to the mission field. Just because Stacey became psychotic doesn't mean you're a lousy counselor. How could anybody have known she was so messed up she'd try to kill you?"

"I'm just not sure I want to go back to counseling and pastoring right now, okay? Maybe this is exactly where God wants us for a while. Actually, I'm enjoying sweating and getting my hands dirty."

"You're sure?"

He peered into her eyes. "For now, I'm dead sure. I don't know how long the Lord wants us here, but I'm certain about one thing. For some reason, God put us here, and I think we're going to find out what that reason is pretty soon. Until then, we just need to sit tight and wait on the Lord to show us what He wants us to do."

"But I hate to see you turn your back on all those years of training and experience."

He put his hands on her shoulders and gave her a comforting squeeze. "I may have taken a break from the pastorate, but I will never turn my back on God. I promise you that."

CHAPTER 24

THE MAUVE SKY WAS fading to black when Stacey James crossed the empty parking lot. Her legs were tired and sore from all the miles she'd walked today. Glancing around furtively, she slid into the shadow of the building, certain she hadn't been seen. She had decided to come at night and take advantage of the cover of darkness.

Now, more than a month after the shooting, Marc had disappeared, and she needed to know where he was. The news reports had said that he and his family had left the area and gone on a sabbatical at some undisclosed location.

Undisclosed, my eye. If anyone knew where Marc was, Liz Simons would. Of course, Liz wasn't exactly going to hand her Marc's new address on a silver platter. But there were other ways to find the information she was looking for.

After burning her clothes in the monster stainless steel grill at Jared's, Stacey had pulled on a baggy pair of his jeans, and was surprised that the fit wasn't nearly as bad as she had feared. After rummaging for a black T-shirt, a black sweatshirt, and a brown leather jacket, she'd left the condo and hiked across town to Heritage Bible Church, lugging one of Jared's gym bags stuffed with several bottles of water, a can opener, and as many cans of food as she could carry. The heavy, awkward bag had slowed her down, but there was no telling how far her journey would take her, and she wasn't about to go hungry.

Circling to the rear of the church, she found a sheltered basement window and shattered the glass with the gym bag full of food. Moments later, she crouched in a small Sunday school room furnished with a round table and tiny, orange plastic chairs. The bulletin board displayed the six days of creation, brightened by fluorescent animal cutouts. Reaching for the door knob, she froze.

Somebody somewhere was whistling. The tune echoed down the empty hallways and sent a shiver down her spine. Her hand instinctively flew to her sagging jacket pocket, heavy with the weight of her gun.

Pressing her back to the cool concrete-block wall, she cursed her luck. Only a janitor could be cranking out "Amazing Grace" at this hour. When the whistling faded away, she decided to leave the bag and return for it on her way out.

Opening the door, she crept down a dark hallway flanked by closed doors on both sides. The walls were tinted by the red aura of an emergency exit sign. Pausing, she listened, fingers pressed to the cool, concrete wall.

She heard nothing.

She entered the church fellowship hall, which was used primarily for church potlucks and wedding receptions. A few months ago, she'd attended a fellowship here and had taken great pains to sit in Marc's line of sight, waiting patiently for his gaze to sweep her direction. Only once had their eyes met, but he'd glanced away coldly, prompting her to storm out in frustration.

Somewhere nearby a door closed.

Pressing her back to the wall, she willed herself to become one with the darkness. From the parking lot, she heard an engine crank several times before turning over. Creeping to the nearest window, she peered out just in time to see a sedan pull out of the parking lot and head down the road, red brake lights glowing.

She decided not to test fate by remaining in the building longer than necessary. She passed through the commercial-size kitchen, grabbing a Diet Coke and a bag of rolls that had been left out on a countertop. The Coke was warm but sublime, and she downed it in seconds. The bread, on the other hand, was old and deserved to be tossed out to the birds, but it was better than nothing.

Ascending a flight of stairs, she crept through the dark hallways toward the pastoral office wing, ears straining for any trace of another's presence. Hearing nothing, she finished her journey, reached

Liz's desk, and skimmed her Rolodex, certain Liz would have Marc's address if anyone would. But she found nothing.

Feeling emboldened, she used a paperweight from Liz's desk to smash the window in Dave Ritchie's locked office door. Rummaging through his desk, she found an address book in his top right-hand drawer. She scanned the T section. Tanner. Taplin.

Thayer.

She read the address repeatedly until she had it memorized, her heart sinking. *Michigan!* How would she ever get there? It was way too far to go on foot. Too bad she didn't still have her car. After the shooting, she'd ditched the white Malibu in a hotel parking lot just blocks from Maralee's, knowing the police would be looking for it. She wondered if they'd found the car yet.

Glancing at Marc's office door, she entertained another impulse. A moment later, the paperweight broke Marc's window, too, and she was inside. She knew Marc's office well and moved quickly past the Western knickknacks she'd never understood. It had always puzzled her that he didn't show off his basketball fame, almost as if that were a part of his life he was embarrassed to talk about.

She snatched a framed portrait of the Thayer family from one of the bookshelves. Rifling through the desk drawers, she found a pair of scissors. Removing the photo, she cut out Marc's face in a neat square and let the trimmings of his family join the broken frame on the floor.

A band of light from the parking lot shone through Marc's window, slashing across Gillian's smiling face. Tempted to take the scissors to Gillian, Stacey chose instead to grind her rival's face into the floor with her heel.

Returning to Liz's desk, Stacey searched through her drawers. She remembered that Liz kept a metal money box filled with proceeds from the church bookstore. Finding the box in the bottom drawer, she used a letter opener to pry the lid open.

Pay dirt! She excitedly stuffed her pockets with bills. Now she wouldn't be tempted to use her credit cards. As long as she used cash, she could go anywhere she wanted without leaving an electronic trail.

On her way to the kitchen to look for more food, she paused to admire Marc's likeness in the red glow of an emergency exit sign. He would be so impressed by the journey she would take to find him. It would be a gesture of her love, a way to patch things up, and he wouldn't be able to turn her away. Removed from the church and from the rules imposed on his life, he could be his true self, the self who loved her and wanted her so badly.

"Very soon," she whispered, imagining herself as the heroine in an old black-and-white movie classic. "Very soon we will be together, my love."

CHAPTER 25

EYES CLOSED, HEAD BACK, Chuck Riley felt the sun baking his face as he prayed for his buddies back in Cincinnati. The small, black notepad where he kept his prayer list rested on his lap, the cool ocean breeze tousling its ink-filled pages.

He knew he shouldn't be out in the sun too long; but one thing he enjoyed best about the Sunshine State was, well, the sunshine. The daily dose of Vitamin D would do him good, Emily kept reminding him. A health fanatic, she was a firm believer in getting at least a half hour of sun daily. She also insisted on his daily drinking eight glasses of water, many of which he covertly poured into her patio plants.

Emily's wicker chair was stationed beside his on the patio, and her face was shielded by a straw hat. He admired her bright, green slacks and her daisy-dotted T-shirt. Across her chest, lying facedown, was one of her favorite Jan Karon novels. From his vantage point, she appeared to be asleep.

Finished praying, he waited a few more minutes until her breathing lapsed into that familiar rhythm he knew so well. He rose slowly, knees creaking, and crept into the condo to his waiting computer. Within seconds, he was logged onto the Internet and had his instant messaging software open.

Juicyfruitcop: Jerry, are you there?

Within seconds came a reply.

Hebrews12race: I'm here. How's Florida?

Juicyfruitcop: Okay, I guess.

Hebrews12race: Just okay? Wanna switch places? I'd take Florida over desk duty any day.

Juicyfruitcop: Come to think of it, you were doing desk duty last week at this time, too.

Hebrews12race: Yeah, it's been really boring around here. I know you're not real keen on your slower pace, buddy, but Florida can't be as boring as this.

Juicyfruitcop: So what's up? What are you doing sitting around? Who's on the Magician Murder case?

Hebrews12race: Aha! So that's why you came chatting today.

Juicyfruitcop: Emily's taking a nap. I thought I'd say hello. So where's the Magician Murder case? Who's on it?

Hebrews12race: Does Emily know you're online asking me these questions? The Magician Murder case is partly the reason you're retired, buddy.

That was the truth, but O'Hearn's bluntness stunned Riley momentarily. A few weeks before his retirement, he'd heard that the unsolved case would be reassigned to some young upstart with a crew cut. He continued typing.

Juicyfruitcop: Look, I gotta know what's going on.

Hebrews12race: Let go of it, bud. This isn't healthy.

Juicyfruitcop: You're right. It's NOT healthy. Some sick loser is out there killing young women. What's healthy about that? Come on, tell me what's going on.

Hebrews12race: All I can do is give you the same answer I gave you last week. Nothing is going on.

Juicyfruitcop: What do you mean, nothing?

Hebrews12race: No new leads. We've done what we can, but this guy knows how to cover his tracks. Trail's going cold again.

Riley paused and listened. Silence. Emily was still asleep. He typed faster.

Juicyfruitcop: Going cold? So does that mean you're not working it anymore?

Hebrews12race: I've still got the file on my desk, but I'm on to other things. I won't be surprised if they pull me off completely one of these days.

Riley leaned back in his chair, his eyes riveted to the computer screen. He rubbed his lower lip with the ball of his thumb. He sat up, fingers flying.

Juicyfruitcop: I know the procedure, Jer, but I sure hate the thought of this file going cold again. When the Magician popped up again after what—thirteen months?—I thought we were going to catch a break.

Hebrews12race: I was hoping too, but you know how these things go.

Juicyfruitcop: Well, keep me posted. If anything breaks on the case, I want to know about it. Anything. Even if it doesn't seem important.

Hebrews12race: I really shouldn't.

Juicyfruitcop: Do it for an old friend.

Hebrews12race: I miss you, buddy.

Juicyfruitcop: I miss you, too. We had some great times together, didn't we?

Hebrews12race: Praise God we're both alive to remember them.

Juicyfruitcop: Still planning to spend Christmas down here with us, right?

Hebrews12race: Wouldn't miss it for the world.

Juicyfruitcop: Seriously, Jer, if anything develops, I want to know. I can't bear to see a case like that gathering dust in a drawer somewhere.

Hebrews12race: So what if something does come up? You can't do anything from down there.

Juicyfruitcop: Sure I can. I still have my mind. I still remember every interview I had, every detail from forensics.

Hebrews12race: It's a wonder you sleep at night.

Juicyfruitcop: Who ever said I sleep at night?

Hebrews12race: So what are you gonna do? Come out of retirement and catch the killer?

Juicyfruitcop: Whatever it takes. Emily will understand.

Hebrews12race: I wouldn't count on it.

The patio door slid open.

Juicyfruitcop: Gotta go. Emily's awake.

Hebrews12race: Stop by anytime. If anything in the case develops, you'll be the first to know.

Juicyfruitcop: Anytime, Jer. Even in the middle of the night. What's beauty sleep when a killer's on the loose?

CHAPTER 26

ON WEDNESDAY AFTER LUNCH, Marc held the spindly top of a small cherry tree steady as Henry Henderson emptied a bucket of water into the gaping hole. Together, they shoveled a mixture of dirt and fertilizer around the tree's roots. After packing the soil down with their feet, girding up the tree's base, they stood back to survey their work.

Marc had to give Henry a lot of credit. In spite of his age, the caretaker barely broke a sweat. From what Marc could gather, Henry had been a busy father of eight. Now all of his children were married and scattered across the globe, but Henry was in no way destined for a rocker on the front porch. At least, not yet. His favorite exercise, he'd said to Marc's surprise, was jump roping.

A stab of pain in his right knee prompted Marc to shift his weight to his other leg. He pulled off his Bulls cap and wiped his forehead on the sleeve of his jacket. The sun shone down with meager light. The weather was mild for mid-November, Henry had said. At least Marc wasn't wearing a heavy coat yet.

"Thanks for your help," Henry said. Hands on hips, he surveyed their work. "You're catching on real fast."

Catching on? I've been doing landscaping all my life, and you know it.
Marc forgave the remark. "Thanks."

"So, which do you prefer—pastoring or landscaping?"

"That's a tough question. I love helping people, but not if they're going to shoot me."

Henry shook his head. "Bruce told Clara and me about what happened. Isn't it amazing—all the fruitcakes in this world? It's a wonder that woman didn't kill you, eh?"

Marc heard someone calling his name and turned. Clara was strolling across the lawn toward them. "Telephone for you, Marc!"

Reaching the Visitor's Center office, Marc found the phone and whooped when he recognized the voice at the other end. "Dave Ritchie? Man, it's good to hear your voice!"

"What other Dave do you know, Shorty?" This had been a standing joke between them, because—as Dave well knew—Marc knew at least a dozen Daves.

"I'm so glad you called. I've been meaning to ask you about my computer cleanup."

"Per your request, Austin sanitized your hard drive, so all those e-mails you were afraid of resurfacing should be history."

"That's a relief. How's the church doing?"

"Actually, attendance has been down, partly due to the media mess, though things have calmed down quite a bit since you left town. Everybody keeps asking when you're coming back."

They exchanged pleasantries about the weather, jokes about the drop in Chicago's crime rate since Marc skipped town, and memories of Saturday morning church basketball league before Marc quit.

"You were our star player, and you know it," Dave said. "Don't even ask me about our season this fall. It's been pathetic without you." He changed the subject, his voice turning serious. "The reason I'm calling. We had a break-in at the church."

"What?"

"Somebody stole all the money out of Liz's money box and broke into my office and yours. We have reason to believe Stacey James was responsible, considering certain evidence left behind."

Marc had hoped the police would have apprehended her by now. "What evidence?"

Dave told Marc about the cut-up family portrait lying on Marc's office floor. "Who else would cut your face out of a portrait like that? It must have been Stacey. Looks like she also went through my drawers and skimmed through my address book. If she did, she probably knows where you are."

Marc's mind ran full speed ahead. Hundreds of miles separated him from Stacey. She'd have to be nuts to come after him across such a long distance, but . . . well, she *was* nuts, wasn't she?

"So what do you think, Marc?"

What anybody with half a brain has to think. "Stacey could be coming after me."

"We don't know that for sure, but if I were in your shoes, I'd be watching my back."

"You've got that right." Marc rubbed his eyes with the heels of his hands, sensing the beginnings of a migraine.

Before hanging up, Dave prayed with Marc over the phone. Marc always felt better after taking time to acknowledge that God was bigger than any problem he might face. After promising to stay in touch, Marc hung up and felt more exhausted than he'd felt in a long time.

Was Stacey coming after him? He didn't know for sure. What he *did* know was that Gillian would be devastated to hear this news and worried sick about his safety. For a split second, he was tempted not to tell her, but then he remembered that keeping secrets had gotten him into trouble before. No, it was best just to be open with her about the situation.

Chances are, Stacey isn't coming after me anyhow.

He found Clara in the Shipwreck Museum.

"Marc, has something happened? You don't look so good."

"I get migraines once in a while. Could you let Henry know that I'm not feeling well? I think I'll call it a day."

Then Marc went to find Gillian with the news.

CHAPTER 27

PEERING OUT THE KITCHEN window, Gillian studied the fall leaves cluttering the ground—another cleanup job for Marc and Henry—and noticed how bare the trees looked already. Fall leaves always reminded her of the cemetery where her babies were buried. She hoped to find time later to write them another letter. Writing her thoughts and feelings seemed to create a special connection.

Meredith and Blaine. How old would they have been today had circumstances been different? How would their tiny bodies have changed and developed?

Tears sprang to her eyes, and she brushed them aside. Facing the kitchen sink, she turned on hot water and reached for a soapy washcloth to scrub the lunch dishes she'd let soak while she worked.

Hearing the back door open, she quickly wiped her eyes and turned to see Marc. "What are you doing home so early?"

He opened the cupboard door and reached for a familiar bottle, a weary look on his face. "I'm getting another migraine."

"I'm sorry." She patted his arm. "Anything I can do? Sometimes a neck massage helps."

Marc shook a couple tablets into his palm. "As long as I can get some quiet for a while, that should help."

She nodded. In general, people had no true understanding of migraines, thinking they were merely bad headaches. They were wrong by a long shot.

She knew the routine by now. Marc would be on his back for the rest of the day in a dark room, and any noise would be like a sledgehammer crashing into his skull. He wouldn't feel better until after the nausea came.

He glanced around. "Where's Crystal?"

"Off to a *Sound of Music* rehearsal."

He filled a glass with water, popped the pills into his mouth, and drank them down. Then he put the glass into the sink and faced her. He seemed to be bracing himself. "Dave Ritchie called. There's something I need to tell you."

He told her about the break-in at Heritage Bible Church. She felt a heaviness in her chest, especially when he mentioned that Stacey had cut his face out of the family portrait.

"I was tempted not to say anything, because I didn't want to upset you," he said. "But I decided that you needed to know the truth."

"I'm glad you told me. I don't like it when you keep secrets from me." She grabbed a coffee mug and scrubbed the living daylights out of it. Soapsuds flew everywhere, but she didn't care. "Stacey *is* coming after you. Where else would she be going?"

"I don't know. But why would she come all the way up here? It doesn't make any sense."

"It makes perfect sense if she's still obsessed with you." She fixed him in a cold stare. "What on earth did you do to make her love you so much?"

He held up a hand to stop her. "Let's not go there, okay? We've been down that road before. There was nothing romantic between us—at least on my side."

"Okay, so then why is she coming here?"

"*If* she's coming here. You're the one who's convinced she is. I'm not."

Gillian sighed. "I'm just being hypothetical. Why would she come after you, if not for romantic reasons?"

He leaned against the countertop, arms folded across his chest. "Beats me. She didn't kill me the first time. Maybe she wants to finish the job."

Gillian strangled the bottle of dish soap. More soap than she needed shot out, splattering the countertop. She wiped up the mess. "No, that's not it. She's still obsessed with you."

"You don't know that."

Gillian faced him. "Sure I do. You say you didn't have an affair with Stacey. Okay, I can accept that. But something happened, Marc, something you don't want to tell me. Maybe you flirted with her. Maybe your conversations became intimate. Either way, something happened. That's why she can't let you go."

He shook his head in exasperation, blowing air through his lips. "For someone who didn't counsel Stacey, you sure seem to know more about her than I do. You think her mind works like yours? Gillian, anyone who has experienced the abuse she's been through is going to be disturbed. Stacey doesn't need any help from me. She's disturbed, she's delusional, and only God can change her. End of story."

"But you encouraged her somehow. You must have."

He threw up his hands. "What! You think I *want* her to come after me? Gill, be reasonable. She tried to kill me, and I have a scar on my chest to show for it. Why would I want to see her again? If I saw her coming, don't you think I'd be running the opposite direction?"

Gillian turned back to the sink and grabbed another mug. It slipped out of her hand and fell into the sink, shattering into pieces. Throwing the washcloth down, she flung her head back, eyes closed. "I know how women work, Marc. Something must have set her off. It's hard to believe you didn't lead her on somehow."

She opened her eyes and glanced at him. He was rubbing his eyes now; clearly the migrane was getting worse. His voice simmered with anger. "I didn't. I'm not lying to you."

"Fine. But please—no more secrets, okay? If you want me to trust you, secrets don't help anything."

Hands on her shoulders, he turned her to face him, his tone softening. "That's why I just told you—so you *wouldn't* think I was keeping secrets from you again, okay?" He sighed. "I know I blew it in Chicago, and I'm sorry. I should have told you about Stacey right away, but that's over now. I'm not keeping secrets from you anymore."

Turning away from him, she glanced out the window, heart hammering. He was still hiding something from her—she could feel it in her bones. She didn't care how delusional Stacey was.

He put his arms around her and pulled her into a hug. "I love you." He kissed her hair.

"I love you, too." She said the words with little feeling, and he seemed to realize it.

Pulling away, he regarded her skeptically at arm's length. "I said I was sorry for keeping secrets from you. You say you've forgiven me, but I'm not sure you really have."

"Forgiveness doesn't equal automatic trust, Marc. It's hard to trust a husband who keeps secrets from his wife. I can't help wondering if there are other things you're hiding from me."

"But I'm *not* hiding anything. I just told you that. What do I have to do to convince you? Beg on my knees?"

That might help. Gillian expelled a sharp breath. "If you want me to trust you, give me reasons to. So far, I haven't seen very many reasons."

Marc sighed and rubbed his eyes again. "Okay, I'll work harder at this trust thing, but that means you need to work with me here. Like, try not to think the worst of me unless you have a real reason to. And then tell me, so I'm not in the dark about what's eating you. I can't control what's going on in your head, but you can."

She bit the inside of her cheek, not wanting to meet his gaze. As usual, he was right. She wasn't letting go of those feelings of betrayal, even though she had no hard evidence to support them. Resentment kept hovering over her emotions like an irritating mosquito. She'd slap at it, drive it away. But it always came buzzing back, thirsty for blood.

She nodded. "You're right. I wasn't being fair."

He pulled her into a hug, and she hugged him back. That was the hallmark of a true friend—having the courage to speak the truth, even when the truth hurt. She was so glad her husband was that kind of friend.

"Why don't you walk out the door and come back in again," she said. "Then we can do a different version of this whole conversation."

They pulled apart, and he smiled at her in spite of the pain evident on his face. "I think we would both do a better job the second time around. Don't you?"

She smiled back. "I'm game if you are."

CHAPTER 28

CRYSTAL FOLDED MOIST HANDS on her lap and tried not to take the rejection personally. The other teens, joking and laughing as they herded into the first two rows of the auditorium seating, acted as if she didn't exist. But why should they? They didn't know her any more than she knew them, at least not yet.

Just be yourself and be friendly, Gillian had told her that morning. *You can't expect to get to know everybody at your first practice.*

While waiting for the practice to begin, Crystal thought of Proverbs 18:24: *A man who has friends must himself be friendly.* Sitting by herself in the third row probably wasn't helping matters. Taking a deep breath and steeling her nerves, she got up and found an empty seat beside a couple of giggling girls.

"Hey, I'm Crystal Thayer." Crystal extended her hand to the closest girl, the one wearing a Bart Simpson T-shirt. She had frizzy brown hair and a bad case of acne. Earbuds sprouted from her ears, her iPod apparently hidden somewhere in the folds of her baggy clothes. The volume was so loud, Crystal could hear a wailing guitar and the thunderous beat of drums.

Frizzy Brown stared at Crystal's hand with distaste, as if Crystal were trying to spread AIDS. "Um, hi."

Strike one. Crystal withdrew her hand. "I guess we're going to be in the musical together, huh?"

"Why else would we be here? This ain't exactly gym class." Frizzy Brown elbowed her giggling friend, who had dyed-black hair and overly thick eye shadow. Her tight black clothes left little to the imagination.

Black Hair studied Crystal from head to toe, her nose wrinkling in disdain. "And you're not exactly dressed for a musical practice either. You must be in the wrong place, girl. I think the June Cleaver look-alike contest is down the hall."

Strike two. Stung, Crystal forced a smile, turned away, and studied the purple stage curtains. What was wrong with her clothes anyhow? Khaki skirt. Striped shirt. Navy cable-knit sweater. She thought she looked fine for a musical practice. Okay, so she wasn't as cool as everybody else in the room, but styles changed so quickly that she rarely gave them much notice.

But music. Well, music was something else entirely. She needed music like fish needed water.

Crystal remembered her last voice lesson with sadness. Her teacher, Maria Rivera, a well-known opera singer, had hugged Crystal and made her promise to keep up with her singing. *Sing in church. Find a local musical. Do something to keep your voice exercised, at least, until you return to Chicago.*

An overweight, middle-aged woman in blue jeans and a white sweatshirt with gold theater masks on it hurried to the podium at the foot of the stage. She carried a clipboard bearing a thick sheaf of papers. The chatter dwindled.

"Hi, everybody. Ready for another practice?"

Groans and mumbles came in response.

Betty Jamison, the director, cleared her throat. "As some of you may have already heard, Tanya Wright has mono and unfortunately won't be able to play Maria in the musical."

Whispers and snickers rippled through the group. Stunned, Crystal wondered what this development could mean.

"I know," Mrs. Jamison said with a sigh. "This is devastating news since the musical is only a couple weeks away. But I think we may have a solution to our problem. I've decided to give the part to Crystal Thayer."

The room turned silent.

Crystal felt her face turn hot.

Mrs. Jamison was smiling at her. "Sorry, Crystal. I know this is a surprise. I meant to talk to you before the practice, but I was delayed. Sorry for startling you."

Crystal somehow found her voice, aware of the many eyes turned her direction. "Um . . . that's okay."

"If you haven't yet met Crystal, she recently moved to the area from Chicago," Mrs. Jamison said to the group, "and she's been in several musicals. In fact, she's even sung Maria before, so she should be able to fill Tanya's spot without any problem. I'm very pleased that she's able to be part of our musical this fall. I hope all of you will go out of your way to make her feel welcome, especially since she's able to help us out at such short notice."

Crystal glanced at the girls sitting next to her. Both appeared to be staring with fascination at something on the floor, their giggles gone.

Today, Mrs. Jamison wanted to start at the beginning of the musical and do a dry run of as much of the music as possible. Or perhaps she just wanted to be sure this newcomer from Chicago was going to work out. Startled, Crystal realized the first song was hers.

The cast assembled on stage, and Crystal stood beside an old upright piano. The pianist, a thin, straight-backed woman with glasses and a hawkish nose, began playing the opening notes of the musical.

Crystal put on her glasses and studied her music. Trying her best not to appear flustered, she took a deep breath and let it out. Asking God for power to do her best, she began to sing.

CHAPTER 29

STANDING AT THE BACK of the auditorium, content to listen from the anonymity of the shadows, Haydon Owens remembered one of the last musicals he'd attended with his mother and recalled her running commentary. *Donny, Rodgers and Hammerstein would roll over in their graves.*

Pressured by his mother, he remembered auditioning for a part in a musical when he was sixteen. She'd been a hit on Broadway. Maybe he would be, too, she'd reasoned. He'd had the confidence to stand in front of an audience—he'd always been a natural performer—but his voice had simply not been good enough, much to his mother's disappointment. One of the judges had written, "Vocal quality too throaty and nasally. Support the tone with proper breathing from the diaphragm." Whatever that meant.

Studying this far-from-promising-looking group of teens, he doubted he would hear anything impressive today. In fact, he was about to leave when a clear, pretty voice silenced the chatter in the room and held everyone spellbound. Someone with obvious talent was singing the first song, "The Sound of Music."

Haydon strained to see. The girl was blonde, pretty, and poised. If she was nervous, she didn't show it. And her voice . . . well, it was angelic, though perhaps overly operatic for *The Sound of Music.*

Blonde hair. Fair complexion. Wire rim glasses.

Recognition buzzed along his nerves. He made fists, driving his fingernails into the palms of his hands to control his rage.

When she was finished, he didn't notice that everyone else in the auditorium had surrendered to hushed astonishment. He was more convinced by the moment that she wasn't who she said she was. That she was someone else. Someone he thought he'd left in Cincinnati.

Someone who should have stayed dead.

CHAPTER 30

ENTERING THE SPACIOUS Cape Cod–style house with Crystal at her side, Gillian delighted in the aroma of freshly baked cookies. "Thank you so much for inviting us over."

"You're welcome." Clara took their coats and headed toward a hall closet. "I thought we'd just enjoy ourselves in the kitchen," she said. "That's where we women spend most of our lives anyhow."

Actually, Gillian thought, *I spend most of my time in the studio working on my calligraphy.* Fortunately, Marc had never seemed to mind that dinner wasn't on the table when he got home. Then again, he probably realized they'd all starve if it were up to him to do the cooking.

"I'm so sorry to hear about Marc," Clara said. "Does he get these migraines often?"

"Thankfully, no," Gillian replied. "But when he gets one, it's usually a doozy."

Gillian and Crystal followed Clara down the hall and into a modest-sized kitchen, where Nicole was seated in the breakfast nook, sipping a cup of coffee. When she saw Gillian, she set down her mug and smiled.

Gillian had heard that Clara collected cows, but now she saw that the remark had been an understatement. Cows were everywhere. Grazing on the salt and pepper shakers. Chewing their cud on the toaster. Being milked on the cookie jar. Cows were even stenciled on the walls.

"Have you ever seen so many cows in your life?" Nicole said. "Take a look at this." She beckoned Gillian and Crystal into the breakfast nook and gestured to a painting on the wall.

Crystal laughed. "A cow Mona Lisa."

"Now I've seen everything." Gillian shook her head.

Actually, she was more interested in the family portraits lining the hallway and hoped that Clara would introduce her brood of children and grandchildren. Gillian couldn't imagine the gumption necessary to raise eight children. Past Clara's unassuming exterior dwelt an inner fortitude rare in this day and age.

She must have a dependence on God that's light years ahead of mine. And she must have a special relationship with Henry, too. It takes two to raise a family, especially one of their size. She couldn't help wondering if Henry ever kept secrets from Clara. Somehow he didn't seem like the secret-keeping type.

Everyone gathered at the table and chose their tea or poured their coffee before Clara asked the blessing on the food. During her prayer, she asked the Lord to bestow extra strength on her third daughter, Lisbeth, and her family as they served as missionaries in Brazil. Lisbeth was near the time of delivering her second child, a son, and the doctor was concerned about her blood pressure.

Of course, it's a boy, Gillian thought after Clara's amen. *Everybody gets a boy except me.*

"I understand congratulations are in order for Crystal here for getting the lead role in the musical," Nicole said, stirring sugar into her Southern pecan-flavored coffee.

Crystal blushed. "Thanks. It's still a big surprise."

"Oh, and just wait until you hear her sing," Clara told Nicole as she patted Crystal's hand. "She sang in church last Sunday. One of those old, beautiful songs you never hear anybody sing anymore. It was soul-stirring."

Crystal thanked Clara for the compliment and quickly changed the topic, asking Nicole about her lighthouse tours. "I've been wanting to know. Where do you get all of your information for the tours?"

"Mainly Old Man Whistler's diary. He kept track of everything." Nicole lowered her voice to mimic an old man's growl. "'Today, it rained. Yesterday, the sky was overcast.' Pretty boring stuff if you ask me. But it's worth reading. Really gives you a clear picture of what life must have been like back then. We live such pampered lives nowadays."

"How did you come to have Captain Whistler's diary?" Gillian asked.

"It was part of his estate and the original is on display in the museum. You can buy a copy at the Visitor's Center, but don't waste your money. You can borrow one of my copies, as long as you don't mind seeing the underlined parts I memorized for my tours."

"Speaking of borrowing things," Gillian said after a sip of mint tea, "Clara showed me some of the beautiful photos you've taken of the lighthouse. I'd like to borrow some of them sometime, if you don't mind. I'm hoping to do some oil painting when I'm not busy with my calligraphy projects and homeschooling Crystal."

Nicole smiled, clearly pleased. "Actually, I think I have some photos with me." She dug into her purse and handed Gillian a stack.

With Crystal looking over her shoulder, Gillian thumbed through shots of the lighthouse from various angles and at different times of the day. "They're beautiful!"

"Thanks. I've been dabbling in photography for . . . oh, a few years now." Nicole took a chocolate chip cookie from a plate in the center of the table. "I usually enter the best pictures in an annual national contest. I've never won anything, of course, unless you want to call getting my pictures published in a cheap calendar 'winning.' Maybe someday, if I stick to it, I'll sell some pictures and make some real money."

In other words, working as a tour guide at Whistler's Point didn't earn "real money," Gillian noted. Since moving to Whistler's Point, she'd wondered why someone like Nicole would choose to live away from family and be a tour guide at a historic lighthouse. Now she wondered if the natural beauty of the Great Lakes had been the main draw. If photography was Nicole's passion, she couldn't have chosen more picturesque surroundings. Nicole was dedicated, too. Just the other day, when Gillian had peered out the kitchen window at the sunrise, she'd seen Nicole strolling along the shoreline, camera in hand.

Gillian paused at a picture of the lighthouse on a dark, moonlit night.

"Oh, my! Look at that fog rolling in." Clara shuddered. "That one reminds me of something out of a horror film, not that I'd ever watch movies like that. I'd have terrible nightmares."

Gillian cut her eyes toward Nicole. "So tell me the truth. Is the lighthouse haunted? I've heard rumors."

"That's what people say. In the middle of the night, the ghost of Harriet Whistler supposedly paces the upstairs bedrooms, wringing her hands and wailing." She smirked. "I wouldn't go that far, but I have seen some weird things. Lights shining from some of the upstairs windows at night. Furniture moved to strange locations. A cool draft even though the windows are closed. Sometimes I feel like someone is watching me. You know that feeling—like someone's eyes are following your every move? Oh yeah, I've had some strange experiences, though I can't say I've ever seen a ghost, in the traditional sense of the word."

Nicole gestured to a framed piece of calligraphy on the wall that Gillian had given to Clara as a hostess gift on their first visit. It was Psalm 46:10: *Be still, and know that I am God.* "Hey, did you do that?"

Gillian nodded. "Yeah, but it isn't very good. I did that one back in college when I was still—"

"Isn't very good? You've gotta be kidding me. It's simply breathtaking."

"Careful, Nicole," Crystal said with a conspiratorial smile. "We don't want my mom getting a big head, now do we? Between us, it's the best stuff you'll find anywhere. That's why she's won several national awards. Her work was even recommended for the annual White House Christmas card."

Gillian studied her tea, wishing Crystal wouldn't gush over her like that. Hating to be the center of attention, she glanced up just in time to see Clara's eyes boring into her.

"Good heavens! You mean the First Lady actually *called* you?"

"Sure, we're old buddies," Gillian couldn't help saying. She laughed at Nicole's serious, open-mouthed response. "Just kidding. She didn't call me personally."

"But it *was* one of her assistants," Crystal said.

"Did you get to do the card?" Nicole asked.

Gillian shook her head with a sigh. "No, but it was an honor to have my work considered, nonetheless."

"I'd say so!" To Gillian's dismay, Nicole was staring at her with a look she could only describe as awe. "I know the White House doesn't just ask any old Tom, Dick, or Harry to do the annual Christmas card."

Feeling herself blushing, Gillian decided to add some cream to her tea. "Look, it's no big deal. I just try to use the gifts God has given me."

Nicole was still staring at her over the brim of her mug, elbows on the table. "A real artist in our midst. I feel highly intimidated now."

"Don't feel intimidated," Gillian said. "Please don't. You're an artist in your own right. You take terrific photos."

Clara took a pan of raspberry scones out of the oven. While they nibbled and poured second mugs of tea and coffee, Nicole talked about her upbringing in New England. She mentioned that she was divorced, but quickly changed the subject, obviously not wishing to discuss details. She'd grown up in a wealthy home, Gillian gathered when she mentioned boarding schools, ballet lessons, and summer trips to Europe.

"I have two older sisters, Chyna and Sabrina. They're both married and, like me, live away from home now. My mom works for an interior decorating studio in downtown Boston. We call each other a lot and send e-mail almost every day."

Nicole obviously enjoyed being the center of attention, deftly making eye contact with each woman in turn. "She's *tried* to persuade me to move home, but . . . well, I like being independent. My dad was president of a prosperous bank, but he"—she paused, her gaze dropping to the tabletop—"he died in a car accident about six months ago."

"I'm so sorry to hear that," Gillian said. *Six months. About the same amount of time since the death of my babies.* She thought about her own grief, about how it clung to her soul like kudzu. "Were you close to your father?"

Nicole nodded, absently folding and unfolding her napkin into halves and quarters. "Yeah, it really hit me hard."

Casting the napkin aside, she made eye contact with Gillian. "Dad and I were on our way to Mackinac Island to stay at the Grand Hotel when it happened. You know Mackinac Island, right? That's where they shot that movie *Somewhere in Time* with Christopher Reeve and Jane Seymour. Anyhow, all of a sudden, there was this big buck right in the middle of the road. Dad had no choice but to hit it."

"Dear, are you okay?" Clara asked. "You look a little peaked."

Gillian was glad that Clara had spoken up. Nicole's face had turned ashen.

Gillian touched Nicole's arm. "Why don't you drink some more coffee?"

Nicole's hand trembled as she reached for her mug. She took a few sips and leaned back in her chair, taking a deep breath and letting it out slowly. "There, I feel better now. I was getting a little light-headed there." She chuckled self-consciously. "Sorry about that. The accident is still difficult to talk about. I guess I haven't gotten over it just yet."

CHAPTER 31

WHILE GARY MORRIS SANG "Bring Him Home" from the international Broadway cast recording of the musical *Les Miserables*, Haydon drove aimlessly. Sometimes during his time off from the library, he hopped in his car and took trips that intentionally went nowhere. It was a habit he had started in high school, and he enjoyed venturing off the beaten path and exploring obscure back roads to find out where they went. His mother had joked that his drive to explore the unknown meant that Christopher Columbus must be a distant relation. *Silly, Mother. Really silly.*

Wearing a winter coat to ward off the nip in the wind, he was glad he'd taken the drive today; he'd needed a break from the maddening solitude of the cabin. Driving relaxed him and gave him an opportunity to think and to evaluate where his life was heading.

He was too far away from Cincinnati now to worry about the police. Haydon Owens was now a thing of the past. He'd shed his identity the same way a snake sheds its skin. Nobody needed to know about his past or why he was living alone in the cabin on Pike Lake. He would fit in, he would stay busy, and he would be fine.

Back to practicing his magic tricks, soon he would perform in public again. He'd begun checking out auditoriums in the area, investigating which ones had the most seating for the spectacle he would provide. Now he just needed to set a date for the event.

The producers of *Masters of Illusion* had been strangely silent since he had mailed them a video a week ago. He'd filmed himself doing a variety of tricks he was certain would amaze them. Perhaps it was time to call and apply some pressure.

Leaning his head against the headrest, he knew why he took these expeditions. The steady hum of the motor always lulled him into a kind of trance. Coming to the forefront of his mind were memories he'd tucked away where he thought they wouldn't do any harm. But with the memories, he felt the rage returning like an old friend he'd said good-bye to, thinking he wouldn't see him again.

But he'd lied to himself. He'd known all along that sooner or later he would be in this situation again.

The girl.

He'd seen her at the practice, and now she was forever on his mind. He'd repeated the pattern enough times to recognize it and know where it would lead. She would haunt his dreams and distract his waking moments until he took action. But could he afford to repeat the pattern? Wouldn't he jeopardize the magic?

The questions were replaced by an anger that made him blind to all else. He thought about Erin Walker, the embodiment of his hatred and revenge, the one who had led him down the dark path to this living nightmare from which he longed to awake. It was her fault.

He remembered stalking her neighborhood, knowing sooner or later he would have her where he wanted her. The event was still fresh in his memory, and he loved to relive it.

Once he'd pulled her into the car and driven away, a blow to the side of her head had kept her subdued, though his heart had raced at the realization that he couldn't possibly let her go.

In that moment, he'd known that she had to die.

Pulling to the side of the road and braking hard, he had reached toward the backseat for something—anything—to end the madness. His fingers had closed around the trick rope he always kept handy to entertain children.

She was coming to. She was staring at him wildly. She was screaming. Someone would hear her.

The rope was all he had. He'd made do with what he had.

"You lied about my parents! You lied about my parents!"

He had screamed the words while committing the act, in a rage unlike anything he'd known before, that had descended on him like a sharp-taloned bird of prey. It had possessed him. Controlled him.

Now the memory of that rage made his right foot heavier, made him more careless about breaking the speed limit. That is, until he realized the last thing he needed was to be pulled over by a cop. He slowed to the posted speed limit and tried to focus his thoughts on something else, on the yellow stripe dividing the lanes and zipping past in a comforting blur.

Finding himself near familiar territory, he turned down a road he knew as well as he knew his own murderous desires. The place was sacred in his mind. He'd always had a strong sense of location and had wept when the place was sold, when he and his parents had been forced to leave and move to Cincinnati.

As a child, he'd known these woods, these bends in the road, as well as he'd known himself. They had been his friends when he'd had no one else.

Returning to the place he knew best from his childhood, he felt as if he'd never left, as if time had stood still while he was gone. It had been home once, long ago. His parents had been on staff here, and they had left him to run wild and explore every nook and cranny of the old place on his own.

Remembering the break in the trees, he slowed to a stop.

Whistler's Point looked exactly as he remembered it—looked time-less, in fact. Of all places on earth, he loved it best. Soon he would return to the lighthouse in the secrecy of night and explore its empty hallways, revisiting the lost childhood he'd left behind.

What would it hurt? He doubted anybody would remember him after all these years.

And the girl. He found out she lived here, too.

How convenient.

CHAPTER 32

SOMEWHERE IN THE BACKGROUND, Willie Nelson was crooning about his lost love who would never come home. The clerk at the North Woods Inn in Newberry squinted at the database on the fingerprint-smeared computer screen and fixed Stacey with an impatient stare. "How many nights do you plan to stay?"

"I'm sorry?"

"One night? Two nights? I need to know."

Stacey flushed under his searching gaze. "Sorry, honey. Actually, I'll be here for three." *That should be long enough to find Marc, find out what his true feelings are, and skip town before anyone's the wiser.*

Suspicion glinted in his eyes when she said she'd pay with cash. "I'm still gonna have to see some ID. What's your name?"

"Mallory Lewis." It was the name of an old friend from high school. She winced at the memories. The less she remembered about those days, the better.

"Okay, here you go, Ms. Lewis." He handed her a form and a pen, and she filled in the blanks with whatever came to mind. Fake address. Fake phone number. Fake license plate number. She'd parked the Buick on the other side of the building, purposefully out of sight of the office window. She doubted the clerk would check the form against her license plate if doing so was inconvenient for him.

"And I need to take a photocopy of your driver's license," the clerk said. "Since you're paying with cash."

"My driver's license?"

"It's standard procedure. I need to keep a photocopy of it on file."

Her mouth turned dry; obviously, she didn't have a driver's license.

After making a show of searching her bag, she did her best to look surprised. "Oh, no. I can't find it. I hope I haven't lost it somewhere. I'll have to go through all my things and see if I can find it." The clerk looked at her for what seemed an eternity. Then he typed something into his computer and handed Stacey her room key. "I'll need to photocopy it at some point. Just bring it by the desk when you find it."

"Mm-hmm," Stacey said. "Thanks, honey."

After giving Stacey directions to her room and mumbling something about hoping she enjoyed the restaurant, the lounge, and the complimentary HBO, the clerk walked into a back room behind the counter.

Thanks, but no thanks, Stacey said to herself. *I don't think I'm going to find Marc in the restaurant, the lounge, or on HBO.*

After checking out the functional but unimpressive room, she sat on the edge of the bed and counted her cash. Biting her lip, she chided herself for spending so much money. She, who'd always had a big bank account and had never had to worry about finances before, was getting skimpy on cash. The feeling was otherworldly.

Why had she decided to rent a room? She could just as easily have broken into somebody's abandoned hunting cabin—but no; she'd been determined to retain at least a modicum of respectability and to behave like a decent, law-abiding citizen. At least for a few nights while she tracked down Marc Thayer.

Ten minutes later, she sank into the bathtub, the water as hot as she could stand, and enjoyed the moment of bliss. The scalding water soothed her aching feet, calves, and thighs; she had walked more miles in the past few days than in the rest of her life combined. Then, realizing she couldn't possibly walk all the way to Michigan, she'd canvassed a used car lot until she found an old Buick that an absent-minded attendant had left the keys in. *He won't be makin' that mistake again.*

She soaked for a half hour before climbing out, her legs rubbery, the skin on her hands white and wrinkled. After rubbing herself extra hard with a towel, she put her dirty clothes back on and studied herself in the mirror. She looked horrible without fresh makeup.

Perhaps she could break into a local pharmacy. Besides, she needed some hair dye to give herself a new look. But each time she broke the law, she realized, she was increasing her risk of being apprehended. She shook her head. Going back to prison wasn't an option; she'd kill herself first.

A noise in the hallway outside her room made her heart race. She imagined policemen crouched just outside with guns raised, ready to knock down the door. After a few moments of silence, she relaxed.

Surely the law hadn't followed her this far north. As long as she continued using cash and her assumed name, nobody could possibly know who she was . . . that is, unless she got careless. Unfortunately, the motel clerk had seen her at her worst—face haggard, makeup smeared, hair going every which way from the wind. It was too late to do anything about him now. If she sniffed danger, she could always sneak away and forget about the three nights she'd paid for up front.

Now she just needed to find Marc—which presented an entirely new challenge. During her long journey north, she'd failed to come up with a feasible plan for how she would contact him once she reached her destination. She couldn't very well just walk up to his house and knock on the front door. First, she was a wanted fugitive. Second, it was just as likely that Gillian would answer the door instead of Marc, and that would create an awkward situation. But neither could she just pick up the phone, call Marc, and say, "I'm here in town, and I want to see you."

Would he be happy to see her? Would he be angry? After all, she *had* killed his dog and almost killed him. But if he truly loved her— something she felt confident about—certainly he would have forgiven her by now. She wondered what he would say when he saw her for the first time since the shooting. Would he look startled? Or would he smile at her knowingly, his eyes tender, and say, "I knew you'd come"?

CHAPTER 33

My Dearest Children,
I miss you so much and wish I could hold you in my arms. Life here has been very hectic of late. Crystal has so much computer work to do and so many musical practices to attend, I don't know how she thinks she's going to keep up. Marc and I often use the Tahoe during the day, so Nicole, the tour guide, has agreed to drive Crystal to her rehearsals, but she can't play chauffeur forever. Marc regrets not bringing the Saturn with us. I suggested we drive to Chicago and bring the car back, but he said that perhaps it's time for Crystal to have her own car.
My little baby driving her own car? I can hardly believe it. It seems like it was just yesterday that I was reading Dr. Seuss to her and she was sucking the tags off her stuffed animals. Part of me doesn't want her to have a car. It's just another reason for her to be away from us.
I'm praying for Nicole. Her father was killed in a car accident, and I sense that she's still hurting. Maybe I'll get a chance to share Christ with her. I hope so. We're going to try to get together for lunch or a walk once in a while. I'd like to develop the friendship.
Well, I must go for now. I think of you often and hold you close to my heart.
Your Loving Mother

CHAPTER 34

MARC GRABBED THE HANDLES and lifted the wheelbarrow, surprised by how much brush and leaves he and Henry had gathered—probably the last until spring. Sensing the wheelbarrow beginning to teeter to one side, he straightened it, feeling his arms strain and his lower back throb. A slight pain in his right knee forced him to favor the leg. Finally in control, he leaned into the weight of the load, edging the wheelbarrow forward, and followed the trail toward the brush pile located at the back of the Whistler's Point property.

He and Henry had hauled a lot of refuse along the well-worn path. Reaching the brush pile, he emptied the wheelbarrow's contents, glad to be rid of his burden.

Wiping the sleeve of his plaid jacket across his sweaty forehead, he remembered countless landscaping projects with his dad and brothers. Working in his dad's business while he was growing up had taught him the importance of working hard and putting in an honest day's work.

After spending the past decade working in an office, he had to admit that exercising and working up a sweat again felt good. Still, he found his thoughts drifting back to his former ministry at Heritage Bible Church, to the ministry he had loved and enjoyed. He couldn't help wondering how the church was faring without him.

They were probably doing just fine. Only his pride tempted him to think otherwise.

He turned his face toward the hazy afternoon sunshine. *Thank you, Lord, for another day. Help me to submit to Your will for me right now, even though it's hard to understand. Show me what You want us to do here. Continue to help Gillian through her grief. Show me how I can help her better and win her trust again.*

His thoughts turned to Dave's recent phone call, and he mulled over the church break-in, wondering if Stacey had found his new address. If so, she knew exactly where to find him.

Deciding he'd wasted enough time, he straightened his back and grabbed the wheelbarrow handles. Doing a one-eighty, he intended to head back the way he'd come, but a flash of movement in the brush up ahead stopped him in his tracks.

No more than twenty feet away, Stacey James stepped into the middle of the path, hands hanging limply at her sides, her expression indecipherable.

So she'd made the trip to see him after all.

For a split second, he was transported back to his master bathroom in Chicago. The barrel of the gun. Stacey's hands jerking upward from the kickback. The deafening report. The searing pain as the bullet plowed into his chest. All caught up in a single moment of disbelief.

The sight of her now pulled the breath right out of him. He dropped the wheelbarrow handles and stepped—or, rather, stumbled—a few steps back.

She was wearing a brown leather jacket and blue jeans, and surprisingly little makeup, if any at all. She thrust her hands deep into her front pockets, making no attempt to hide or flee. He saw no gun—in fact, nothing she could use to harm him. So why then was she here?

A small smile played on her lips as the breeze tousled her hair, scattering blonde strands across her face. She looked weary, the wrinkles around her eyes deeper than he remembered. Perhaps she hadn't been sleeping well. Not that he would sleep soundly if he knew the law was hounding *his* steps.

"Hi, Marc."

Flabbergasted by her casual greeting, he glanced down at the wheelbarrow as his mind raced. He wondered where Henry was. Henry knew he was taking a wheelbarrow load to the brush pile. In a few minutes, he'd wonder what was taking Marc so long, and hopefully he'd come to investigate.

Stacey must have sensed his wariness. "It's okay, Marc. I'm not here to hurt you." She pulled both hands from her pockets and raised them, palms facing forward. "I don't have a gun."

He somehow found his voice. "Then why are you here?"

"To talk."

"To talk." He heard the disbelief in his own voice, but wasn't sure how else he was supposed to feel. She *had* tried to kill him. What assurances did he have that she wouldn't try to hurt him again? Why else make the long trip?

He shrugged. "Talk about what?"

She took a few steps closer. "Us, Marc. We need to talk about us."

Us? He didn't know what to say.

"I love you." She said the words with deep feeling, her eyes misting with emotion. "In fact, I've always loved you. Do you love me?"

Marc swallowed hard. She could be lying and have a gun tucked into the back waistband of her jeans. The wrong answer could be his death sentence. "Stacey, I love you as a sister in Christ, as someone I've done my best to help and counsel from God's Word."

"But do you *love* me—you know, like a man loves a woman?"

He blinked. "Stacey, I'm a married man. You know that."

She shook her head as if refusing to listen. "That doesn't matter, honey. I want you to be honest with me. I've sensed for a long time that you have feelin's for me. You can't hide how you feel from me any longer. I came all the way here to hear the truth from your lips. Now I want you to be honest with me."

I have *been honest.* Marc recalled having the same conversation on the day he'd told her that Liz Simons would be her new counselor. Stacey clearly wanted more than he could give. A married man, he was devoted to his wife. He simply couldn't fill the romantic void she was seeking to fill, and he wanted her to stop thinking he could. What was there not to understand?

God, please open her eyes. Help her to see the lies she's been believing. He remembered what Liz had said; perhaps Stacey *did* see a little bit of her father in him. He didn't want her to perceive his words as cold rejection; if she did, she could turn violent again.

Glancing toward the lighthouse, hoping to see Henry, he gathered his thoughts. "I *am* being honest, Stacey. I love my wife and have romantic feelings *only* for my wife. I don't have feelings for you in that way."

Taking a few steps closer, she shook her head and bit her lip. He could tell her emotions were creeping dangerously close to the edge. He felt himself sweating.

"Marc, nobody's watchin'. It's just you and me. You don't have to hide behind your church or pretend anymore. You can tell me the truth. You want me, don't you?"

"I'm not pretending. I don't have feelings like that for you. I never have. I'm afraid"—he shrugged—"that you've misunderstood me. Apparently you've misunderstood my care and concern for a long time."

He hesitated and took a breath, trying to make her see. "I *do* care about you, Stacey, but not as a lover. I care about whether you decide to walk with God and obey Him as you know you should. I care about your being faithful to the husband God has given you. I care about all those things."

She reached out her hands imploringly. "We could go away—now. You and me. You don't love Gillian—I know you don't. Leave her and come with me. You don't need to live a lie anymore."

Marc stared at her; she hadn't heard a single word he'd said. What did he have to say—or do—to help her see? "You don't realize what you're saying."

Another step closer. "Yes, I do."

"Stacey, you're living in a fantasy world. Just look around." He spread his arms, taking in their surroundings. "This is reality. I live here with my wife and daughter. I *love* my wife. I'm sorry if what I say hurts you, but you need to wake up and take a hard look at reality. We need to put this matter to rest once and for all. You shot me—don't you remember? If you loved me as you say you do, why did you do that? It doesn't make any sense."

Stacey stared at him as if her eyes had been opened for the first time. Confusion marred her features. She opened her mouth, then closed it. She stared at the ground, as if looking for an answer there.

Glancing up, her eyes flaring, she cried, "You're lyin'! I don't believe you."

"I'm not lying! It's the truth. It has always been the truth. Why can't you accept it?"

Henry appeared on the path behind Stacey. He froze, his face confused, his eyes wary.

Marc hoped his facial expression was enough to help Henry see that he had come at a good time but was also stepping into a potentially dangerous situation.

Stacey must have heard Henry on the path or seen the dart in Marc's gaze. Wheeling around, she turned and fled, brushing past Henry and disappearing into the trees.

CHAPTER 35

STACEY FUMBLED WITH THE key, fired the ignition, and hit the gas. The sedan's wheels spat gravel and dirt before finding purchase. As the car shot forward, she gripped the steering wheel, trying to see through her blinding tears. She raced down the dirt road that wound within walking distance of Whistler's Point.

Marc's words kept replaying in her mind like a looping sound bite. *I'm not pretending. I don't have feelings like that for you. I never have.*

How could he say those words? How could she have been so deceived? The compassionate look in his eyes, the caring tone of his voice during counseling—could she have been so mistaken? No, it was too unbelievable. Her mind couldn't grasp it. No matter what he said, she knew he cared.

She shook her head. But none of it mattered anyhow. At least, not now. Right now she needed a place to hide.

Soon the cops would be swarming over every inch of the area, looking for her. She knew she couldn't return to the motel. That's the first place they'd look.

Where should she go? Perhaps she should head toward the highway and get out of Dodge. Then again, she hated to leave so abruptly after traveling so far to see Marc. If only she could think.

I don't have feelings like that for you. I never have.

Brushing aside tears, she drove for ten minutes, turning down unfamiliar roads at random while trying to remember the way she'd come so she could find her way back to the highway. Eventually, she left the pavement and explored a meandering dirt road that ventured deep into the woods. The washboard effect of the rutted track made her teeth rattle. Through the trees flashed the occasional silvery blue reflection of a lake. Every fifty feet or so, the road curved randomly to the right or the left, as if the road builders had kept changing their minds.

She hit the brakes when she glimpsed a small dirt driveway branching off the main road to the left. At the entrance of the driveway stood a fancy wooden sign with a name carved in elegant script: "Traveler's Rest."

The name fit her mood. She just wanted a private oasis to rest, to hide from the police, and to decide what to do next.

Turning into the driveway, she parked the car, got out, and grabbed the bag of canned goods. She walked along the driveway deeper into the trees and ascended a steep rise that left her breathless. An unseen stream or river gurgled somewhere in the distance.

At the top of the hill squatted a brown A-frame hunting cabin. A single front window, like a single eye watching her, revealed a dark interior. The parking area to her right was empty, except for two covered snowmobiles parked on a trailer. A few feet beyond the parking area stood an outhouse. Her nose wrinkled at the thought of no indoor plumbing.

It now occurred to her that she'd forgotten to consider the timing of hunting season in the North Woods, but no one appeared to be home, and amazingly the side door was unlocked. Apparently, this deep in the woods, either nobody feared burglars, or the place offered nothing worth stealing.

The ancient door creaked on its hinges. She stepped inside, leaving the door ajar to provide additional light.

"Hello, anybody home?"

Silence.

The stale air was tinged with wood smoke. Two additional windows on the back wall contributed to the meager light. Stacey squinted to make out a potbellied stove, a set of bunk beds lining the far wall, and a dusty card table that she assumed doubled as a kitchen table. To the left hung a row of cupboards, probably filled with garage sale–quality plates, silverware, and other odds and ends. On the far wall, a mounted deer head with impressive antlers stared down at her with questioning black eyes, clearly not amused to see her trespassing.

Stacey slung the bag of food to the floor and folded her arms, suddenly cold. Yes, it was a typical bachelor pad—certainly not as nice as Jared's condo, but it would have to do. First, she'd open all the windows to air the place out. Perhaps she'd clean a little too, but maybe the place was always this dirty. What did a bunch of men care anyhow?

Men! What a mistake she'd made traveling here to see Marc.

Her stomach growled, reminding her that she'd skipped lunch. Wisely predicting that Marc would call the police after her appearance, she'd packed everything she needed in the car. Still stocked with plenty of canned goods, she wouldn't go hungry.

First, the windows, then she'd eat. She moved to the nearest window and stopped. A Bible lay on the closest bunk bed.

I care about whether you decide to walk with God and obey Him as you know you should. I care about your being faithful to the husband God has given you. I care about all those things.

Marc's words echoed through her mind as she replayed their meeting. He'd said his care was limited to her spiritual welfare, but he had to be lying. Had to be.

Sitting on the edge of the bunk bed, she slid her hand across the front cover of the Bible, wiping away the dust. Back home, she would sometimes turn to the book of Psalms for the comfort no one else could provide. But how could she turn to God now, after she'd turned her back on Him so many times? Certainly He didn't approve of why she was here in the first place.

She tried not to listen to the gentle prodding in her heart, but she knew God was talking to her. Stubbornly. Persistently. And she knew what He was telling her.

Stacey, I love you. I love you. I love you. *My love is all you need. Why can't you see that? Just reach out to Me. I want to fill that empty place inside you.*

Stacey sprang away from the Bible, as if stung. No, she wasn't ready to open her heart to Him. Not now. Maybe later.

Thirsty, she left the cabin and headed into the trees, following the sounds of the river. Along the way, she almost tripped, blinded by her tears.

CHAPTER 36

DONNY, DONNY, DONNY. LIFE is so short. We can't afford to waste what little time we have left.

Sitting on a stool behind the counter at the library, Haydon glanced at the clock and sighed, his mother's counsel ringing in his ears. He hated working the afternoon hours, because they seemed like such a waste of time. He would rather be home practicing his magic tricks, but he had to pay the bills somehow.

He was also weary of listening to Marjorie's endless chatter. All she talked about was an online college course she was taking in American literature and the research she was doing for a paper on the life of William Faulkner, whoever he was. Well, at least it was Thursday, and he'd have the weekend off.

The glass doors swung open, and three high-school girls breezed in, giggling and talking loudly. The blonde one in the middle said goodbye to her friends, who headed toward the room with the computers and the Internet access. She was approaching the checkout desk.

Realizing who she was and that he couldn't let her see him, he eased into the back room where they stored all the DVDs and videos. If he stood in the doorway just right, he could hear the conversation without being observed. He heard Marjorie's cheerful voice as she greeted the girl.

"Hi, I'm looking for the soundtrack to *The Sound of Music*. Do you have it?"

Just to hear her voice made his nerves buzz.

"Tape or CD?" Marjorie asked.

"CD."

"I'm pretty sure it hasn't been checked out. Let me check our holdings." He imagined Marjorie was looking up the CD on the database. "Yes, it's here. Just check the recordings. You'll find it under 'Soundtracks.'"

A beat passed. "Sorry, this is my first time here. Where do I go?" Marjorie gave her directions.

A couple of minutes later, the girl returned with the CD and handed it to Marjorie. "I'm new to the area and don't have a library card yet."

"No problem. What's your name?"

"Crystal Thayer. Is it hard to set up an account?"

"No, it's simple." Marjorie had gone over the policy with Haydon just yesterday. "I'll need your driver's license or some type of ID proving you live in this county."

"Oh. We just moved here a few weeks ago from Chicago, so my license is from Illinois."

"Well, do you have anything else. Maybe a student ID?"

"No, my mom is homeschooling me up here, so I'm not going to the high school. My parents are working at the Whistler's Point lighthouse. Honest. I wouldn't make something like that up."

"Mm-hmm," Marjorie said. "Well, okay then. I guess your Illinois license will have to do."

Haydon heard Crystal digging into her purse and took a peek. Something about the shape of her face against her blonde hair sent sparks sizzling along his nerves. Overcome by rage, he dug his fingernails into his palms, trying to gain control. The anger dissipated but not by much. He moved back out of view.

Crystal handed Marjorie her driver's license, and Marjorie scrutinized the information. "Hey, it's your birthday," she said after a long moment. "Happy birthday!"

While Marjorie processed her account, Crystal made conversation. "Did you know that the local teen theater group is doing *The Sound of Music*?"

"I do recall hearing something about that," Marjorie said.

He shook his head. *Get a life, Marjorie. That's all anybody's been talking about.*

"You should come. It'll be at the high school auditorium the weekend before Thanksgiving."

"I'll have to check my calendar."

"Someone else had the part of Maria, but then she got mono, so now I've got it. It's such a big surprise. God is so good, isn't He? Isn't it amazing the way He surprises us sometimes?"

Crystal, you have no idea.

He imagined Marjorie handing her the new library card and running the CD through the scanner. "There you go. You're all set."

"Thanks, you're a big help."

"Good luck on the musical," Marjorie called.

Haydon waited a full minute before carrying to the front desk a pile of returns that needed to be sorted.

"Oh! There you are," Marjorie said. "Where'd you disappear to?"

"I had to use the little boy's room," he lied.

Marjorie shrugged and picked up the ringing telephone. Moments later, she was off on another mission.

Crystal Thayer's personal data still glowed on the screen, drawing him like a moth to a flame. He stared at the information for several moments before pulling himself away. He glanced at the clock, calculating the minutes until his replacement would arrive. He'd been watching Crystal from a distance for long enough.

It was time for a closer look.

CHAPTER 37

SITTING AT THE KITCHEN table behind a candlelit, white-frosted birthday cake, Crystal smiled as Gillian snapped a couple more pictures. It wasn't every day that her daughter turned seventeen, and Gillian had every intention of making the day memorable. It was Thursday after supper, and they were celebrating the special occasion together as a family.

After they sang "Happy Birthday" and Crystal blew out the candles, Marc handed her a box wrapped in brown, grocery-bag paper. "From me."

"Wow, Dad!" Crystal exclaimed. "I just love the *creative* wrapping paper you chose. In fact, I think I might save it and use it for your birthday. What comes around goes around." With a sardonic smile, she tore the paper away instead of folding it neatly as Gillian always did. "Flannel shirts! Just what I always wanted. Now I can look like a real Yooper."

Gillian revealed an ornately wrapped package she'd been hiding behind her back.

"Mom! Another gift? Good grief. I can't believe how you two spoil me."

"The only child always gets spoiled." Marc grinned.

Crystal tore away the paper and opened the box to reveal a DVD of *The Sound of Music*. "Thank you so much!" She hugged Gillian.

A smile on his lips, Marc exchanged knowing glances with Gillian. "We have one more gift for you, but you need to step outside to see it."

Crystal raised her eyebrows in curiosity as Marc and Gillian led her to the driveway, where a shiny, blue Cutlass Ciera was parked. Marc handed her the keys. "Here you go. Now Nicole doesn't have to keep chauffeuring you to practices."

Crystal stared at Gillian, eyes wide. "No way! You're kidding, right?"

Gillian laughed. "Do you think we'd kid you about something like this? Well, are you going to just stand there, or are you going to take a look inside?"

Crystal jumped up and down, clapping her hands, and ran to the car to check it out. "I can't believe it! Wow! I don't know what to say." Bending at the waist, she peered through the window at the car's interior.

"As you can see, the car's used and pretty old," Marc said, "but I've been assured that it runs perfectly fine. I even have a guarantee."

Crystal crushed her parents in a massive hug. "I love you, Mom and Dad. This is awesome!"

"Okay, everybody back inside for some cake," Marc ordered. "I've been dying for a slice."

"Is that so?" Gillian smirked. "I didn't think you'd have any room for cake after all the steak you ate."

Marc had cooked perfectly seasoned fillets on the charcoal grill. *When did he ever have time to do that in Chicago?* Gillian was pretty certain the answer was *never*.

CHAPTER 38

STACEY LINGERED BESIDE THE massive, sprawling oak, her eyes on the Thayer house, certain no one could see her in the opaque blackness of night. She shivered in the chilly breeze. The police had apparently left after searching the premises of Whistler's Point, because she saw no sign of them anywhere.

Earlier, peering past open drapes, she'd watched the Thayers celebrating Crystal's birthday in the dining room. Occasionally, she'd seen glimpses of Marc as he stepped outside to check the meat on the grill. She wanted so badly to speak to him again, but she'd felt too nervous to make her move, especially after their disappointing meeting that afternoon. At one point, Marc, Gillian, and Crystal had stepped outside to look at a car parked in the driveway, one that Stacey hadn't seen before.

She knew she was taking a big risk just by coming back. Just because she didn't see cops didn't mean no one was watching the house in case she was stupid enough to return.

Perhaps she *was* stupid. But after enduring a few hours of maddening solitude at the cabin and God's insistent tugging on her heart, she'd decided to return to Whistler's Point to be near Marc. Now that he unquestionably knew her true feelings and had had a chance to think about it, maybe he would change his mind about her. Then again, she'd already declared her love in so many notes and e-mails that her feelings for him couldn't have been a mystery.

Perhaps he *did* care more than he was letting on, but maybe he just needed time to figure out how to dump Gillian. Leaving his wife and daughter couldn't be an easy decision. Perhaps conflict raged inside his soul, pitting commitment to his marriage against his love for another woman.

She hoped her suspicion was true. At least then she would have a chance. Only a chance, perhaps. But a chance nonetheless.

I don't have feelings like that for you. I never have.

She shrugged off the memory of his words. His statement couldn't be true. Perhaps if he just saw her one more time, but she needed to find a way.

Something flickered at the corner of her eye. She huddled close to the tree, certain she'd seen movement to her right.

Somebody was out there in the dark.

A man. His shape was unmistakable.

Ice coursed through her veins. She held her breath, wondering if he was a cop. But he wasn't heading her direction. He was striding purposefully toward the white house where the Thayers lived. Who was he? One of the groundskeepers?

She watched as he crouched behind a shrub about twenty feet from the house's back door. The light shining out through the windows provided enough illumination for her to make out his shape more clearly.

The man raised something to his face. What was he doing? Goose bumps broke out on her arms.

She knew she needed a closer look. Perhaps the man was so distracted by what he was seeing that he wouldn't notice her.

Steeling her resolve, she sprang from cover, darted to a stand of trees closer to the house, and waited a full minute before sneaking a peak.

The slim, blond-haired man didn't appear to have noticed her. He was intently watching the house through binoculars.

Binoculars? Is he a Peeping Tom?

She wondered what he was seeing that could so totally transfix him. A golden glow dominated a section of the house's main story. From her angle, she could peer through the window and see into the Thayers' living room. An antique-looking floor lamp. A burgundy couch. A dark green wingback armchair. The shifting, bluish glow on the ceiling from a TV.

Her breath hitched as a familiar figure came into view.

Marc.

He stood beside the wingback chair, with a mug in his hand, apparently talking to someone she couldn't see.

Then Crystal moved into the frame, put her arm around her father, and kissed his cheek before leaving the room. What a lucky girl Crystal was to have a father like that!

Moments later, Gillian appeared, put her arms around Marc, and peered up at him with a smile. They kissed.

Stacey expelled air out of her mouth and looked away. She couldn't stand to watch.

The moment passed. She stole another glance. Now he was hugging her.

Oh, good grief! She looked away, feeling like a Peeping Tom herself.

I love my wife and have romantic feelings only for my wife. I don't have feelings for you in that way.

She felt tight bands compressing her chest. Perhaps Marc *had* been speaking the truth. But feelings for that plump redhead who wasn't nearly as attractive as she was? She had to admit the possibility that he might truly love his wife. Love went beyond attraction for some people.

Stacey stole a glance at the man hiding behind the bush. He wasn't watching Marc and Gillian. A light had turned on upstairs, and he was aiming his binoculars at an illuminated upstairs window.

The blinds were open, but from her angle, Stacey could only discern shadows dancing across a spinning ceiling fan.

He's watching Crystal! In spite of the sweatshirt and leather jacket, the breeze made her shiver. *Why is he watching Crystal?*

Stacey had seen the talented young lady around church plenty of times, sometimes viewing her as a younger version of herself before her father abandoned the family for another woman. Young. Naive. Ambitious. So clueless about how the world really worked.

Another woman.

Stacey sucked in some air. For a split second, she was Crystal's age. So idealistic about finding the right husband. So idolizing of her father, who could make no mistakes in her eyes. Time fell away from her, and she was snared by memories long dusty in the files of her mind.

*   *   *

Her father was throwing clothes into a suitcase.

"Where are you going, Dad?"

He didn't look at her. At his temple pulsed a single vein. "Another speaking trip."

"But you're always going on speaking trips. Can't you stay here with us? Maybe we could go for a walk—just the two of us—the way we used to."

His mouth was set in that familiar, fierce set of his jaw. "No time for that." His brown eyes slid to her face then just as quickly pivoted back to the open drawer. "You know how important this is to me."

Oh yeah, she knew. Ever since he'd had a speaking engagement at an evangelistic rally in Atlanta, everything had changed. Stardom appeared to be going to his head, fueled by talk that he might be the next Billy Graham. Pastoring no longer satisfied him, and he rarely filled his own pulpit anymore. He wanted to be a superstar, and people seemed more than willing to fulfill his dream. Meanwhile, she and her mom secretly wondered if they'd ever have him back.

He muttered something about getting his shaving kit and headed down the hall. Lingering in the doorway, Stacey glanced at his open suitcase and saw a small pink box partially hidden under his boxer shorts. It was a perfume her mom had said she loathed. So who was it for?

Perhaps there was a logical explanation. Maybe the gift was for his sister, Aunt Jenny, or someone else in the family. Looking back later, the memory was a rebuke. She should have seen the signs, but she couldn't believe her own father could fall as so many had before him.

*   *   *

Stacey shivered, aware that she was standing beside a tree outside Marc Thayer's house. A stranger was watching Marc's daughter through binoculars, a stranger who could mean her harm.

Perhaps Marc loved her; perhaps he didn't. That didn't matter anymore. Seeing Crystal as a younger version of herself made her realize her mistake. Her insistence on coming between Marc and Gillian could consign Crystal to the same grief another woman had inflicted on her years ago.

She realized *she* was the other woman, and she could be condemned to repeating the past and hurting others if she didn't alter her path.

Hugging herself to ward off the chill of the evening, she vowed to break the pattern. The past would not repeat itself—she would keep it from happening. She would prevent Crystal from suffering as she'd suffered her own father's fall from grace.

The best thing she could do, she realized, was to turn her back on Marc Thayer. He'd made his intentions clear; he wanted nothing to do with her idea of love. Somewhere in the recesses of her heart, she also knew God was telling her that pursuing Marc wasn't His best for her life either. Never had been.

Earlier, she'd given in and read a few verses from the book of Psalms, an intense battle raging inside her. Marc had always told her that it was never too late to do the right thing, but she felt buried under a heap of bad choices, too soiled to see the point of crawling away. And still the battle raged.

Pursue Marc. Obey God. Pursue Marc. Obey God.

God had won the war.

She had to let go. Walk away. Now. Before she changed her mind.

She'd head out west somewhere—she'd always wanted to see the Pacific Ocean. But first she needed to warn Marc about the stranger watching his daughter. Perhaps she'd even go to the police and turn herself in. Then she'd tell them about the stranger watching Crystal Thayer, perhaps doing enough good to somehow atone for the harm she'd already done.

Stacey glanced at the young stalker. This time his head swiveled her direction.

She pulled herself behind the tree, her heart thumping in her ribcage. Had he seen her?

She ventured another look. He was staring right at her, and an unexplainable and overwhelming sense of evil froze her blood in her veins.

A Peeping Tom, no. Something far worse.

He was rising and leaving the bush behind. He was striding directly toward her.

She reached for her pocket. *Oh no!* She'd left the gun in the car.

Abandoning the tree, Stacey ran. Forget the police. She'd run to the front door and warn Marc right now.

Footfalls thudded behind her. A hand grabbed her arm.

She wrenched herself free. Rounded the corner of the house. Saw the front porch. *She was going to make it!*

Something tripped her. She went down, but he was down, too.

Springing to her feet, she raced up the steps, pushed the doorbell. Chimes echoed in the house. Relieved, she tried to catch her breath.

Something closed around her neck and yanked her backwards, wrenching her off her feet. Her hands flew to her neck.

She was being dragged off the porch by a rope. She couldn't breathe.

She gagged, grabbing at the rope where it bit into her neck. She flailed her legs, trying to find some leverage to fight back.

She couldn't see her attacker as he grunted, hauling her like a sack of potatoes out of the front yard and past the side of the house, beyond view of the front porch.

Even as she felt her life slipping away, Stacey imagined Marc opening the front door. Peering into the night. Wondering who had rung the doorbell.

If only she could scream. At least then he could hear her and know what had happened. But she couldn't make a sound. The end came with silence as she struggled for one last breath.

CHAPTER 39

ON FRIDAY MORNING, Gillian, Crystal, and Marc were in the kitchen finishing breakfast when they heard the front doorbell. Taking a last gulp of coffee, Marc pecked Gillian on the cheek and went to answer the door.

"Shouldn't have had that second cup of coffee," he said as he walked out of the room. "Henry's probably wondering if I overslept."

Gillian busied herself with the dishes, but when she heard an unfamiliar voice coming from the living room, she dried her hands on a dish towel and went to see who the unexpected guest was.

Reaching the living room with Crystal at her side, Gillian stiffened when she saw a burly police officer standing near the open door, talking to Marc and scribbling something on a small notepad.

"What's this all about?" Gillian suddenly felt cold.

The blond officer, his face pitted from acne, turned to Crystal and Gillian with a smile that was cordial but not overly friendly. "I'm Sheriff Nate Dendridge with the Luce County Sheriff's Office. As you know, my men have been searching everywhere since yesterday for Stacey James."

With the preparations for Crystal's birthday, Gillian had managed to put Stacey out of her mind after Marc's confrontation with her and the sheriff's search of the premises. At the time, it had been a jolt to have her worst fears come true. In the back of her mind, she'd always known that Stacey would come looking for Marc. She hoped the sheriff had good news. The sooner the police apprehended Stacey and put her back in jail, the sooner life could get back to normal. Whatever normal was. Life had been anything but normal since the twins died.

The sheriff gestured to the couch and chairs. "Do you mind if I take a load off?" Not waiting for an answer, he claimed the nearest wingback chair and sank into it with a sigh. "That's better. It's already been a long morning."

Crystal chose the other wingback while Gillian sat on the couch next to Marc, facing the sheriff. Right away, she sensed something was wrong.

"So how is the investigation going?" Marc asked after an awkward pause.

Sheriff Dendridge tapped his pen against his notepad and studied their faces. "We found Stacey James."

Marc sighed. "I'm so glad."

"Now hold on. It's not quite what you think. We found her all right. The problem is, she's dead."

Gillian grabbed Marc's hand. His fingers were cold, and there was a tremor in his voice as he said, "*What?*"

"One of your maintenance men stumbled across her body about an hour ago," the sheriff said.

The blood had drained out of Marc's face. "Henry?"

Sheriff Dendridge nodded. "It appears she was strangled, probably sometime last night."

Gillian bit the inside of her cheek. *Last night. What were we doing last night?*

"Where did they find the body?" Marc asked.

The sheriff's eyes flickered momentarily. "See, that's the strange thing. Where exactly did you see her yesterday?"

"At the brush pile where we dump grass clippings and leaves," Marc said. "That's where she approached me."

"Approached you?"

Gillian felt a heaviness in her chest. Why was the sheriff asking these questions? Surely he already knew the answers after their thorough police report yesterday.

Marc said, "I dumped a wheelbarrow full of brush, turned around, and there she was."

"Do you mind showing me exactly where this meeting took place?"

"Not at all." Marc pushed to his feet, glanced around as if confused, and headed toward the door.

Gillian was going to follow them, but the sheriff intercepted her, something telling in his eyes. "Just your husband," he said in a low voice.

CHAPTER 40

THE OVERCAST MORNING WAS crisp, and steam drifted from Marc's mouth as he led the sheriff down the worn path. He wondered what was so special about the brush pile, but the truth evaded him. The sheriff was studying him intently as they walked and exchanged small talk about the weather.

Closer now, Marc stopped. Crime scene tape encircled the compost area. Two deputies turned and stepped toward them.

Then Marc knew.

His eyes flicked to what the deputies had been studying on the ground. As he closed on the last few yards, a tight knot squeezed his gut.

Stacey James lay facedown in the brush pile, a rope pulled tight around her neck, its frayed end dangling past her tousled blonde hair to the middle of her back. The cord looked like a white gash against her brown leather jacket. Her unnaturally white hands were frozen near her neck, as if she'd been trying to free herself when the end came. Thankfully, her face was turned away.

Marc thought he was going to throw up. Or pass out.

Stepping back, he bent at the waist, hands on his knees. Trying to breathe, he felt his gorge rise. An army of black dots invaded his peripheral vision and then retreated. He was going to be okay. He wiped clammy sweat off his forehead.

Fixing his eyes on Sheriff Dendridge's boots, he realized the sheriff had known all along what they would find at the end of the path. He'd asked Marc to accompany him to the brush pile for one reason. *He thinks I killed her.*

The knot in his gut squeezed even tighter, but he straightened up and filled his lungs with crisp air that helped to clear his head.

"Now, I understand you and Ms. James had an argument here yesterday," the sheriff said with an air of satisfaction. "Why don't you start at the beginning and tell me all about it?"

⁂   ⁂   ⁂

Gillian felt cold as she stood on the front porch, Crystal's arm around her. The sheriff was leading Marc down the front porch steps toward the police cruiser. The sheriff turned as if to answer Gillian's fears.

"Just routine, ma'am. It seems as though your husband was the last person to see Ms. James alive."

The sheriff had said Marc wasn't under arrest and that he just wanted to ask him some questions. Marc, of course, had agreed. Gillian didn't see any handcuffs, but there was no mistaking the tone in the sheriff's voice. Marc didn't really have any choice.

Marc gave Gillian a reassuring nod. "Look, everything will be fine. I'll call you later, okay?" He paused, frowning, as if reading her mind. "Now don't worry. You heard what he said. It's just routine."

Gillian forced a smile and nodded. The last time she'd seen a policeman was at the hospital on the night Marc almost died. His appearance was like a harbinger of her worst fears. Making a quick decision, she said, "We're coming, too."

CHAPTER 41

MARC HAD READ THAT during police interviews, most cops spent time chatting and making the interviewee feel at ease before swinging the sledgehammer. Sheriff Nate Dendridge had apparently skipped that class at the academy.

Dendridge sat across from him at a wood-grain, Formica-top conference table in a cramped interview room that lacked proper ventilation. Marc wiped his forehead on his sleeve. Dendridge was noting his discomfort with great interest, but Marc's perspiring had nothing to do with guilt. The room was simply too warm and cramped. Ever since the car accident in which the Jaws of Life had been used to free him, Marc had always hated closed-in spaces.

Dendridge leaned forward, intruding into Marc's personal space, his bloodshot eyes scary enough to make anybody sweat. "Understand that you're not under arrest," the sheriff said. "You can go anytime you want to."

This was just an interview for information purposes, he said. But it was clear to Marc that this was more than a friendly chat.

The sheriff's breath reeked of sour coffee. "You and your family seem to be the only folks within a couple hundred miles who even know Stacey James. Why don't you start at the beginning and tell me all about her?"

Marc detailed the events in Chicago. He told the sheriff about Stacey's flirtations, about the church discipline meeting and her anger, about the shooting and Stacey's escape. He also described Stacey's rape accusation and the resulting media frenzy.

"So why did you and your family decide to move up here to work at Whistler's Point?"

"To get away from the media circus. The leadership at the church where I was serving thought it wise for us to leave town for a few months . . . so things could settle down."

The sheriff stared Marc down. "So *did* you try to rape Stacey James? There *is* a possibility she shot you in self-defense."

Marc didn't blink. "Absolutely not. Request reports of the crime scene evidence. I think it'll be very obvious to you that she broke into my house, killed my dog, messed the place up, and waited for me to come home so she could shoot me. You won't find any evidence that I tried to rape her or that she shot me in self-defense."

The sheriff shook his head. "That's because there was never a physical exam. If the police had found Ms. James and done an exam, then we'd know for sure, wouldn't we? She probably healed since then, and of course now she can't tell us her side of the story." He stared Marc down again. "Which is all very convenient for you, isn't it? Now nobody will ever know the truth."

Marc kept his anger in check. "I didn't rape Stacey James. I didn't kill her either."

"Mm-hmm." The sheriff chewed on the end of his pen. "Let's back up. Did you try to contact Ms. James after the shooting?"

Marc hesitated. "Yes."

"How?"

"I mailed a letter to her current mailing address."

The sheriff raised an eyebrow. "A love letter?"

Marc tried to hide his distaste for the line of questioning. "No, Stacey and I were not romantically involved. I just wanted her to know that I'd forgiven her."

"For shooting you."

"Yes, I wanted her to know I'd forgiven her as God has forgiven her. And I encouraged her to read her Bible and seek the Lord for help."

Dendridge smirked at the God-talk. "But that was all? You didn't send her any other letters?"

"No, that was the only one."

"And you put your return address on the letter so she could find you, right?"

"No, I sent the letter to a friend on staff at the church. He mailed the letter for me from Chicago. See, I didn't want Stacey to know where I was. My location was a secret, and I have no idea if she even got the letter."

"Now hold on. If your location was a secret, how did Ms. James know where you were?"

"There was a break-in at the church. My pastor friend, Dave Ritchie, called and said somebody had stolen money from my secretary's desk and had broken into my office and taken a photo of me. That's why they thought Stacey was the one responsible. The person had also broken into Dave's office, rummaged through his drawers, and possibly looked through his address book. If Stacey was the thief, that explains how she knew where I was."

"Did you call her?"

"No."

"Did she call you?"

"No."

"We know she was staying at the North Woods Inn on Wednesday night, using a phony name. She was also probably driving a stolen car. Did you try to see her?"

"No."

"Did you contact her or try to meet her at the motel?"

"No. I didn't even know she was in town."

Dendridge leaned back in his chair, folding his brawny arms across his chest. His bloodshot eyes never left Marc's face. "Well, we'll track down your phone records. We'll find out if she called you or if you called her. Then I'll know if you're lying to me."

He wrote something down on his notepad. "So why do you think she drove up here?"

Marc knew the answer to this question was the most damaging of all. "To find me, I guess. I can't think of any other reason. Dave suggested that Stacey might try to track me down, but I didn't really take him seriously. I couldn't imagine that she'd actually take a trip like that, but I guess I was wrong."

"Did Ms. James contact you before your meeting with her yesterday?"

"No. Yesterday was the first time I'd seen her or communicated with her since the shooting."

"Okay, why don't you tell me again about your meeting with her yesterday."

Meeting? The sheriff had used the word twice as if Marc had scheduled the encounter. He gathered his thoughts. "Henry and I had just finished cleaning the grounds. I took a wheelbarrow full of leaves to the brush pile. I dumped the leaves, turned around, and there she was."

"Just like that?"

"Just like that."

"What did she say?"

Marc felt himself blushing. "She said she loved me and wanted to know if I loved her, if I had feelings for her. I told her I cared for her as her counselor at the church, and that was all. I told her I didn't have feelings for her like that, but you have to know Stacey. She lived in a fantasy world half the time. Remember, I was her counselor for a while. To say she was disturbed would be an understatement."

The sheriff chuckled. "A real psycho, huh?"

Marc glanced away, not seeing anything funny. Stacey had problems, certainly, but she was a living soul just like everybody else. Part of him had always loved her as a sister in Christ who needed help. When her death sank in, he knew he'd have a good cry. But not right now. Too bad for Dendridge. He would have enjoyed seeing tears.

The sheriff asked, "How did it make you feel to see her again?"

"I was alarmed. Remember, she almost killed me in Chicago. It was certainly a shock to see her again."

"Were you afraid she might hurt you?"

"Of course. She said she didn't have a gun and didn't intend to hurt me, but I couldn't tell for sure. I thought she might be hiding a gun somewhere in her clothing. If I gave her the wrong answer, I wasn't sure what she would do. She could shoot me again. So yeah, you could say I was worried."

"Henry says he came along as you two were arguing."

Marc nodded.

"Could you tell me what the argument was about?"

Marc sighed. "Stacey insisted that I loved her, even though I told her I didn't. She wanted me to abandon my wife and daughter and run off with her. The whole thing was absurd, and she wasn't making sense. If she loved me, then why shoot me? I tried to help her see how ridiculous she was being, but she wouldn't listen. She got mad. I got mad. That's what Henry saw."

"Then she just ran off."

"I think Henry scared her, and she probably knew I'd call the police—which I did."

The sheriff leaned forward in his chair. His face bore a pleased look, as if he knew something Marc didn't. The look was unnerving. "The bottom line is this: no one else in this whole region had a reason to want Ms. James dead, except you. So we've got motive."

"But I didn't kill her."

Dendridge shook his head. "She tried to kill you, Mr. Thayer. When she showed up, you realized you had your chance for revenge."

"No!"

"Henry saw the two of you fighting. You wanted her dead."

"No!"

Closing his eyes, Marc leaned back in his chair and prayed. Not for Stacey—it was too late for her. He prayed for Gillian and Crystal. He prayed for control.

"Then look where you left the body—in an out-of-the-way place where she might not be found for days."

"That's ridiculous. Henry and I dump stuff in that brush pile almost every day, and look what happened—Henry found her this morning."

"But who else even *knows* about the location of the brush pile? Henry said only you and a couple other groundskeepers would have known."

"That's true." Marc chewed his bottom lip. The location was an interesting detail. Who would have killed Stacey and thought to leave her body there? Perhaps someone else had witnessed his argument with Stacey. Perhaps whoever had killed her had intentionally left her body in the brush pile in an attempt to point the finger at him.

"Where were you last night, Marc? The medical examiner says Stacey was killed sometime between 8 PM and 2 AM."

"I was with my family the entire evening. We were celebrating my daughter's seventeenth birthday. You can ask either one of them. I think Gillian and I went to bed around eleven."

The sheriff wrote all of this down. "Did you leave the house at all last night?"

Marc hesitated. "Well, yeah. Around six, I grilled some steaks on the outdoor grill. Later, Gillian and I showed Crystal the used car we'd gotten her for her birthday." He paused, trying to remember. "Then before bed, I took out the trash."

"Which would have been when?"

"I'm not sure. It was late. I'd forgotten to do it earlier and realized that if I didn't do it then, I'd never do it. I forget things sometimes. Just ask my wife."

"Were you outside the house any other time?"

"No."

"Do you recall anything unusual about last night? Did you notice anyone outside? Hear or see anything unusual?"

Marc had forgotten a detail until now. "The doorbell."

"The doorbell?"

"Yeah, someone rang the doorbell. But when I went to see who it was, there was nobody there."

"Nobody at all?"

"That's what I just said. Nobody."

"Any idea what time that would have been?"

Marc tried to remember. "Around 9 PM, I think. I'm not sure. Gillian might know better."

Marc replayed the event in his mind and puzzled over what it could mean. Who had rung the doorbell? And why ring the doorbell and run away before he opened the door?

CHAPTER 42

THE UNADORNED LOBBY OF the Luce County Sheriff's Office was lifeless, as if nobody in the region ever committed a felony. Sitting in the waiting room, surrounded by outdated but functional decor, Gillian glanced at Crystal, who was slouching, arms folded across her chest, and looking more worried by the moment.

Gillian checked her watch. It was getting close to noon. More than two hours had passed, and Sheriff Dendridge was still questioning Marc.

The situation seemed surreal, as if at any moment a group of friends would leap out of their hiding places, shouting, "Surprise!" and they would all enjoy a joke planned for Crystal's birthday. Except nobody was hiding behind doors, and no streamers or balloons were hanging from the ceiling.

Catching herself tracing letters on the vinyl seat with her finger, Gillian folded her hands. She longed for her calligraphy pens, for anything to help her focus on something other than Stacey's murder and whatever Marc was enduring in the interview room down the hall.

But she supposed Marc's meeting with the sheriff was of little importance in the bigger scheme of things. His interview would surely be over soon, but nobody could bring Stacey back to life. As much as she had disliked Stacey, the news of her death shocked and saddened her. Another soul had passed into eternity. Had Stacey even been a believer?

She recalled Marc's pale face when the sheriff gave them the news of Stacey's death. She'd heard the tremor in Marc's voice and gripped his hand comfortingly. It was only natural that he would grieve for Stacey. No one else had poured his life into hers like he had.

Gillian stared at the bland walls and counted the ceiling tiles. Why were they taking so long? Surely there weren't enough reasons to interview Marc for two of the longest, most agonizing hours in recent memory.

Shortly after reaching the Luce County Sheriff's Office, Gillian had called Nicole, who had recommended a good lawyer for Marc. Within a half hour, Sandra Millford, a businesslike, middle-aged woman with thick, gray hair, had arrived and set Gillian's mind at ease. At least, at first.

"This is just routine," she'd assured her and Crystal after glancing through the preliminary police report. "There's nothing to worry about. Everything will be fine."

But now, as the interview room door opened and Sandra came out, her face looked drawn and haggard. Taking a seat across from Crystal and Gillian, she scanned the notes she'd scrawled on a yellow legal pad.

Hooking a lock of hair behind her ear, Gillian studied Sandra expectantly, trying to be patient. Crystal wasn't as patient.

"So what's going on? It's been at least two hours. It's almost time for lunch. When are they going to release him?"

Sandra hesitated, her brown eyes betraying nothing. "I'm afraid things are more complicated than I had thought. The medical examiner believes Stacey was strangled sometime between 8 PM and 2 AM. By your husband's own admission, he took out the trash sometime during that window of time."

Gillian nodded. "He did. I remember."

"Well, you see, that means Marc doesn't have an alibi. He could have been somewhere outside your house at the time of Stacey's murder."

"But he was only gone a few minutes," Gillian pointed out.

"The strangling wouldn't have taken more than a few minutes." Sandra took a breath. "Mrs. Thayer, be aware that the sheriff may want to ask you a few questions. He may also request a warrant to search your house for evidence."

Gillian swallowed hard. *God, what is happening?*

"Is there anything else you can tell us?" Crystal asked.

"I'm afraid the sheriff has a pretty strong circumstantial case against Marc. He had opportunity, means, and motive. I know all about his connection to Stacey James. Even the location where the body was found is suggestive, since Marc had talked to her there earlier in the day."

"But Marc didn't do anything." Gillian felt bone-weary.

"You have to look at the case from the sheriff's point of view," Sandra said. "Since there's only your husband's word—obviously Stacey can't give testimony—we have to use other evidence to determine the truth. A lot can make or break a case—and there's a lot more than fingerprints nowadays. There's a whole list of things that can incriminate or exonerate a suspect: DNA, blood, fibers, semen."

Gillian's stomach clenched. "Are you telling us Stacey was raped?"

Sandra shook her head. "The medical examiner used a rape kit. There's no evidence that Stacey was sexually assaulted."

Gillian closed her eyes, allowing some relief to seep in.

"But there *was* some sort of evidence at the scene," Crystal said. "That's what you're telling us, right?"

Sandra nodded. "The forensics team found something under Stacey's fingernails. Sometimes a victim claws her attacker during an assault. It's premature for anyone to say for certain whose DNA it is until the more advanced tests come back from the lab. The tests could either help Marc or hurt him. It all depends on what's under Stacey's fingernails.

"In the meantime, like I said, the circumstantial evidence against Marc is very strong." She paused and touched her tongue to the middle of her upper lip. "I'm sorry, but Marc has been arrested."

This can't be happening! Gillian shook her head.

Crystal pulled Gillian close and held her tight. "It's going to be okay, Mom. We'll get through this together."

Sandra stood, her image rippling and distorting as Gillian's eyes filled with tears.

"I'm very sorry," she said. "I'll do everything I can to get Marc released, but I'm afraid he'll have to spend the weekend in jail. His arraignment is Monday at 10 AM, so maybe we can get him out on bail at that time."

Gillian sighed, and Sandra touched her arm. "Let's just take things one step at a time, okay? We'll know a lot more after the DNA tests come back from the lab and after the medical examiner has finished his autopsy. If he finds hair samples, fingerprints, or other evidence of a third person—someone other than Marc who appears in one of the national databases as a known offender—Marc could be cleared right away. In the meantime, we just need to sit tight and wait."

And pray. Pray as if our lives depended on it.

Sandra handed Gillian her business card. "I know this is unsettling, but believe me, everything will work out. I'll be in touch. If you have any questions—any at all, night or day—please call me. Otherwise, I'll see you Monday morning at the arraignment."

CHAPTER 43

HE CREPT DOWN A dark, narrow alley with moonlight providing the only light. It was enough for him to make out the shape of the body lying twisted and forsaken behind an overflowing Dumpster. Sirens wailed in the distance, making him realize how far he was from help, from safety. If he called out, would anyone hear him?

Perhaps she'd called out, even pleaded. Perhaps she'd offered her body to save her life, to stall for time.

Nobody would ever know. Whatever means of persuasion she'd tried had fallen on deaf ears.

Without bending down for a closer look, he knew she was dead. The angle of her head, her closed eyes, the rope pulled tightly around her neck—he'd seen this scene before and felt that familiar twist in his gut.

No, God, no. Not another one. Please make it stop.

Movement flickered in his peripheral vision. He whirled around, clutching at his throat.

Too late.

A rope was around his neck, and his unseen assailant was pulling it tight.

He wrestled with his foe, but couldn't see who it was. The face was hidden in shadow.

He couldn't breathe. Flailing his arms, he tried to break the killer's hold.

* * *

Riley woke with a start, his heart coming out of his chest.

The phone rang again.

He sat up, startled. His mind searched for the road out of the haze. Emily's hand gripped his arm like a vice.

A phone call. In the dead of night.

That could mean only one thing. Something terrible had happened to someone he loved. His daughter, Samantha? Darrell? The twins? A car accident? A burglary?

He grabbed the receiver, his mouth desert dry. "Hello?"

"Riley, it's me."

O'Hearn? "Is everything okay?"

"Sorry to call you in the dead of night."

Riley smiled at O'Hearn's choice of words, an inside joke from years ago, and felt some of his tension slipping away. "So what's up? It must be important."

"It is. I wanted to call you right away. We think the Magician Murderer struck again."

An orange-hot poker stabbed Riley's stomach. This news was no surprise really. The perp had never been caught; it was only logical that he would strike again eventually, though Riley had entertained a fantasy that the killings had stopped at the moment of his retirement. "You called me in the middle of the night to tell me that?"

"Look, buddy, just listen to me. Another strangling, yes, but this one was different. It wasn't in Cincinnati."

Now Riley was awake. "Not in Cincinnati?"

"No, in Michigan."

"Michigan?"

"About as far north as you can get, as a matter of fact."

Riley's mind raced. If the killer was not "geographically stable," the term that forensic psychologists used for someone who commits several crimes in the same geographical area, he was now a transient serial killer. "Do you realize what this means?"

"Uh-huh. He broke his pattern. He's out of his comfort zone. He could have been careless, could have left something important behind. This is big."

"Why do you think it's him?"

"This may take a little time, so hear me out."

Riley rolled his eyes. He was wide awake now and not about to get back to sleep anytime soon. "I'm listening."

"Well, you remember DiMarini, don't you? Left the department a couple years ago to go back to Illinois—his wife wanted to be closer to the grandparents, or something. Anyhow, he's with the Cook County Sheriff's Department now, outside of Chicago somewhere, and he calls me tonight. Seems some sheriff in Upper Michigan—a town called Newberry—called him and was asking questions about a pastor from Illinois who was shot by a woman he counseled. Maybe you remember hearing about it on the news a month or so ago. Big story for Chicago."

Rubbing his bald head, Riley had only a vague recollection of the story. He wondered where all this was going.

"Anyhow, this same pastor got arrested today—no, make it yesterday now—for strangling the same woman who had shot him."

"Okay."

"Now get this. Whoever strangled this lady didn't use just any rope. What kind of rope do you think he used?"

Riley's breath caught in his throat. "How can you be sure?"

"DiMarini said the sheriff from Michigan mentioned some sort of 'trick rope'—just mentioned it as an aside, but DiMarini worked the Erin Walker case, as you'll recall, and his little ears perked up. He knew we'd be interested in that particular detail, so he gave me a call."

"Has anything been said to the folks in Michigan?" Riley felt his pulse accelerate. "Because somebody needs to tell them."

"I *did* tell them. I called the local sheriff—guy named Dendridge. He's got the pastor arrested as a suspect and frankly just likes to hear himself talk. I told him about the possible connection to the murders in Cincinnati, but you know how it is. Small town. The first murder in, what, fifty years? A sheriff looking for stardom. Probably an upcoming election affecting his judgment. He wouldn't listen to me."

"Somebody needs to check out that suspect and see if he's our guy from Cincinnati. Man, Jer, he's got a gold mine in his lap, but doesn't realize what he's got!"

Riley imagined bumbling cops traipsing all over the crime scene, destroying or contaminating critical evidence. Just the thought was enough to make him feel ill. He rubbed his lower lip with the ball of his thumb.

"Anyhow, I knew you should know right away," O'Hearn said. "After all, you *were* the lead investigator."

"Thanks. You did the right thing calling me."

"So what do you think we should do?"

"Did you call the FBI? The perp's crossed state lines. I bet they'd be interested."

"I called Mitch Reed at Quantico. He's interested, but he doesn't have any agents available right now."

Availability is probably only part of the picture. It was a case that had gone cold, a trail that could end up going nowhere. He empathized with the bureau's reluctance to spend expensive man hours on an investigation that could be nothing but a waste of time. "And?"

"He said they might be able to send somebody in a couple weeks."

"A couple weeks!? This isn't the kind of development you can wait on." Riley heard the fire in his own voice. "I mean, by the time they cut through the red tape and send somebody up there, the trail could be cold. A top investigator needs to be on the scene right now."

"Hey, buddy, you're preaching to the choir."

"Sorry, Jer." Riley rubbed the sensitive skin on his balding head. "Somebody needs to do something now. Delay could be the kiss of death."

"I'd go if I could, but I've got critical cases I'm working on here. My boss would never give me the time away. Do you know anybody who might be available?"

Riley realized what O'Hearn was implying. Riley had time—and a compelling interest in the case; but he'd retired from that kind of life. He'd promised Emily a relaxing retirement, and there was no guarantee this wouldn't turn into a protracted investigation leading to another frustrating dead end. Emily had just been saying—was it just last night at dinner?—how happy she was that he no longer had to jump every time a new case or clue came in. He knew she would just tell him to let it go, to let the younger dogs chase the fox. But, oh, how he hated to leave things undone!

Here was a potential break with a killer who was out of his comfort zone, who might have left behind a clue he'd been careful to cover up in Cincinnati. It was an opportunity to go after the guy before the trail turned cold again, and it could be his last chance to solve the case and pick up the pieces of a failure that would hound him to his grave unless God provided a way for him to redeem himself.

After promising O'Hearn he'd get back to him, Riley hung up. Emily was leaning back on her elbows, a question in her eyes, her face pale in the moonlight that streamed through the window.

"What was that all about? The Magician Murderer?" she asked. "I thought somebody had died."

He sighed. "Somebody *has* died. Somebody's daughter. In Michigan."

"And Jerry thinks local law enforcement is going to mess up the investigation?"

Riley related the conversation, surprised by Emily's interest. "Sounds like we've got a hothead sheriff who won't listen to reason. Some things just never change."

"But you could set things right. You could bring justice for all those girls, couldn't you?"

He couldn't hide his surprise at her words. "I would certainly do my best."

"I think you should do it."

He blinked, not certain he'd heard her. "You think I should do it?"

"Call it your last shot at the case. The fact that you never caught the killer has weighed on you ever since you left the force. You've been off the job, but not fully retired. Am I right?"

He could only nod, his throat tight.

"In fact, I hate to say it, but I think your mind has been more on your past failures than on your present and future prospects." Without giving him a chance to reply, she added, "Maybe it's time to finish the job, hon. It looks like God's giving you a second chance."

Actually, a fifth chance, he thought, counting the victims. He looked her in the eye. "But I was determined to put the case behind me, to push the pressure aside so we could have a nice retirement."

Sitting up, she faced him. "And we can still have a nice retirement when your mind is on retirement. But your mind is on a killer who needs to be brought to justice and on families who need closure and vindication."

"But I'll have to leave you here alone for a few weeks. Maybe even longer."

She smiled sadly. "When you're finished, I'll be here waiting."

"It also means I'll have to put my gun back on. You hate it when I'm in danger. Won't you worry about me?"

"Every blessed minute."

He hesitated. "Before I go tearing off to who knows where, I think we should talk to the Lord and make sure this is what *He* wants. What do you say?"

She put an arm around him. "I was just waiting for you to say the word."

CHAPTER 44

MORNING LIGHT SLANTED THROUGH the barred window and landed in a warm, bright square at Marc's feet. He stuck his hand-cuffed hands into the light and watched the way dust motes and shad-ows danced across the cold, concrete floor. The sun reminded him of warm summer days back home, but he didn't feel any warmth.

He felt cold. So very cold.

He studied his scuffed shoes and shifted uneasily in his Day-Glo orange jumpsuit with the words *Luce County Jail* stenciled in black letters across his back. The suit was too large for him, reminding him of hand-me-down clothes he'd worn as a boy. The suit made him want to burrow down inside and hide away for a while so he could sort all of this out. Wiping a hand across his face, he realized he needed a shave.

He clasped the Bible he'd requested from the guard and tried to pray. Somewhere down the hall, a TV or radio was blaring a political talk show. Tomorrow, he would be arraigned—whatever that meant. Right now, he longed to be in church. It was Sunday, after all.

He sat up straight, stretched, and pushed his shoulders back. His back ached.

It felt like an eternity had passed since his interview and arrest on Friday. Setting the Bible on the cot beside him, he replayed in his mind for the umpteenth time his interview with Sheriff Dendridge.

He hadn't felt alarmed at first. Dendridge had seemed cordial enough, but his questions had become increasingly accusatory, more indicative of where things were headed. Around eleven o'clock, he had sat numbly while Dendridge informed him he was under arrest for the murder of Stacey James. They had read him his Miranda rights and asked him to sign a form indicating he understood them. And then they had put him in handcuffs.

At that point, Sandra Millford, a lawyer Marc assumed Gillian had hired for him, had come into the room. She had explained his rights and clued him in on the circumstantial evidence against him. He had listened patiently, wide-eyed, wondering when somebody was going to take the handcuffs off. He couldn't have been more surprised when Sandra told him he would be spending the rest of the weekend in jail. Somehow he'd thought that with a lawyer involved he'd be able to go home until things were cleared up.

Sandra had been helpful to a point. She'd been the public defender in Luce County for twenty-odd years, but what Marc needed was for her to pretend she was teaching criminal law basics to a classroom of third-graders. He didn't know a thing about police procedure, about how long he would have to stay here, about what was going to happen to him next. What he *did* know was that he'd been arrested for a murder he didn't commit, and no hope of release was in sight.

Adding insult to injury, they'd taken his fingerprints and mug shot and stuck him in a holding cell with a couple of lowlifes, who had moved to the other side of the cell when he came in. Finally, he'd been granted a phone call to Gillian, who had apparently been waiting in the lobby for him all morning and had just returned to Whistler's Point when the phone rang.

"Marc, are you all right?"

"I can't believe this is happening. I don't know why they have me in here."

"Marc, it's the circumstantial evidence. Surely Sandra explained it to you."

"Who did this, Gill? Who killed Stacey?"

"I don't know."

"What's going to happen to me?"

"Your arraignment's on Monday. That's when formal charges against you will be made. The judge will probably grant bail. If we pay that, then you can go home."

"How much is bail?"

"Sandra said for a murder charge it'll be more than we can afford."

"So then what?"

"Then we wait for the trial."

A trial? Could things possibly get any worse?

"Something else you need to know. Sheriff Dendridge sent a couple of men back over here with a search warrant. They're searching our bedroom as I speak."

"That's just great!"

"Don't worry. We'll get through this somehow. Have you prayed and asked God for help?"

"Of course." The truth was, ever since his arrest, he'd been questioning why a loving God would allow this to happen to him. He knew it was an immature way to assess the situation, but he'd stopped walking in the Spirit the moment they put handcuffs around his wrists.

"Thanks for calling." He didn't know what else to say. "I love you."

"I love you, too. Don't worry, okay?"

"I'll try not to."

"Remember, God has a purpose."

"I know, but I sure wish I could see it."

※　※　※

As Sunday morning dragged on, Marc read random verses from Psalms to calm his nerves, to remind himself that God was somewhere in all of this foolishness.

The thought was hard to believe, but he had to believe it. The alternative was unthinkable.

Remembering his latest Bible study, he turned to the book of Habakkuk. Evil men in Israel were flourishing, and the prophet Habakkuk wanted to know when God was going to do something about the problem. God's answer was that He was going to judge Israel by the hand of the Babylonians, a nation even more wicked than Israel. In the end, however, the Babylonians would be judged as well, and Habakkuk simply needed to trust God, though the situation made little sense from a human standpoint.

But that was the point: Sometimes God's plan doesn't make sense. We simply need to trust Him when we don't understand.

Marc closed his eyes. *God, none of this makes sense. None of it. An evil man is walking the streets as a free man, and I'm in here paying for his crimes. Are You going to bring this killer to justice?*

Sensing that someone was watching him, Marc opened his eyes and glanced up. Outside the cell, a balding, white-haired man in his sixties or early seventies was studying him inquisitively. The short, stocky man had a deeply wrinkled face, putting him well past his prime, but his warm, brown eyes had a twinkle that said, "Don't judge me by appearances. I can surprise you."

"Is that Marc Thayer?" the white-haired man asked the guard, his eyes still on Marc.

"Yep, that's him."

The man shifted his weight and took a step in the direction of Marc's cell. Dressed in a dapper navy suit complete with brown penny loafers, a white dress shirt, and a power burgundy tie, he looked out of place in a jailhouse.

He looks like an insurance salesman, Marc mused. The man had that fat, contented air about him that speaks of money, experience, or both. *Or maybe he's just somebody's grandfather.*

"I'd like to ask him a few questions," the man said over his shoulder to the guard.

The deputy disappeared through a door. A moment later, the door opened, and Sheriff Dendridge appeared, disapproval written all over his face.

The old man faced Dendridge, hands spread, and said in a diplomatic voice, "Look, Sheriff, I know this is your jurisdiction so far. I'm not trying to weasel my way in, okay? I just want to get at the truth. Like I told you on the phone, I know the guy I'm looking for. I've seen his work too many times. It isn't going to hurt anybody if I just ask your suspect here a few questions. Besides, I flew all the way from Florida—at my own expense, I might add—to talk to this man. That's how much this interview means to me. If he's the killer, I'll know it."

Dendridge chewed his lower lip. "You're retired, Riley. You have no official business here, and I've already interrogated him. It's an open-and-shut case."

The man called Riley peered up into Dendridge's bloodshot eyes. The sheriff was probably a foot taller than he was, but no match in terms of spunk or determination. "I don't mean to be patting myself on the back here, Sheriff, but I don't think you realize who you're talking to. I was a homicide detective in Cincinnati for more than thirty years. I hunted murderers every day. I could ask you how many murderers you've put behind bars, but I won't. Just think about it.

"The fact that certain evidence has appeared in this murder means that I might be dealing with someone I've been after for the past several years. He strangled four women in Cincinnati, and I almost caught him. Now this evidence alerts me to the possibility that this killer has left his home court in Cincinnati and has struck outside his comfort zone. I don't believe in coincidence."

Dendridge was shaking his head.

Riley stepped closer to the sheriff, his face turning red. "You let me talk to this man, or I'm calling Mitch Reed at the FBI."

Dendridge bristled. Swearing under his breath, he pointed a finger at Riley. "Eat your heart out, but I'm filing a formal complaint against you."

"File away."

"Your questions won't come to anything." Growling, Dendridge marched away—to the apparent amusement of Riley, who suppressed a smirk.

Marc's head was spinning as the deputy unlocked the cell and escorted him out. He'd been wrong by a long shot. A homicide detective—this guy? He wondered what the detective could possibly want with him.

CHAPTER 45

GILLIAN OPENED HER SONGBOOK and tried to sing—she truly did. But the words kept getting caught in her throat. She couldn't recall a Sunday since she'd been married when Marc hadn't been at her side, holding the songbook for her and belting out the song in his sometimes off-key baritone. As if to underscore her loneliness, Crystal had chosen to sit with some of her youth group buddies in the back. Thus, Gillian stood in her pew on the far right side like a small, weathered tree rising from the middle of a desolate meadow.

Faithful as ever, white-haired Melody Crenshaw was bent over the old piano, employing her gnarled, arthritic fingers in spite of chronic pain. Poor Melody. Gillian didn't feel half as bad when she reminded herself how fortunate she was. *Imagine trying to do calligraphy with fingers like that!*

Smiling Tony Gerber, the song leader, was swinging his arms around in bizarre maneuvers that could only be described as figure eights. Gillian had long since given up trying to understand the significance of his gestures. Thanks to a brief stint taking flute lessons as a child, she knew enough about time signatures to realize that Tony didn't have a clue what he was doing. But glancing around at the other parishioners crowding the small auditorium, she realized that nobody seemed to care. And why should they? This was the Lord's day, a time to focus on God, not on the foibles of other people.

Stung by this reminder, Gillian saw her critical spirit for what it was: a feeble attempt to elevate herself by pushing others down. She identified the trap and breathed a silent prayer, asking God to forgive her negative thinking and to replace it with positive reminders of His goodness. Knowing she couldn't truthfully sing the words of the hymn, she put the songbook down, closed her eyes, and reminded herself of good things.

Jesus died for me on the cross and rose again. He saved me from my sin. My sin is separated from me as far as the east is from the west. Nothing can separate me from the love of God. God has given me all things pertaining to life and godliness. He will never allow more difficulty than I can handle. He will never leave me or forsake me. He will—

Hearing the shuffle of feet, Gillian opened her eyes. Clara Henderson stood at the end of the pew. She slid in next to Gillian, a smile on her lips. She gave Gillian a little pat on the shoulder as if to say, "You don't need to say a word, dear. I know what a difficult morning this must be for you without Marc at your side. In fact, that's why I'm here."

Clara took Gillian's songbook and lifted it up for both of them, contributing a wobbly but determined soprano.

> Be still, my soul: thy God doth undertake
> To guide the future, as He has the past.
> Thy hope, thy confidence let nothing shake;
> All now mysterious shall be bright at last.

Clara kept singing, but Gillian was still cemented to that last line. *All now mysterious shall be bright at last.* So all of those troubling things that were confusing now would make sense someday? Was that what the song meant? She certainly hoped so, because little was making sense to her lately.

After a male duet, Pastor Randall approached the pulpit and began a sermon on the trap of thanklessness, based on Romans 1. But Gillian could hardly concentrate on what he was saying. She kept thinking about Marc and wondering how he was doing. Had he had breakfast yet? If not, he'd be starving right about now. She hoped the cot hadn't been too hard. Otherwise he'd have a backache for the rest of the day.

After the message drew to a close and Pastor Randall closed in prayer, Gillian didn't move. Others were on their feet and heading toward the exit, but she remained seated. The sounds of their shuffling shoes were interspersed with bursts of laughter and words of encouragement. A few paused to tell her they were praying for Marc, and she thanked them for their concern. But she didn't feel like getting up. Not yet. She'd come, expecting to meet God and find solace. But something was missing.

Clara had lingered, her head bowed, mouth moving. Finally, she looked up and smiled at Gillian, patting her shoulder again. "Dear, you need to talk to someone, don't you? You look like you're about ready to burst. Why don't you just tell me what's on your heart?"

So Gillian began to talk, and what began as a tiny trickling stream was soon a gushing torrent, as if from a fire hydrant. She told Clara everything: about the death of the twins, about Stacey's infatuation with Marc, about the discovered love letter, about Marc's shooting and the rape allegations, about Stacey's murder, about Marc's arrest.

"It just feels like more than one person can bear," Gillian concluded.

"That's why God wants you to cast your burdens on Him," Clara said. "He'll carry them for you."

"I know."

"Do you? You seem determined to carry these burdens all by yourself. Telling me was a good start, but why don't you let them go?"

Let them go. "You make it sound so easy."

Clara shook her head. "No, trusting God with our problems is never easy. We're too full of pride, thinking we can handle them on our own. We can cast our burdens on Him and five minutes later take them right back again. That's why the Christian life is such a minute-by-minute process." She shrugged. "You say you don't feel like you can bear these burdens on your own. Then don't. Let them go. Be free."

Be free. Gillian closed her eyes. *God, I can't carry these burdens anymore. They are too much for me to carry. I give them to You now and trust You to do what You feel is best.*

Gillian looked up to see Clara's gray eyes brimming with hope.

"Now you've shared many burdens with me," Clara said. "Do you mind if I take them to the Lord?"

Tears filled Gillian's eyes as Clara began to pray, her confident voice and gentle words revealing a child who truly knew her Father.

CHAPTER 46

ENTERING THE SAME STUFFY interview room where he'd talked to Dendridge on the night of his arrest, Marc realized something big was up and that the old detective had been busy. On one wall stretched a large map of Cincinnati. Black lines had been drawn to connect four red dots, creating a rectangular pattern. Marc assumed the red dots indicated crime scenes.

Another wall was dominated by four large portraits of young women about Crystal's age. They were attractive girls, but not impressive. All had blonde hair and blue eyes, and they wore wire rim glasses. They looked like the girl next door. Unassuming. Small town. Naive.

Something sucked at his heart to see their innocent faces. They had smiled for yearbook photographers, for fathers at birthday parties, for friends at the amusement park. Like their peers, they'd expected to go on to college, to find a job, find Mr. Right, get married, have a family of their own, and live happily ever after.

Those were dreams that now would never come true.

A third wall, directly facing the interview table, was covered with grisly crime scene photos. Though Marc averted his eyes once he realized what they were, he couldn't help glancing at a few of the pictures as he sat down on a metal chair at the table. What he saw sickened him.

The detective took a seat across from Marc at the table. Leaning back in a squeaky metal chair, he unwrapped a stick of Juicy Fruit gum and folded it into his mouth.

Now that they were confined to such a small room, Marc felt

smothered by the overpowering aroma of Riley's cologne. It was either Ralph Lauren Polo or Chaps. Marc always got the two mixed up.

"So you're probably wondering what this is all about." Riley eyed Marc quizzically.

Marc blotted sweaty palms on the thighs of his jumpsuit. His long legs barely fit under the table. "You could say that."

"I'm retired Sergeant Chuck Riley, but you can call me Riley, okay? As you've probably gathered, I was a homicide detective in Cincinnati for a good many years. While there, I hunted a serial killer I'm still trying to track down. Have you ever been to Cincinnati?"

"No."

"Are you married?"

"Yes."

"Any criminal record?"

"No."

Riley locked eyes with Marc. "Realize that with your name and Social Security number, I can verify everything you're telling me. I would advise you to be completely truthful."

"I am." Marc wondered why Riley thought he was lying. Or maybe he just treated everybody this way.

"Have you ever met a girl named Erin Walker?"

Marc thought a minute. "Doesn't ring a bell."

"Got any children?"

Counting the ones in heaven? "One daughter. Crystal's sixteen." He caught himself. "Sorry, seventeen. Her birthday was on Thursday."

"I've got a daughter, too." Riley shook his head sadly. "I pray every day she won't cross paths with this monster."

Marc wondered if Sergeant Riley was a religious man, but didn't have an opportunity to ask. More questions came in rapid-fire succession. Marc reminded himself that he was a suspect and that these pressure tactics were intended to unnerve him. Riley asked about his background, his education, his places of employment, his addresses of residence in the last decade.

Marc answered every question as best he could. He told Riley about his brief stint in professional basketball and about the accident that had closed the door on his dream. He described his pastoral background, summarized his last few years in Chicago, and mentioned his need to get away for a few months—though he left the reason purposely vague.

Riley's face brightened. "So, you're a Christian?"

Marc broke into a grin. "You bet. Since my accident. God got my attention."

"I'm a Christian, too." Riley told Marc about an altar call at a Christian camp when he was eight years old. He described a fire-and-brimstone message that had left him quaking in his seat, desperate for the assurance that he would someday go to heaven when he died.

"So I prayed right there, trusted Christ as my Savior, and became a child of God." Riley closed his eyes and nodded as if the memory were a movie playing in his head. "Oh, yeah, it seems like only yesterday."

Marc was surprised to realize that Riley reminded him of his own father. A gruff exterior covering a heart of gold. The difference was that Marc's dad was still an unbeliever, and a wall had gone up between them shortly after Marc's conversion. His father had always pulled for him to make it big in the NBA, and Marc's decision not to try to come back after the injury and to pursue the pastorate instead had been too difficult for his dad to accept. Marc prayed every day that he and his father would be reconciled someday.

"I can look you in the eye and say with confidence that you're not the man I'm looking for," Riley said after a sigh. "First, the only evidence against you is circumstantial. Second, I have forensic evidence linking this murder to another perpetrator with a clear M.O. and a series of unsolved murders committed in Cincinnati. Third, what I can tell so far is that you weren't anywhere near Cincinnati when the other murders occurred. Of course, I'll need to do some checking to be sure. But that's good for you and bad for me. It means I've got a lot more work to do."

Marc felt a measure of relief, but he wasn't sure what kind of pull Riley had in Sheriff Dendridge's jurisdiction.

Riley seemed to sense Marc's wariness. "Now don't you worry about a thing. You just leave the sheriff to me. As soon as we're done here, I'll do what I can to get you out of here today. Of course, you'll have to promise to stay in town in case you're needed for more questioning, and you'll remain a suspect until the real killer is caught."

Marc didn't try to hide his relief.

Riley leaned back in his chair. "Nope. You don't fit the profile at all. I'm looking for a loner, someone who probably had a troubled childhood. Maybe abusive. Probably had a domineering mother, a distant father."

"You're sure it's a man?"

"Serial killers are rarely female. He's a man, all right. Probably a high school dropout, possibly dishonorably discharged from the military. Someone who knows how to use a computer and the Internet."

"Which could be just about anybody these days."

Riley shrugged. "Yeah, but this guy's a pro. Weeks before each murder, he cyber-stalked each girl. Sent threatening instant messages and e-mails. Harassed them. Even went through their garbage."

"But you can track down e-mails and instant messages these days, right?"

Riley grimaced. "Normally, yes, but this guy knows his stuff. He knows how to hide on the Internet, but there are always other ways to track him down."

"So then why hasn't he been arrested yet?"

Riley glanced away. "Because a hotshot homicide detective in Cincinnati messed up and couldn't crack the case." He raised guilty eyes to Marc's. "Yep, you guessed it. That would be me."

"Sorry, I didn't mean—"

"Hey, it's okay. I'm only telling you the truth. We all make mistakes, right? Mine was being blind to what was staring me in the face. Anyhow, the guy vanished without a trace—'Now you see him, now you don't,' as they say."

Riley turned serious, his eyes hard. "I investigated more than one thousand leads that went nowhere, and then I reached the agreed-upon date of my retirement and had to walk away from it all. That was only about a month ago, and I've thought about the case every day since. When my old partner called to tell me about this case here in Michigan, it looked like we might catch a break. I'm planning to meet with the medical examiner who conducted Stacey's autopsy and see what he learned. Maybe our guy was careless for once."

"So you're sure it's the same guy?"

"That's what it looks like. I have every reason to believe the killer moved into this area and assumed another identity. Probably thought he could hide in a small town where he wouldn't be noticed and heal himself of his compulsions. But in my experience, it never works that way. A serial killer, once he's developed a taste for death, rarely stops killing unless either he dies or someone stops him. That's why I'm here—God help me—to stop him once and for all."

Marc heard a rap on the door. The door opened, and a young sheriff's deputy handed Riley a manila folder. Whispers were exchanged, but Marc couldn't make out the words.

The door closed. Biting his lower lip, Riley opened the folder and glanced through a sheaf of documents that Marc couldn't see. Immediately, Marc sensed something was wrong. The relaxed atmosphere in the room had been replaced by a thread of tension.

Riley leaned back in his squeaky chair and rubbed his lower lip with the ball of his thumb. "It appears that things might not be as simple as I'd thought." He leaned forward, staring Marc down. "Why didn't you tell me about this rape allegation in Chicago?"

CHAPTER 47

BENT OVER THE TABLE in her studio, Gillian was working hard on another calligraphy project, but nothing seemed to be going right today. Stiffness wrestled her hand into a knot. Putting down the glass nib pen, she massaged her wrist and sighed.

It was a simple project with a familiar passage of Scripture: Philippians 3:13–14.

Forgetting those things which are behind and reaching forward to those things which are ahead, I press toward the goal for the prize of the upward call of God in Christ Jesus.

She had scripted those verses dozens of times, even blending different ink colors on the parchment paper. The project should have been old hat, like riding a bike. But it wasn't. Not today.

So what's wrong with me today? Well, what do you think, silly? Marc's in jail.

Tomorrow she would attend his arraignment and see if he would be coming home anytime before Christmas. This morning had been strange—going to church without Marc at her side. Thank goodness Clara had been there to provide some comfort. And though she rarely worked on Sunday, firmly believing in treating Sunday differently than other days of the week, she'd decided that doing some calligraphy would help get her mind off Marc and their troubles.

She remembered Clara's words: "We can cast our burdens on Him and five minutes later take them right back again."

God, is that what I'm doing? Taking my burdens back?

She pushed away from the table, her eyes straying out the window to the overcast, chilly world outside. Reaching for her mug, she sipped her tea. She missed her flower garden and regretted that they hadn't moved to Whistler's Point at the beginning of the growing season instead of at the end.

What would normally be blooming in her flower garden right now? Chrysanthemums, certainly. And her red dahlias, of course, until that first hard frost withered them and made them look like the Wicked Witch of the West.

On the stereo, George Winston was playing one of his meditative solo piano pieces she so enjoyed. The song was "Black Stallion" from the movie by the same name. Normally, the music soothed her, but not today. Today, she felt as tense as a wire.

She glanced at a pile of mail she needed to sort through. Biting her lip, she wondered why so few of the other pastors' wives in Chicago had taken the time to write her. Certainly they knew she was going through a difficult time since the shooting. Just a simple "hello" would have been nice.

But I never really fit into their group. They were all gifted in ways she couldn't relate to. They played the piano, sang in church, counseled other ladies around the clock, and even held Bible clubs in their backyards. Nothing against those ways of serving, but they weren't for her.

Maybe it's because I'm an artist. Art glorifies God just as much as playing the piano does, but people don't normally see it that way.

Memories of "The Road Not Taken," a poem by Robert Frost, stirred in her memory.

> Two roads diverged in a wood, and I—
> I took the one less traveled by,
> And that has made all the difference.

Gillian thought the house seemed strangely quiet today. Crystal was upstairs trying to do homework, but there was little hope of concentrating on homework, or much else, with Marc's future hanging in the balance.

The phone rang and Gillian caught it on the second ring. It was her mother, responding to her voice mail. She sounded confused. Gillian imagined her mother's white curls jiggling in her agitation.

"Honey, are you okay?"

"I'm holding up all right, Mom." Gillian sipped her tea and set the mug aside. She was feeling much better since her prayer session with Clara; she'd never heard anyone pray with such passion.

"What on earth is Marc doing in jail? I got your message, but it didn't make much sense to me."

Gillian told her mother about the murder and Marc's arrest, but she omitted mentioning the damning circumstantial evidence. She reviewed the shooting and Stacey's unlikely trip to the North Woods to see Marc. "Mom, it has to be nothing more than a simple misunderstanding. Marc was apparently the last person to see Stacey alive. In the absence of any other suspect, I guess the police look at people like him first. They have every right to suspect him because of the shooting, but he'll be cleared soon. I'm sure of it."

"We'll be praying."

"I know you will."

"Please call when you have more news."

"I will."

"Are you doing okay otherwise?"

Am I doing okay? She missed Meredith and Blaine as much as always, but since their move, she hadn't been crying as often. And because she hadn't been crying, her headaches hadn't been as frequent. Perhaps Marc was right. Perhaps the change of scenery *had* done her good.

"I'm doing well, Mom. I've been developing a friendship with Nicole, the lighthouse tour guide, and Clara, who also helps run the lighthouse. And we're enjoying our small Baptist church very much. And I have plenty of projects to keep me busy."

"That's great to hear. Well, I won the battle on that book cover I told you about. I didn't have to lower the neckline after all."

"That's encouraging to hear, Mom. So what happened?"

"Oh, beats me. The art director finally listened to the voice of reason, I guess. Decided he'd rather go to sleep at night with a clear conscience."

"You get to keep your conscience clean, too."

"Well, you know me. I wasn't about to bend on this one. They could have canceled my contract and called some other artist for all I cared."

"Glad to hear it, Mom." Gillian reached for her mug and sipped her tea.

"Well, I need to go. Please call when you have more news."

"I will, Mom. Love you."

"Wait. What are you sipping?"

"Earl Grey tea. I think I'm an addict."

"Well, there are worse things to be addicted to. You know I'm a coffee person through and through. Can't abide tea. Tea is for weaklings."

Gillian smiled and shook her head. "Good-bye, Mom. I love you."

After hanging up, Gillian regretted giving her mother hopes she didn't believe in herself. Remembering the sheriff's curt, accusatory manner, she didn't have any assurances that Marc would be coming home soon.

She glanced at the clock and turned her attention back to the parchment paper that was attached to the tabletop at an angle for writing. *Forgetting those things which are behind.*

Yes, Lord, but it's so hard. How can I forget? Is it even possible to forget? Am I even supposed to forget?

Lately, thoughts of Meredith and Blaine had filled her every waking moment, her heart yearning for their coos and their tiny grasping hands. She supposed those longings and a sense of guilt were a normal part of the grieving process, but lately the feelings had been stealing her joy and making her question God's goodness for the hundredth time. Consequently, every time she tried to pray, she felt like such a phony.

Eight months ago, she'd been painfully but happily pregnant, ankles swollen, sciatica causing her hands to turn numb and wake her in the night. But the discomfort had been worth every moment of expectant dreams and wishes for her babies.

So what had gone wrong? Why had her babies died? Could she have done anything differently to prevent the tragedy?

If only it made sense, Lord. But it doesn't make sense—none of it. Please teach me how to let go. I don't believe I should forget my babies, but neither do I want their memory to be a stumbling block to my future.

On several occasions, she'd noticed how Crystal resented her over-protective nature. She didn't want to hinder her daughter from pursuing her dreams, but part of her wanted to lock Crystal away from the harsh world. She hated to see Crystal learn from all the pokes and slights of life. Wouldn't it be better to hold her close so she wouldn't get hurt?

Reaching back with both hands, Gillian cradled her stiff neck. She realized she'd been sitting too long with her head bent over the parchment. After rubbing in some Bengay, she'd write another letter to her babies and then go for a walk. It would give her time to sort through her feelings and pray for help before going to the evening service without Marc at her side.

⁕ ⁕ ⁕

Gillian followed the sandy path down to the shoreline, where choppy waves had churned foam amid the pebbles and driftwood. The overcast sky was the color of slate, and the stiff wind cut through her thin windbreaker, making her regret not grabbing something thicker. The scent of winter was in the wind. Soon snowflakes would swirl through the air, and the lake would begin icing over.

She was crouched, choosing a few pebbles to toss into the water, when she heard someone call her name. She turned.

It was Nicole, descending the path to the beach. She was adorned in jeans and a jacket. "I don't have much time," she said. "I've got an appointment in town; but Clara told me about what happened yesterday. I can't believe the police arrested Marc. How are you holding up?"

"I'm feeling a bit shell-shocked, to be honest."

Strands of black hair fluttered across Nicole's face, and she brushed them aside. "Well, who wouldn't be? I remember after my father died, the police asked me tons of questions. His death was obviously an accident, but I guess it's their job to look into every possibility."

"I guess this is a test to see how much I trust our legal system. I'm afraid I don't trust it nearly as much as I thought I did."

Nicole glanced at her watch. "I'm sorry, but I really do have to run. But I wanted to let you know I'm thinking of you and Marc. Also, you asked if I could give Crystal a lighthouse tour as a homeschooling outing. I'd be happy to."

"Great. After the tour, I'm assigning her to write a paper about the experience. Would you be willing to look it over—you know, to make sure she gets her facts straight?"

"Sure. No problem. Talk to you later." Nicole gave a little wave and headed back up the path the way she had come.

Gillian watched her go, wishing they had more time to talk. She knew Nicole's grief was lurking just beneath the surface, wanting so badly to come out. Perhaps they would have a chance to talk again soon and about more than the American legal system.

Lord, I know You can help her.

Turning back to the beach, she thought she heard a familiar voice—but it couldn't be.

"Gillian!"

She swung around. At the top of the hill stood Marc and a stocky, white-haired man in a navy suit.

CHAPTER 48

GILLIAN HATED TO MISS the evening service, but sometimes there were exceptions to faithful attendance, and this was definitely one of them. She reached for the telephone, knowing Clara was planning to keep her company at the service in Marc's absence. Clara was thrilled to hear that Marc was out of jail, and she made Gillian promise to call her during the week and let her know how things were going. Gillian promised and hung up.

Taking a seat on the living room couch beside Marc, she listened to his story and couldn't help whispering a silent prayer of thanks to God. She cast appreciative glances at Chuck Riley, the grandfatherly man with the mahogany-brown eyes. The retired homicide detective interrupted Marc now and then to add insights of his own and explain why Marc had been released. The news seemed too good to be true.

Gillian listened to Riley's chilling account of the serial killings in Cincinnati, about the magician's trick rope used in the slayings, and about the same type of rope used in the murder of Stacey James.

"No, ma'am," he said after taking a sip of the hazelnut coffee she'd brewed. "Your husband isn't the man I'm looking for. Even with circumstantial evidence connecting Marc to Stacey James, there's a pattern here that points to my perpetrator from Cincinnati."

"Thank you for getting involved. Marc's release is a miracle."

Riley's eyes narrowed. "Well, the case isn't over yet, and neither is Marc's involvement, I'm afraid. I had to step in and use some persuasion. The sheriff doesn't want to accept the fact that this murder is connected to the ones in Cincinnati." He winced. "I just hope I wasn't too hard on him. Sometimes you have to say what needs to be said, but I certainly didn't intend to dishonor the man in any way."

Marc shook his head. "I thought you were fine. If you hadn't used some forcefulness, I'd still be in that cell they had me locked in." Leaning his head against the sofa cushion, he closed his eyes.

Marc looked exhausted, his face pale and stubbly, the tiny wrinkles around his eyes deeper than Gillian remembered. He probably longed to take a long, hot shower and crash into bed.

The phone rang. Gillian got up to get it.

"That could be a news reporter," Riley said. "Just tell them you have no comment, and they should leave you alone."

Sure enough, the call was from a female reporter from a newspaper in St. Ignace. After Gillian identified herself, the reporter said, "We have information that your husband was released today. May I ask him a few questions about the murder of Stacey James?"

"I'm sorry, but he's not available at the moment," Gillian said.

"Would you like to comment for your husband?"

"No, I wouldn't."

"Okay, then maybe you can tell me something else. Maybe you can answer some questions about the rape your husband was accused of committing in Chicago."

Gillian's fingers tightened around the receiver. Riley was shaking his head, mouthing "no comment," but she couldn't help herself. "My husband never tried to rape anybody, and there's no evidence that he did. Now, if you'll excuse me . . ." She hung up more forcefully than she'd intended.

"Prepare yourself for some attention," Riley said as Gillian resumed her seat next to Marc. "There aren't a lot of reporters up here in the North Woods, but murders don't happen every day. I spoke to a couple of reporters at the sheriff's office who were from a TV station in Detroit. The story may gain national attention, especially once the link to the Magician Murders gets out."

Gillian thought they'd left the media circus in Chicago. Now it was coming here? *That's just great!*

Riley glanced at his watch and said he needed to go. Rising, he grabbed his suit coat from the back of the chair beside him. "Thanks for the coffee, Mrs. Thayer."

Gillian stood. "Please, call me Gillian."

"My, that's a pretty name! Sorry I can't stay. I have meetings with the sheriff and the medical examiner tomorrow, and I need to do a little research before then. I'll let you know how it goes."

Marc stood and pumped Riley's hand. "Thanks for everything. I was afraid I was going to be locked up for a while until you came along."

"Just thank the Lord for that," Riley said. "I was down in Florida when I heard the news, and quite frankly I wasn't sure what my wife would say about my getting back involved in all this. But God began prompting my heart, and you know His voice isn't one you can easily ignore. I knew I had to get up here as quickly as possible. It appears I was just in time."

"If you need help—help with the investigation or whatever—just let me know," Marc said. "I don't know what I can do, but I'm willing to do what I can. How long will you be in town?"

Riley shrugged. "A week or so at the most. It all depends on what I discover while I'm here. The results of the DNA tests should clear you once and for all. We'll have to wait and see." He paused, a look of chagrin teasing his face. "Why does something tell me things aren't going to be that simple? This guy's elusive, but I feel like we're real close this time."

Gillian followed Marc and Riley outside and said good-bye to Riley before watching him drive away. Marc grabbed her hand, lacing his fingers into hers. It was both a comforting feeling and a reminder of answered prayer.

CHAPTER 49

AT TEN O'CLOCK ON Monday morning, Riley entered the unassuming, brown-brick structure that housed the Luce County Sheriff's Office. Riley approached the front desk and asked for the sheriff. Moments later, Dendridge appeared, his sour face telling Riley everything he needed to know.

Riley shook the sheriff's hand—a formality that offered scant cover for their mutual dislike. "I'd like to see the evidence in the Stacey James murder case."

Dendridge shook his head. "Afraid not. That material is sensitive and being held for the district attorney. You're not here in any official capacity, and I don't have to show you anything. In fact, I'd prefer that you go back to Disney World."

The stonewalling was no surprise. No one likes to be shown up, and the sheriff had clearly resented Riley's initiative in securing Marc Thayer's release. "Then maybe you could answer some questions for me, Nate. Look, no hard feelings. We both want the same thing—to catch the guy who did this."

Dendridge crossed his arms across his chest and took a deep breath. "What do you want to know?"

"The murder weapon points unequivocally to the guy I've been chasing for the past four years, but the victim profile's all goofed up. I'm hoping that means my guy made a mistake—that he's thrown us something we can nail him with. That's why I want to see what you have."

Dendridge expelled a sharp burst of air. "Okay, why don't you come on back to my office."

When the two men were safely ensconced behind closed doors, the sheriff pulled out the Stacey James case file and slid it across the desk to Riley.

"The forensics are pretty straightforward," Dendridge said. "Ms. James was found lying facedown in a compost pile behind Whistler's Point. The rope was still around her neck. Not many defensive wounds—I think he caught her from behind; but there were some marks on her neck, apart from the rope, of course." He pointed to one of the crime scene photos in the file. "You can see those little crescent-shaped bruises where she dug her fingernails in, trying to loosen the rope."

"Any chance she nicked the killer?"

"DNA tests are still out," Dendridge said, "but we should have results in soon. We did find some tissue under her fingernails. It was probably her own, but she could have nicked the killer,' as you say, during the struggle."

Riley nodded. Wishful thinking probably, but maybe they'd catch a break. "Like I said, the trick rope is a definite fingerprint for my perp from Cincinnati, but there's a lot that doesn't make sense. In the past, this guy has gone after blonde-haired, blue-eyed high school girls, with wire rim glasses—we're four for four on that score—so the selection of Stacey James doesn't add up. She's blonde-haired, blue-eyed, but she's also what? Thirty-six, thirty-seven?"

"Yeah, thirty-seven," Dendridge said.

"And from what Marc Thayer says, she doesn't wear glasses. So we've got some inconsistencies that I'm hoping will point us to a break in the case. When a killer breaks his pattern, there's a good chance he got careless with something else."

"Spare me the lecture on serial killers, Detective. I've been sheriff in this county for—"

Riley threw his hands up in front of him, palms outward. "No need to get your feathers ruffled, Sheriff. I'm just trying to lay out the facts for you so maybe you can help me spot the clue that's going to bust this thing wide open."

"Okay, fine," Dendridge said, shuffling some papers on the desktop. "What else do you want to know?"

"In the Cincinnati cases, the perp always stalked his victims before he moved in for the kill. But the cops in Chicago tell me that Stacey James has been on the lam for the past month or so—ever since she shot Thayer. So unless this guy's magic includes clairvoyance, there's no way he could have known she'd be in the area. That's why her death seems almost random—like she got in the way somehow."

"Either that or your perp's not the guy," Dendridge said. "Let's not forget we've got a suspect with proximity, motive, and opportunity that you helped to spring from our custody."

"Look, Sheriff, with all due respect, Marc Thayer did not kill Stacey James. Of that one thing I'm certain." He tapped one of the crime scene photos showing a close-up of the noose around Stacey's neck. "This trick rope is a signature that's every bit as distinctive as John Hancock's."

"So what you're saying is that it's just a coincidence that Stacey James's body was found less than a hundred feet from Marc Thayer's front door."

"No, I'm not overlooking that connection, but the guy I'm looking for kidnaps his victims, transports them in his car, strangles them at an unknown location—presumably in his car—and then dumps the body at a secondary location. If Stacey James was in the vicinity of Whistler's Point—which we know she was, since Marc Thayer encountered her there on Thursday—it's possible the killer saw her somewhere out there, maybe offered her a ride, and then killed her and dumped her up on the property."

"So how does that explain the drag marks, Detective?"

Riley sucked in his breath. "What drag marks?"

The sheriff smiled, as if delighted he knew something that Riley didn't. "Yeah, we found a drag pattern starting in the front yard near the front door and progressing to the south side of the house where it ended near some bushes. It appears that she was strangled there and then carried to the brush pile."

"Now we're getting somewhere," Riley said, leaning forward. "Marc Thayer told me that somebody rang the doorbell on Thursday night. But when he opened the door, nobody was there."

"Right. But how do we know he's telling the truth? He could have grabbed Stacey, dragged her to the side yard to avoid being seen, and strangled her. We also know he reportedly left the house to take out the trash. So much for his alibi."

Riley shook his head. *This sheriff is one stubborn guy.* "No, that doesn't work. Gillian Thayer corroborated the doorbell ringing, and she said that Marc came right back. By the way, did your CSI grab a print from the doorbell? That might shed some light for us."

Sheriff Dendridge pushed back from the desk and clasped his hands behind his head. His face was fire-engine red. "No, I don't think we dusted for prints on the doorbell." He reached for the phone. "I'll send somebody out there right away and see what we find. Is there anything else I can do for you, Detective?"

"No, I think that's all for now." Suppressing a smile, Riley closed the case folder, set it back on the desk, and walked out of the room.

CHAPTER 50

UNDERWATER AND ABLE TO see only a few feet in the murky depths, Haydon struggled against the handcuffs. He checked his waterproof watch to measure how much time had passed and frowned. The escape this time was taking longer than usual. In a moment, he would be free of the handcuffs, but he always experienced a few seconds when panic knocked at his door.

The water was freezing.

To ensure a real test, he'd tossed the handcuff keys on the dock before jumping in. He *had* to get the cuffs off—his life depended on it. Of course, even if he couldn't get the cuffs off, it wasn't the end of the world. Like Houdini, he was an excellent swimmer and could get to the surface and survive in the water for hours, even while handcuffed.

At last, his long fingernails worked to his favor, and he felt the lock yield under his pressure. The cuffs sprang open. Lungs aching, he squirmed his feet out of the chains wrapped around his ankles and kicked hard, propelling himself to the surface.

✳ ✳ ✳

Twenty minutes later, he was drying off in the cabin, listening to the original Broadway recording of *The Secret Garden*, and planning the rest of his day. He noted that he was running low on groceries and decided to do some shopping soon.

He also planned to call the producers of *Masters of Illusion*. He was surprised they hadn't called him back and asked him to appear on their show.

He also needed to call the high school and book the auditorium for the first weekend in December. Soon he would need to design fliers and begin sending press releases to the newspapers. Soon people would see a show they'd never forget.

He paused at one of the bedroom doors, wondering if he had time for a visit with Houdini. He shook his head. Not today.

The cops were no closer to catching him here than they had been in Cincinnati. But that realization didn't erase his blunder a few days ago. In fact, he didn't even know who Stacey James was other than that she'd been at the wrong place at the wrong time. TV news reporters said she was a fugitive from Chicago the police had been trying to apprehend. Weird.

Why she'd been lurking behind the Thayers' place was still a mystery to him. He'd known only one thing: she'd seen him watching Crystal with the binoculars and couldn't be allowed to share that knowledge with anyone. It was spur of the moment, not his usual carefully planned and executed arrangement, but his instincts were now well honed, and they hadn't let him down.

But the woman's death was a needless distraction. He regretted drawing police attention to Whistler's Point—but, again, it couldn't be helped. He'd just have to be extra careful, extra clever with his next moves. But he'd find his opportunity, of that he was certain.

Entering his bedroom, he sank into the chair in front of his bank of computers and found the file he was looking for. Moments later, Crystal Thayer's smiling face filled his screen. He touched the screen, adding fingerprints to the hundreds already there.

In an instant, anger descended on him like a taloned beast of prey. He drove his fingernails into his palms, seeking control. His mother's words helped him relax.

Patience, Donny. Patience. Jerk the hook too quickly and the fish might get away.

CHAPTER 51

RILEY WOLFED DOWN A fast-food lunch and reached the office of Gerald Muller, the medical examiner, a few minutes before his three o'clock appointment. A fastidious man in his fifties, Muller wore thick-rimmed glasses that seemed to swallow his haggard face and made his watery, blue eyes appear several times their normal size. Polite and friendly, he was thorough in describing the findings in Stacey James's autopsy and didn't hesitate to answer Riley's questions.

While Muller talked, Riley vigorously chewed a stick of Juicy Fruit and sifted through a thick file of data. Time of death, sometime between 8 PM and 2 AM, was undisputed. Asphyxia by strangulation was substantiated as the cause of death due to the tiny petechial hemorrhages under Stacey's eyelids.

Other than a few bruises, assumed results of her struggle, Muller had found no other wounds on Stacey's body, discounting the neck abrasions caused by the rope and tiny neck cuts caused by her own fingernails. DNA samples from the scrapings under Stacey's fingernails were still out—so no chance yet to look for a match in the database of known offenders.

Riley's throat tightened. There had to be something here. Something more. He felt his hopes deflating like a leaky balloon. *God, please show me what I'm missing.*

He studied the reports and photos again. Drummed his fingers on the desktop. Swallowed hard.

He sensed that Muller was watching him patiently. The buzz from the overhead fluorescent lights was the only sound in the room. Riley cleared his throat. "So that's it. You don't have anything else to show me?"

The medical examiner spread his hands. "I'm very sorry. I wish there was more I could say. Due to the high-profile nature of the murders in Cincinnati, and the apparent link here, I plan to double-check my findings and examine the body one more time. The second exam may turn up something else."

Riley hesitated. "Please don't be offended, but I have another idea. Do you mind if I get a second opinion? I know some experts at the FBI who have offered to take a look at the body for me."

Muller shifted uneasily in his chair. "Well, I don't know—"

"I've been working on this case for a very long time. It would mean a great deal to me personally if they could examine the body. Please understand that I'm not questioning your skills or findings in any way. But you know what they say about another pair of eyes—"

"I understand." Muller offered a wan smile. "But I'll need to clear your request through the sheriff first. The woman's husband wants the body shipped to a mortuary in Chicago, but I can't release it until the physical exam is finished. It might delay the funeral if we have to wait for these FBI guys to come in."

Riley bit his lip. Sheriff Dendridge could say no to his request—after the fingerprint fiasco, he could go either way. Riley would just have to wait and see.

"By the way, Doc, do you know if they came up with anything off that doorbell?"

"Ah, yes, the doorbell," Muller said. "As a matter of fact, they did. It was only a partial, but enough to make a match with our victim here, Stacey James."

Bingo! So Marc was telling the truth, and now we know it was Stacey who rang the bell.

Riley closed his eyes and played the scenario out in his mind. *Stacey goes to the door and the perp catches her from behind—but not before she rings the bell. So he had to be right there, and he had to have a reason why he didn't want her to see the Thayers.* He shook his head. *What's the connection? C'mon, Riley. Be objective. Don't paint yourself in a corner.* Then he thought of something he'd almost forgotten. "Hey, Doc, let me ask you another question. When you saw the body for the first time, were Stacey's eyes open or closed?"

Muller didn't hesitate. "Closed."

"And no one would have closed them at the scene?"

Muller flushed. "Absolutely not. We have very strict rules about that. Nobody touched the body before I got there, and I can assure you—"

"Hey, I'm not questioning anyone's competence here. I have to ask these questions, okay?"

Muller pushed his glasses back onto the bridge of his nose and pursed his lips. "That's all right. Go ahead."

Riley's mind raced. All the victims, except for Erin Walker, had been found with their eyes closed, suggesting the killer's remorse for the slayings. But why remorse for the last four slayings and not for the first? What was so special about Erin Walker? Why had the killer left her eyes open? He'd shown more hate for her than for the others. But why?

The clock was ticking, and he was running out of options. Now that the killer had broken his pattern and was taking new risks, all bets were off. Something in Riley's gut convinced him that unless he intervened, he would soon be investigating yet another murder.

Disturbing questions continued to gnaw at him. Stacey had known the police were looking for her, and yet she rang the Thayers' doorbell at risk of her own arrest. Why? What had she intended to tell them? And what was the Magician Murderer doing at Whistler's Point?

CHAPTER 52

AT PRACTICE ON MONDAY, Crystal was trying to remember her lines, to put energy into her singing. The stage lights were blinding, but she tried to ignore them and channel her energy into her performance.

"Very good." Betty Jamison, invisible behind the blinding lights, clapped her hands. "Now let's do that scene again. Remember, Crystal, you're feeling very uneasy about being governess for the von Trapp children. When you sing this song, you need to communicate that anxiety in your voice."

Betty rubbed her forehead. "The choreography appears to be fine. You're doing a fantastic job of learning the moves with such short notice. Now let's start again at the top."

It was the song "I Have Confidence," and Crystal felt far from confident, but she poured as much energy into the number as she could.

Twirl around with the suitcases, smile and look brave, swing to the right, punch the air, support that high note coming up.

Fifteen minutes later, the rehearsal was over, and she felt exhausted, eager to be on her way. But she decided not to rush off as she had after previous rehearsals. Some of the girls in the cast had spread the word that she was a religious snob who looked down her nose at everybody around her. She intended to prove them wrong. But mingling with the other cast members only emphasized how little she had in common with any of them, though she tried her best to be sociable.

After all, she knew that being in the musical needed to be more than just a fun opportunity for her, more than just another rung on the ladder of her musical career. These other kids needed Jesus, and she wanted to show His love through her life, no matter how difficult that might be. Still, this certainly wasn't like the youth group she'd left in Chicago. She felt like the only ray of light in a dark, hopeless place.

Hanging around backstage, she exchanged small talk with Jill, Russ, Trevor, and other members of the cast who seemed to have become more accepting of her in recent days. They were curious about the murder at Whistler's Point and figured Crystal would have the inside scoop. Crystal was glancing at her watch, thinking it was about time to go, when something sharp scraped against her back. She leaped out of the way.

"Hey, watch where you're going, Eric!" Jill cried. "You almost knocked Crystal down. Be more careful next time!"

A guy about Crystal's height was wrestling with a large, fake fireplace to be used in the set of the von Trapp living room. He was slim and blond-haired, his matching goatee wispy.

As he adjusted his grip on the fireplace, Eric ducked his head, his eyes cutting toward Crystal's face before quickly darting away. "Um, sorry. Didn't mean to hurt you or anything."

Crystal's back still throbbed; she wondered if she'd have a bruise. "Hey, it's no big deal. I'm fine. Really." She paused. "You know, I don't think we've met before. I'm Crystal Thayer."

He ducked his head again, his eyes doing everything but meeting her gaze. "Eric White. Nice to meet you." He paused. "I'd be pretty stupid not to know who you are, having the lead role and all."

"The fireplace goes over there," Jill said, pointing across the stage. Eric looked hard at Jill, then began pushing the set piece in the other direction.

Jessie, the girl who was playing Liesl, chuckled and shook her head. At least ten necklaces—some gold, some silver, some with lapis lazuli—dangled around her too-skinny neck and swung down over her green sleeveless T-shirt. "So now you've met Eric White, our newest member of the stage crew. A real piece of work, huh?"

"So, like I was saying before we were rudely interrupted," Jill said to Crystal, "are the police going to catch this killer or what? I think I'd be a little freaked knowing the killer did the deed right behind my house."

"I can't believe something like that could happen around here," Jessie said. "I mean, this ain't Chicago or New York City."

Crystal wished she could have closed her ears to what Jessie said next, and she tried not to wince visibly at her foul mouth. A few of the kids knew Crystal was "religious" and had been noticeably curbing their language around her, but Jessie so far seemed pretty clueless. *Maybe Jesus will give her a clue.*

Glancing around, she noticed Eric standing near the fireplace. He looked pretty lonely. She recognized the body language.

She always tried to be cautious when talking to guys, not wanting to give the wrong impression. But part of her always sought out the loner, the rejected, the least of the cool.

"Hey, I haven't seen you around before today," Crystal said as she approached Eric.

His eyes darted to the floor as soon as she drew near. "I signed up late."

Crystal extended her hand and tried not to grimace at his sweaty palm. He was probably just nervous, not knowing anybody. "Well, it's great to have your help with the production. I'm kind of a late addition myself."

Eric glanced up and seemed to gain confidence from what Crystal had said. "I love musicals, so when I heard about this one, I knew I had to be part of it."

"Well, it's great to have you here. See you around."

He nodded.

Betty gathered the cast and gave instructions for the next rehearsal. "Be sure to check the forum on the Web site for other announcements. Oh, and don't forget to greet Eric White. He's new, helping out with the set." She glanced around the room. "Oh, I guess he must have left already. Well, be sure to greet him at the next rehearsal. Okay, see you next time, regular time. Don't be late."

Crystal said good-bye to the others and left the auditorium. She hit the speed-dial button on her cell phone as she headed toward her car, so she could let her mom know she was okay. She didn't notice a figure hiding in the shadow of the building.

Watching her.

CHAPTER 53

AT BREAKFAST ON TUESDAY, Gillian ate hurriedly and said she had a calligraphy project she needed to get in the mail right away. After she drove off in Crystal's car, Marc picked up the newspaper she'd been reading and stared at the front page.

Suspect Released in Whistler's Point Slaying.

He read the article, expecting to see an account of how the evidence against him just didn't add up, but he was shocked by the obvious slant taken by the writer. With growing incredulity, he read several damaging quotes, offered by Sheriff Dendridge, that left little doubt the sheriff still believed Marc was the killer.

He wiped a hand across his face and muttered under his breath. "Physical evidence. There's no physical evidence."

"Did you say something, Dad?" Crystal, who was washing dishes at the sink, glanced his direction with mild interest.

Marc hadn't realized she was standing there. "No, uh . . . I'm fine." Not wanting her to see the article, he folded the newspaper in half just before she came to clear Gillian's dishes.

"Oh, I've already read that," she said. "No use hiding it."

"I wasn't *hiding* it."

"Yes, you were. I saw you." She smirked. "Isn't it silly? They think you strangled Stacey James just because she shot you in Chicago. Revenge is, like, so juvenile."

Marc tried to rub away his growing headache. He hoped it wouldn't develop into another full-blown migraine. The last one had been bad enough.

After stacking the dishes in the sink to soak, Crystal took a seat across from Marc and warmed her hands around her coffee mug. "Man, Dad, you've been in the newspaper already twice this year. At this rate, your name is going to be a household word in no time."

"Huh?" He glanced up, distracted.

"Yeah, you know. Ted Bundy. Jeffrey Dahmer."

"You think I'm a murderer?"

"I'm just kidding, Dad. But that's what everybody's going to think—that you're one of those crazies who goes around strangling people and then chopping them up into—"

"Hey! I'm eating here—do you mind? Besides, don't you have a rehearsal . . . or something else you're supposed to be doing right now?" He could barely taste his Golden Grahams. Not that it mattered. He had such a bad taste in his mouth right now that nothing would be palatable.

The phone rang, and Marc got up from the table.

"I'll get it." Lately, the phone had been ringing off the hook, thanks to the many reporters who'd come to town for the big story. Marc wondered if any of them were really interested in the truth.

It turned out to be just an annoying sales call. After hanging up, Marc called Riley at his hotel. "We need to talk."

"Uh-oh. You aren't going to confess on me, are you?"

"*Confess!* Of course not. I'll tell you all about it."

✳ ✳ ✳

The Daily Grind coffee shop was located at the edge of town near the rumbling highway. The coffee was superb, and normally Marc would be enjoying every sip, but today it was just a formality.

Sitting across from him in the corner booth, Riley taste-tested a white chocolate mocha frappuccino and smiled blissfully. "I think I know why we're here," he said. "Did you read the morning paper?"

"Uh-huh."

"Then you know what everyone's thinking."

Marc hated the look in Riley's eyes. It appeared the detective concurred with the general sentiment, notwithstanding his efforts to get Marc out of jail a couple of days ago. Marc heard the futility in his own voice. "I don't really care what everybody else thinks. Right now, I want to know what *you* think."

"Coffee isn't really the beverage you should be drinking right now. You need something . . . uh, soothing," Riley said.

"You didn't answer my question."

"What I think really matters?"

"Matters to me. Matters a lot."

Riley didn't blink. "Of course I believe you're innocent, Marc. But until the DNA test comes back or something else comes up to clear you, you're the sheriff's number-one suspect. You had motive and opportunity. They found the victim on your brush pile."

"Yeah, he's already told the world he thinks I'm guilty."

Riley spread his hands. "So what makes him think he can speak for the world? If you're arrested again and this thing goes to trial, a jury will decide your fate, not a rush-to-judgment sheriff."

"A jury could find me guilty. People aren't too bright sometimes. Just look at the O. J. Simpson murder trial."

Riley held his peace.

"I've had enough of being falsely accused. It's happened to me twice in the last couple months. Do you have any idea how that feels?"

Riley took a sip. "No, I don't know how it feels, but don't think you're the only one. Inside our prisons are lots of people who've been falsely convicted. Thankfully, through DNA testing that wasn't available until recent years, more of the innocent ones are being set free."

Marc slammed his fist down on the tabletop, making the salt and pepper shakers dance a jig. "I went through this in Chicago. Now I'm going through it here. I've had it!"

"Marc, try to save some of that passion and energy. You're going to need it when I tell you what I want you to do."

Marc let his coffee cool, waiting for the detective to finish his thought.

Riley sipped his frappuccino, taking his time. Finally, he said, "I'm going back to Cincinnati."

"*What!* I thought you were sticking around here until the killer's caught."

"No reason to. The key to catching this guy is in Cincinnati, not here. I know that now."

"I'm not sure I understand."

Riley rubbed his forehead. "See, it's like this. This predator cut his teeth in Cincinnati. Stacey James's murder is a piece in the puzzle, certainly, but the puzzle was created long ago in Cincinnati. Do you understand?"

"Give me some time."

"With every serial killer, the past is connected to the future. Nobody just decides one day, 'Hey, I'm going to start strangling people.' Something happened a long time ago, in the killer's childhood or early adulthood; something that molded his psyche and made murder the next logical step."

Riley took a sip and swallowed. "In serial killings, the first murder is always the most important, and the first forty-eight hours are the most critical. If you don't catch a break right away, the trail often goes cold. Which is what happened—four times over. The first victim was a girl named Erin Walker. I know where she lived, I've spoken to her mother, and I've interviewed her teachers."

"And?"

Riley rubbed his lower lip with the ball of his thumb. "I missed something. Things didn't add up. I wasn't seeing the whole puzzle. I'm going back for another look."

"Okay, so you're going back to Cincinnati. But what does that have to do with me?"

"While I'm gone, I want you to investigate Stacey James's murder here."

Marc burst out laughing. "Wait a minute! I'm a pastor, not an investigator—and I'm the primary suspect, to boot. I don't even know where to start."

"Tired of people thinking you're guilty?"

"Yeah."

"Here's your chance to clear your name. The sheriff's clearly not looking to do it for you. Find out who the killer is, and people will leave you alone."

"You make it sound so easy."

Riley's face turned serious. "It's one of the toughest things you'll ever do, but it has to be you. You're the only one in town who believes you're innocent, and you're the only one I can trust." He glanced around the shop uneasily as if spies were lurking in shadowy doorways. "We may have already lost our window of opportunity, but while I'm gone it can't hurt to have you looking for information and possible connections between yourself, Stacey James, and the killer. Based on the evidence I've seen—and I'm not suggesting you're involved somehow, but there's some connection and we have to figure out what it is."

Marc shrugged. "So, what do I do, just walk into the sheriff's office and ask him to tell me everything he knows about the case?"

"No, leave the sheriff out of this. I can tell you what you need to know to get started. I'll give you a list before I leave. You'll have to discover everything else on your own."

Marc sat silently for a moment. "Why are you telling me this? I'm accused of murder."

"Because I trust you," Riley replied. "I know you didn't do it and I need some help."

Marc still felt lost and inadequate. He took another sip of lukewarm coffee and gazed across the room.

"Look, use your imagination and ask Gillian to help you," Riley said. "Think of it as a project for you to work on together. Start at Whistler's Point. Someone killed Stacey there. Maybe somebody saw whoever did it prowling around. Ask your friends out there if anybody suspicious was seen hanging around the grounds."

Marc was starting to catch on. "In other words, be a Perry Mason."

"Or a Hercule Poirot or a Sherlock Holmes—whichever persona you prefer. Do you like puzzles? Because, Marc, you're about to begin the most difficult puzzle of your life."

"I feel pretty overwhelmed. Would you mind if we prayed about it?"

Riley nodded, his serious eyes softening. "I was going to make the same recommendation."

CHAPTER 54

GILLIAN STROLLED ALONG THE Lake Superior shoreline, her attention absorbed in the rippling waves. Seagulls swooped overhead, their hungry cries echoing over the water. The fresh air had a cleansing effect on her troubled mind.

The morning had been eventful. Marc had come home from a meeting with Chuck Riley, all fired up about helping him with the investigation into Stacey's death. Then, after lunch, he and Henry had left to purchase supplies for next spring's landscaping. Ten minutes ago, Crystal had sped away in the Cutlass, seemingly oblivious to the blue cloud of smoke billowing behind her. She had her cell phone and had promised to call Gillian and let her know when she made it safely.

She was off to another rehearsal, which only added to Gillian's apprehension now that a killer of young women was on the loose. Though Crystal's participation in the musical was a wonderful opportunity for her, Gillian also felt uneasy about the spirit of independence the used car had fostered. She'd felt pangs of sadness the first time Crystal drove off alone. Part of her had wanted to chase after the car, to admonish Crystal once more to be careful.

My dearest children, Crystal is the only baby I have left. I have a right to be protective, don't I? A quote by Benjamin Franklin pushed against her troubled thoughts: "Do not anticipate trouble, or worry about what might never happen. Keep in the sunlight."

Keep in the sunlight.

Crystal could take off whenever she wanted to now. She made enough money with her Internet business to afford the gas and car insurance. But the car wasn't what bothered Gillian. Not really.

Now I'm all alone.

She felt lonelier than she'd felt in a long time. Crystal had her rehearsal. Marc had his landscaping—and now this investigation, whatever that meant. *And me? I have my calligraphy projects and Crystal's homeschooling lessons.*

Certainly both pursuits promised to keep her busy, so why did she feel a black hole yawning in her heart? Was it because she missed Chicago? She shrugged. Maybe she just needed some herbal supplements. She had hoped the walk would help.

Sometimes exercise can soften a sour mood, but can it mend a broken heart?

✳   ✳   ✳

Gillian was heading back to the caretaker's house to fix a cup of tea when she spotted Nicole strolling toward her at a fast clip. Lighthouse tours had dwindled now that it was the middle of November, with bracing winds and brooding skies. Soon Whistler's Point would be closed for the season, and Nicole would be packing her things and heading to Boston with her dog to spend the winter with her mother.

"Hey!" Nicole called. "Want some company?"

"Sure," Gillian called back. "But what about your tours?"

Nicole closed the distance between them. "It's a ghost town today. Clara decided to close the place early. She says things are only going to get slower."

The local children had been back to school for months, and the fall colors had long since faded, taking the tourist trade with it. Gillian felt a pang of sadness at the thought of Nicole's leaving.

If we return to Chicago for Christmas, I might not see her again. What do I really know about her? It seems like we've had so few opportunities to talk.

"Where you off to?" Nicole had traded in her turn-of-the-century dress for a black turtleneck, a green parka, blue jeans, and Rockports.

Gillian gestured ahead. "Just down the shoreline. Every day, weather permitting, I walk fifteen minutes down and fifteen minutes back." She ducked her head self-consciously. "I'm trying to lose weight."

"Aren't we all? Do you mind if I join you?"

"Not at all."

As they set off at a brisk pace, Nicole stuffed hands into her pockets, tossing her head to shift the black hair blowing around her face. "They say walking is the best form of exercise. Gets the heart pumping without straining those joints. They say it prolongs life."

Gillian smiled. "I suppose. But when the Lord decides it's your time to go, it's your time. There's nothing you can do to stop it."

"But what about my dad? Wouldn't you say his death was premature?"

Careful, Gillian thought. Clara had told her that Nicole didn't like people banging her over the head with the Bible. "I think God has a date in mind for each of us, but we don't know what it is. His timing is always perfect, even though His ways are sometimes difficult to understand. In human terms, your dad died years before he probably should have. But on God's timetable, he died right on time."

Nicole stared out to sea, an edge in her voice. "I'm sorry, but I don't see it that way. I just can't. I mean, why would He decide that my dad should die so young?"

"I can't answer that, but I do know that God's wisdom is greater than ours. Why not trust the One who is stronger and knows better?"

"But how do you know He knows better?"

"Because God has given me the faith to trust Him and believe what the Bible says."

Nicole shook her head. "I don't think I could ever have that kind of faith. I'm not sure I want it, either. Why live my life at the whim of some distant, detached being?"

"God isn't some distant, detached being. Faith tells me that everything happens for a divine purpose, that everything that happens to me is Father-filtered."

"Father-filtered?" Nicole frowned. "Okay, now you're talking way over my head."

"Sorry. What I mean is that nothing can happen to us unless God first gives His permission. That doesn't mean He *causes* evil, but sometimes He allows evil things to happen. There's a difference."

"Like Stacey James's murder?"

"Uh-huh."

"Like my dad's accident?"

"Yes."

"But how can God allow those bad things to happen and still be good and all-powerful? That's what I don't understand. He could stop them. So why doesn't He?" Nicole sighed and shook her head. "It just doesn't work."

The sandy shoreline stretched before them like a blank piece of parchment at the beginning of another calligraphy project. *Lord, where do I begin?* Gillian prayed. Then she remembered something her mom had told her years ago. *Sharing Christ should be as simple as telling your life story.*

"Can I answer your questions by telling you a little bit about my background?" Gillian asked.

"Sure."

"When I was a little girl, I went to church because my parents and friends told me I was supposed to, but I didn't really know God. Later, as a troubled teen, I realized I didn't have any purpose in life. Life without God is pretty meaningless if you think about it. If we're just here on this planet by ourselves, then what's the point?"

Nicole nodded.

"Anyhow, I was just wandering aimlessly through life like the next person. To fill the emptiness, I started drinking. I began using drugs. I even ran away from home and was living with a guy for a while. I caused my parents a lot of heartache."

Nicole glanced at Gillian in surprise. "But you're a pastor's wife."

Gillian laughed. "I *am* a pastor's wife now, but that's because of God's goodness, not because of anything I've done. I'm not proud of my past."

The memories stung like a scrape under antiseptic. "My boyfriend said he loved me, but it was infatuation. Nothing more. We were just kids, and the romance didn't last. We moved in together, but as soon as I got pregnant, the ride was over. He said he wasn't ready to be a father. A couple days after I told him the news, he drove off and abandoned me."

"What a jerk! What did you do?"

"I did one of the hardest things I've ever had to do. I called my parents and begged them to let me come home. They forgave me before I even asked them to and let me return to my old bedroom as if nothing had happened. But then I had to face all my old friends, and by then everybody knew I was pregnant. Then, to make matters worse, I miscarried."

Nicole's eyes widened. "Oh, Gillian!"

Gillian nodded. "It was the worst time of my life, but the best time of my life, too." She recalled Charles Dickens's famous opening words to *A Tale of Two Cities*. "It was the best of times, it was the worst of times."

"What do you mean?"

"See, before then, I thought I was a pretty good person. I hadn't done anything *really* bad. I hadn't killed anybody. But then I saw the real me, saw how wicked I really was, and realized only God could save me."

Nicole shook her head. "It's hard to imagine. You're always so . . . well, perfect."

"Far from it. I turned to God and asked Him to forgive me, and I've never been the same since. He changed me from the inside out, and I know He's with me always."

"Okay, but what does that have to do with everything being 'Father-filtered'?"

"The Bible says if I'm God's child, nothing can happen to me unless it's first filtered through the Father, unless God gives His approval. God won't allow *anything* to happen in my life unless He has something good in mind. Do you understand?"

"Even bad things? Like your stillborn twins?" Nicole bit her lip. "Sorry, Clara told me. I hope you don't mind."

Gillian gulped back a rush of fear and sadness. She shook her head. "It's okay."

"It must have been terrible."

"It *was* terrible. After I married Marc, we had Crystal right away. But after that, I couldn't get pregnant, no matter how hard we tried. Finally, after more than a decade of fertility therapy, I became pregnant with twins." Gillian glanced at the crashing waves and took a deep breath, holding back the torrent of tears.

"So what went wrong?"

Gillian cleared her throat and gazed into Nicole's dark eyes. "If only I knew. I've asked myself that question so many times I've lost count. In the ultrasounds, the twins appeared to be fine. Everything seemed to be on schedule, right up to only a few weeks before their delivery. But then something went terribly wrong."

Gillian stopped walking and closed her eyes. She saw the nurses' shocked faces. Heard the silence in the delivery room.

The silence.

No cries. No words of congratulations. And then she saw . . .

She shuddered and felt Nicole's hand on her arm.

"Gillian, are you okay?"

Gillian bent over, hands on her knees. She felt the world tilting and struggled for balance. She took some deep, measured breaths, waiting for the moment to pass.

My dearest children, what happened to you? What did I do wrong? It must have been my fault.

Tears welled up again. She felt her chin trembling.

"I'm sorry if I brought up painful memories," Nicole said.

Gillian opened her eyes and blew out her breath. "I'm okay now." She wiped her eyes and straightened.

"You're sure?"

"Yeah, I'm fine. It isn't easy to accept . . . to really believe God let it happen, but I choose to believe there was a reason."

They continued walking.

"Remember what I told you about my dad's accident?" Nicole asked. "I think I was partly to blame."

"What do you mean?"

"Just before the accident, we were arguing about my divorce, and Dad wasn't looking at the road. If he'd been looking at the road, he might have seen the deer. But he was looking at me."

"But you can't blame yourself for what happened."

Nicole stopped and faced her. "I know you're right—in my head." Her hand fluttered to her chest as tears pooled in her eyes. "But here—" She shook her head and turned back toward the lighthouse.

Walking beside Nicole, Gillian studied the profile of a beautiful, broken woman. *Lord, speak to her.*

"Tell me what it is," Nicole said abruptly. "There's something different about you and your family, but I can't figure out what it is. I remember when you had me over for dinner and Marc prayed over the food. It was like . . . like he was really talking to God. Like God was actually in the room."

That's because He was. "There *is* something different about us, Nicole," Gillian said. "That's what I've been trying to tell you."

"And then this whole killer-on-the-loose thing. I mean, the way you and your family have handled the stress. Anybody else would have been a basket case by now, but something seems to be giving you guys special strength."

"It's Jesus, Nicole. I don't know how else to explain it except to say that it's Him." Gillian glanced at her watch. "Why don't you come back to the house with me for some tea? I could open my Bible and show you what I mean."

"I think I'd like that."

"And if I start banging you over the head with a Bible, you'll stop me, right?"

Nicole laughed. "Absolutely."

CHAPTER 55

SITTING AT HER COMPUTER that evening, Crystal was trying to write a report about the lighthouse tour Nicole had given her that afternoon before rehearsal. But she hated writing, and the words simply refused to flow. Then she began working on the design of a new Web site, but her creativity was coming up dry. A chat with Ryan always cleared her head, so she sent him an instant message. She was beginning to think he wasn't online when her computer chimed and she saw his reply.

Charliedude824: Wuz up?

"Charles" was Ryan's middle name, and 824 stood for his birthday, August 24. Her own handle, Java4Jesus, was a play on her growing affinity for coffee and a computer programming language common on Web sites.

Grinning, she typed, "Beginning to think u you weren't home."

Charliedude824: What else would I be doing but chatting with u?

Java4Jesus: Can think of lots of things. Playing basketball. Practicing your karate.

Charliedude824: Karate hurts. Banged my right elbow yesterday. Can barely bend my arm.

Java4Jesus: Boo hoo! Poor cwyin' Wyan. Did little boy get boo-boo?

Charliedude824: Could u kiss it better?

Java4Jesus: Kiss your elbow? I'll pass.

Charliedude824: LOL. J/K. So what r u up to?

Java4Jesus: Web stuff. What else? Zzzzz.

Charliedude824: If u don't like it, why do it?

Java4Jesus: Pays for gas, insurance, car repairs. No gas, and I can't go to practice. No practice, and I can't sing and dance like Julie Andrews.

Charliedude824: Who says u need to practice?

Java4Jesus: U r sweet!

Another instant message popped up on Crystal's screen, startling her. The message was from someone named Houdini409. She vaguely remembered accepting a chat invitation from that handle a few days ago. Ever since she'd visited the cast Web site and submitted material on the forum, she'd been getting IM'd by everybody.

Charliedude824: U there?

Java4Jesus: Got an IM from somebody I don't recognize.

As she read the message, a tickle of electric current ran down the back of her neck.

Houdini409: I'm watching you.

Smirking, Crystal thought the message sounded amateurish. This was obviously somebody's idea of a silly joke. Probably Russ, the prankster from the musical cast. He was the type to do something creepy like this. He probably thought he was flirting with her.

She typed a reply: "Oooooo. Like, I'm soooo scared."

Houdini409: You should be.

Java4Jesus: Do I know u?

Houdini409: Of course you do. Don't play games with me. Games can get out of hand.

Java4Jesus: Don't know what u r talking about.

Houdini409: Go ask Stacey James. She'll tell you about games. Oh, that's right. Silly me. Stacey's dead, isn't she?

Crystal stared at the screen. Did this creep know something about Stacey's death?

Charliedude824: Still there?

Java4Jesus: Somebody's playing a sick prank on me. Just a sec. I'll send u what he sent me.

Charliedude824: He?

Java4Jesus: Some creep called Houdini409. He's not very nice.

Houdini409: Still there?

Java4Jesus: Yep.

Houdini409: I know who you are. You can call yourself Crystal Thayer all you want, but you and I know
the truth.

Crystal's heart constricted. The creep knew her real name. That
was no big deal if it was Russ, but what if it wasn't? She recalled seeing stories on the news about perverts preying on girls through cyber-
space. Was this guy one of those perverts? If so, how did he know her?

Charliedude824: Crystal?

Java4Jesus: Yeah.

Charliedude824: Don't reply to him. He's got a sick
sense of humor.

Java4Jesus: But what if he's just a joker from
the cast? I'll be the laughingstock at the next
rehearsal.

Charliedude824: Just don't, k? This could be
serious.

Java4Jesus: Good grief. It's just an IM. He can't do
anything.

Charliedude824: If he knows yr name, he can find
out where u live.

Houdini409: You there?

Crystal's fingers hovered over the keyboard. This guy was giving
her the creeps, but she felt far from frightened. If anything, she felt
driven to find out more about him. If she could find a way to slip him
up, to get him to reveal himself . . . Her fingernails clicked on the
keys.

Java4Jesus: You're a pretty sick person, Russ.

Houdini409: Who's Russ? I'm not Russ. But if I'm sick, it's because you made me this way.

What's that supposed to mean?

Crystal began typing: "How did I make u sick? I don't even know who u are."

Houdini409: Of course you do, Erin. Stop pretending. You're just wasting time, and you don't want to waste what precious little time you have left. Be a good girl and don't try anything stupid. Remember, I'll be watching.

Java4Jesus: Don't know what u mean. And my name isn't Erin. Think u got me mixed up with somebody else.

Crystal let the moment pass. No response. She waited a few more seconds. Still nothing.

Charliedude824: What's going on?

Java4Jesus: Think he left.

Charliedude824: What did he say?

You don't want to waste what precious little time you have left.

She imagined a creepy sing-song voice repeating those words like a litany. The last line had unsettled her more than she cared to admit.

Remember, I'll be watching.

She glanced at her only window. The horizontal blinds were drawn. No one but God could see her right now. She took a deep breath and blew it out.

Charliedude824: U OK?

Java4Jesus: Everything's cool. The creep left.

Crystal felt herself trembling. Was this for real? Should she tell her parents? At the next rehearsal, she'd seek out the prankster. If there was someone on the cast with Houdini409 as a handle, she'd track him down. But she had a gnawing suspicion that he wasn't a prankster after all. That he was someone else.

Someone who was watching.

CHAPTER 56

ON WEDNESDAY MORNING AFTER breakfast, Gillian was sitting in her studio, getting ready for another morning of homeschooling, when she remembered that she had promised Marc she would go with him today to investigate something about Stacey James's murder. She still thought the whole thing was crazy—the closest Marc had ever gotten to police work was watching reruns of *Perry Mason*—but he was so determined to clear his name that she couldn't help but say yes when he'd asked for her assistance.

The telephone rang, and she reached for the cordless.

"Oh, hi, Clara. I was going to call you this morning."

"Well, I've been thinking about you," Clara said. "How are you doing?"

"Oh, pretty good."

"That bad, huh? 'Pretty good' usually means 'not so good.'"

"Not this time. Things couldn't be better actually. Marc's home. I even had a chance to talk to Nicole about Jesus."

"Terrific! I'm so glad things are going better for you. Just be sure you're not resting on good circumstances. Rest on Jesus. Then when circumstances aren't so good, you'll have a solid rock to stand on and enduring joy no matter what's happening in your life."

"Good advice."

"It's easy to say but hard to live. I know." Clara chuckled. "Don't think I've mastered the art of trusting because I certainly haven't."

"Hey, thanks again for spending extra time with me on Sunday. That meant a lot."

"Well, I'm always here if you need someone to lean on, okay?"

"Okay."

Moments after hanging up, Gillian heard a knock on her door. It was Marc.

"I figure we can cover more ground more quickly if we work together," he said.

"Okay, but what do we know about criminal investigations, Marc, other than what we've read in mystery novels or seen on TV? Zilch."

"So we'll be the blind leading the blind." Marc leaned against the doorjamb, arms folded across his chest. "But I've got a list of things that Chuck said I should do, people to talk to."

As if seeing the dubious look in her eye, he said, "C'mon, it'll be interesting. And at least you'll get to spend some extra time with me."

"Well, if you put it that way. But first I need to arrange with Crystal to move our homeschool schedule to this afternoon. And I'm not sure how I feel about just leaving her here alone this morning."

"She'll be fine. She can just work on her Web design stuff—which is what she'd rather be doing anyway, right? And she's got her cell, so she'd only be a call away."

"Okay," Gillian said. "Just give me a minute to go talk with her, and I'll be right back down."

✳   ✳   ✳

While he and Gillian sped toward town in the Tahoe, with Gene Autry singing in the background, Marc filled her in on his investigation at Whistler's Point. He'd already talked to Clara, Henry, and the other groundskeepers who might have noticed a stranger prowling around the property. But other than Henry's glimpse of Stacey's argument with Marc, nobody had seen her or noticed anything out of the ordinary. The Magician Murderer had strangled Stacey outdoors at night—a location and time that guaranteed few witnesses.

But "the perp," as Riley often called the killer, may have made other appearances during daylight hours. Like everyone, he had to go grocery shopping and buy gas. More than likely, he'd made an appearance near the North Woods Inn, where Stacey had gotten a room. But Riley had already checked out that location, and nobody remembered seeing anyone suspicious. Because the Magician Murderer was from Cincinnati, where he'd last struck only last month, locals here wouldn't know him well; in fact, he was probably new to the area.

"I think our best bet is to check out every location where someone new to town might go," Marc said.

"Now who exactly are we looking for here—Stacey or the Magician Murderer?"

"Both." Marc gestured to a folder lying on the backseat. "Grab that folder."

Gillian reached for the folder and opened it, but stiffened when she found an enlarged snapshot of Stacey James smiling back at her. Riley had made several copies of the photo to assist their investigative efforts, but Gillian closed the folder quickly, her skin cold, not wanting to see the dead woman's face.

"Chuck said if we find people who remember seeing Stacey," Marc said, "they might remember a stranger who crossed paths with her. If we find out where she went, we might find him, too."

Killing two birds with one stone, Gillian thought. What Marc said made sense, but she wondered how many wild geese they'd have to chase before finding any useful information. She was glad she had worn comfortable shoes. This investigation could take some time and demand a lot of pounding the pavement.

Eyeing the folder again, she tried to sort through her feelings about Stacey James. The woman had tried to seduce and kill her husband. Weren't her feelings of revulsion for Stacey normal? Yet she felt rebuked for not having more compassion. If not for God's grace, couldn't she have walked the same path?

*   *   *

Before dropping Gillian off at one of the few grocery stores in town, Marc reviewed the type of questions she should ask. Confident she understood, Gillian grabbed a photo of Stacey, turned to wave, and headed toward the supermarket while Marc drove to the nearest bank.

Inside the store, the gray-haired checker popping bubblegum at the first cash register squinted at the photo and shook her head. Nope, she'd never seen that woman before. When Gillian asked if other employees could look at the photo as well, the checker rounded up as many employees as she could find "without disrupting normal operations"—not that the place appeared even remotely busy—but nobody recognized Stacey James.

Gillian headed down the sidewalk toward the center of town, stopping into various shops along the way. If Stacey James had ever shown her face in downtown Newberry, everybody Gillian talked to needed a dose of ginkgo to boost their memory function. A few minutes later, she spotted the Tahoe and waved. Marc did a U-turn and pulled alongside the curb.

"Any luck?" Marc said as Gillian hopped into the car.

"No. How about you?"

Frustration swelled in Marc's voice. "Nothing either. Surely somebody somewhere must have seen her." Marc put the car in gear and drove south.

"Hey, what about the library?" Gillian said, pointing to a brick-and-glass-sided building they were passing.

"Stacey booked a room at the North Woods Inn for three nights and appeared to have one goal—to see me. It's unlikely she would have taken the time to apply for a library card."

"Maybe she needed Internet access. Who knows? At least it's somewhere we haven't checked."

Marc shrugged and pulled quickly to the curb. "I guess it's worth a shot."

CHAPTER 57

HAYDON'S HANDS TREMBLED AS he gingerly opened the aged cover of the small book and perused its pages. The library frequently received book donations, but he never expected to find such a treasure amid the pile of trashy romance paperbacks: Harry Houdini's *Miracle Mongers and Their Methods*.

He sat at the counter, the box of used books at his feet. Marjorie wasn't around to spy on him, so he had time. Without thinking, he began humming "Memory" from the Broadway musical *Cats*.

He read the title page: "Miracle Mongers and Their Methods: A Complete Exposé of the Modus Operandi of Fire Eater, Heat Resisters, Poison Eaters, Venomous Reptile Defiers, Sword Swallowers, Human Ostriches, Strong Men, etc., by Houdini."

As he excitedly skimmed the preface, his eyes came to rest on the following words:

> I do not feel that I need to apologize for adding another volume to the shelves of works dealing with the marvels of the miracle-mongers. My business has given me an intimate knowledge of stage illusions, together with many years of experience among show people of all types. My familiarity with the former, and what I have learned of the psychology of the latter, has placed me at a certain advantage in uncovering the natural explanation of feats that to the ignorant have seemed supernatural. And even if—

Haydon glanced up as the front door opened and a vaguely

familiar-looking patron entered the foyer. When she noticed him at the counter, she headed in his direction.

Average height. A little on the chubby side. She wore casual khaki dress slacks and sensible brown shoes. Wavy, shoulder-length red hair spilled over the collar of her green winter coat.

As she approached the counter, she smiled and engaged him with attractive green eyes. She had something in her hand—a photo, he realized, as she brought it up for him to see.

He knew both faces—the face in the photo and now the face of the woman in front of him—but he told his eyes to lie. Deception came easily in his line of work.

"Hi, you may have heard about the murder of Stacey James," the woman said.

He nodded. Who hadn't?

"The police found her body out at Whistler's Point. I'm investigating her death and was wondering if maybe you might have seen her here at the library."

He began shaking his head before she finished her last sentence. "Nope, never seen her before."

The corners of the woman's mouth turned downward, reflecting obvious disappointment. "Do you mind telling me if she had an account here?"

He hesitated. "Are you with the sheriff's office?"

"Nope. Just doing some research on my own."

He knew her husband, Marc, was the prime suspect in Stacey's murder—a fact that thrilled him. As long as the police had their sights on someone else, they wouldn't be looking for him.

"Oh, I'm sorry, but I can't discuss another person's records without an official request from law enforcement. It's library policy."

"That's okay. What if someone wanted to use your Internet access? Do they need to have a library card?"

"Yep. Locals get free access since they pay taxes. Outsiders have to pay. I know—it doesn't seem quite fair, but that's often how life is, isn't it?"

The woman bit her lower lip, her eyes straying off to the rows of bookshelves before she turned her gaze back to him. "May I ask the head librarian if she's seen Stacey James here?"

He paused. "That would be Marjorie." He pointed toward the stacks. "Her office is down there."

Watching as the woman walked toward the back of the library, Haydon drove his fingernails into his palms, trying to calm down. What was Crystal's mom doing here asking questions about Stacey James?

CHAPTER 58

THE PLACE SEEMED STRANGELY deserted for a Wednesday morning. Because the library shared facilities with a local school, Gillian had assumed the place would be bustling with kids. Quite the contrary, actually. Perhaps they were all in class right now.

It wasn't a big library, so why was she having such a difficult time finding this Marjorie's office? She went up one stack of books and down another, surprised to see more popular adult fiction than she'd expected. Not that she read anything popular; she mostly stuck to the classics. The computer lab had more computers than she'd expected, too.

Gillian paused and considered. Stacey couldn't have used a computer. She would have had to establish a library account first, and if she was traveling under an assumed name—which Marc had learned from Riley she was—she wouldn't have had the proper identification. In short, she had probably never set foot in the place. But still, it wouldn't hurt to ask the librarian if she'd seen Stacey. If only she could find the woman.

She entered the Local History room and spotted a door to her right. She turned the knob, and the door opened to reveal a dark room beyond.

Well, this can't be it. Puzzled, she headed toward another row of books. *He did say there was an office back here somewhere, didn't he?*

Just then she heard a footfall. Somebody was coming. "Hello?" she called out.

No answer. Maybe the sound had been her imagination.

She headed down another row of books, looking for the librarian's office, which had to be here somewhere.

More footsteps, this time two rows over. And a humming sound. A low voice, humming a familiar tune.

A shiver ran down her neck. Rounding the corner, she shrieked.

The male librarian with the black-frame glasses leapt back in surprise. "Oh, sorry," he said with a curious little laugh. "Didn't mean to startle you. You're looking a little lost."

Hand to her chest, Gillian felt her heart slowing down. "I couldn't find Marjorie's office."

The young man shook his head apologetically. "Sorry, I forgot. Marjorie stepped out and won't be back for a few hours. But if you give me your name and number, I can give her your message. Then, if she remembers anything, she can call you."

CHAPTER 59

RISING FROM HIS DESK, Jerry O'Hearn crossed the small office to the doorway and gave Chuck Riley a bear hug that left him breathless.

"You're a sight for sore eyes." O'Hearn sat on the edge of his desk, his rolled-up shirtsleeves revealing freckled arms. "Things just haven't been the same since you left."

"Sorry to hear that." Taking a seat across from O'Hearn's desk, Riley realized he wasn't being entirely truthful. Part of him felt flattered that he'd been missed. He glanced around the office at O'Hearn's treasured collection of stock-car racing miniatures, which lined his bookshelf and windowsill.

"We need to get something straight before you dive into this." O'Hearn's brown eyes were serious, his brown hair thinner than Riley remembered. "I'm not giving these files to you, understand? If word gets out that I'm helping you with this case, my head could be on a platter. I have other cases that gotta take priority."

Riley nodded. "Understood. You aren't giving the files to me—which is true. I'm going through them on my own, and you don't need to get involved." He shrugged. "I wouldn't worry, Jer. By now, the bigwigs already know about my being here, thanks to that loud-mouthed sheriff in Newberry. In fact, I'm surprised they haven't hidden the files in anticipation of my arrival."

"Nobody's hidden the files as far as I know. Yesterday, I made sure they were still there and found them, sure enough. In some ways, I wish they *would* disappear. I've never known a series of murders to cause so much heartache."

O'Hearn led Riley down a hallway that opened into a large room dominated by office cubicles and the continuous drone of ringing telephones. People were coming and going, the place buzzing like a beehive. Recognizing Riley, a few people paused to say hello, but nobody questioned his presence in his old stomping grounds.

Moments later, he and O'Hearn descended a flight of stairs to the basement where inactive case files were stored. Rows of floor-to-ceiling metal shelving units and dusty filing cabinets lined a windowless room where bare lightbulbs hung from cobwebbed ceiling joists. A musty smell assaulted Riley's nostrils.

"Now, I've still got the Amanda Forbes file in my office, of course, but you said you wanted to go back to the beginning," said O'Hearn. "So it's down to the dungeon for you."

Not missing a beat, Riley went straight to the Magician Murder files. Documents from the unsolved murders had filled a filing cabinet to capacity and had overflowed to several stacked cardboard boxes. The sight of the filing cabinet and boxes, now piled four feet high, made Riley's stomach tighten. Perhaps somewhere hidden in those files lay a clue that could save someone's life. Time was of the essence.

O'Hearn helped Riley heft the boxes to an old, unused desk, and Riley cleared the dusty desktop to create work space. Using boxes from the case as his chair, Riley opened the filing cabinet's first drawer and removed a thick stack of manila folders. He placed them on the desktop.

Grasping the wattles of skin at his neck, O'Hearn eyed him as if uneasy about leaving him alone.

"You better go," Riley said, "before your boss starts wondering where you've gone. I don't want you getting your hands dirty. You've done too much already."

Turning to leave, O'Hearn said, "I'll bring you coffee. That's the least I can do."

"I'll drink anything you can spare, but don't wait up. I'll probably be here all night, unless what I need jumps out at me—which isn't likely." Riley glanced at his watch and winced. "It's already after two. That's what I get for eating lunch."

O'Hearn waved good-bye, and Riley heard his friend's feet shuffling up the stairs.

Before opening the first folder, Riley sighed. He closed his eyes and asked God to show him what he'd missed before. He knew these files like the back of his hand and felt like he was returning to an old piano piece he'd memorized for a recital years ago when he was a child. He knew the piece—remembered it well—but needed practice. He just needed to clear the cobwebs away.

And, boy, are there cobwebs down here.

The files contained interview transcripts, crime scene photos and reports, affidavits, the works. Somewhere in the files, he would find samples of the trick rope, copies of an unidentified fingerprint that had been found at the Meghan Leland crime scene—a fingerprint that hadn't found a match in the Automated Fingerprint Identification System database. But that had been a while ago. Later, he would run the fingerprint again, but he didn't expect to get a hit.

First, Riley decided to review the interview transcripts—particularly those in the Erin Walker case. Along with the transcripts was a form on which were listed the phone number and address of Erin's mother. It might be useful to call her, to see if she would be willing to talk to him again, though he dreaded even picking up the phone.

Just seeing the woman's sad, haunted eyes again would only underline his failure. During the first few days after Erin's murder, he'd been so optimistic about cracking the case. He'd never dreamed at the time that the murder investigation would drag on for four years and wind up going cold.

Riley bowed his head. *Please, Father, open my eyes and show me what I've missed. I can't do this without Your help.*

CHAPTER 60

AT SEDER'S PIZZA CHALET, Marc ordered a late lunch while Gillian found the bathroom, washed her hands, and went in search of a quiet corner table. Shedding her coat, she took her seat and sighed, glad to be off her feet. After the library, they'd checked more banks, gas stations, the Ace Hardware, the Ben Franklin, and she couldn't remember what else. As she had feared, they'd come up empty-handed.

Marc appeared moments later, raving about how good the pizza smelled. He plunked down kitty-corner from Gillian and said, "I hope the food here tastes as good as it smells because I'm *really* hungry."

Fifteen minutes later, their large supreme pizza arrived, sans the green peppers, which Marc despised. Taking Gillian's hand, he blessed the food before they pulled slices onto their plates.

While they ate, Gillian suddenly realized they were alone, just the two of them. What a strange feeling! She recalled their September anniversary trip to downtown Chicago to see *Fiddler on the Roof.* Had that been their last real date?

She steered her eyes back to her pizza, realizing that she'd been staring at Marc. Another second, and he'd ask her what was up.

As if on cue, he said, "I just realized we haven't had a date like this in a while."

She couldn't help smiling. "I was just thinking the same thing." How many times had they both thought the same thing at the same moment? Too many times to count. Just one of those quirky things about being married.

"We should go out together more often." He grabbed her left hand, the one she wasn't using to eat her pizza. She squeezed his hand back and felt transported to another day seemingly ages ago.

✳ ✳ ✳

They'd been casual friends for a year at Bible college before something mysteriously changed. Perhaps it had begun the day Marc invited her to accompany him to the snack shop and then walked into a telephone pole while looking at her for her response. Whatever the reason, everything had changed after that. She came out of class at the end of the day, and there he was, waiting for her with that boyish grin plastered on his face and a goose egg over his left eye.

A few lunch dates later, she'd told him the honest truth about her painful past. Amazingly, her history of regrets hadn't repelled him. "Hey, everyone makes mistakes," he'd said. He was more interested in what she believed God wanted to do with her life in the future.

The following summer, his parents had invited her to join them on their annual family getaway to a condo in Hilton Head, South Carolina. After pizza one evening, she and Marc had strolled barefoot along the sandy beach and looked for shells, a favorite pastime for tourists. The rest of his family, as if taking their cue, were seemingly nowhere to be found.

He'd asked if he could hold her hand, and she'd said yes. His squeeze was warm and tight, and she'd felt a little weak-kneed just by the closeness of his physical presence. He was tall after all, and many girls on campus agreed that though he perhaps wasn't the most attractive guy on campus, he was definitely somewhere on the list.

Then Marc had pretended he'd seen something unusual; letting go of her hand, he'd taken off at a jog, sand wisping up behind his feet. Bending over, his long tan legs dark against his white shorts, he'd picked something up and dusted it off. When she'd caught up to him, curious about his discovery, he'd said, "Wow, look at what I found!"

He'd handed her a seashell, just one among many they'd already seen, and it appeared to be nothing unusual. But then something had caught her eye and dazzled her in the sunlight. Her breath had caught in her throat.

A ring. A diamond ring.

She'd clutched it in her palm and for a moment overlooked the significance. Finances had always been tight in her family, and she was concerned about the financial loss if she dropped the ring in the sand and lost it.

Then she'd realized he was smiling at her, and she wasn't sure what glinted more—the diamond ring or the sparkle in his eyes. He had knelt in the sand in front of her, and she still couldn't believe what had happened next.

"Gillian Marie Canfield, will you marry me?"

✳   ✳   ✳

Marc was squeezing her hand, and the present came crashing back like a wave at Hilton Head. She was back in Seder's Pizza Chalet, sitting next to her husband and the father of her children. God's good gift.

His cornflower blues were probing. "What is it? You seem a thousand miles away."

She glanced down with a smile, twisting the diamond ring on her finger. "Actually, I was. I was just remembering the pizza we had at Hilton Head. Remember?"

He wiped his mouth on a napkin. "Can't say I remember much about the pizza. All I could think about was the beautiful redhead sitting next to me and the diamond ring burning a hole in my pocket."

"Remember how sick you were the semester before?" She put down a piece of crust and met his eyes. "Sacrificing your health just so you could work third shift and save enough for the ring."

He sucked down some of his Pepsi and winked at her. "I'd say you were worth it." He slid another slice of pizza from the tray and cleared his throat. "Actually, that day at Hilton Head has been on my mind for the last couple of months."

"Oh really?" She smiled at him playfully.

"In fact, to be perfectly honest, getting together with you today wasn't just about the investigation. I had an ulterior motive."

She searched his face, finding mystery in his eyes and wondering what it could mean.

He dug into his pants pocket and plunked something down in the middle of the table.

Her hand flew to her mouth.

A seashell. Could it be *their* seashell? Had he kept it all these years?

He chuckled. "Well, are you going to just sit there gawking, or are you going to take a look inside?"

This can't be happening! She grabbed the seashell, and a ring with a diamond much larger than the one on her engagement ring tumbled into her hand.

Her eyes filled with tears as he took the ring and slowly slipped it onto her right hand. She grabbed her napkin, trying to mop up the deluge now coursing down her cheeks.

Marc's eyes were moist as he leaned toward her. His kiss was anything but a casual peck.

As his warm hand cradled her neck, his eyes peered deeply into hers. "You're worth it, Gillian Canfield Thayer. You've always been worth it. And if I had it to do all over again, I wouldn't change a thing."

CHAPTER 61

LIGHT WAS FADING FAST, and Nicole knew she needed to hurry. Checking her camera's aperture, she peered through her viewfinder and positioned the sun to her left, balanced by the emerald waters of Lake Superior and the "diving rock" to her right. She clicked the shutter and lowered the camera, admiring the sunset with satisfaction. In a few days, she hoped to show Gillian where she went for her best shots and how she composed them.

Gillian. Nicole shook her head, unable to comprehend losing twins the way Gillian had. She was still amazed that Gillian wasn't angry at God for taking her babies away. Or if she was angry, she was pretty good at not showing it. Gillian had admitted to having bad days now and then, had said that writing letters to her babies helped her get through the worst of her grief. *Like my grief is anything compared to hers.*

She considered taking another shot, but hesitated, finding herself strangely distracted today. She hadn't been herself since her conversation with Gillian yesterday. And now everything in her life seemed . . . well, off balance. Unsettled. Not quite the way it used to be. As if God were reaching down from the heavens, giving her a good shake, and saying, "Hey, don't forget that I love you."

Gazing into the darkening sky, she discerned the first pinpricks of pulsating stars. *Do You really love me, God? Did You really send Jesus to die just so I could know You?* The thought blew her away.

Glancing at her watch, she realized she needed to get home to Mirabella before the dog left a nasty rebuke on the kitchen floor. She had a lot of thinking to do during her drive home. Gillian's words about

God's love rose inside her like a comforting embrace; they were something she'd been needing for a long time. Lately, she'd been feeling so fearful, so uncertain about her life and future.

If there truly was a point to the universe, she wanted to know what it was. And strangely, she was certain she now knew the answer.

She had lied when she told Gillian that she preferred living alone, that the divorce from Luke was really no big deal. *I actually hate being alone, and I miss Luke so much. Why doesn't he call? Why doesn't he care? I never did anything to drive him away. What's wrong with me anyhow?*

Striding toward her car, Nicole glanced at the lighthouse and froze. A light glowed from a window on the third floor—which was odd because she distinctly remembered turning off all the lights before locking up the place for the night. Her pulse quickened as she drew nearer to the front door.

From her angle now up close to the lighthouse, she caught a better glimpse into the third-floor room. Past the lacy curtains, a shadow moved, dancing across the wall.

Someone's inside!

Heart in her throat, she headed to the caretaker's house and knocked on the door, wondering if the Thayers were even home. She knew they'd been gone most of the day, but perhaps they had come home before the prayer meeting.

When the door opened, Marc looked surprised to see her. "Hey, Nicole. Is something wrong?"

"Call the police! There's an intruder in the lighthouse!"

CHAPTER 62

LINGERING IN THE DARK where no one could see him, Haydon listened as the police searched every inch of the place. The lighthouse echoed with the shuffling of feet, the creak of old floorboards, the murmur of voices, and the opening and closing of countless doors. Once he heard someone knocking on the wall just inches from where he stood concealed in darkness. *You can't find me,* he thought with a delicious shiver of delight. *Not where I'm hiding.*

He chided himself for being careless, for leaving the light on. The fact that his presence had been detected could possibly change everything now. Someone would be watching the lighthouse more carefully; coming and going would be more difficult, more risky.

Years ago, when his parents had been caretakers at Whistler's Point, he'd found the recess behind the bookshelf by accident while looking for a hiding place from his drunken father. Learning to hide from the predictable beatings had begun his obsession with concealment, which had led to an interest in becoming an escape artist. In a twisted sort of way, he had his father to thank for his life's work.

He listened intently until he was certain the police had gone and no one was lurking inside the lighthouse except him. Maneuvering out from behind the bookcase, he prowled the dark hallways alone. The light he'd so carelessly left on would only reinforce the legend that the lighthouse was haunted by Harriet Whistler's ghost.

In the plush Victorian bedroom called "Emily's room," he pushed aside the stanchions intended to keep visitors from touching the valuable furniture and crawled atop the creaky, antique bed that he'd pretended was his as a boy. It still stood in the same place, angled toward the tall window, as if positioned by a sly act of fate.

He slid under the soft covers. They hadn't been dusted in some time, but he barely noticed. Lying on his side in the fetal position and resting his head on the pillow, he peered through the rippled, antique glass of the window at the starlit sky, just as he had done so many times as a child, dreaming of the famous magician he would someday become. The setting conjured memories and emotions he hadn't experienced in some time. His chin trembled.

If only he could go back to those simple, carefree days before the trouble started . . .

He imagined his mother's presence, pictured her tucking him into bed and singing him a lullaby in that husky voice that had been famous long ago. Closing his eyes, he felt her soft lips brush his forehead.

Go to sleep, Donny. You know your mother loves you, don't you?

Yes, Mother. I know.

CHAPTER 63

AS TRUDY WALKER REACHED for another Kleenex, Riley asked himself again whether interviewing Erin's mother a second time had been a wise decision. He glanced at O'Hearn, who gave him an encouraging nod.

I guess it's too late to be second-guessing myself.

It was only about nine o'clock in the morning, but Riley was already feeling uncomfortable as he and O'Hearn sat shoulder to shoulder on the worn loveseat in the Walkers' tiny living room. Sitting across from them in a rocking chair, Trudy blotted her red-rimmed blue eyes and puffed on a cigarette. The smoke was bad enough, but Riley was doubly cursed; his eyes were also itchy from the blasted cat, which had reluctantly given up its napping spot for them.

Beside the loveseat stood a curio cabinet filled with Hummel figurines. They reminded him of a girl he'd dated long ago, whose mother had collected Hummels. He'd always thought the chubby German children needed to cut back on their Wiener schnitzel.

"Even after all these years," Trudy said, "I can't live a day without thinking about my Erin." Her careworn face was a study in unfulfilled dreams. "Would you like to see her room?"

"No, that's fine," Riley said, "but thanks for offering." The bedroom, which he'd seen several times before, was little less than a shrine. Nothing had been altered since Erin's death. He got the chills every time he saw it.

Trudy had lost her beauty long ago, her voice husky from cigarettes, her face worn and listless. She seemed to have one foot stuck in reality and the other firmly planted in another world, a world dominated by the daughter she could never have back.

She didn't blame Riley, of course, but he couldn't help feeling pangs of guilt at his unsuccessful investigation. The case had begun with her, and now here he was, back where he'd started, like a stubborn child who refused to learn. Was he just a glutton for punishment? *Father, please help me learn something new today.*

"I can't even go to a hairdresser without weeping my eyes out." She smiled sadly and peered down at her hands, at fingernails bitten to the quick. "Isn't that ridiculous? But I can't help it. Just seeing a curling iron reminds me of Erin. She wanted to be a beautician, you know."

Riley exchanged knowing glances with O'Hearn. Yes, he knew all about Erin's interests; knew about her father, who had almost qualified for the Olympics; knew about Trudy's alcoholic binges; knew more than he cared to know.

He studied Trudy's face, willing her to understand. "I'm here to learn what I didn't find out before, Mrs. Walker. There's something I missed the last time we talked, but I don't know what it is. I'm hoping you can tell me something I don't already know about Erin, about the last few days before her death."

So, predictably, she told him everything he'd heard before—about Erin's classes at school; about her best friend, Sheryl; about her taking a couple of neighborhood children to a musical on the night of her abduction and murder.

"Can you go further back?" He forced patience into his otherwise impatient tone. "Can you backtrack to the last few months before Erin's death? Were there any big events in her life, anything out of the ordinary?"

Trudy's eyes lit up. "A Britney Spears concert. Oh, she loved Britney, all right. Had all of her CDs. Even had her autograph."

"And the concert was where?" O'Hearn asked.

"In Chicago. At the United Center. She spent the weekend with her cousin, Felicia. Felicia's the artsy type—plays the violin—and didn't want to go to the concert. She now goes to Yale, which is an Ivy League school. I'd hoped Felicia would rub off on Erin, but it didn't take. And now it doesn't matter." She reached for yet another Kleenex.

Felicia. That was a name Riley hadn't heard before. He scrawled the name down in his notepad and asked for Felicia's address and telephone number. Trudy promised to give him both before they left.

He heard the *tick tick tick* of the clock on the fireplace mantel and reminded himself of the precious minutes ticking by and of the fact that he wasn't learning much that was new. He wondered if Marc's investigation was faring any better than his.

O'Hearn spoke up. "Anything beyond the daily activities of going to school, babysitting, and cutting hair?"

Trudy Walker rubbed her forehead as if to massage the wrinkles away. "Well, she cut her own hair, did it up real pretty."

Riley's spirits plunged to earth. He glanced surreptitiously at his watch.

"See, she wanted to look extra special," Trudy said.

Riley glanced up. "For a boyfriend perhaps?"

"You haven't been listening to me." Impatience growled in her voice. So she wasn't the only one weary of this conversation that was going nowhere. "I told you before—she didn't have a boyfriend. She wanted to look nice when she took the stand."

"The stand?"

"The trial, of course. You remember. I told you about her testifying in court. The Owens case."

The Owens case. A murder case.

Now he remembered. Erin had testified against Walter and Virginia Owens. Riley had read the court transcript so many times, he could have recited it backward. He was certain he'd gone down this path before without finding any new leads, but it wouldn't hurt to revisit it again.

Cautiously optimistic, he turned to a clean page in his notepad, his pen poised. "I want to know all about this trial. Everything you can remember."

Father, please.

She rose. "How about some coffee? This is going to take a while."

CHAPTER 64

AT LUNCHTIME ON THURSDAY, Gillian told Marc he had a message from Riley to call him. Within seconds, he had Riley on the line.

"Hey, Marc. Just checking on how you're doing."

"I'm glad you called. How are things in Cincinnati?"

"I'll get to that in a minute. How is your investigation going?"

Marc hesitated. "Not so great, I'm afraid." He brought Riley up to speed on the events of the previous day, their investigative efforts at Whistler's Point and Newberry, and the disappointing results. "I thought if we found someone who had seen Stacey, he might remember a stranger prowling around. Maybe we'd even get the killer's name."

"Well, I already know his name," Riley said. "At least, I'm pretty sure I do."

Marc succumbed to a moment of stunned silence. "You *what?*"

"You know that interview I had with Trudy Walker today?"

"Uh-huh."

"I thought it was going to be a big waste of time, and it was at first. Then she reminds me that Erin was the key witness in a big murder case. We'd explored possible connections at the time, but hadn't found any leads. Somebody knocked off an old lady in some type of investment scheme. Erin saw a couple entering the old lady's house the night before the old lady was found murdered. Her testimony was critical in putting the killers behind bars."

"Killers *plural?*"

"Yeah, there were two of them. Walter and Virginia Owens. They both got life in prison. And get this—they left behind a son. Turns out he's an amateur magician."

"You're kidding!"

"I'm pretty sure he's the Magician Murderer, Marc. He had a strong motive to want Erin dead."

"So what happened to him?"

"He disappeared, and nobody seems to know where he went."

"And now he's here in Newberry. So what's his name?"

"Haydon Owens."

"If you know his name, I assume someone is going to arrest him?"

"That's where things get dicey, I'm afraid. I already checked some of the databases here. There's no record of a Haydon Owens after he left Cincinnati. He must have changed his identity."

"And if he changed his identity, we're at a dead end, right?"

"Not necessarily. I have a lead. Haydon's father, Walter, died in prison, but his mother, Virginia, is still alive in a state correctional facility upstate from me."

"So that's where you're headed next?"

"Yep. I'm interviewing her in a couple hours."

"Do you think she'll tell you where Haydon is?"

"*If* she even knows where he is, I hope so."

"I'll be praying."

"Please do. In the meantime, I'm sending the most recent photo of Haydon to Sheriff Dendridge. He'll canvass the area and get the photo in the newspaper and on TV. Could you check on it for me?"

"No problem."

"Maybe somebody has seen this guy, though I bet he's changed his appearance unless he's completely stupid. But I don't think that's the case. I think he's smart, maybe smarter than we are. But we'll catch him. Oh yeah, we'll get him. You can bet on it."

CHAPTER 65

AT THE FRONT DESK of the Ohio Reformatory for Women, a stony-faced woman confirmed Riley's special clearance, set up by O'Hearn beforehand, before vaguely motioning him toward the visiting area. Not that he needed directions. He'd been in plenty of these places and knew his way around pretty well by now.

A uniformed guard led Riley through a metal detector and directed him to a tiny room with a cubicle and a Plexiglas window that sealed him off from the room beyond. Telling Riley he had a half hour, the guard left and closed the door behind him. Riley eyed the intercom system on the wall and the tiny camera staring down at him from the ceiling.

Sitting on a hard, plastic stool, he studied the Plexiglas that would separate him from the mother of Haydon Owens. The glass was unusually clean this morning; someone must have washed it recently. Usually, he could count the handprints of small children who wished to touch their mothers.

Folding a stick of gum into his mouth, he stared past the glass to the door, which now opened to reveal a black-haired woman in her mid-sixties. She wore baggy, orange coveralls that reminded him of burlap. The coveralls seemed incongruous to her slim figure, her permed and obviously dyed black hair, and her fresh application of makeup.

As she stepped toward the chair on her side of the glass, Riley wondered if she had done herself up especially for him or if she looked this way all the time. There was the hint of celebrity in her face, the look of a woman who'd been on the stage or before the camera.

Sitting across from him, she gave him a pleasant smile, as if the two of them were sitting in a candlelit restaurant, romantic music playing in the background. He noted the sinuous way she moved, the way her eyes studied him; she knew men, perhaps a little too well.

"Good morning," he said.

"Good morning to you, too." There was a musical quality to her husky voice.

"You *are* Virginia Owens?"

"The one and only, though my friends call me Ginny." She rested her chin on her folded hands, doing magic with her eyes. "You know who I am, don't you?"

He knew all about her, but preferred she tell him herself.

When it was obvious he wasn't going to say, she said impatiently, "Broadway. Thirty years ago. You don't look like the Broadway type at all. For a minute there, you reminded me of an agent I once knew."

"I'm sorry. I don't know anything about Broadway." He'd seen the movie version of *Oklahoma* but would have been stumped if asked to hum one of the songs.

She leaned back in her chair and sighed. "Figures. I should have known I was just wasting my time."

"I'm sorry. You were expecting someone else?"

"I thought maybe you were the guy who wanted to re-release my recordings." She shrugged. "Just as well."

"Ah, so you're a recording artist?"

"I *was* a recording artist. I'm still a singer—ask any of my cell mates when I'm taking a shower—but everybody here sings the blues. That's not my style, but nobody nowadays wants to hear anything else." She got up as if to leave. "Look, I don't know who you are, and I don't want to waste my time or yours, okay?"

"Wait. Don't go."

She eased back down with a grunt. "All right, I'll stay a little longer. I don't get to talk to men very often, and you're not half bad to look at."

Riley laughed and pointed to his wedding band.

"Yeah, I see it. Big deal. Married men are more fun anyhow." She paused with a simper. "So if you aren't here about my recordings, why are you here?"

"Your son, Haydon."

She glanced away and looked as if she might get up again to leave; but after composing herself, she steered her eyes back to his face. "So how is dear Donny?"

"I was hoping you could tell me."

"You're a cop, aren't you?"

"Retired."

Bitterness hardened her face. "Why should I tell you anything about my son? Losers like you got me locked up here in the first place."

Riley ignored her. "Your son's in trouble, serious trouble. I don't want to hurt him, understand. I just want to help him. But I can't help him if I don't know where he is."

"Ah, so he's missing, huh?" She chuckled mirthlessly. "Good for him. I hope he stays missing for a long, long time."

Riley rubbed his lower lip with the ball of his thumb. "Was Haydon your only child?"

The change in subject matter seemed to take her aback. "Yep. Spoiled rotten, I'm afraid. Unfortunately, when I was singing all over Broadway, I didn't spend the time with him I should have. And his father was a drunk most of his life and resentful because of my success—not much help there." She shrugged. "Then when my voice gave out, well, we headed up north so I could recuperate."

"Up north?"

"Upper Michigan, the U.P., near Lake Superior. It's beautiful. Ever been up there?"

More recently than you know. Riley knew her husband had worked in Whistler's Point. Haydon would have been a boy then.

"So Haydon was an only child. But you always wanted to have a daughter, didn't you?"

"Well, of course. Every mother wants to have a daughter, but it doesn't always work out that way."

"Someone's daughter just died, Mrs. Owens."

She stared at him, lips slightly parted, as if unsure of how to respond. "I'm sorry to hear that, but what does that have to do with Donny?"

"Haydon killed her."

No surprise registered in her glistening, black eyes. "Donny never killed nobody."

"Sure he did. That blonde girl who gave testimony in court against you and your husband. Remember her?"

"Erin Walker." She spat the name as if it were poison on her tongue. "Of course I remember her. She's the reason I'm locked up in this god-forsaken place."

"She gave testimony against you, didn't she? The jury believed her and put you and your husband away for the rest of your lives."

Ginny cursed under her breath. "She was a little liar. I've hated her for years."

"You wanted her dead, didn't you?"

She studied him, as if wondering what kind of game he was playing. "I think anybody who's been falsely accused would feel the same way."

Ah, so she still maintains her innocence. He couldn't help smiling. He knew all about her case; she was guilty, all right. They had fiber evidence, fingerprints, DNA, the works. "When was the last time you heard from your son?"

"I don't know. Maybe six months ago."

"E-mail?"

She smirked. "They don't let us do e-mail in a place like this. You should know that."

"You love your son, don't you?"

"That's a stupid question. Of course I do."

"And he's an obedient son, isn't he?"

"He's always been obedient." A wary look crept into her eyes.

"Obedient enough to kill for you?"

Her eyes flared. "Look, I never said anything to him about killing that Walker girl. Whatever he did, he did on his own without any help from me."

"But you know he killed her, don't you?"

She wet her lips. "I don't think I should say anything else without my lawyer present."

"Your attorney is more than welcome. In fact, I think he'd like to hear this, too. I have strong circumstantial evidence against your son,

Mrs. Owens. I can't plant a wire on you—they'd never let you out of here for that—but if you were to testify against your son or reproduce letters in which he confessed the murders to you or get him to talk about his crime on the telephone, I could talk to my superiors and see if they're willing to work a deal. Maybe get you out of here someday while you're still able."

He knew she'd been sentenced to life without possibility of parole. If she was at all intrigued by his offer, she didn't show it. Her eyes were hard, her feelings buried deep beneath a sad, weary face that had once been admired under the bright lights of a Broadway stage.

He leaned forward. "Can't guarantee anything, of course. But you think about it. Think about it long and hard."

She just watched him, eyes flickering.

"In the meantime, I'd like to find out where your son is. You see, Erin Walker isn't the only one he's killed. There've been four more murders—four young women who had nothing to do with Erin Walker—and we believe Haydon was involved in all of them."

Ginny raised an eyebrow but said nothing.

"Details in the latest murder tell me he's getting careless and desperate. He will look for another victim—another innocent victim—if we don't find him first."

Something inside her broke. Her voice quavered. "Donny's a good boy. I told him the computer classes would help him find a better job. I told him the magic wouldn't do him any good, that it would only lead to a dead end, but do you think he would listen to his own mother? I told him to wait, to let me find him a good wife, but he wouldn't listen. He had to go looking for glory. He had to—"

"Mrs. Owens, I'm not sure you heard me. Haydon has killed *five* women. Someone else may be in danger *right now*. Do you want another daughter to die? If you tell me where Haydon is, we can save someone's life."

Her eyes moistened as her gaze drifted away. "I knew something was wrong. I knew the trial would shatter him. He was never the same after that."

"Do you know where he is?"

She smeared tears away, her emotions under control again, and fixed Riley with a hard stare. "If you think I want to see my son locked up in a place like this, think again."

"We're right on his heels, Mrs. Owens, and the net's tightening."

"But things can't be quite as neat and tidy as you'd like to make out, are they? That's why you're here, isn't it? You need something else to cinch the deal. Otherwise we wouldn't be having this conversation."

Riley kept his face impassive, betraying nothing. She wasn't stupid. So far, everything he had on Haydon *was* circumstantial; he would need hard, solid evidence to put him behind bars. If he could find Haydon, he could get his fingerprints and DNA. He *could* cinch the deal, as she put it.

"We're going to catch him sooner or later, with or without your help, so your participation isn't crucial. But like I said, if you cooperate, I could investigate a deal that could get you parole."

Ginny shook her head, a husky chuckle resonating in her throat. "You've got the wrong guy. My son does simple vanishing tricks. He'd never strangle anybody, least of all with a magician's trick rope."

The fact that the rope was a magician's trick rope was a detail law enforcement had withheld from the media. Riley locked eyes with her. "Whoever said anything about a trick rope? Ma'am, I think you know a whole lot more about this case than you're telling me."

She stared at him, stricken. Rising, she turned and disappeared through the door. A guard closed the door behind her.

CHAPTER 66

TEN MINUTES AFTER THE abrupt ending to his interview with Virginia Owens, Riley was on the phone with his friends at the FBI. Once they heard his story, they didn't need much persuading to see the importance of getting a subpoena to seize Virginia Owens's mail.

"You understand what I'm saying?" Riley said into his cell phone as he drove to Columbus. "She's probably been corresponding with her son. We have a golden opportunity here to track him down."

Special Agent Mitch Reed sounded tired but understanding. "Look, Chuck, we've got to get a judge to issue a subpoena, and these things take time."

"Yeah, yeah, I know. But someone's life may be in jeopardy. I would think that—"

"Look, I should have word soon."

"How soon?"

"Soon. That's all I can say."

Realizing he was strangling the steering wheel, Riley forced himself to relax. "Sorry to be so pushy, Mitch. It's just that I've been waiting a long time for this kind of lead. It's hard not to rush forward, and—"

"Hold on, Chuck."

The phone went silent for a moment before some cheerful elevator music began to serenade Riley. He rolled his eyes and checked his watch.

Fortunately, Mitch Reed's bass voice soon returned to the line. "Good news. I should have the subpoena within the hour. If Virginia Owens has been corresponding with her son, we'll find his address. The prison is already monitoring her personal phone calls. We'll get the recordings of those as well."

Riley sighed. It was too good to be true. "You've got my number. Call me as soon as you learn anything."

"I will. Talk to you later."

Riley closed his phone and offered a prayer of thanks.

Thank you, Father. I could never have gotten to this point without You.

He checked his watch. It was after three. He had plenty of time to drive to Columbus, where he could catch a flight via Detroit to the grandly named Chippewa County International Airport in Sault Ste. Marie. From there, he'd drive to Newberry, about an hour away. It would be a late night, but it would be worth it. He could hardly wait to see Marc's face when he told him the news.

CHAPTER 67

As Marc drove them home in silence, Gillian kept her eyes fixed out the passenger-side window, where not even a single pinprick of light pierced the impenetrable blackness. She was again reminded of how remote Whistler's Point was and how easily someone could be in peril without anyone knowing.

She pushed the dark thoughts aside to make room for happier ones. Crystal's opening-night performance had exceeded everyone's expectations, including her own. Gillian's heart swelled with pride when she remembered how confidently Crystal had performed on stage, her clear, controlled voice holding the audience spellbound. Her performance had even rivaled her previous appearance as Maria in Chicago. Crystal's voice teacher, Maria Rivera, would have been proud.

That was my daughter, Lord. My daughter. Thank You.

Gillian sighed. What an evening! She and Marc had joined Pastor Randall and his wife for dinner at a supper club before taking in the performance from the front row.

When your daughter has the lead role, I guess you can expect certain privileges.

Gillian glanced at her watch and tried to shake off her apprehension. It was almost half past ten. Crystal had promised them she'd drive home shortly after changing out of her costume and checking in with Betty Jamison for a brief cast meeting.

"Do you think we should have waited for Crystal and followed her home?" Gillian asked, breaking the silence. "Maybe I should call her."

Marc shook his head. "I'm sure she's fine. The whole cast was still there when we left, and she said she'd drive straight home."

"I suppose you're right." She glanced at Marc, wondering why he was so quiet tonight. Was something on his mind? "I noticed that you and Pastor Randall talked quite a bit during intermission."

"He's getting up in years, and he's tired."

Gillian laughed. "Well, who wouldn't be? How many years has he been a pastor up here? Thirty-five years?"

"Forty-two to be exact."

Gillian shook her head, unable to fathom so many years—not to mention cold winters—in the North Woods.

"I can't help wondering who's going to take his place when he re-tires." He paused. "You know, Gill, maybe this is the type of place where we could serve."

She studied his face in the dim glow of the instrument panel to be sure he wasn't joking. "You mean, you want to stay up here in the woods? Don't you miss Chicago?"

"Well, sure. But there's something about this place. And the people are so needy."

"People are needy everywhere, Marc." She wanted him to meet her gaze, to grasp the full import of her words. But he kept his eyes on the road. "Where are you going with this?"

Marc wiped a hand across his face. "Pastor Randall told me he's thinking about retiring. He asked me to consider serving for a while on an interim basis until they can find someone to serve on a more permanent basis."

She stared at him. "You're serious."

The steady hum of rubber on pavement mingled with the purr of the engine.

Marc nodded. "It would only be temporary."

"Well, that's good."

"But you never know. It could become more permanent down the road if that's how the Lord leads." He finally glanced in her direction and met her gaze. "I know. I can see it in your eyes that you don't like the idea. But we don't have to commit to anything right away. It's just something to think about."

Something to think about. For months she'd been longing to return to Chicago, and now he was telling her this? But she had to admit that living at Whistler's Point had its perks. She enjoyed seeing Marc throughout the day, and he had more time for family life—something that had been sorely lacking in Chicago. If they moved back now, would anything be different, or would he just get sucked back into the rat race?

Something to think about.

❋ ❋ ❋

After reaching the caretaker's house, Gillian put a kettle on the kitchen stove, and they enjoyed a cup of tea. A half hour later, standing at the kitchen counter, she peered out the window into the dark, opaque night and shivered. Only a week ago, Stacey James had been strangled outside their house, and the killer had never been identified. Did that mean he'd left the area? Or was he still prowling around outside somewhere? Could he be watching her right now?

Marc came up and hugged her from behind, his chin resting on her shoulder.

"She's late," Gillian said.

"Relax. I'm sure she's on her way."

Gillian reached for her purse to get her cell phone. "I'm calling her."

"Give her fifteen more minutes. C'mon, Gill. She's seventeen."

She heeded his advice, but watched the clock like a hawk. When the time was up and Crystal still wasn't home, Gillian couldn't scramble to her purse and call her fast enough. She listened to the phone ring, her eyes fixed on the peeling wallpaper in the corner of the room. One ring. Two rings.

C'mon, Crystal, where are you? Pick up!

Five rings. Six rings.

She glanced at Marc. "Why doesn't she answer?"

He didn't say a word, his face impassive, but she knew what he was thinking. *Gillian, you're just being an overprotective mother as usual. Crystal's a big girl.* Yeah, well, Stacey was a big girl, too, and look what happened to her.

Gillian snapped her phone shut and began to pace the room. "I don't like it. Something's wrong."

She imagined Crystal crouched on the side of the road trying to change a flat tire. A stranger was approaching silently from behind.

She tried calling Crystal again. Still no answer. She folded her arms across her chest and ran her hands up and down her arms. She couldn't get warm.

"Marc, do you think you could—"

"Go look for her?" He nodded, an understanding glint in his eyes. "You're right. It's late, and we should know where our daughter is right now."

CHAPTER 68

AFTER MARC LEFT, GILLIAN called Betty Jamison, the director of the play, and felt embarrassed when she heard a sleepy voice answer on the other end. "Please forgive me for calling you so late," Gillian said. "Crystal should be home by now, and we don't know where she is."

"That's strange," Betty said. "Everybody left the theater over an hour ago."

"Perhaps you saw her leave with some of her friends?"

"Crystal has been working hard at getting to know some of the other cast members. Lately, she's been talking to Eric a lot. Maybe she was with him. I don't remember."

"Eric?"

"Eric White. He's on the stage crew. He's really very good and seems to have more stage experience than he's letting on." She paused. "Sorry. Here I'm rambling, and you're trying to find your daughter, who, by the way, did a fantastic job on opening night."

Gillian's heart swelled. "Thanks."

"I'm sorry I can't be more helpful. We had a brief cast meeting to touch base. Everybody seemed tuckered out and talked about how much they were looking forward to heading home and going to bed."

Gillian thanked Betty for her help, hung up, and went upstairs, heading down the hall to Crystal's bedroom. She felt uneasy about poking around her daughter's room, but perhaps Crystal had left something on her desk indicating where she might have gone. She frequently referred to the electronic to-do list she kept on her computer's desktop.

Gillian sat at Crystal's desk and faced her computer monitor.

Moving the mouse, she noticed that the computer appeared to be in standby mode. The screen slowly brightened, and Crystal's colorful desktop glowed to life. Glancing around the screen, she didn't see anything resembling a to-do list. What she *did* notice was a minimized box in the lower right-hand corner. The box was blinking orange as if communicating some type of alert.

Glancing at the door, wondering if Crystal might walk in at any moment, Gillian clicked on the blinking box. A window popped up on the screen. Someone had recently sent Crystal an instant message, which meant she was logged onto the Internet right now.

> **Houdini409:** You better hide. I'm coming for you soon.

Gillian's breath hitched in her throat. The planet seemed to tilt beneath her, and she struggled for equilibrium.

Houdini.

The Magician Murderer.

There had to be a connection.

God, no!

Lurching from Crystal's desk, Gillian dashed down the hall and stumbled down the stairs to the kitchen.

My baby! The Magician Murderer's after my baby.

At the bottom of the stairs, she glanced around helplessly, her nerves frayed. Where was her purse? She remembered putting her cell phone back inside. She needed to let Marc know, to hear him apologize for thinking she was just being an overprotective mother.

There it was, on the kitchen table. She reached for the purse, her shaking hands accidentally knocking it to the floor. Cosmetics, loose change, and a small bottle of hand cream spilled out. Her blue cell phone skidded across the hardwood floor.

She snatched up the phone, her hands trembling, and dialed Marc's number.

Somewhere in the house, she heard Marc's familiar ringtone.

Following the sound upstairs to the bedroom, her heart sinking, she slumped onto the edge of the bed in defeat. Marc had changed his clothes and must have grabbed a more casual jacket on the way out, leaving his cell phone here.

She couldn't call Marc. She couldn't do anything.

Except pray.

＊   ＊   ＊

As Marc sped down the road toward town, becoming more worried by the moment, he spotted a familiar Cutlass Ciera and felt himself relax. Flashing his lights at Crystal, he pulled over to the shoulder. He was reaching for his cell phone to call Gillian with the news when he realized that he'd left it at home.

The Cutlass Ciera did a U-turn and pulled behind the Tahoe. Crystal hopped out.

Marc got out of the Tahoe and strode toward his daughter. "Where have you been?" He regretted the anger simmering in his voice but was unable to disguise it.

Crystal's forehead was furrowed in confusion. "I got held up for a while."

"Why didn't you call and tell us? Your mother's been worried sick."

"Sorry. Some of us decided to stay late and spend extra time on our lines. What's the big deal?"

"The big deal is that your mother's been trying to call you, and you haven't been answering your phone. That's why we got you the phone, so this sort of thing wouldn't happen."

Forehead furrowed, Crystal dug into her purse and found her phone. "Oh, that explains it. Sorry, I left the phone on vibrate, not wanting it to go off backstage during the performance."

Marc reached for her phone. "Do you mind if I borrow it for a sec? I need to call your mother before she goes into cardiac arrest."

＊   ＊   ＊

When Marc and Crystal reached Whistler's Point and ascended the steps to the front porch, Gillian bolted out the door and threw her arms around Crystal, pulling her close.

"I'm okay, Mom," Crystal said. "I'm sorry for scaring you like that."

They pulled apart, and Gillian pressed a trembling hand to Crystal's face. "It doesn't matter. I'm just glad you're okay."

Marc noticed Gillian's tear-stained face. "What about *you*, Gill. Are you okay?"

Gillian wiped her face. "No, I'm not okay. There's something I didn't tell you." She turned to Crystal. "I saw something on your computer, Crystal. Something terrible."

"Why were you in my room?" Crystal asked, a slight edge to her voice.

"I'm sorry, sweetie. I didn't mean to snoop, but I thought maybe you'd left something on your electronic to-do list to explain where you were. I saw something else."

Gillian led them into the house, and they climbed the stairs, quickly crowding into Crystal's small room. Studying her computer, Marc read the instant message and felt his stomach clench. He glanced at Gillian and saw visceral fear reflected in her eyes. Hadn't Riley said that the Magician Murderer cyber-stalked his victims before the murders?

Marc's cell phone rang, making Gillian jump. Marc grabbed the phone, wondering what else could possibly happen tonight.

It was Riley. "I've got important news. I'm sorry for calling so late. I hope I didn't wake you."

Marc scratched the stubble on his chin. "No, you're fine. We haven't gone to bed yet. In fact, it's unlikely we'll be getting to sleep anytime soon. We've got a real situation here." He told Chuck about the instant message and didn't need to point out its possible implications.

Riley's voice pulsed with urgency. "Go lock your doors, Marc. Lock all of them and close the drapes. Now."

"Okay, I'm doing it as we talk." Marc turned to leave Crystal's room, Gillian's concerned eyes watching him go.

"Got a gun?"

"Yeah." The stairs slid under Marc's feet.

"Then go get it."

"Okay."

"Did you call the police yet?"

"No."

"Don't worry about it. I'll call them for you. You need to keep Crystal safe."

Marc drew the drapes on the kitchen windows. "So this is really that bad?"

"It's worse, Marc. Look, just stay put. I'm on my way. I flew into Sault Ste. Marie, and I'm driving to your place now. I should be there sometime between twelve-thirty and one. Wait up for me."

It's not like any of us are going to sleep anyhow. "Okay, Riley."

"We're going to catch this killer, Marc. Do you hear me? He just made his last threat."

CHAPTER 69

SITTING ON CRYSTAL'S BED, holding her daughter close, Gillian checked her watch and sighed. It was after 1:00 AM. Normally, she never would have been able to stay awake this late, but ever since Marc had told her about his phone conversation with Riley, she'd felt wired. The police had arrived moments ago and were watching the house while they waited for Riley to arrive. Their presence at least gave her some relief.

She glanced past the computer, which now felt evil to her, and took in Crystal's bookshelf crammed with Web site programming and design manuals. In contrast, the smiling faces of opera singers Cecilia Bartoli, Beverly Sills, Kathleen Battle, and Kiri Te Kanawa adorned her tackboard.

Gillian shook her head. Computers and classical music. What a weird combination!

"Mom, you *can* go to bed, you know," Crystal said.

"You really think I could sleep at a time like this?"

Crystal sighed. "Don't you think everyone is overreacting just a tad?"

Gillian pulled back and peered into her daughter's eyes. "No, Crystal, I don't think we are. Your father and I know some things that Riley told us. We decided not to tell you because we didn't want you to be upset."

"Well, don't you think it's high time somebody told me what's going on? I'm not a child, you know."

Gillian told Crystal as much as she felt she could tell her. She finished by saying, "Now do you understand why we've been concerned about you? It didn't help when you changed your plans tonight without telling us."

Crystal was staring off into space, obviously stunned by the news. "Sorry, I guess I should have called you."

Reaching out, Gillian tucked a lock of blonde hair behind Crystal's ear. "Sweetie, I know you didn't mean to scare us, but the situation being what it is, you just can't be too careful. You're a beautiful girl, and there are evil men in this world. Someone murdered Stacey James, and the police haven't caught him yet. That's why you need to be extra careful."

Crystal steered her gaze back to her mom. "You're right. Ryan has told me to be careful like a thousand times."

"Have you been in touch with him lately?"

"Yeah, we do the whole Facebook and chat thing a few times each week. He's doing great."

Gillian smiled. "I'm glad you guys are staying in touch. Ryan's a sharp guy who really loves the Lord."

Crystal grinned. "You don't have to tell me that, Mom. I know. I miss him like crazy."

"But from what I hear from Mrs. Jamison, you've been spending time with this Eric White character."

"Oh, Eric." She shrugged. "He doesn't have many friends. I thought I'd be nice to him."

"Does he know about Ryan?"

"Oh yeah. I've told Eric all about Ryan."

"How well do you know Eric? Do you think he'd send you a chat message like that?"

"I don't know him well, but I don't think he would have done anything like that. At first, I thought somebody on the musical cast was playing games with me. But it isn't anybody from the musical, unless somebody's lying. I asked everybody."

Her eyes widened in desperation as she fell into Gillian's arms. "The creep won't leave me alone, Mom. He keeps sending me these nasty messages." She paused. "He says he's going to kill me."

* * *

Gillian and Crystal headed downstairs when they heard Marc greeting Riley at the front door. Entering the kitchen, Gillian greeted the detective, whose face looked fatigued yet strangely energized. Without further delay, Riley asked Crystal to show him any conversations she'd had with Houdini409. Crystal had already printed out her chat logs, and Riley spread them out on the kitchen table, studying them closely while everyone looked on. Reading the first chat conversation, Gillian felt her skin prickle.

You don't want to waste what precious little time you have left.

"I don't mean to frighten any of you," Riley said, "but we are very fortunate we found out about these chat messages when we did." He glanced at Crystal. "And, young lady, you're lucky to be alive. Chat messages just like yours were found on the computers of all the victims I've investigated. The difference is, you're alive, and they aren't."

"Mom told me about what's going on," Crystal said. "You mean, the same guy who went after those girls in Cincinnati could be coming after me?"

"That's exactly what I'm saying."

"Wow. I thought somebody was just playing a joke or something."

Riley nodded. "That's probably what those other girls thought, too."

"What happens now?" Marc's face was ashen.

"Things may feel like a circus for a while. Sheriff Dendridge is sending a couple of deputies over right now. Obviously, they'll need to take Crystal's computer."

"But what about my business?" Crystal cried.

"Your business will have to wait." Marc's voice was edged with fear. "It's more important that you're safe and that the police try to track this guy down."

Riley nodded. "This is one sick monster. With the exception of Stacey James, he's always cyber-stalked his victims before he killed them. During the weeks leading up to the murders, he even stole their trash. That's probably how he learned so much about them."

Crystal turned silent and folded her arms across her chest. Gillian could tell she was upset about losing her computer, but she was also pretty sure her daughter understood the gravity of the situation.

"The sheriff is also starting around-the-clock surveillance," Riley continued. "From now on, an officer will be parked in front of your house twenty-four seven. I'd rather not take any chances."

Gillian nodded, her fear somewhat lessened by a sense of gratitude. "But what about the musical?"

"Starting tomorrow, she'll have a police escort to and from the performances."

I'll be there, too, and I won't let her out of my sight, Gillian thought.

Crystal was shaking her head, eyes on the ceiling, clearly shell-shocked. Life as she knew it had just ended. "How long is this going to last?"

"I wish I knew," Riley said. "A forensics team will be studying your computer. The killer is a computer expert and knows how to hide, but they might find something on your hard drive. If they do, we might catch this guy right away."

Crystal looked far from encouraged. "And if they don't?"

Riley shrugged. "Then we wait. With the increased security, he might leave you alone and go after somebody else. Or he might still try getting to you somehow. Officers will be watching around the clock, but until this guy's caught, we'll need to take special precautions. I'll give you a can of Mace to keep with you at all times."

Gillian bowed her head and rubbed her forehead, sensing the beginnings of a headache. *God, this can't be happening.*

Ten minutes later, the sheriff's deputies arrived and took Crystal's computer away while she looked on sullenly, Gillian's arms around her. "I still don't get why they want my computer," she said.

Riley smiled patiently. "You work with computers, so this is good for you to know. Each e-mail message and instant message bears an important piece of information called the 'sender's Internet protocol address.' This IP address enables investigators to track down the sender's identity through his Internet service provider and ultimately through his phone or cable company."

"Wow! That's all there is to it?"

Riley shook his head. "Unfortunately, not always. There are ways to hide. For example, a lot of hotels offer free Internet access now. Someone could log on anonymously from the hotel parking lot, create a bogus e-mail address, and send threatening e-mails that way, too. Nobody would be able to track him down."

"Amazing!"

"But I don't think the Magician Murderer works that way," he said. "I think he uses special software to hide his tracks, perhaps software he custom-wrote for himself. Whatever it is, it's sophisticated."

✷ ✷ ✷

Riley led Marc around the house and checked all the windows and door locks. Another police car pulled into their driveway and slowed to a stop. It gave Gillian some comfort to know that the man sitting behind the wheel was watching out for them, but she wondered how they would get any sleep tonight, knowing some crazy person wished Crystal harm.

Pushing the drapes aside, she peered out the window and wondered who could be out there in the dark, watching them. Riley had said the killer was showing an unprecedented level of desperation. He'd strangled Stacey outside their house. But what was stopping him from venturing inside? And if he tried getting to Crystal, would he do so tonight? Tomorrow? Next week?

Gillian gripped the drapes until her knuckles turned white. *Whenever it is, he'll have to get past me first.*

CHAPTER 70

UNABLE TO SLEEP AFTER seeing Crystal's performance in the musical, Haydon rose and stealthily made his way to the old caretaker's house. There he observed the Thayer family's activities as best as he could past drawn drapes and closed blinds, as he had done countless times before.

Peering around the tree where he was hiding, Haydon was surprised to see a parked police car and a deputy watching the house. So Crystal had narked on him. That meant she was scared, a fact that thrilled him. He wanted her to be scared.

The police surveillance made his entrance more challenging but not impossible. He was up to the game. In many ways, the challenge would make his victory all the more triumphant.

He'd never gone after a victim inside her own home before, and the possibility of such a challenge excited him. His mother's voice whispered in his ear: *Desperate times call for desperate measures, Donny.*

Just then, the tall shape of a man's form crossed one of the windows, making his pulse race. Marc Thayer was a problem, but one he could easily eliminate.

An orange glow suddenly emanated from behind Crystal's blinds. He imagined what she would have thought had she known that the policeman sitting in his car was asleep and that he was standing just beneath her window.

Plotting her demise.

He could have easily reached the roof's overhang by climbing the tree and lowering himself down one of its limbs. Within seconds, he could be through her window and upon her before she could make a sound.

But no, he thought with a smile. He had other plans. She would never see him coming.

CHAPTER 71

MARC TRIED TO PERSUADE Gillian to go to bed as usual, assuring her that Crystal would be fine with police protection and really needed her rest for Friday night's performance. But Gillian insisted on spending the rest of the night in a sleeping bag next to Crystal's bed. She didn't care if Marc thought she was overreacting; she wasn't letting Crystal out of her sight. She expected Crystal to be irritated by being treated like a little girl, but to her surprise, Crystal had just the opposite reaction.

"Cool! We can pretend we're camping. I just wish we could cook s'mores or something."

In the process of unrolling her sleeping bag, Gillian stopped. "Well, why not? I've got graham crackers and Hershey's downstairs, and I'm pretty sure I've got marshmallows in the pantry somewhere. Let's go look."

Giggling like silly schoolgirls, they ventured downstairs and searched the kitchen cupboards. Gillian was bent over, pushing the lazy Susan around in search of the marshmallows, when she sensed someone at her back and jumped.

"Do you know what time it is?" Marc had changed into a T-shirt and running shorts and stood with his toothbrush clutched comically in his hand. "It's after two. Are the two of you going to get some sleep or what?"

"We're going to try to, Dad." Crystal grinned at him while clutching several Hershey's chocolate bars. "We just wanted a snack."

"Uh-huh."

"Would you like a s'more?" Gillian offered.

Marc's expression told Gillian that he was certain she'd finally lost her mind. "No thanks. Good night."

⁎   ⁎   ⁎

Somehow, they slept, though Gillian wasn't sure how they managed after their nocturnal feast. They talked for a while about all sorts of topics that mothers and daughters should talk about more often but rarely do. Exhaustion must have finally kicked in because Gillian woke to the sound of the silly cowboy ditty ringtone on Marc's phone.

She sat up in alarm, stiff from sleeping on the floor, and wondered where she was. Then everything came back to her like a sledgehammer to the back of the head. The news of Crystal's stalker. The police protection. Her decision to sleep on the floor beside Crystal's bed.

Crystal was still out cold, an arm flung over her pretty face. The window blinds were oozing toward gray. Glimpsing the alarm clock and realizing it was after seven, Gillian got up, donned her housecoat, and crept downstairs.

Hearing Marc's voice, she found him in the kitchen leaning against the counter, his cell phone to his ear. "I understand," he was saying. "Of course."

Sunlight was streaming through the kitchen window, casting tall shadows across the floor. She lingered in the doorway, not wanting to interrupt Marc, but he noticed her anyhow. After hanging up, he turned toward her, his stubbly face pale, his eyes bloodshot. No mystery who'd gotten the least sleep.

"Long night?" She ran fingers through her hair, wondering if she looked any better than he did.

"Kind of hard to get shut-eye when you know some magician psycho is dead set on strangling your daughter."

Gillian padded toward the sink. "I'll make some extra-strong coffee. I think we both could use it." She looked in the cupboard for the grounds.

"That was Dave Ritchie," Marc said to her back. "Apparently the medical examiner is going to release Stacey's body today. He called to let me know about the funeral. Bruce wants me there."

Keeping her back to him, scooping coffee into a filter, Gillian said nothing. How many times had they had this conversation before? It was one thing to care about others; it was another to let them rule your life at the expense of your own family.

She didn't need to hear what he said next because she already had his lines memorized. *I really ought to be there, Gill. After all, I was one of Stacey's counselors. It's only right that I'm there to comfort the grieving family. I'm sure you understand.*

"I'm not going," he said.

She turned, measuring spoon poised in her hand, certain she'd misunderstood.

"You heard me. I'm staying here. How could I leave now when we've got a killer practically on our doorstep?"

Rushing toward him, unable to contain herself, Gillian buried her face in his chest and wrapped both arms around him in a massive hug. Finally, he was putting her and Crystal first. He must have realized how badly they needed him.

But what had changed his heart?

When they pulled apart, he kissed her, and something awoke inside. She didn't know what it was. It was a part of her she thought had died long ago. Standing in the kitchen in an embrace, just the two of them, the light reflecting off her new diamond ring, she reveled in the intimacy of the moment.

Something had changed between them. Perhaps she was just overtired; she wasn't sure. But whatever it was—it was right. She felt like she finally had her husband back after all those rocky years. He was staying, and she wasn't letting go.

Part 3

THE HUNTED

I fled Him, down the nights and
*   down the days;*
I fled Him, down the arches of the
*   years;*
I fled Him, down the labyrinthine
*   ways*
Of my own mind; and in the midst
*   of tears*
I hid from Him, and under running
*   laughter.*
Up vistaed hopes I sped;
And shot, precipitated,
Adown Titanic glooms of chasmed
*   fears,*
From those strong Feet that followed,
*   followed after.*

                —Francis Thompson,
              "The Hound of Heaven"

CHAPTER 72

From: Houdini409@internetmail.com
To: Java4Jesus@emailbox.net
Subject: I'm watching you

Your days are numbered. Prepare to meet your maker.

LEANING BACK IN HIS black leather chair, Haydon eyed his bank of monitors and measured the words in the e-mail he was composing. He inserted a couple more sentences, then deleted them. He played with adjectives and adverbs, carefully measuring the nuance of each word, but finally deleted them as well.

He wanted just the right effect.

He particularly hesitated over the word *maker*. If he capitalized the word, he would be conceding the existence of God. He smirked. *God is dead, and that's just fine by me.* The word remained in lowercase.

Five minutes later, satisfied, he hit the Send button and watched his e-mail disappear somewhere into an invisible world of computer codes; routers; and phone, DSL, and cable lines. It was a world where he felt the most comfortable, a world where he could hide without detection.

Resting his head against the back of his chair, he imagined how Crystal would feel when she received his e-mail. Would his words hit the mark?

Since yesterday, he'd been sending her chat messages, but she didn't appear to be using her instant messenger anymore. Or if she was, she wasn't responding. So he'd resorted to e-mails. Those were more traceable than instant messages, but he knew he'd cloaked himself well.

He silently thanked his mother for recommending the computer classes years ago. Quickly past the basics, he'd entered a technological world mastered by only a few.

He closed his eyes and imagined Crystal Thayer's blue eyes, her blonde hair, her wire rim glasses. Since the opening performance of *The Sound of Music*, he hadn't been able to get her off his mind. After the play, unable to sleep, he'd driven to the lighthouse. He couldn't delay the visit a moment longer. The visit was still vivid in his memory.

But he wanted more than a memory. He realized it was almost time to make his move.

Not long now.

CHAPTER 73

TRUE TO THE FORECAST, a cold front swept in on Friday, bringing a bracing chill that sailed right through Gillian. Snow was in the forecast. Lots of it. But the play went off without a hitch on Friday night. A policeman escorted Crystal to the performance, which Marc and Gillian attended, and then they all caravanned back to Whistler's Point. They waved to the policeman who was watching their house as they went inside.

Saturday came without event. No strange calls. No suspicious visitors at their front door. No intruders on the property.

Nothing.

Had the killer given up on Crystal? Gillian hoped so, but a strange sense of foreboding told her their ordeal wasn't over yet. She knew she wouldn't relax until the last performance was over and until they were all safe in Chicago for Christmas. But that was still weeks away. A lot could happen before then. *God, please protect her.*

For the Saturday matinee, Crystal had reserved seats so Marc and Gillian could sit with Nicole and the Hendersons on the front row. Gillian realized the matinee was her last chance to see Nicole, who would be flying to Boston tomorrow to spend the winter with family. She would return to Whistler's Point in the spring, when the tourist season began again. *But we won't be here, will we?* Gillian thought.

For the first time, the thought of not returning to the North Woods filled her with profound sadness. The place had grown on her, and she couldn't dismiss the fact that she had mixed feelings about leaving.

Every day, she prayed Nicole would turn to Christ, but she wasn't going to pressure her. Nicole had promised to e-mail and to visit a good Bible-believing church that Gillian had found for her in Boston.

✳ ✳ ✳

Though Crystal had done a fine job on Friday night, Gillian thought she especially shone during the Saturday matinee. After the final curtain call, Gillian and Marc rushed backstage with Nicole and the Hendersons to congratulate Crystal on her fine performance.

"Did you like it?" Crystal asked after Gillian hugged her.

"What a silly question," Gillian said. "Of course we did. You were wonderful, as usual."

"You seem so natural on stage," Nicole said. "Weren't you nervous?"

"Well, yeah. I always feel a little nervous at first. But once I get into the story, I just let myself go."

A thin young man stood awkwardly at Crystal's side. He looked oddly familiar, but Gillian couldn't place him.

"Oh, Mom, before I forget, this is Eric White. Remember? I told you about him. All the cool lighting effects you saw tonight were his idea."

Gillian hid her distaste at Eric's sweaty handshake and assumed he was just nervous. "It's very nice to meet you, Eric."

"Actually we met once already, at the library," Eric said.

So that's how she knew him. "Oh, yes. I remember now. You work there."

He nodded, leaving an awkward pause in the conversation. "I need to go take care of some things. I'll see you later, Crystal."

"At the cast party, right?"

"I wouldn't miss it," Eric threw over his shoulder as he walked away.

Gillian turned to Crystal. "Cast party? What cast party?"

Crystal sighed. "Remember, Mom? I told you about it on Monday."

Gillian glanced at Marc, shaking her head. "Good grief. I forgot all about it." She turned to Crystal. "We said you could go, didn't we?"

"Yeah, Mom, you did. But don't worry. A policeman will be watching Mrs. Jamison's house, and there'll be a crowd. I'll be safe. Eric said he'd drive me home."

"No offense to Eric," Marc said, "but you're supposed to have a police escort, remember?"

Crystal rolled her eyes. "For crying out loud, Dad. How long is this going to go on? I can't have a policeman at my elbow for the rest of my life."

"It's only until this guy's caught," Marc said. "Look, why don't you come with us? We'll drop you off at the cast party. Then, when the party's winding down, just call me, and I'll come pick you up. The weather's supposed to be bad tonight. I'd feel better if I drove you."

Not really having a choice, Crystal nodded reluctantly. "I'll go tell Eric I don't need a ride."

* * *

Gillian pulled Nicole into a hug, her throat tight. "Promise me you'll stay in touch." Standing at Nicole's car, they pulled apart.

"I'll e-mail or call every week. I promise." Nicole wiped tears away with her fingertips. "And thanks for your talks, Gillian. Seriously. You may not realize how helpful they were at the time. And I'm still thinking about what you said."

Gillian nodded and glanced away, fighting an overwhelming sense of disappointment. She so badly wanted to see Nicole turn to Christ. She hated to see her new friend leave without making that important decision. *But God does the saving*, her mom had told her so many times. *All we can do is open our mouths and speak the truth.*

Gillian took a deep breath and touched her arm. "Well, take care of yourself, okay?"

A low was coming in, and the bracing wind tousled Nicole's black bangs as she opened her car door. She turned. "I should be saying the same thing to you. Let me know when the police catch this monster, okay? I want to know Crystal's safe."

Gillian nodded as Nicole climbed into her car and started the engine. She felt Marc's arm around her, his squeeze comforting. She waved as Nicole drove away.

* * *

After dropping Crystal off at Betty Jamison's, Marc and Gillian headed back to Whistler's Point in the Tahoe. It was after 3:30 PM, and the sky was heavy with snow clouds. As they drove, Gillian peered at the sky and bit her lip. What if the weather became worse than the weatherman had predicted? What if the forecast of eight inches of snow really meant a couple of feet? She didn't like the idea of Marc and Crystal's being out on the roads with severe weather headed their way.

She thought about the party and wondered if there would be beer or loud music. Then she reminded herself that Betty Jamison was hosting the party. Certainly, the high school teacher wouldn't be serving alcohol to minors, and a wild party didn't seem consistent with what she knew about her.

Simmer down, she told herself. *Sooner or later, Crystal has to start making choices on her own.* But she couldn't push her uneasiness aside. She didn't know what was bothering her, but something didn't feel right.

A flutter of white drifted down from the sky and swirled against the windshield. Gillian peered at the snowflakes in dismay, a sinking feeling in the pit of her stomach. The snow predictions had been accurate after all.

CHAPTER 74

RILEY PEERED OUT HIS hotel room window with concern. Heavy snow had begun falling an hour ago, and the ache in his knees was confirmation that a big storm had descended upon the region.

Earlier, he had called Emily and told her how the investigation was going and how much he missed her. After hearing her eternal optimism and a passage of Scripture from her devotions, he had promised he'd be in touch and said good-bye.

He had barely hung up when his cell phone chirped. It was Sheriff Dendridge.

"Good news for Marc," he said. "His phone records checked out. No suspicious phone calls to or from anyone who could have been Stacey James. Anyhow, I guess that pretty much gets Marc off the hook. We have no forensic evidence connecting him to Stacey's death. And there are no phone records or anything else to show he even knew she was in town until she showed up to see him."

"Glad to hear it," Riley said.

"Also, I just got off the phone with Mitch Reed." Apparently, the sheriff had been informed of the FBI's subpoena on Virginia Owens's mail and phone calls. "And I'm afraid I've got bad news. The only mail Virginia Owens has received from her son, Haydon, came from his old mailing address in Cincinnati more than two months ago. He hasn't been in touch with her since."

The sheriff sounded sympathetic this time, instead of secretly triumphant that Riley's investigation was stymied. In fact, miracle of miracles, he'd even agreed to Riley's request that the FBI forensics team examine Stacey's body, though they hadn't found anything the medical examiner hadn't already seen. "Hey, I'm sorry—I really mean it. I'm afraid this investigation isn't going to be as quick and simple as we'd hoped."

If Riley were a swearing man, as he'd been years ago, a few colorful words would have come in handy to describe his mood at the moment. But the Holy Spirit pricked his heart, reminding him of God's sovereignty. Dendridge was listening, and Riley realized his response could show the sheriff how a Christian responds to trouble.

He didn't exactly say, "Praise the Lord!" but he *did* say, "Thanks for letting me know."

Riley hung up, impressed by the sheriff's police work. He turned back to his room, where manila case file folders representing the Magician Murders investigation were organized in neat piles across the floor. For all he knew, Dendridge had leads he wasn't sharing with him, but that was okay. What did it matter? Riley didn't care who made the arrest. As long as Haydon Owens was apprehended and God got the glory—that's what was important.

Sighing, he shook his head. Was his own investigation going anywhere? Posters of Haydon Owens had blanketed the entire county, but so far the only tips the sheriff's office had received had gone nowhere. Owens was either in the area and no longer resembled the man in the poster, or he had been spooked by the posters and, realizing the police were closing in, had packed his bags and fled to some other out-of-the-way town to start over. Riley hated to consider the possibility.

Father, please don't let it be so. He's gotta be here. Please show me how to find him.

An uneasiness he couldn't explain gnawed at his gut. He reached for his coffee, which he'd sweetened with hazelnut creamer, and took a sip. Staring at the files, he rubbed a hand across his balding head. There had to be something here he'd missed, but he'd read through these documents countless times. What could there possibly be that he hadn't seen before?

His gaze landed on a folder crammed with information about Harry Houdini, the famous American magician who had reached the zenith of his popularity in the 1920s. Four years ago, after learning about the e-mail and instant messages to Erin Walker bearing the

Houdini handle, Riley had researched the life of Houdini, hoping for greater insight into the Magician Murderer's psychological profile. At the time, the research had failed to unveil any earth-shattering revelations. Still, he didn't regret doing the research; he'd learned long ago that a seemingly unimportant detail can sometimes crack a case wide open.

Sitting at the cramped, walnut veneer desk, Riley opened the folder and began glancing through printouts from various Web sites. He remembered his original surprise at finding so many diverse sites about the escape artist's life.

Some had featured black-and-white photographs representing the span of Houdini's life. Others had offered photos of the magician's many daring escapes from various handcuffs and prison cells. Especially famous for escaping from handcuffs, Houdini had challenged anyone to find a pair from which he couldn't escape. The illusionist had also escaped from various trunks, even a large milk container.

One photo from 1909 showed Houdini making a wild leap from a bridge into the Seine River in France, his wrists handcuffed before him and secured by a chain to his neck. According to the accompanying news article, the water was nearly freezing, but within minutes Houdini broke the water's surface, lifting the handcuffs in an upraised fist.

Riley sipped his coffee. A history buff, he found the information fascinating, but the review wasn't leading him any closer to finding Haydon Owens. Shuffling through the papers, he reread Houdini's biography:

> Born in Budapest, Hungary, on March 24, 1874, Ehrich Weiss—"Harry Houdini" was not his real name—moved to Appleton, Wisconsin, with his family. He grew up in poor conditions and began performing tricks at an early age to supplement the family's income. One trick involved picking up needles with his eyelids. Later, he—

Riley froze as his mind turned over the name Ehrich Weiss. *But why does that name sound familiar now?*

Ehrich Weiss.

Eric White.

Where did I just see that name . . . very recently?

A memory marshaled him to his feet. He reached for another folder and pulled out a sheaf of papers.

On top of the stack was the program from Crystal's play. Gillian had proudly told him about Crystal's fine performance in *The Sound of Music* and had shown him the program. In all of the commotion about the threatening messages from Houdini409, the program had gotten mixed in with Crystal's chat logs and he had taken it with him.

Yes, there's something here. Something I saw . . .

Opening the program, he skimmed the text until he found the name he was looking for. Was it only a hunch or something more?

CHAPTER 75

CRYSTAL REGRETTED TEARING HERSELF away from the party—she was getting along with everybody so well—but snow was piling up outside. After the cast had watched the video of the best performance and wolfed down enough hot dogs, soda, and chips to feed a small army, Betty Jamison encouraged everyone to leave early due to the severe winter storm the local meteorologist was no longer predicting but promising. Crystal called Marc and asked him to pick her up.

"Good grief," she told Mrs. Jamison after hanging up. "I feel like a sixth-grader—asking my dad for a ride like this."

"It's only until the killer's caught. I think you were brave to finish the musical after everything that has happened."

Crystal shook her head. "I don't know. I think everybody is over-reacting just a little bit. Don't you?"

"I guess in a situation like this, it's better to overreact than to underreact."

"I suppose you're right."

A half hour later, most of the cast had left, and Crystal started to feel awkward. She glanced at her watch and wondered what was taking her dad so long. Suddenly, her cell phone chirped. She glanced at the caller ID.

"Dad, are you okay?"

"I'm standing in snow up to my ankles, but otherwise I'm fine." His voice penetrated a haze of static. "The Tahoe's in a ditch, but at least I missed the tree."

"I'm glad you're okay. Where are you? I'll ask the policeman outside if he can send you a tow truck."

After Marc gave Crystal directions, she pulled on her coat and ran outside to the policeman sitting in his idling car outside Betty Jamison's house. She told him what had happened, and he agreed to call for a tow truck right away and send it Marc's way.

This wasn't Officer Stenholm, the cop who had driven her to her performances the past two days. She supposed they all took different shifts.

"But wasn't your dad going to pick you up?" the cop asked in a gravely voice. "How are you going to get home?"

"I don't know."

"Why don't you come with me? I'll drive you home. We could even pick up your dad on the way." He smiled and extended his hand. "By the way, I'm Officer Gibbs. Glad to meet you."

Crystal shook his hand. "I'm Crystal Thayer. Are you sure you don't mind?"

"Not at all."

"Okay, I'll be right back."

Returning to Mrs. Jamison's house, Crystal called Marc and filled him in. Marc agreed to call Gillian with the news so she wouldn't worry. Five minutes later, Crystal said good-bye to Mrs. Jamison and headed to the police car.

What a gentleman, Crystal thought when Officer Gibbs opened her door and closed it behind her. After he got in his side, she glanced at the young officer with the bushy mustache. "You know where Whistler's Point is, right?"

He nodded. "I could drive there blindfolded."

CHAPTER 76

AT WHISTLER'S POINT, GILLIAN put the kettle on the stove for tea and stood at the kitchen sink, peering out the window as snow drifted down like confetti. Already, several inches covered the ground, and the sky looked dark and menacing. Wondering how much more snow would fall before Crystal and Marc came home, she regretted the fact that they were out in this weather.

The phone rang. It was Riley. "You got home safely," he said. "That's good. It's nasty out there."

"Yeah, and Crystal and Marc are still out in it. So what's up?"

"Do you have an extra program from Crystal's show? I was looking at one there the other night when I first got back, and I'm afraid I accidentally took it with me. I've got it here."

"No problem. I've got another one over on the desk. What's going on?"

"Look at the page that lists the crew. One of the stagehands is named Eric White. Do you know him?"

"Yes, I met him last night. Why?"

"It's hard to explain."

The kettle was sputtering, but she ignored it. "I'm listening."

"Okay, here's the short version. When Haydon Owens, aka the Magician Murderer, stalked his victims through the Internet, he used the screen name 'Houdini409.' You know who Houdini is, right?"

"Sure, a magician who was popular back in the early 1900s."

"Owens collects Houdini memorabilia. In fact, he's a bona fide Houdini nut, according to his former landlord. His apartment was jam-packed with Houdini stuff."

"Okay, I don't see the connection, but I'm listening. Go ahead." Gillian poured boiling water into her mug and let the Earl Grey steep.

"While you were at the matinee, I reviewed some research I had done online a few years ago, and something caught my eye. 'Harry Houdini' wasn't Houdini's real name. It was 'Ehrich Weiss.'"

She had never heard that name before. "So—"

"*Weiss* is German for 'white,' so—"

"Eric White!" Her pulse quickened. "So you think this guy on the stage crew could be Haydon Owens?"

"I know it seems like a long shot, but look at it this way. The sheriff plastered Owens's mug all over town, but nobody seems to have seen him. My guess is that he altered his appearance and changed his name. Given his obsession with Houdini, is it possible he would have changed his name to Eric Weiss or White? How many people do you think would know Houdini's real name?"

Not very many. "Thank goodness Crystal's safe. Eric was probably at the cast party this afternoon, but that broke up early due to the weather. Marc was going to pick Crystal up, but his car slid off the road."

"Is he okay? Is there anything I can do?"

"He's stranded, but he called and said a tow truck is on its way. A policeman is bringing him and Crystal home. They should be here soon. What are you going to do?"

"I'm going to call the sheriff and request an arrest warrant for Eric White," Riley said. "A hunch isn't enough for a warrant, but maybe we can pick him up on suspicion. The sheriff should know where Eric lives. Pray that he's home. If he is, and in fact is Haydon Owens, then we can pick him up and hopefully close this case right away."

"I hope you guys catch him. It would be great to know Crystal's safe."

"The next time I call you, it could be all over."

"Praise God!"

After they hung up, Gillian took a sip of her tea. With the snow piling up, she decided to take out the trash so she or Marc wouldn't have to deal with it later. Grabbing the bag from under the sink, she headed to where the trash cans were kept alongside the garage. When she got outside, they weren't there. Puzzled, she looked toward the end of the driveway, wondering if Marc had left them out by the road. No containers.

Then she remembered what Riley had said about the Magician Murderer stealing trash before he went after his next victim. Gillian shivered.

CHAPTER 77

THE POLICE CAR SWERVED as Dendridge wrestled with the steering wheel. The rear tires found momentary traction, and the car righted itself on the shoulder of the snowy road, just missing the grasping limbs of a pine tree. Riley held onto the dashboard and gritted his teeth. He'd been praying for Crystal, but wondered if he should be praying for himself instead.

Snowflakes swirled against the windshield, combining with the halo of fog on the inside of the glass to cut visibility to no more than twenty or twenty-five feet. The defroster was blowing full blast, but it was more noise than action. All Riley could see out his window was the faint outline of trees. This was not just an early season snowfall; it was a blizzard unlike anything he'd seen in Cincinnati.

The police radio crackled and buzzed with bursts of static. Occasionally, Riley heard voices, but they made little sense. He wondered if the sheriff was on the right frequency.

Dendridge barked into the radio. "Dendridge here. We're almost there. Is backup on the way? Repeat. Dendridge here. We need backup at Pike Lake. Do you copy?"

He waited for an answer, but static was his only reply. He swore.

"I got through to Gillian Thayer earlier just fine," Riley said, "but maybe the storm's worse up here."

"Maybe you're right." The sheriff's gaze locked on Riley. "Got a gun?"

"Of course."

"Then it looks like it's just you and me."

After talking to Gillian earlier, Riley had called the sheriff and told him his suspicions about Eric White. At first, Dendridge had seemed skeptical of Riley's hunch that Eric White and the Magician Murderer were the same person. He'd also laughed outright at Riley's request for an arrest warrant—that is, until he received a troubling call. Deputy Stenholm, the officer in charge of watching Crystal at the cast party, wasn't responding to his radio. In fact, both he and his police car had mysteriously disappeared.

Something was wrong.

As long as Crystal wasn't with Eric White, Riley knew they had nothing to worry about. But now nobody knew where she was. Eric had been at the cast party, too, but where was he now? Nobody knew that either. Had he stolen the police car and abducted Crystal? It was a possibility.

No longer laughing, the sheriff had gotten the arrest warrant and swung by to pick Riley up on the way. Now Riley chewed his gum hard and wished the sheriff could go faster as anxiety clawed away inside him. *Father, please keep her safe.*

He toyed with the idea of calling Gillian back, but decided not to worry her with something they weren't sure about. Maybe Stenholm had simply gotten stuck in the snow somewhere and his radio calls were no longer getting through the storm.

It was after 5 PM, and the sky was growing darker by the second. If it had been nighttime, they never would have seen the road sign. The sign was caked with snow, the words "Pike Lake Road" barely visible.

"This is where Eric White lives," Dendridge said. "You know, I made a few calls about this guy before I picked you up. He works at the library and lives here. Beyond that, nobody knows anything about him. But everybody has a past, right? Nope. Not this guy."

Riley strained to see beyond the whiteout. Fine, black lines etched themselves across the white canvas of the landscape. Tree branches materialized out of the falling snow. Then the cruiser was among the trees, which provided some shelter from the falling snow and improved visibility.

Riley rubbed some of the fog off the windshield with the cuff of his jacket and studied the road up ahead; in a couple of hours, no one would realize that a road was even here. Nobody had passed this way, at least not recently. Then again, if Eric White had driven this way, the snow could have covered his tracks by now, given the volume still coming down.

Another pencil-thin outline emerged from the white landscape. It was the peak of a roof. Black lines shot to the ground, revealing walls. The green, single-story house squatted forlornly at the end of the drive. Beyond the house stretched an expanse that Riley guessed was Pike Lake. No police car in sight.

The cruiser rolled to a stop. Without being told, Riley knew they would leave the car here and proceed the rest of the way on foot. His mouth turned dry as he took in the small house and realized that he'd never been closer to catching the Magician Murderer. Could his journey finally end here?

Dendridge reached down and unsnapped his holster, checking his firearm to make sure it was loaded. Riley pulled a .38 Smith and Wesson out of his jacket pocket.

Stepping into more than six inches of snow, they left the car's doors standing open.

Dendridge signaled Riley to cover the house's rear while he checked the front.

Riley skirted the perimeter of the house, the caking snow slowing his progress, his knees creaking. Snowflakes lashed at his face, and he regretted not having grabbed a hat, but at least he had gloves. He'd moved to Florida to get away from this stuff, but now here he was, back in it again. This snow was about as bad as he'd ever seen.

He found the back door and pressed his back against the siding, pointing the nose of the .38 toward the door. Anyone exiting the house would be naked to him. He heard Dendridge pounding on the front door.

Minutes ticked by. Finally, Dendridge appeared around the corner of the house with a flashlight. "No answer, and the front door's locked."

Riley tested the handle on the back door and found it locked. He peered through the door's window. "I see a kitchen. No signs of life, but no way to tell for sure. This is our way in."

They had no choice. Crystal could be struggling for her life inside.

Dendridge stepped forward and smashed the nose of his pistol into the glass on the door. Reaching through the broken window, he unlocked the door and swung it open. Both men stepped into the kitchen in combat stance, guns ready. The house was warm.

"Police!" Dendridge shouted. "Anybody home?"

Silence was the only reply.

Riley shone his flashlight around the kitchen. A refrigerator stood to his right, a stove to his left. The counters were bare, except for a microwave, a knife set, and a coffeemaker. Nothing appeared unusual. The room was immaculate.

The sheriff eased down a hallway with Riley at his back. To the right were two closed doors; to the left was only an open door into the bathroom. Dendridge took a look inside and peeked behind the shower curtain. Nothing.

Riley felt sweat beading on his hairline. *Father, please let her be okay.*

They entered the living room at the front of the house, another tidy room with 1960s décor.

No Eric White and no Crystal Thayer.

Whirling around, Riley tried the first door on the hallway and found it unlocked. He slammed the door open and stepped back, tightening his grip on the Smith and Wesson. When there was no immediate response, he reached inside with one hand and flipped on the wall switch, revealing a plainly decorated bedroom.

Along one wall stood a double bed covered by a solid navy bedspread. The bed was flanked by a nightstand and a four-drawer dresser.

Occupying the opposite wall was a bank of computers and other electronic equipment that Riley didn't recognize. The monitors were dark, but blinking amber lights indicated the computers were probably on standby. It was the kind of computer system he would have expected the Magician Murderer to use. They'd know for sure once they got some computer techs out here.

Dendridge studied a couple of framed photos on the dresser top and motioned Riley over to see.

The handsome young man in the photograph had curly, black hair; attractive, dark eyes; and a small-featured face with an infectious smile. He looked wholesome and moral, the kind of person you could trust. Riley immediately saw the resemblance to the pictures of Haydon Owens that Dendridge had plastered all over town.

"Bingo. Well, now we know for sure that Owens and White are the same guy. But where is he? And how are we going to track him down in this blizzard?"

"I don't know," Dendridge said. "But he hasn't been here for a while, from the looks of things. Maybe if we head up to—"

Riley held up his hand. He'd heard something.

Through the wall seeped the murmur of music and voices from the second bedroom, the only room they hadn't checked. Perhaps a radio had been left on. Whatever it was, the sound gave Riley the creeps, as if someone were lurking in the house after all.

This time, it was the sheriff's turn to throw the door open, his pistol pointed at the gaping doorway.

The voices and music grew louder. Then Riley heard another sound. A clicking sound—something he couldn't quite put his finger on, yet it sounded familiar. A sliver of ice slid down the small of his back.

Dendridge swore. One step behind him, Riley saw the reason for the sheriff's dismay. The bedroom had been transformed into a shrine. The clicking sound came from an old film projector, its large wheels turning. On a white screen on the far wall, the projector was broadcasting a black-and-white silent film.

Riley recognized Harry Houdini from the Internet photos. On the screen, the magician was hanging upside down by his feet while jungle natives in grass skirts were lowering him into a large pot over an open fire—no doubt a presentation of one of his many daring escapes.

Lining the walls on either side of the screen stood enclosed, illuminated glass cases with Houdini artifacts on display. Words had been engraved on small, gold plates, describing in meticulous detail what each piece was as well as its role in the escape artist's life. Rare books Houdini had written, handcuffs and other restraints from which the magician had escaped, even a large milk can—all of it was here. Framed photographs chronicling Houdini's life from boyhood to his death hung on the walls.

Riley's head jerked around when the projector's reel came to its end with a loud *click click click*. The projector snapped, an unseen mechanism rewound the film reel, and the projector began playing *Terror Island* again.

He wondered why anyone would exit the house and leave the lights on and the projector running. Glancing around the room, he wondered if this private screening was intended solely for them. Was someone hiding in the house, as yet unseen? No, they had searched the place and hadn't found anyone.

Eric White *was* Haydon Owens, the Magician Murderer. But where had he gone?

Hearing the sheriff curse again, Riley rushed over to see what was the matter. In the corner, beside a glass case displaying Houdini's death mask, stood a stone statue of a woman in a long robe. She appeared to be in mourning.

"That came from a cemetery," Dendridge said. "I'd bet my badge on it."

"Maybe from Houdini's gravesite," Riley said. "It would be logical to place it beside the death mask. I knew Owens was a Houdini fan, but this shows a compulsion."

Dendridge rubbed his jaw. "He's nuts all right. Maybe Houdini's corpse is around here somewhere, too."

"It looks like he settled for a memento, but you never know."

"We won't know for sure until my men search this place from top to bottom. Maybe there's a basement or a crawlspace we haven't seen."

Riley held his gaze. "If they find a body, let's pray it's only Houdini's."

CHAPTER 78

WIPERS SWEPT ACROSS THE police car's windshield, but did little to improve visibility. The snow was coming down so hard and fast that the wipers barely had a chance to clear the flakes away before others took their place.

Through the glass, the road was indiscernible against a wall of white that met a brooding sky. Thankfully, the trees flanking the road gave a sense of where the road was supposed to be. Crystal could tell that the snow wouldn't be stopping anytime soon, and she wished she could get home before the heavens dropped whatever else they were holding back.

She was relieved that Officer Gibbs was driving her home, though he seemed to be driving slower than necessary. At this crawling pace, it could take an hour to get out to Whistler's Point. But even that would be better than sliding off the road as her dad had done. She just hoped they would reach him soon; hopefully, he was staying warm inside the Tahoe while he waited.

Officer Gibbs's police radio crackled with static and the occasional burst of voices. Apparently, nothing they said was important, because he seemed disinterested. Finally, he shut the radio off and turned on the CD player. Crystal recognized the original Broadway soundtrack recording of *The Phantom of the Opera*. An odd choice for a cop.

"So you're staying at Whistler's Point, huh?" He kept his eyes fixed straight ahead. At least he was attempting conversation; the car was too quiet, even with the music.

"Yeah."

"Like it?"

"It's okay."

"Not great? Just okay?"

"My family and I are from Chicago. No offense, but that's where I'd rather live."

"You brought some real class this place has been needing for some time. I saw the musical on Thursday night." He glanced in her direction, his eyes warm. "You were incredible."

Her face turned hot, and she glanced away. "Thanks."

"The North Woods isn't for everybody."

"That's for sure."

"But it's a great place to hide."

She studied him, wondering what he meant.

"I mean, if you were a big-time criminal and needed to get away from the law, you'd want to come to a place like this. The crime rate is so low up here, nobody expects crime when it happens."

The snow bore down in swirling, angry gusts. The wipers squeaked as they shoved away the latest accumulation.

"Like Stacey James, for example," Office Gibbs continued. "I'm sure she never expected some psycho to strangle her. It's peaceful up here. Nobody expects violence." He glanced her direction. "I bet you wouldn't expect anything bad to happen to you either."

Crystal's skin prickled. "Why should I?"

"Because violence can happen to anybody at any time just when they least expect it. Everybody has to be prepared for surprises, especially up here in the woods. I mean, look at this place. Nobody with half a brain is going to be out on these roads right now. The odds of somebody driving by and seeing us right now are practically nil."

He slowed the car to a stop just beyond an intersection and put it in park. Crystal peered out the windows, wondering where they were. In the background, Sarah Brightman and Michael Crawford were singing "The Point of No Return." The song, one she always skipped due to its seductive overtones, always gave her the creeps. "Why did we stop?"

Officer Gibbs ignored her. When he spoke, his voice changed and reminded her of someone she knew. "I hope you like surprises because I'm not who you think I am."

Officer Gibbs removed his hat and pulled off a brown wig.

Heart slamming into her throat, Crystal unclasped her seatbelt. She reached for the passenger door handle and jiggled it. *Locked!* She slammed her hand into the lock button. The door still wouldn't open. Then she remembered that the man had closed the door behind her. Had he jammed it somehow?

Officer Gibbs dug his fingers into his face, peeling away skin that wasn't skin and a nose made out of latex and putty.

Crystal grabbed her purse from where it lay on the floor at her feet. Inside was the can of Mace that Riley had given to her.

As Officer Gibbs stripped off his mustache and extracted a set of false teeth, the transformation was complete. When Crystal looked up, still fumbling with her purse, she was staring into the cold, black eyes of Eric White, and a rage she couldn't comprehend.

"E–Eric, what are you doing? You're—you're scaring me."

Without a word, he pulled out a length of white rope. Crystal felt herself begin to shake.

His face had gone slack, expressionless, but his vicious eyes locked onto hers. "There's no one around to help you, Erin, and there's no point in trying to get away. It's just you and me again."

"Who are you?" Crystal struggled to tame the quaver in her voice, but she was shaking so hard now that it was all she could do to say anything. "And who is Erin?"

"You've got a big mouth, Erin. I tried to shut you up, but you wouldn't listen. You kept coming back. Now I have to shut you up for good."

CHAPTER 79

MARC HELD AN ARM in front of his face, trying to ward off the blast of snow the wind drove down without mercy. From the vantage point of a cozy living room window, the tableau of snow-sprinkled pines would probably have looked pretty. But it seemed far from pretty to him right now. *At least I'm getting my exercise*, he thought.

He'd warmed himself in the Tahoe long enough, waiting for the tow truck he was now certain would never come. Getting dangerously low on fuel, he'd finally shut off the engine, grabbed a flashlight, and started walking. Anything was better than sitting in the stranded vehicle and waiting for help. He debated whether to call Gillian, but why worry her? Perhaps the tow truck was somewhere ahead.

Around the next bend, he expected to see more snow and a road meandering endlessly through the trees. But what he saw instead was an old, brown Monte Carlo creeping down the road toward him, black exhaust billowing out of its tailpipe. The snow was so deep that the car's tires were blazing their own trail, and snow was scraping the car's undercarriage. The snow was simply too deep for driving; it was a miracle the driver hadn't gotten stuck.

Marc waved as the car approached, longing to get out of the cold that was made more bracing by the merciless wind. The car pulled alongside Marc and rolled to a stop. The driver's window slid down.

"Hey, Mr. Thayer! I never expected to see you out here."

Marc could hardly believe his eyes. It was Crystal's boyfriend. "Ryan Brodski! What are you doing here?"

Ryan smiled. "I drove up here to surprise Crystal. I saw the play this afternoon, but then she took off before I could see her, and I don't know where she went."

"She went to a cast party."

"Well, that explains it. I finally decided to try finding Whistler's Point, but I got lost a couple times. I'm not even sure where I am. This is the right way, isn't it?"

Marc nodded. "Did you see a tow truck or police car heading this way? My vehicle slid off the road a ways back, and I'm waiting for my ride."

Ryan shook his head. "Haven't seen anybody except you. Hey, you look cold. Wanna get in?"

"That sound great."

Marc cleared a pile of trash off the passenger seat and eased inside. The heat felt good. "Why don't you turn around and head back the way you came. I'm wondering what happened to that tow truck. A cop was supposed to pick me up, too, but that was a while ago."

Where is everybody?

CHAPTER 80

CRYSTAL'S HAND FOUND THE can of Mace in her purse. She pulled it out and pointed it at Eric's face, but before she could trigger the nozzle, he slammed her hand into the dashboard. The can dropped to the floor. Crystal grabbed at the rope and tried to twist it from Haydon's hand, but he was stronger. His face had morphed into a hideous mask of evil.

He wrenched the rope away from her, shoved her back against the car door, and began clambering across the seat after her.

Crystal swung her purse at his head, but he blocked it with his arm and landed heavily on top of her. Flailing with her arms, she screamed and tried to get out from underneath his weight. Pulling her knees up in an effort to curl into a protective ball, she caught him square in the groin.

Cursing and groaning, Haydon rolled off the seat into the footwell, writhing in pain. In that split second, through the window over his shoulder, Crystal thought she saw headlights reflecting off the snowy trees outside.

"Somebody help me!" she screamed. "*Please!*"

By now, Haydon had recovered and was coming after her again. With strong and practiced hands, he slipped the rope around her neck and began to pull it tight.

Crystal clawed at his face, his hands, the rope, but he was too strong.

She felt the noose tightening on her throat. He was choking her. She couldn't breathe.

She hammered at his arms with her fists, but he wouldn't let go. The rope only grew tighter. Stars danced before her eyes.

God, please help me!

CHAPTER 81

AS RYAN STEERED THE Monte Carlo carefully along the slippery and elusive roadway, Marc continued to scan up ahead for any sign of the tow truck. The snow had eased a bit, but it was still coming down hard enough to obscure visibility.

The road curved sharply to the right, and as Ryan negotiated the turn, Marc suddenly spotted a police car on the shoulder up ahead. Its lights were off and snow had begun to accumulate on the roof, back window, and trunk.

"That's strange," Marc said as Ryan pulled alongside the cruiser. "It looks like someone abandoned ship out here. But where—"

Just then, through the driver's side window, Marc saw a dark shape rise up and lurch forward. In the same instant, he was certain he heard a scream that was suddenly cut off.

Crystal!

He leapt from the car and yanked at the door of the police cruiser.

Locked.

Acting on pure instinct and adrenaline, Marc dashed back to Ryan's car and grabbed the suitcase he'd seen lying on the backseat. A split second later, he was pounding it against the driver's side window, a mix of rage and desperation driving him on.

More screams issued from the car.

Oh, God, please!

Ryan appeared at Marc's side and grabbed the other corner of the suitcase. Without a word, they swung the suitcase back like a battering ram and plowed it into the window again. With a muted crack, the safety glass gave way and crumbled into the front seat.

Marc unlocked the door and wrenched it open. Reaching inside, he grabbed the closest thing he could get his hands on. It was an arm, and Marc yanked on it for all he was worth. A male voice cursed, and the attacker tried to elbow Marc away.

His breathing labored now, Marc grabbed the belt around the wiry man's waist and recognized the sheriff's deputy's uniform. Officer Stenholm was assaulting his daughter.

His anger bursting into flames, Marc tugged at the belt with strength he didn't know he possessed. Gravity and pure rage worked in his favor. The man in the uniform toppled backward out of the car and into the snow.

As Marc scrambled to regain his balance on the slippery roadway surface, he saw the attacker's rage-twisted face. It wasn't Officer Stenholm at all. Instantly, Marc realized who he really was.

Haydon Owens.

The Magician Murderer.

As Haydon struggled to his feet, Marc tried to catch him in a wrestler's hold. But as he stepped forward, his feet went out from under him and he went down hard, flat on his back, the wind knocked out of him. He tried to breathe, his gaze lost in the treetops.

Haydon advanced, peering down at Marc as a smile tugged at his lips, his breath frosting white. As he raised his boot to smash Marc's face, something struck him from behind, toppling him like a felled tree.

Ryan!

Marc rolled to his side in time to see Haydon trying to push himself to his knees. Just then, Ryan's right leg shot out, and his foot plowed into Haydon's face with a distinctive crunch of cartilage. The killer went sprawling.

Ryan half-crouched in a classic karate stance, ready for more action, but Haydon only groaned and rolled over, cupping his hands under his bleeding nose.

Marc rose shakily to his feet, breathing hard, his lower back burning like fire. Exhausted, he leaned against the cruiser for support, aware of his trembling hands and the aftertaste of rage that had finally burned itself out. What had come over him? Blowing air out of his lips, he silently thanked God for holding him back. Then he went to find Crystal.

CHAPTER 82

THE SOUND OF SHATTERING glass registered somewhere in Crystal's fading consciousness. She was aware of a weight lifting off her, and the roar of angry voices. Doubling over, she clutched at her throat, loosening the rope and gasping for breath. She heard a scuffle in the snow beyond the open door, but didn't have the strength to lift her head.

When someone grabbed her arm, she shrieked, and then stared in confusion. "Dad!" Her neck burned. It hurt to talk. "How did you find me?"

Sliding across the seat toward her, Marc wrapped his arms around her and held her tight.

"I'm so glad you're okay." Marc kissed her forehead. "A few more minutes . . ."

She was surprised to see tears in his eyes.

"How do you feel?" he asked.

"Not so good." She smoothed tiny flecks of glass out of her hair, her neck aching. "Where's Eric?"

"I wrenched him off of you, and then Ryan finished him off."

"Ryan?" Crystal shook her head in confusion. "What do you mean, Ryan?"

Ryan Brodski leaned in through the open driver's side door and greeted Crystal with a big grin on his face.

"He won't be going anywhere, Mr. Thayer," Ryan said. "I knocked him out and I think I might have broken his nose."

He turned to Crystal. "You okay?"

"I think so, but how . . . ?"

"I'll explain later," he replied.

Marc removed the rope still around Crystal's neck and handed it to Ryan. "Here. You better tie him up."

While Ryan left to work on Haydon, Crystal felt herself calming down. "We've gotta call the police," she said, then remembered she was sitting in a police cruiser.

Marc shook his head. "No cop in his right mind is going to be out here in this weather, and I'm not sure I could even tell them where we are."

"But we've gotta do something, Dad."

Ryan returned with a look of triumph on his face. "I've got him tied up pretty good."

Marc turned on the police radio and tried talking into it, but could rouse nothing more than staccato bursts of static. The bad weather was no doubt affecting reception. He pulled out his cell phone and tried it. He shook his head. "No signal," he said. "At least not from here." He slipped the phone back into his jacket pocket. "I'll try again later."

Just then, Crystal heard the roar of an engine and glanced out the back window of the car. Turning her head made her neck throb. Through the swirling snow, flashing yellow lights were approaching on an adjacent road.

"Dad, it's a snowplow! Stop the driver and see if he can help us."

"No way," Marc said. "He'll run me over before he even sees me."

"Oh no!" Crystal cried. "He's approaching the intersection. It looks like he's going to go right on by."

"I'll get him to stop," Ryan said, springing away from the police cruiser and jogging toward his own car.

"What are you doing?" Marc exclaimed.

Ryan didn't answer. He jumped into the Monte Carlo, cranked the engine, and jerked the gear shift into reverse. The car lurched backward into the intersection, a barrier in the path of the snowplow.

Her arm around her dad, Crystal watched in disbelief. *God, please make the plow stop.*

CHAPTER 83

AT THE KITCHEN TABLE, Gillian paused from her letter writing to start praying.

Something was wrong. The policeman who was supposed to bring Marc and Crystal home should have arrived an hour ago. Marc had called and told her about the ride, but why hadn't he called since?

God, where are they?

She tried to remember the last time she'd spent earnest, prolonged time in prayer beyond blessings over meals and five-minute rituals after morning devotions. Perhaps it had been in October, when Marc was in the hospital, teetering on the brink of life and death.

She wondered why she hadn't prayed sooner. *Why, Lord, do I need a crisis before I get on my knees? Where are Marc and Crystal? Please keep them safe.*

The phone rang, making her jump. It was Marc. She heard a lot of static, but at least his words were coming through.

"Marc, why haven't you called? I've been worried sick."

She listened in stunned disbelief as he described what had happened. Her hands began to shake. "Is Crystal okay?"

"She's alive, but her throat and neck are pretty sore. I'm taking her to the hospital so someone can look her over. Naturally, she's pretty shaken up, too."

"I'll meet you at the hospital."

"No, just stay put. The roads are terrible. It won't do anybody any good if you get stuck somewhere."

"Marc, I'm coming. I need to see her."

"Okay, I'll come by and pick you up. Watch for a big snowplow."

"What?"

"I'll explain when we get there."

CHAPTER 84

"SHE'LL BE FINE," SAID Dr. Jim Taylor, a middle-aged man with salt-and-pepper hair. "No damage to the trachea. No damage to the muscles, tendons, or blood vessels in the neck. She'll have some soreness and bruising, but other than that, she just needs to rest."

"Can I go home now?" Crystal asked from the examination table at the Helen Newberry Joy Hospital.

The doctor nodded. "Sure, as long as the police are finished asking you questions."

After the doctor left, Crystal headed to the bathroom to change back into her clothes. Sitting beside her bed, Gillian felt relieved beyond words, though she'd winced at the sight of the nasty rope burn around Crystal's neck.

Thank You, Lord!

The door swung open, and Riley stepped in, his eyes filled with concern. "The sheriff and I just got back from checking out Eric White's place, and we heard the news," he said to Marc. "How's Crystal?"

Marc didn't bother getting up from his chair. He looked exhausted, and Gillian could tell he was ready to get home and go to bed. "She'll be fine after a few weeks. Chuck, this is Ryan Brodski, a good friend of Crystal's. He drove up from Chicago to make a surprise appearance at the musical and didn't realize he was going to help save her life."

Ryan raised his eyebrows. "Well, it wasn't just me. I think Mr. Thayer here had something to do with it, too."

Riley shook Ryan's hand. "You did a very heroic thing today—both of you did." He glanced in Gillian's direction. "Hey, Mom, how are you doing? Holding up okay?"

"I'm fine," she said.

Am I? Since arriving at the hospital and hearing that Crystal was going to be okay, she'd felt sapped of energy. She caught herself tracing calligraphy letters on her chair's armrest with her finger and folded her hands in her lap. She could hardly wait to get everyone safely home and put this ordeal behind them.

Crystal came out of the bathroom and greeted Riley with a shy smile and a self-conscious wave.

"Hi, Crystal. I'm happy to see that you're okay," Riley said. "Did you give the police a statement?"

She nodded. "I told them everything I could remember. They said they'd call if they needed anything else. Later, I'll have to testify at the trial."

Riley raised his fist in jubilation, as if the reality of what had happened had begun to sink in. "I'm sorry for what you've all been through today. But we've finally got our man. That was smart of you to bring him in on the snowplow. He's Haydon Owens, all right, and he's not going anywhere."

Gillian smiled at him in relief. The Magician Murderer was finally behind bars, and Crystal was going to be okay. It almost seemed too good to be true.

*   *   *

Snowflakes lashed the windshield without mercy as Marc drove Gillian and Crystal back to Whistler's Point in the Tahoe. A tow truck had pulled the SUV out of the ditch, and it appeared to be running fine. They had dropped Ryan off at the hotel where he had booked a room. Despite Gillian's repeated invitations for him to join them at Whistler's Point, he had insisted on spending the night in town since Crystal wasn't feeling up to company. Riley had stayed in town to interview Haydon Owens, but said he'd join them later, weather permitting.

Gillian's stomach growled, and she glanced at her watch. It was almost seven o'clock and she'd forgotten all about supper. Suspecting that Marc and Crystal would also be hungry, she mentally created a simple menu.

Snow had fallen thick on the highway, despite the efforts of the snowplows, and she was grateful for the four-wheel drive. Because of the hazardous conditions, however, the trip took twice as long as usual. Exhausted, she looked forward to a long, hot bath.

When Marc pulled up in front of the caretaker's house, Gillian could tell that something was wrong. She was certain she had left the kitchen light on, and the light outside the garage, but the house was completely dark.

"There's probably a tree down on the power lines somewhere," Marc said. His voice was grim with fatigue as he toggled the light switch inside the back door.

Gillian felt her way across the kitchen and grabbed the telephone. "The phone's dead, too."

"No electricity means no heat," Marc said.

"We could stay in the lighthouse," Crystal suggested. "There are plenty of fireplaces in there. As long as we have firewood, we should be okay."

"I guess we have no choice," Gillian said. She wondered when the challenges of this day would ever end.

"Let's round up candles and flashlights," Marc said. "We'll need to find sleeping bags and extra blankets, too. I think we're going to need them tonight."

As Gillian and Crystal gathered supplies, Marc took one of the flashlights and went upstairs to the master bedroom. He returned a few moments later with his Glock pistol and a box of ammunition.

"But Marc, Haydon's in jail," Gillian said. "He can't hurt us now."

Marc shrugged, a flicker in his eyes. "Maybe so, but I'm not taking any chances. Not after what happened today."

CHAPTER 85

SITTING AT THE INTERVIEW room conference table, Riley peered into the eyes of pure evil. Haydon Owens met Riley's gaze with an insolent stare, as if he were in a state of denial. He slouched in a metal folding chair, arms folded across his chest, a sour look dominating his pale face.

He still wore the police uniform he'd stolen earlier from Officer Stenholm, who was at the hospital recovering from a bad concussion. Betty Jamison had found Officer Stenholm lying unconscious in a snowbank behind her house, arms tied behind his back. If she hadn't found him when she did, Riley surmised, he wouldn't have survived the night in the cold.

Riley studied Haydon's face. He'd seen a few photos of him and knew he could be charming and attractive when he wanted to be; but now was not the time for smiles and polite conversation. Besides, his black-and-blue nose had swollen to twice its normal size. That high school kid had clobbered him good, and Riley couldn't help surveying the damage with amusement.

Riley warmed his hands around a cup of hot coffee. He had run out of Juicy Fruit but wasn't about to trek into the storm for more. There were more pressing matters.

While one officer manned a video camera in the corner, a second officer read Haydon his Miranda rights and asked him to sign a form, indicating he understood his rights.

"Do you wish to speak to me without an attorney present?" Riley asked. "You can, you know." He slid the form back across the table and indicated where Haydon needed to add his initials to waive his right to an attorney.

Haydon just stared at him with dead, emotionless eyes.

"So that's it then?" Riley tried not to show his annoyance. "You're going to stonewall us? You know it's over. Why don't you talk? Your silence isn't going to help anyone."

Haydon shook his head ever so slightly.

Riley rolled his eyes. "Look, pal, I just want to ask you a few questions, but it's not like I'm fishing for clues here. I've got direct testimony from the girl you tried to strangle this afternoon, plus statements from her father and her friend. I've been to your house and seen your computer setup—which, by the way, will be a gold mine for the boys in the computer crimes unit. And the sheriff's got a team out there right now, sifting through the rest of the evidence. We've got the ropes, and some trash, and who knows what else. And to top it all off, I've got a fingerprint that I'm betting will tie you in to a string of murders in Cincinnati. Not to mention the DNA sample that's on its way to the lab as we speak. Now, can I ask you a few questions, or do you want to do it the hard way?"

Haydon just smiled.

Getting up, Riley glanced at the other officers. "Take him to his cell, guys. I'm not wasting my time." He turned to Haydon. "If you change your mind, just ask for Riley. I'll be here."

CHAPTER 86

OH, DONNY. POOR DONNY. What have you done now? Think your mother's gonna bail you out this time? Think again, buster.

In the semidarkness, Haydon sat on his cot, elbows on his knees, and hummed the tune to "Gethsemane" from *Jesus Christ Superstar*. He stared at the floor of his cell, his mother's husky voice echoing in his skull.

If only he could get the voices out of his head. And the memories. He mentally ticked off the minutes, feeling impatient but knowing there was nothing he could do. At least, not yet.

The jail was strangely quiet. Down the hallway rang the distant closing of doors, the scuffing of shoes, the mutter of voices.

Apparently, he had the whole wing of the jail to himself, but that wasn't surprising now that they knew who he was. Soon they would be analyzing his chromosomes and DNA and puzzling over the strange anomaly known as the Magician Murderer.

He smiled, delighting in his newfound notoriety. In the morning, reporters would be camped out on the front steps, waiting for a look at him.

The crazy man. The serial killer.

All his life, he'd longed for crowds to adore him as the greatest magician alive. Now he realized he'd gain the fame he'd always coveted, but for an entirely different reason. The fact that a lot of people were suddenly interested in him, Mr. Nobody, fed a hungry place in the secret recesses of his heart.

But this wasn't the way the story was supposed to end. Erin was still alive, and he'd never left a job unfinished before. He could hear his mother's counsel ringing in his ears. *Donny, when you've got a job to do, you do it.*

Haydon drove his fingernails into the palms of his hands. *Yes, Mother, I always do what you tell me to do. Like a good son, I followed your instructions. But you didn't realize what you were starting, did you?*

He couldn't help feeling a little proud of his masquerade earlier. After Crystal told him that her dad would pick her up from the party, thwarting his plan to get her alone, Haydon had gone to the cast party with the disguise paraphernalia handy, in case the right opportunity presented itself. Then when Mrs. Jamison had told him that Crystal's dad was stranded on the side of the road, he'd known the right moment had come. Who else would take Crystal home but the policeman watching Betty Jamison's house?

He'd had to move quickly to put on the disguise and switch places with Officer Stenholm. It still amazed him how easily he'd taken the cop's place. The shocked look on Crystal's face when he had removed the disguise had been priceless. He would never forget that look. The realization that he was going to kill her.

Haydon studied his surroundings with a smirk. These idiots thought they could contain him in this joke of a cell; they didn't realize their gesture was an insult to who he was. If they truly knew him as well as they thought they did, they would have realized their mistake.

For a moment, he felt regret about his magic show, which he'd been forced to cancel as soon as he saw the wanted posters with his mug plastered all over town. The show would have been too risky, especially with the police looking for him. It was time for a low profile, but fate hadn't cooperated. Yet what did it matter? Now that they had him in custody, the show would have been canceled anyhow. But the show wasn't over yet, was it? What mattered now was what he did next.

What will you do next?

He reached his arms behind him and clasped his hands, stretching his back. Inside his head whispered the sentence Houdini had scrawled in many of the books in his vast library: *My brain is the key that sets me free.*

Haydon had studied every book Houdini had written and had mastered every trick Houdini had perfected.

He'd show them. He'd show them all.

He felt pent-up rage returning and tried to calm himself. No need to rush. *Haste makes waste*, his mother had always said. He did a few breathing exercises to relax himself.

My brain is the key that sets me free.

He reclined on his cot and ignored the meal turning cold on the tray at his feet. He stared at the ceiling. Then his plan came into focus.

CHAPTER 87

ARMS FILLED WITH FIREWOOD, Marc knelt beside the blazing fireplace and stacked the logs in a neat pile for later. Candles had been stationed around the parlor, where Marc, Gillian, and Crystal had decided to camp out for the night. Compared to other rooms in the lighthouse, the parlor was small, yet it offered plenty of space for the three of them. And because the parlor was an interior room, Gillian reasoned, the cold wouldn't be as bad here.

Clad in her green winter coat, she sat on the floor with her back resting against an antique couch, the fire warming her face. Finally, after the tense and event-filled week, she experienced a sense of relief that all would be well now. The police had Haydon in custody, and Crystal was safe. *Praise God!*

On her lap, she held Riley's police scanner, which he'd given her the last time he was at the house. Before locking the house for the night, Marc had grabbed it, thinking they could tune into weather reports—that is, if they could figure out how the contraption worked.

A couple of feet away, Crystal lay on a second couch, wrapped in a sleeping bag. The rise and fall of her resting form, the sigh of her steady breathing, indicated she was asleep.

Closing her eyes, Gillian thanked God that Crystal was okay. *She could be in heaven with Meredith and Blaine right now.*

Putting another log on the fire, Marc stood back to watch it burn.

"You saved Crystal's life today," Gillian said softly.

"Well, it wasn't just me. If Ryan hadn't shown up when he did, we never would have found the car." Marc sat down beside her and put his arm around her, pulling her close. "It was the Lord and His perfect timing." He peered into her eyes. "A couple more minutes, and Crystal—" His voice trailed off, and their minds filled in the blanks.

Gillian shivered, and he held her tighter. Resting her head on his shoulder, she said, "I love you."

He kissed her forehead. "I love you, too."

"I'm so glad you didn't go to Stacey's funeral."

"Me, too."

"You don't know how much it means to me that you stayed."

"I always want to be there for you, Gill. After God, you're the most important person in my life. Do you realize that?"

She nodded. "But you can say it as often as you want. It's nice to hear."

The antique clock on the mantel ticked away the moments. The burning logs crackled and popped. The warmth of the fire permeated every inch of her, wrapping her in a warm embrace. She closed her eyes.

In spite of the fire's warmth on her face, she felt tentacles of cold creeping into the room. Marc seemed to feel the draft, too. He pulled an unzipped sleeping bag around them. They cuddled.

Wisely, she'd thought to grab pillows and snacks. *We'll be okay for tonight*, she thought. *But if this blizzard lasts more than a few days, then we're in trouble.*

Marc got up. "I better go find more firewood. What we have won't last the night." He left, closing the door behind him.

Gillian turned the scanner on, but hearing only static, she tried another frequency. Still nothing. Then she thought she heard voices, but they sounded too far away and too garbled to be understood.

Shrugging, she turned off the scanner and reached for the bags of potato chips and dried fruit. The snacks were a poor substitute for supper, but they would have to do. Several mouthfuls later, her stomach satisfied, she stared into the fire. The dancing flames mesmerized her.

She caught herself nodding, the fatigue of the day weighing her down in a sleepy stupor. Her last coherent thoughts were a prayer.

Thank You, God, for sparing Crystal's life. Thank You, thank You, thank You . . .

* * *

She was walking down a long, dark tunnel alone, hands pressed protectively to her swollen belly. Inside her, life breathed. If the tiny mouths had spoken, she would have heard them. But they were silent. Peaceful. And why not? They had nothing to fear.

A dark shadow fell across her path, and a cold hand reached toward her, reached *into* her. Malevolent fingers probed past muscle and sinew, searching for the life that breathed unseen.

Her children cried. Whimpered. Screamed for her to do something.

Somehow she was with them in that dark, quiet haven they knew so well, seeking the menace that was causing them pain.

Suddenly, she saw him.

The man in black.

He was wrapping something around the necks of her babies. Weaponless, he was using their umbilical cords, and her children were screaming. They couldn't breathe.

She ran hard, knowing she had to stop him. "Meredith! Blaine!" she cried. "Hold on! I'm coming. I won't let him—"

* * *

Gillian jerked awake, cheeks wet with tears, the aftertaste of potato chips sour in her mouth. How long had she slept? Alarmed, she glanced around the room and rubbed her eyes. One of her legs had fallen asleep, and hot needles pricked her calf. Repositioning her leg for better circulation, she waited for the discomfort to pass.

Seeing that the fire was little more than glowing coals, she rose on stiff legs and put on another log, using the poker to stoke the flames. They licked up hungrily.

She glanced at her watch: 10:17 PM. She'd been asleep for more than an hour. Apparently, she'd been more exhausted than she realized.

Turning, she studied Crystal, the rhythmic sound of her breathing filling the room. She was still asleep.

Poor dear. She must be exhausted.

Gillian looked around.

Where's Marc? Why hasn't he returned with more firewood?

Hating to leave the fire unattended, she nudged Crystal awake. "Sweetie, could you watch the fire? I'll be right back."

Startled from a sound sleep, Crystal peered up at her, eyes wide, then nodded and lay back down. Sleep reclaimed her.

Determined not to be gone long, but curious about Marc's continued absence, Gillian grabbed a flashlight and left the warm, comforting room, closing the parlor door behind her. Shining her flashlight down the dark hallway, she understood the fear Nicole had experienced on numerous occasions—sensing that someone in the lighthouse was watching her.

"Marc?" Her voice echoed hollowly in the silence of the place. "Marc!"

There was no answer.

Inching down the hallway to the foyer, she checked the front door. It was still locked. She peered out the tall side windows to where they'd parked the Tahoe for the night. It was covered in white, and the snow was still driving down hard.

Heading down another hallway, she stepped into the dining room. "Marc?"

Gillian tripped on something and stumbled painfully to her knees. The flashlight clattered from her hand. An oblong shadow lay stretched across the floor beside her. The shadow moaned.

"Marc?" She reached for where his head should have been and felt something wet. Without seeing, she knew it was blood.

Marc moaned again.

Gillian rolled him onto his back. Grabbing the flashlight—thankfully, it still worked—she examined him. His eyelids fluttered. He groaned again. "Marc, are you okay?"

He lifted his head and gazed at her groggily. "Hurts bad."

"I bet it does. You've got quite a bump on your head. What happened? Did you trip and fall?"

He groaned. "There's somebody in the house. He hit me."

"What do you mean? Who hit you?"

"I heard him coming up behind me, but I didn't see his face."

A chill snaked down Gillian's spine. "Are you sure?"

"Yeah. Didn't you see him?"

"No, I haven't seen anybody except you." Glancing around the room, she studied the shifting shadows in the narrow beam of the flashlight. Firewood littered the floor where Marc had dropped it.

"I think it might be him," Marc said.

"Might be who?"

"Haydon. I think he might be here." Marc reached down to the waistband of his jeans. "The gun. He must have taken my gun, too."

Small hairs rose on the nape of Gillian's neck.

And if he is here, we now have no means of protection.

She kept her voice steady. "Can you get up? Just lean on me. There you go. Good."

Together, with his arm slung around her neck, they shuffled down the hallway. She wondered if he'd sustained something worse than a bump on the head; he seemed to be having balance problems.

She felt desperate to get back to the parlor, not wanting to leave Crystal alone for another second.

When at last they reached the door of the cozy room, she was relieved to see Crystal where she'd left her. Still asleep.

She helped Marc to a chair, and he sighed as if expending his last bit of strength. Giving him a wad of Kleenex, she ordered him to press it to the wound on his head. Then she scurried to the parlor door, took a last, fleeting glance down the corridor, and closed the door. She turned the lock.

Aware of her wildly pounding heart, Gillian tried to calm down. Haydon Owens was locked in a jail cell. It couldn't possibly have been Haydon who hit Marc. But if it wasn't Haydon, who was it? What had happened? Who had attacked Marc? Perhaps Marc *had* tripped and just didn't remember. Nothing was making sense.

Grabbing the police scanner, she turned it on. Longing to hear another human voice, she tuned to the frequency Riley had used, but heard only static in reply. She listened and waited. *Somebody. Anybody. Please.*

But there was only static. Disappointed, she turned the scanner off.

Then another sound made her jump. It was the silly cowboy ringtone blurting from Marc's cell phone. Startled, she fished it out of his coat pocket. She was amazed that the call had gotten through.

"Gillian!"

It was Riley. "Chuck, it's so good to hear your voice. I didn't think anybody could get—"

"Where are you?"

"In the lighthouse. There's no power, and the phones are dead. But at least—"

"Get out"—static swallowed his voice— "lighthouse!"

"What's wrong?"

"Haydon escaped." The phone crackled with static. ". . . coming after you."

Gillian's heart would not slow down.

More static. The call was breaking up.

"Chuck, I'm losing you. What do you want us to do?"

"Get . . . Tahoe"—static—"Drive to town. *Now!*" Raw fear resonated in his voice. "Do whatever . . . need to do"—static—". . . out of there!"

CHAPTER 88

RILEY FINISHED HIS EMERGENCY message to Gillian and hung up, wondering if she'd even heard his final instructions. He'd heard her breaking up on the other end, fear and desperation ringing in her voice. He felt so powerless to help her. *Father, please protect them.*

Peering into Haydon's empty cell, he shook his head. What a fool he'd been not to have realized what Haydon was capable of. Haydon fancied himself as the next Houdini, and Houdini had been a master escape artist. Add to that an old jail that badly needed updating, and his escape almost seemed inevitable.

Fifteen minutes ago, one of the deputies had gone to look in on Haydon, only to find an empty cell. It was hard to believe he could have squeezed into a ventilation duct above his cell, but with the cell door still locked, it was seemingly the only way he could have gotten out.

The police had set up roadblocks on all roads leading out of town, but Riley had a strong suspicion that Haydon was long past the roadblocks and would be heading to the lighthouse to take care of unfinished business.

But when exactly had he escaped? How much of a head start did he have? Was he already out at Whistler's Point?

Feeling a hand on his shoulder, Riley turned to peer into the sheriff's bloodshot eyes. "Let's go," Dendridge said. "I've got men and four-wheel-drive trucks ready."

Riley grabbed his coat. "He may have been gone for an hour or more, and he wouldn't have hesitated to steal a vehicle."

"Then we're wasting time. Let's go."

CHAPTER 89

GILLIAN LEAPED TO HER feet as a burst of adrenaline coursed through her veins. "Marc, we've got to get out of here. Now!"

When Gillian repeated Riley's warning, fear registered in his eyes. He got up weakly from his chair, his face pale. "Where to?"

"The Tahoe. I don't want to wake up Crystal. She would only be terrified by all this. Can you carry her?"

"I'll try, but something's wrong with me. Everything's blurry, and I feel like I'm going to throw up."

Gillian grimaced. *Does he have a concussion, or something worse? Maybe a fractured skull?* Could their situation possibly get any worse?

Marc somehow found the strength he needed. While he hefted Crystal, still wrapped in her sleeping bag, into his arms, Gillian spread out the logs in the fireplace, their undersides a bed of glowing embers.

Gillian unlocked the parlor door and opened it. Glancing at Marc, she realized they had no weapons, nothing they could use to defend themselves. If only they still had Marc's gun.

What if Haydon is waiting for us? What if he comes for us right now?

Then she remembered the fireplace poker and grabbed it. It was better than nothing. Holding the flashlight in her other hand, she led the way.

Shadows shrank before them. All she could hear were her footsteps ringing on the hardwood floor and Marc's grunts as he shifted Crystal's weight in his arms.

No sign of Haydon.

Reaching the front door, Gillian swung it open to the elements. The Tahoe was blanketed with several inches of snow.

Gillian opened the passenger-side door and helped Marc maneuver Crystal onto the seat. "I'll drive," she said.

While Marc got into the backseat, Gillian made her way around the front, grabbing onto the hood of the SUV for balance, and pulled herself into the driver's seat. She reached for the keys Marc had left in the ignition earlier and gasped.

"They're gone! The keys are gone."

CHAPTER 90

THE TRUCK SWERVED, AND Dendridge wrestled it back onto the road. Riley grabbed the armrest, praying silently. The truck's high beams illumined what seemed like millions of snowflakes. They struck the windshield like hungry bugs out for blood.

C'mon, faster, Riley thought. *Father, please let us be in time.*

As if reading Riley's thoughts, Dendridge said, "I'm doing the best I can. There must be a foot of snow."

"What a night to be out on these roads!" exclaimed a young deputy from the backseat. "Nobody should be driving in this. I'd give anything to be home with my wife right now."

I'd give anything to be at Whistler's Point right now. Riley chided himself again for having missed seeing the obvious. *If only I'd been paying attention, I could have prevented this. If anything happens to the Thayers, it'll be on my head.*

He closed his eyes and prayed, muttering quietly, lips moving. A favorite Bible story in Judges 10 came to mind. During a great battle, God had caused the sun to linger in the sky longer than usual, giving the Israelites the time they needed to defeat their enemies.

"Hey, you okay?" The young deputy's voice broke into Riley's thoughts. "What are you doin'?"

"Praying." Riley glanced back at him. "God's in control of the snow. He can get us there quicker if He wants to. If you want those folks at Whistler's Point to be okay, you might try praying, too."

CHAPTER 91

FEAR COILED AROUND GILLIAN'S heart. Standing in the foyer, she studied Marc, who was straining with Crystal's limp body in his arms and looking more ill by the moment. "What do we do now? Haydon must have taken the keys to keep us from leaving. He's definitely here somewhere."

But why doesn't he come for us? she wondered. *Where is he?*

Marc shook his head from side to side, as if to clear the cobwebs. "Follow me. Time for plan B."

Gillian wasn't content until they had found the most out-of-the-way first-story bedroom they could find and put Crystal in one of the old beds, pulling the blankets up to her chin. Amazingly, she had stayed asleep through all the moving and jostling around. She must have been exhausted by the day's ordeal.

The bedroom, once intended for a hired servant, was located beside the kitchen, the oak door blending in with matching cupboards and the entrance to a food pantry. Maybe, just maybe, Haydon wouldn't look for them here.

Sitting on the edge of the bed, Marc cradled his head in his hands, clearly not himself. Suddenly, he reached for a nearby wastebasket and vomited. An inadvertent groan escaped his lips as he wiped his mouth on his coat sleeve, his pale face glistening with sweat.

Gillian bit her lip as the sour smell permeated the room, making her stomach clench. What were they supposed to do now? Marc obviously needed medical attention.

As if summoning what little strength he had left, Marc lifted his head and peered into her eyes. "You stay here with Crystal. I remember

Clara saying something about flares stored in the cellar for emergencies. I could shoot them off and bring help."

She shook her head. "You're in no condition to do anything. I'll go get the flares. Besides, if Haydon finds Crystal here, you'd protect her better than I could." *If only Ryan were here.*

"Gillian, there's a dangerous killer out there. I can't let—"

Grabbing the wastebasket, he retched again. Then to her dismay, he crumpled to the floor.

Alarmed, Gillian sprang to his side and shook his arm. "Marc, are you okay?"

He didn't respond. His eyes were closed, his face a sickly white. Had he fainted?

Frantically she reached down and put her fingers on his throat. When she sensed his pulse, clear and strong, her anxiety disappated but not by much. Marc needed an ambulence.

Gillian fished Marc's cell phone from his pocket to call 911, but the phone had no signal. She put the phone in her pocket and pressed trembling hands to her face.

Oh, God, now what? What am I supposed to do?

"Mom, what is it? What's wrong?" Crystal said from the bed.

Gillian handed the poker to Crystal. "Take this for your protection. Your father passed out, but I think he's going to be okay." *I hope he's going to be okay.* "I need you to watch him while I go for help."

Crystal glanced around the room as if lost. "But where are we? What hap—"

"I think Haydon's here in the lighthouse somewhere. He must have hit your father."

Crystal's eyes widened.

"I have to go for help. If Haydon comes here, use this." She wrapped her hands around Crystal's hand that held the poker. "Do you understand?"

Crystal sat on the edge of the bed and nodded. Steam drifted from her mouth as she stared at Marc's crumpled form.

"I know it's cold," Gillian said. "Those extra blankets on the bed will help. Put one over your father and see if you can wake him, okay? Lock the door behind me and don't open it for anyone."

Gillian felt herself tear up. *No, you have to be strong. God will help you through this. You know what you need to do. Don't feel. Just do.* She steeled her resolve. "Do you understand what I want you to do?"

Crystal nodded, looking so much like a lost little girl. Gillian hesitated, her gaze flicking to her daughter then back to Marc. Now going after those flares and finding help were even more critical. If his condition were serious, how much time did she have? Hours? Minutes?

God, please let him be okay. Please help him to hold on.

She kissed Crystal's forehead. "I love you, sweetie. I'll do anything to protect you."

She kissed Marc's clammy cheek. Then, crossing the room, she stepped out into the hallway and closed the door behind her. Darkness fell on her in a stranglehold, but she pushed aside her fear and prayed that Haydon wouldn't look for Crystal down here.

Lingering on the other side of the bedroom door, Gillian strained to hear the tiniest of sounds. She heard nothing, but silence was deceptive. Somewhere in the dark lurked a monster who had claimed five victims and had almost taken Crystal as his sixth.

Righteous indignation sparked inside her and roared into an inferno. She imagined hunting Haydon down and blowing him away with a machine gun. But she had no gun—in fact, no weapon to speak of, unless she counted her flashlight. And what could she possibly do alone?

Anger dissolved into fear. Somehow, Haydon had escaped from the county jail and had returned to Whistler's Point. That meant only one thing: he wanted Crystal, and he was looking for her now. Somewhere in the dark, he was searching the lighthouse room by room.

And I'm the bait. He'll hear me first. He'll come after me.

Before her fears could talk her out of her plan, she inched down the dark hallway. Now that her eyes had adjusted to the dark, she kept the flashlight off, not wanting to announce her whereabouts to Haydon should she encounter him along the way.

Wincing as the floorboards creaked and groaned beneath her feet, she entered the dining room, skirted the oak table, and stepped into the sitting room, her feet making *swishing* sounds on the carpet. The grand piano and other furniture rose on either side of her like dark, looming shapes best not left to the imagination. With each step, she wondered if Haydon was waiting around the next corner.

Bracing herself, she entered the far hallway and inched her way along the wall, feeling for the cellar door. Still no sign of Haydon. And no other sound or movement. Finally, her hands found the small door, which she found unlocked when she tested the handle. A dusty miasma assaulted her nostrils as she pulled the door open, and she faced a darkness as impenetrable as granite.

Clicking on the flashlight, she splayed her fingers across the lens and shone the mellow beam down a narrow set of steps. She closed the door behind her and descended creaky steps that betrayed her presence to anyone who might be waiting below.

Reaching the cellar floor, she thought she heard a sound and flicked off the flashlight, listening intently. It couldn't have been any darker, and the air was stale and unwelcoming. Turning on the flashlight and cupping it again in her hand, Gillian surveyed a room crowded with miscellaneous junk: an old washing machine from another era, a broken push lawnmower, a fancily carved wooden chair missing two legs. Ancient cobwebs whose hosts had long since died and shriveled up hung from the massive floor joists overhead.

Studying a wooden shelf fastened to the stone wall, she glimpsed a bag of clothespins, an oil can, a glass bottle filled with a variety of drill bits and screws, and a steel box on which someone had scrawled the word "Flares."

She extinguished the flashlight, certain this time that the sound she heard wasn't her imagination. Fine hairs rose on the nape of her neck as the floorboards creaked directly above her head.

Now the footsteps moved off to her right and paused near the stairs she had just come down.

Grabbing the box of flares, she looked around frantically for a place to hide. Hearing the cellar door open, she scurried behind a dust-covered bookshelf and crouched against the stone wall.

Someone was coming down the stairs.

CHAPTER 92

HER HEART POUNDING AND her breath coming in short, quick gasps, Gillian flattened herself against the bookshelf and pressed the back of her hand to her mouth, trying to quiet her breathing.

The intruder moved across the room, his shoes barely making a sound. But it was enough for her to discern his location. He was only yards away. "Erin, where are you?" he called. "I know you're down here."

He's delusional. He's looking for someone he's already killed.

"You can't hide from me," he spoke to the darkness. "I grew up here, and I know all the hiding places. You might as well come out. I'll find you eventually."

Reaching behind her, expecting to feel more stone wall, Gillian felt . . . nothing. Easing backward without making a sound, she bumped into a stone step.

Stairs?

Then she realized that before turn-of-the-century renovations, this had been the original cellar entrance.

The footsteps stopped.

Gillian's muscles ached, but she didn't budge. Didn't breathe. What was he doing? Listening?

Then she heard the scramble of feet. He was coming for her!

Heart beating out of her chest, Gillian turned on the flashlight so she could see, clutched the flares, and raced up the stone steps.

A double wooden door stretched at an angle above her head. Aiming a shoulder at the point where the two halves came together, she plowed into the door. A sharp pain shot down her arm, but the door didn't budge.

At the bottom of the steps, Eric White peered up at her in surprise, obviously expecting to see Crystal. Shining the flashlight down the stairs, she was pleased to see his disappointment.

Meeting his stare, Gillian felt herself shaking, but not from fear. White-hot anger boiled inside her at the thought that this man had tried to kill her daughter, the only child she had left in the world. *How dare he!*

"I don't want you," he said. "I only want your daughter. Tell me where she is."

It was the emotionless voice of a man who had killed so many times that he'd become hardened to natural feeling. His callous words made her even angrier, if such a thing were possible. Anger was the only weapon she had left, but was it enough to overpower him?

"How dare you hurt my husband and daughter!" Gillian heard her voice shaking. "You're crazy if you think I'm going to tell you where she is."

He advanced up the first two steps, a thin, white rope taut between his hands. If he had Marc's gun, he wasn't using it. His unblinking eyes were glazed as if he were more machine than man.

"Tell me where she is, or I'll kill you."

She shined the flashlight into his eyes, and he drew back, momentarily blinded. It was the moment she needed.

Drawing back the bolt she'd missed seeing before, she slammed her shoulder into the door again. The old wood shuddered, and a flutter of snow fell down through the gap.

Gillian sucked in a quick breath and shoved again. This time the door gave way, and an icy wind swept into the cellar as she stumbled up the last two stairs into the dark, wintry world beyond.

Behind her, Haydon raced up the steps and lunged for her legs, but he was a split second too late. Dashing outside, Gillian flung the heavy door down on top of her pursuer. In snow up to her calves, she fled.

CHAPTER 93

THE WIND SHRIEKED LIKE a wounded animal. Snow drove down with a vengeance, stinging Gillian's face and eyes. Pressing her back against the lighthouse's brick facade, she tried to calm her pounding heart, her breath frosting white.

Peering around the corner, she watched the cellar door for several minutes. He wasn't coming after her. At least, not now.

Sick fear soured in her stomach at the thought that Haydon was still inside, looking for Marc and Crystal's hiding place. She was wasting time. *Hold on, Marc, hold on.* They needed her help, and her gloveless hands would get frostbit if she braved the elements much longer. She chided herself for leaving her gloves somewhere along the way.

Opening the metal box, she saw the flare gun and a single flare. After taking a few seconds to figure out how to load it, she pointed the flare gun at the dark sky and pulled the trigger. The blast flung her arm back with surprising force. The flare sped toward the heavens, pausing in midair before exploding in a burst of incandescent white.

She cast the gun into the snow before considering the best way to get back into the lighthouse. Returning to the cellar door wasn't an option. Perhaps if she—

The swoop of the lighthouse's revolving beacon startled her. With the power outage, she hadn't expected the beacon to be working; seeing it now, she assumed it was operating on battery power. Then a thought struck her.

The townspeople often spoke affectionately of the lighthouse's beacon as one sure thing that hadn't changed in more than one hundred years. The light had always been there, even through the most violent of storms.

But what if she turned the light off? Perhaps someone—maybe even the Coast Guard—would notice and come see what was the matter; that is, if they were foolhardy enough to defy the weather. Maybe it was a silly idea, but she had to try.

Certain that Haydon would never expect her to enter the lighthouse through the front door, she decided to take a chance.

Please, God, did we leave the door unlocked when we came back in?

Creeping up close to the front door, she gently tried the handle. With a muffled click, the pin released and the door eased open.

Safely inside, every one of her senses on edge, she quietly closed the door against the howling wind and stood in the foyer in silence, pausing to let her eyes adjust to the dark.

It felt so good to be out of the cold. She flexed her fingers, wondering if the warmth would ever return to them.

She resisted the impulse to check on Marc and Crystal to make sure they were okay. Haydon knew she couldn't stay outdoors forever. Once he knew she was back inside, he would be even more determined to eliminate her. Even now, he was waiting somewhere in the shadows of the cavernous place, listening for her first move. One thing was certain: she'd never lead him to Crystal.

During her flight, she'd dropped the flashlight somewhere in the snow—no doubt lost until spring. As she edged down the front hallway to a storage closet to look for candles, she heard two antique clocks gonging a discordant duet. She peered at her watch. Eleven o'clock.

Lighting a candle and putting the other in her pocket for safekeeping, she pressed on toward the staircase leading to the lighthouse tower. All the while, she tried to recall Bible passages to calm her nerves and remind herself of God's presence, even in dire circumstances. But she couldn't remember a single verse—she who had scripted countless verses in calligraphy.

Finally, Psalm 16:8 came to mind, and she clung to it like a lifeline. *I have set the LORD always before me; because He is at my right hand I shall not be moved.*

Passing the parlor where her family had basked in the fire's warmth only an hour ago, she paused and listened. She didn't hear anyone, but she knew Haydon had to be somewhere. Waiting. Watching.

As she turned a corner, she accidentally brushed up against the wall, knocking a framed piece of artwork to the floor with a clatter. Shuddering at the noise, she noticed that the painting had concealed a hole in the wall. She looked closer.

From the hole, a single, black eye peered back at her.

Gasping, she drew back.

The eye disappeared, and something moved inside the wall as if a wild animal were trapped inside. Somehow, Haydon was inside the wall, and he was coming after her.

Not looking back, she raced toward the tower and came to a small, steel door. A chain was wrapped around the door handle and secured by a padlock. The padlock lacked a key.

Her heart sank. There had to be a way inside. *God, please . . .*

Moving the candle closer for a better look, she realized that the C-shaped bar of steel pivoted freely from its base—the padlock wasn't locked. Relieved, she removed the lock and chain, opened the door, and entered a small, cylindrical room.

In the middle of the room, a circular staircase wound upward and out of sight. Closing the door behind her, she regretted that she couldn't lock it from the inside.

She crossed to the black steps and looked for the power source for the revolving beacon. Seeing nothing, she began her ascent, one hand tight on the cold railing, footsteps ringing hollowly on the cast-iron steps.

The steps rose and angled to the right above her, limiting her vision to only a few feet at a time. On her left was a painted white wall, punctuated periodically by small, round windows that reminded her of portholes. Outside the windows, the night was too black for her to see anything beyond the panes.

Her leg muscles burned, and her breathing became labored as she continued her ascent. The steps seemed to go on forever. Losing count, she wondered how many more could possibly be left.

A clang of steel stopped her in her tracks. Below, someone had opened the door leading to the tower. She heard the steady, metallic rhythm of footsteps ascending with a purpose. Gillian instantly regretted having chosen to climb the tower. The footsteps could only be

Haydon's, and there was only one way up or down in the lighthouse tower.

She was trapped!

Heart racing, she peered up the steps, wondering how much farther she had to go. *And when I reach the top . . . then what?*

Maybe two minutes had passed since she'd begun her ascent. At least that much time separated her from Haydon.

Two minutes to think and to plan. She quickened her pace.

The stairs ended at a trapdoor, which Gillian easily pushed open. She pulled herself up into the small, octagonal lantern room, which she remembered from her first day at Whistler's Point. She closed the door and surveyed her surroundings.

In the center of the room stood the rotating electric beacon that had turned endlessly since 1968, replacing the original light that had to be wound. The light hummed and spun clockwise, its white light strobing across the water. Some wires led to a mechanism at the light's base, but she saw no switch, nothing obvious, for turning the beacon off.

Snow pelted against the glass panels that rose from her waist to the ceiling, encircling the room and providing a breathtaking view of Lake Superior on clear, sunny days. A small door to her right opened onto a catwalk that wound around the top of the tower, but there was at least a foot of snow on the catwalk by now.

At any moment, Haydon would reach the trapdoor. Peering around frantically, she wished she had the poker she had left with Crystal. But she had nothing with which to defend herself.

She still had the candle in her hand, and another was in her pocket, but what use could they serve beyond illumination?

She studied the trapdoor, but saw no way to lock it. If she sat on top of it, her weight would hold it down. But for how long? Haydon would eventually push her off.

Moving to the other side of the beacon, she positioned it between herself and the trapdoor and set her candle down.

Why not face him? I have no place to hide.

CHAPTER 94

FATHER, PLEASE PROTECT THEM, Riley prayed.

The truck swerved again—this time sliding off the road completely. Dendridge cursed colorfully as Riley pushed his door open into a snowbank and climbed out, his legs deep in snow. The wind blasted his head, and he shivered. Why did he keep forgetting to wear a hat?

Dendridge pressed on the accelerator, but the tires only spun in the snow. The SUV was stuck.

The officers in the back spilled out of the vehicle and began searching for some way to block the tires. Another SUV pulled up on the shoulder of the road, and three other officers got out to help. One of the men hooked a chain to the axle of the SUV that was stuck in the snow and dragged the other end back up to the SUV on the road.

More delays, Riley thought, his ears numb. *Father, please help us get there in time.*

Something caught his eye, and he glanced to his left as a white flare lit up the night sky.

CHAPTER 95

GILLIAN HEARD THE TRAPDOOR squeak open, and Haydon Owens climbed into the lantern room. He still had a length of rope in his hand, and his intentions were obvious. Gillian began to wonder whether he actually had Marc's gun, but maybe strangling was just more his style. Her left hand went involuntarily to her throat, and she suddenly felt even colder than before.

Gaining his bearings, Haydon fixed his eyes on Gillian, and she crouched slightly to avoid his direct gaze. He looked surprised, and Gillian realized that once again he had mistaken her for Crystal. He also seemed puzzled, as if wondering why she had led him up here.

Why indeed.

The energy she'd burned climbing the stairs would work in his favor. Her legs were burning, but he didn't look remotely fatigued by the climb. But now that they were face-to-face, she didn't feel afraid of him. Not anymore.

I have set the LORD always before me; because He is at my right hand I shall not be moved.

"It's all about hate, isn't it, Haydon?" She spoke over the hum of the beacon. "Long ago, somebody ticked you off, and you never forgave her."

The hatred in his eyes grew more intense, if such a thing were possible. He spat on the floor and muttered a name between clenched teeth.

"Erin Walker."

"How did she hurt you?" "She lied to a jury and said my parents had murdered someone. My parents were locked away for the rest of their lives, and my father died in prison—all because of her."

"So you strangled her."

"Yes." His eyes betrayed not a scintilla of human compassion. There was no regret. No remorse. Nothing. "But she keeps coming back."

Gillian couldn't hide her curiosity. "What do you mean?"

He glanced down at the rope, pulling it tight between his hands as if to demonstrate his resolve. "I keep seeing her, everywhere I go." He lifted his hate-filled gaze to hers. "I see her in Crystal."

Gillian stared at him in disbelief. "You think Erin Walker is somehow reincarnated—is somehow living—inside my daughter?"

"I see her."

Gillian couldn't help laughing in spite of her circumstances. "But that's ridiculous. Don't you realize that?"

For an instant, he seemed to waver, as if seeing the truth for the first time. As if he could turn his back on the past and walk away from all this.

If only he would, she thought.

Something hardened in his eyes. "No." He shook his head as if refusing to hear the voice of reason. "Erin has returned. And Erin must die."

"But it's all a mistake—you have to see that. Erin is already dead, Haydon. It was a mistake for you to kill those other girls, and it's a mistake for you to go after my daughter. And it all began with someone you couldn't forgive. Don't you see?"

As she spoke, she remembered that she, too, had harbored an unforgiving spirit—toward Marc. She had held onto resentment about something—about someone—beyond Marc's control. Thank God, the conflict was resolved now, but for a while she'd been just like Haydon. It was only a matter of degree.

"Erin doesn't deserve to be forgiven," he said.

"But who are you to judge? Don't tell me you've never made a mistake. Nobody has ever had to forgive you for doing something—for saying something—wrong? For making a mistake?"

He shook his head, his face twisted, as if a battle were raging in his mind. Finally, with a sigh, he said, "It's too late. You don't understand."

"I'm *trying* to understand." Gillian sensed that she was gaining some leverage in the conversation, but she knew it was tenuous. Until a minute ago, Haydon had been trying to kill her; now he was confiding in her. None of it made sense, but maybe it didn't have to. Maybe he just needed someone to extend mercy to him. She remembered a quote from the novelist George Eliot: *We hand folks over to God's mercy, and show none ourselves.*

Every minute he spent baring his heart to her was one less minute he was hunting Crystal. Perhaps Riley was on the road now, coming to their aid. The more time she occupied, the better.

Just keep him talking. Don't stop.

Drawing himself up, Haydon stepped toward her. "I don't want to hurt you, but I'll kill you if I have to. I want Erin. Tell me where she is."

Like a soap bubble popping on a blade of grass, whatever advantage she had gained was gone. The aggression was back.

Gillian slid to her right, keeping the beacon between herself and Haydon. She drew herself up. "Her name is Crystal—and why should I tell you where she is? I don't want my daughter to die."

"If you don't help me, you're only an unnecessary distraction." He began to edge around the beacon.

"But if you kill me, how will you find her?"

"I don't need your help. You would just save me time."

The callousness of his words made her tremble. "But why kill Crystal? What good would that do? Erin has always returned before. What makes you think that killing her this time will make any difference?"

Indecision clouded his eyes. He was so close to seeing the truth. *God, please open his eyes.* "Wouldn't you like to be rid of Erin forever? You can, you know."

He was listening, but he was also still trying to get closer to her. Gillian continued to slide to her right to keep the distance constant.

"There's only one way. You have to let her go. You need to forgive her."

Haydon took another step toward her. "I'll never forgive her. And you'll never get out of here alive if you don't tell me where Erin is."

Gillian's heart sank. Crystal and Erin were the same person in his mind, no matter how hard she tried to persuade him otherwise. Reaching behind her, she felt the latch of the door leading to the catwalk. "You don't have to live with hate, Haydon. Jesus can forgive you if you ask Him to. Then He'll teach you how to forgive others so you can put the past behind you."

"Jesus." He spat the name as if it were a bad taste in his mouth. "I don't need Him. He never did anything for me. You're the one who should be praying to Jesus." He lunged toward her.

Gillian opened the door, and the wind seemed to tear it out of her hand. Not looking back, she stepped onto the catwalk and pressed forward, the snow heavy around her legs.

A stiff, icy wind buffeted her head, and snow lashed her face. Ducking her head, she grabbed the railing. It was so cold—it felt like fire on her gloveless hands.

She glanced back. Haydon was coming toward her, arms raised to shield his face.

She inched farther down the catwalk against the shrieking wind. All around her was pitch black, except for the moments when the lighthouse beacon swiveled past. The combination of her sneakers, the snow, and the iron deck of the catwalk made for treacherous footing. Several times she had the feeling that if she loosened her grip on the railing she would topple into the blackness below.

Haydon had closed the distance between them, and he was now close enough to reach for her. Releasing one hand from the railing, Gillian tried to push him away, but he grabbed her wrist.

Snow stung her eyes, momentarily blinding her. She bowed her head, unable to see as tears fell in runnels down her cheeks.

With a deft flick of the wrist, Haydon looped the rope around her neck and pulled it tight. A searing pain erupted in Gillian's throat and neck, and she slipped to her knees, losing her grasp on the railing. Instinct kicked in and she reached for her neck, digging her fingers into her skin in a desperate effort to loosen the rope. She began to see bright flashes of light as her lungs cried out for air.

God, please help me!

Clawing at Haydon's wrists, she tried to pry his hands away from the rope. But he was behind her now and she couldn't break his grip.

As the darkness began to close around her, something cracked above the shriek of the wind like the snapping of a tree limb.

She felt the rope slacken and she lurched forward, sliding on the icy, snow-covered catwalk. She landed on her back and loosened the ligature from around her neck. Stumbling to her feet, she coughed, gagged, and sobbed as fresh air poured into her lungs.

When a hand tightened around her arm, she whirled around, arms flailing at her attacker.

A strong hand closed around her wrist and held her at bay. A familiar face loomed out of the lashing snow, illumined by the passing flash of the beacon.

Riley! Thank God!

Gillian stared at him in disbelief.

Holding a pistol off to the side, Riley grabbed her with his free hand, keeping her from losing her balance as the last bit of strength drained from her legs.

Haydon lay crumpled in the snow at Riley's feet, his face contorted in pain as he clutched at a wound in his shoulder, his rose-red blood staining the freshly fallen snow.

CHAPTER 96

MARC AND CRYSTAL WERE waiting for Gillian at the bottom of the stairs. At the sight of their expectant faces, a fresh sob burst from her throat. They were okay! Throwing her arms around them, she burst into tears.

She embraced Marc and Crystal for what seemed like an eternity before pulling away to wipe the tears and slush from her face and push back her wet, stringy hair. She knew she must look a sight, but she hardly cared. Her fingers throbbed, and she rubbed her hands together, trying to warm them.

Marc still looked pale, but at least he was conscious. He pulled her into a hug and kissed her.

"Mom, are you all right?"

"No, but I will be."

"What happened up there?"

Gillian pressed a hand to her daughter's face. "I'll tell you later, sweetie."

Moments later, as the Thayers stood in front of the lighthouse with the snow continuing to fall, Sheriff Dendridge and another policeman emerged from the front door with Haydon, now handcuffed, walking between them. His face was white with pain and shock, and he shuffled slowly toward one of several police vehicles.

Riley finished a conversation with one of the sheriff's deputies and turned toward Gillian and Marc. What remained of his thin, iron-gray hair clung to his bald head, and he looked exhausted.

"We found Haydon's diary and some letters," he said. "Looks like his mother ordered him to commit the first murder. We may never understand the rest."

"I might be able to fill in the blanks," Gillian said. "He and I had a talk before he chased me onto the catwalk. He basically confessed everything to me."

"Then I'll need to get your statement," Riley said. "Haydon's shoulder wound isn't serious. He'll stand trial for sure. How are you holding up?"

She smiled weakly. "Let's just say you came at the right time. How did you know where to find me?"

"Well, we saw your flare, which let us know you were in trouble. Then, when we got to the lighthouse, I glanced up at the beacon, which was the only light in the middle of a whole lot of darkness, and I saw you and Haydon up in the lantern room. Fortunately, I was able to figure out how to get up there, but those stairs just about killed me. I'm way too old for that kind of workout."

As Riley talked, he glanced over at Marc in time to see him reach for his head and crouch down in the snow. "Hey!" Riley shouted to one of the officers nearby. "Somebody get over here and help this guy."

Gillian helped Marc to his feet and looked at him with concern as the officer came to escort him to one of the SUVs, where he joined Crystal in the warmth of the interior.

"An ambulance is on the way," the officer said to Gillian. "And by the look of your neck, ma'am, I'd say you should be examined, too."

Gillian tentatively touched her fingertips to the raw skin at the side of her neck. "It's probably just rope burn." She forced a smile. "Crystal probably has it worse than I do."

"Nevertheless, you should let a doctor take a look anyhow, just to be—"

Just then, a commotion erupted by the police vehicles. Gillian jerked her head around in time to see Haydon bowl over Sheriff Dendridge and head-butt the other officer before dashing through the snow toward the lake, his hands still cuffed behind him.

The sheriff's officers responded in force. "Freeze!" one of them shouted. Only yards behind Haydon, he raised his gun.

"Hold your fire! Hold your fire!" Dendridge's voice echoed into the night. "Surround him! He can't get away."

CHAPTER 97

EVEN AS HE RAN, Haydon worked the cuffs, ready to spring them open when the time was right. But he waited, knowing that his final trick would be more dramatic if he left them on a little longer. He raced toward a familiar cleft of rock that jutted out over the churning water of the lake.

The headlights from the half-dozen or so police cars back at the house provided just enough light for him to see where he was going. Their beams were like a spotlight, illumining his ultimate performance. *Perfect.*

Numb to the cold, he was aware only of the raw, searing pain in his shoulder. His arm was stiff, but he could move it enough for what he had to do. Without looking back, he knew the police were closing in from behind, none too eager to let him get away.

But they won't shoot me, he thought. *I'm too valuable alive.*

His feet encumbered by the snow, he scrambled across the rocky cleft and poised on the precarious edge, the bracing wind tousling his hair. Thirty feet below, the frigid waters of Lake Superior churned in the darkness. Beyond the ice-encrusted shore, ice floes resembling slivers of glass stretched as far as the eye could see in the flashes of light from the Whistler's Point beacon. If he'd had time to admire the view, he would have said it was beautiful.

He glanced back only once to make sure they were watching. He was a performer after all, and he needed an audience. They didn't want to miss the show.

In his mind's eye, he pictured Houdini in France in 1909. Standing on a bridge overlooking the placid waters of the Seine River. Peering down. Bracing. Leaping.

Except, this time it wasn't Houdini. It was him, Haydon Owens.

He was Houdini, and he wasn't afraid.

A smile tugged at his lips. He gathered his wits and leaped, toes pointed down.

The dark, angry water rose to meet him. Exploded around his feet. Enveloped him with an icy embrace. Closed over his head with a frigid impact.

CHAPTER 98

A SPLASH.

The officers were shouting.

Dendridge was cursing.

Gillian jerked forward. "What's happening?" she asked Riley. "I can't see what's happening!"

Raised voices trailed down toward the lake.

"I can't believe it!"

"No way!"

"He jumped into the lake. A thirty-foot drop, at least."

"Call the Coast Guard!"

"Get some lights down here. Quick!"

Gillian squinted into the darkness, wishing she could see. *No, it isn't possible,* she thought. *Nobody in his right mind would do such a thing.* How could he hope to survive in the freezing water?

Riley's face had blanched. "I can't believe it," he said, more to himself than to anyone. "I just can't believe it. Houdini pulled the same stunt in France, right down to the handcuffs." He shook his head, his eyes meeting Gillian's. "But don't worry. Houdini may have survived his own stunt, but I don't think Haydon's walking away from this one."

CHAPTER 99

RILEY PACED THE LIVING room of the caretaker's house like a caged tiger. Marc and Gillian looked on from the couch, where Gillian was resting her head against a pillow, a cold compress on her sore neck. Marc had a large gauze bandage on the back of his head and strict orders to stay off his feet and get some rest. To Gillian's relief, the doctor had said that Marc's concussion wasn't serious and would heal quickly.

Sheriff Dendridge had called a half hour ago with some good news. Haydon's fingerprints matched the ones on file, which meant he was, in fact, the Magician Murderer. Unfortunately, Haydon's body had not yet been recovered from the lake, which meant he was still officially at large.

"Nobody knows where Haydon is," Riley said. "The police and the Coast Guard have been searching for him around the clock. Sheriff Dendridge said he'll call when he has something new to report. I guess all we can do is sit tight and pray that somebody finds him."

"What I haven't been able to figure out," Marc said, "is how he got here after he escaped from the jail."

"He stole a police SUV," Riley said. "We found it parked behind some trees a quarter-mile from here. He traveled the rest of the way on foot, wanting to surprise you."

Oh, he was a surprise all right, Gillian thought.

Marc had his arm around Gillian, and she snuggled against him, so glad to have him home and more or less in one piece. Crystal was asleep in her bedroom, and Ryan had decided to wait at his hotel until Crystal woke and felt more sociable. So it was just the two of them and Riley in the living room.

It had been a crazy Sunday morning after umpteen police interviews, endless calls from reporters, and an anxious call from the Hendersons. On a trip downstate after yesterday's matinee, they'd heard the story on the news and had been worried sick about Marc and Gillian. Nicole had also called, and Gillian had been happy to report that they were all safe.

"I won't sleep here until he's found," Gillian said. "If Haydon's alive, he'll come back—I know he will. Crystal and I will never be safe until he's caught."

"The Coast Guard may never find him, but I wouldn't worry." Riley spread his hands. "Lake Superior is like a small ocean. Have any idea how cold that water is this time of year?" He shook his head. "Nobody could last more than an hour in that water. As far as I'm concerned, Haydon committed suicide when he jumped into that lake. Besides, he had a bullet wound in his shoulder and handcuffs on. How could he possibly swim?"

"The important thing," Marc said, peering into Gillian's eyes, "is that you and Crystal are safe. We don't have to stay here tonight. We can always stay somewhere in town under police protection if you want to."

The phone rang. "I'll get it." Riley pushed to his feet.

He returned moments later, an expression of relief etched on his face. "That was Sheriff Dendridge. The Coast Guard found Haydon about a mile offshore on an ice floe. He's confirmed dead."

Gillian pressed her face against Marc's chest. "Then it's finally over."

Marc squeezed her tighter. "He'll never hurt anybody ever again."

Gillian sighed with relief. Next Thursday, they'd celebrate Thanksgiving—and what a time of thanksgiving it would be! She couldn't remember ever feeling more thankful to be alive.

Settling into the rocking chair, Riley leaned his head back and closed his eyes. He took a deep breath and blew it out.

"Hey, you okay?" Marc asked.

Opening his eyes, Riley smiled. "I'm fine. I'm just letting the relief settle in and thanking God for His goodness. This was the toughest case of my life, and I've prayed a long time for this day. Now that it's here . . . well, I guess it hasn't really sunk in yet."

"What will you do now that the case is closed?" Gillian asked.

"First, I'll share the news with the victims' families so they can experience some closure. Then I'll return to Emily in Florida and get on with my retirement. In fact, she's probably worried sick about me. I'm going to call her with the news right now."

＊　＊　＊

After Riley left the room, Marc pulled Gillian closer, glad for the moment to be alone with her. He could have been a widower this morning, but God had spared her life.

Gillian sighed. "Marc, I'm so glad it's over. We've lost enough children. I don't know if I could have handled losing another one. Crystal came so close—"

"I know, but it's over now. Try not to think about it. There are no 'what ifs' in God's plan."

"I know. But still. When I think about how close she came to death. Losing the twins was bad enough."

"How are you doing these days? With the twins, I mean."

She glanced at him, surprise glinting in her eyes, then looked away.

"I know we haven't talked much about the twins since—" He sighed. "I thought if I mentioned them, you would only feel worse, so I decided not to talk about them. But I didn't want you to think I wasn't grieving, too."

Gillian didn't answer.

"You need to talk about them, don't you?"

She nodded as tears filled her eyes. They spilled onto her cheeks, and she smeared them away. "Absolutely."

"I felt awkward talking about them, so I . . . I avoided the subject. But I realize I was only being selfish, that you needed to talk about them. Will you forgive me?"

She peered into his eyes. "Of course I forgive you."

"So tell me the truth. How are you doing?"

"Today—not too bad. Other days—absolutely terrible. Sometimes my arms physically ache because I want to"—she hesitated—"to hold them so bad." She bowed her head. "I'm sure that probably sounds silly to you. You can't possibly understand—"

"Yes, I do. I want to hold them, too. Every day."

She looked up. "You do?"

He nodded. "Gill, I want you to be honest with me about something. Do you blame yourself for what happened to Meredith and Blaine?"

She nodded. "It's hard not to feel like I did something wrong, that I was deficient somehow. I mean, why did they have to die? It doesn't make any sense."

"But you heard the doctor. You know there's nothing you could have done differently."

"I know, but still—"

"God's in control. Don't blame yourself."

"I'm trying not to."

"Then don't." He hesitated. "Besides, this doesn't have to be a dead end for us. There are other ways to have children."

Her eyes locked onto his.

He realized he had her attention now. "You know, we haven't even talked about adoption."

Tears pooled in her eyes, but he could tell they weren't tears of sadness. They were tears of hope.

✳   ✳   ✳

Riley dialed his home number and waited impatiently through two rings.

"Hello?"

He recognized her voice, so comforting, like a warm blanket. Picturing her in his mind, he couldn't wait to hold her in his arms. "Hey, it's me."

"Something's wrong," Emily said immediately. "I can hear it in your voice."

"No, nothing's wrong. Everything's right. The Magician Murderer is dead. I'm coming home."

Emily was silent, and Riley wondered if something was wrong. Then he realized she was crying. "I'm so happy," she finally said through her tears. "So very happy."

EPILOGUE

Six months later

HEAVING A BOX INTO the back of the already crammed U-Haul, Gillian wiped a sleeve across her damp forehead. She took a long, hard look at the beautiful Victorian that now belonged to a perfect stranger. The feeling was . . . well, she wasn't sure how she was supposed to feel. A year ago, if anybody had asked her if she'd ever part with this house, she would have said he was crazy.

But so much in my life has changed since then.

She had a restored marriage, not one plagued by suspicion and resentment. All along, Marc had loved her deeply, but she'd held him at arm's length, not letting him into the secret recesses of her heart. She'd let bitterness and anger get in the way, skewing her view of God and of herself. At odds with God, she'd been at odds with everyone around her.

Especially with Marc.

And something else had happened, too. Something exciting. She and Marc had begun adoption paperwork. She knew they had a long road of legal fees and red tape ahead, but the hope of holding a baby boy in her arms thrilled her beyond words.

Crystal trudged down the sidewalk, another box in her arms. Blonde strands of hair clung to her damp forehead. "Any more room?"

Gillian shook her head. "Nope. It'll have to go in the Tahoe."

Putting the box down, Crystal studied her mom, head tilted. "Hey, you okay? You look like you just lost your best friend."

"Maybe that's because I have." Gillian studied the front porch and remembered the many mother-daughter talks she and Crystal had enjoyed on the front porch swing while sipping herbal tea.

In the front garden plot, she glimpsed tall purple and golden irises, about ready to open. She regretted that she wouldn't be here to see the blooms and hoped the new owners would appreciate her gardening efforts. "I have so many wonderful memories of this place. I guess I'm having a hard time saying good-bye."

Putting an arm around her mom, Crystal hugged her. "But, hey, we'll be making new memories in a brand-new place, right? That sounds pretty cool to me."

Gillian watched her daughter return to the garage for another box, marveling at how much she'd matured in just the last few months. When she and Marc had told her about their decision to move to the Upper Peninsula so Marc could take Pastor Randall's church upon his retirement, Crystal had soberly nodded and said that that was fine with her as long as Ryan could visit once in a while.

Lately, she'd begun programming Web sites pro bono for a legion of struggling missionaries who couldn't afford expensive Web site fees. As far as her singing . . . well, Gillian knew Crystal would be making beautiful music wherever she went. She couldn't help it.

Locking the front door, Marc descended the front steps and strolled toward them, his gaze fixed on the house key in his hand. "Guess it's a little late to be having second thoughts, huh?" He glanced at Gillian. "Hey, you okay?"

Gillian nodded, her throat tight. "Before we go, there's one more thing I need to do. We talked about it yesterday, remember?"

He embraced her and kissed her on the forehead. "Of course. Take as long as you need."

Getting into the Tahoe, Gillian pulled the door closed behind her. Through the open window, she said, "I'll be back in a half hour."

"We'll be waiting."

In the rearview mirror, she watched Marc and Crystal wave good-bye. Then Marc pulled out a basketball, and Crystal tried to block his layup as he drove to the hoop. The ball sank into the net, and Gillian smiled.

Another blessing to add to the long list. Marc was playing basketball again.

✷　✷　✷

Laying a bouquet of wildflowers at the foot of each headstone, Gillian stepped back and fixed the sight in her mind. She knew she probably wouldn't be back to the cemetery for a long time.

Don't forget, the wind rushing in the treetops seemed to whisper to her. *Don't ever, ever forget.* As if such a thing were possible.

Of all the challenges she'd faced in their move to the North Woods, saying good-bye had been the toughest. How could she leave her babies behind? The fact was, she couldn't—not in her own strength, that is. God had enabled her to take each difficult step. And wherever He led her, His grace would be there, too. Just enough to provide what she needed for each day.

She knelt at Meredith and Blaine's graves and touched the stones with her fingertips. She didn't bother wiping her tears away; there was no point. Good-byes had always been hard for her, but it was okay—even necessary—to cry. If she didn't have a good cry now, she'd always regret it later.

She thought of another mother who was probably grieving today. Virginia Owens. She'd birthed a son into the world with high hopes that his life would be a success, certainly never expecting his final outcome. *But without God, what chance do any of us have of living a life of true success?*

Gillian breathed a prayer for Virginia Owens.

Reaching into her pocket, she pulled out a sheaf of letters. A year ago, she'd ordered two stones, engraved with Meredith and Blaine's names written in calligraphy by her own hand. Now she used the stones as paperweights to hold the letters down.

Sure, the letters to her babies had begun as a form of therapy and weren't evil in themselves, but sometimes she'd found herself calling out to her babies instead of praying to God, as if beseeching their help from beyond the grave.

Forgive me, Father. Some of those letters were prayers I should have offered to You. You were there to help me, but I turned my back on You so many times. Thank You for forgiving me. I need You now more than ever. Please give me strength for the journey ahead.

Minutes ticked by, and the strength that had propelled her this far seemed to vanish from her limbs. She knew if she didn't finish what she'd set out to do, she would be tempted to spend the rest of the afternoon here. The rest of the day. The rest of her life.

And, Father, could You give my babies a kiss for me? I know they're safe in Your arms, but I miss them so much.

She listened to the trees, to the rustle of their leaves, and felt jealous. She would be gone, but the trees would remain here and grow taller for many years to come. So close to her babies. Their roots would burrow down into the cold, dark place where her children slept . . .

She realized if she didn't leave now, she never would. Remembering the journey ahead, she stood, kissed her fingertips, and touched the headstones one last time.

Meredith. Blaine. Good-bye, my dearest children. I know I'll see you again . . . someday.

A poem by Christina Rossetti seemed appropriate:

> Remember me when I am gone away,
> Gone far away into the silent land.
> Better by far you should forget and smile
> Than that you should remember and be sad.

With strength only God could provide, Gillian brushed the last tears away, turned, and walked toward the Tahoe, resolving not to look back. For an instant, sorrow stabbed her soul as if she were leaving her children behind, abandoning them to cold nights and bitter winds. Then she reminded herself that they weren't here. Not really. God was watching over them, His protective arms holding them close, His love infinitely better and more true than anything she could have provided here on earth.

As she strolled through the warm grass, the sun beating down on her neck, the wind stirred the trees, filling the air with the sound of rushing leaves. Closing her eyes, she imagined waves crashing on Lake Superior's shore. She pictured the Whistler's Point lighthouse rising against the cobalt blue of the water like a castle.

No, I'm not leaving anyone behind, she thought. *I'm going home.*

READING GROUP GUIDE

1. After Gillian discovered Stacey's love letter to Marc, she quoted a Bible verse to help her through her crisis. What verses do you turn to for comfort when something has turned your life upside down?

2. Did Gillian deal with her grief over the loss of her twins in a biblical way? If you could have counseled Gillian, what would you have told her to help her deal with her grief? (For help, see Isaiah 41:10; Jeremiah 29:11; Romans 8:28; and 1 Corinthians 10:13.)

3. We learn that Marc decided to avoid basketball due to losing his temper when he played. But when Marc heard a vandal ransacking his house, he yielded to his anger and stepped into a dangerous situation that almost cost him his life. Have you ever put yourself in a bad sitiation because you acted out of anger? What should you have done instead?

4. At one point in the story, Gillian confessed that she wasn't sure what she believed in anymore. Have you ever doubted your faith in God? What helped strengthen your faith?

5. Marc kept several secrets from Gillian that strained their marriage. Is it ever right to keep secrets from your spouse? Why or why not?

6. Gillian observed that the family's move to Whistler's Point made little sense in human terms. Has God ever redirected your life in a way that didn't make sense at the time? What did God teach you through the experience? Looking back, were you able to see His plan?

7. Gillian was distressed to see that Marc had stored his pastoral books in the basement of the caretaker's house. When she confronted him, he replied that he needed some time and space to evaluate how God was leading him. Is it ever appropriate to take a break from Christian service?

8. In Florida, Chuck Riley regretted leaving unfinished business and still wanted to catch the Magician Murderer. During the course of the story, God led Riley to finish the job. Do you have any major projects in your life that you have left unfinished? Do you believe God wants you to finish them?

9. After Marc rejected Stacey, she fled to a deserted hunting cabin to regroup. But even then, she couldn't run from God. Has God's Word ever pursued you or stopped you in your tracks when you were dead set on going your own way?

10. God uses the words of other believers to encourage us in the Christian life. After Marc rejected Stacey's declaration of love, she kept remembering his words; in the end, the truth of his words helped shatter her delusions. Has God ever used the words of another believer to help you come to an understanding of a situation?

11. Before Stacey's death, she decided to stop pursuing Marc Thayer and to warn him about Haydon. Her act of seeking to warn the Thayer family led to her own demise. Have you ever stood at a crossroads between what you wanted and what was more important for the good of others? Did you make the right choice?

12. Gillian was an overprotective parent, almost to the point of driving Crystal away. Are you overprotective of your children? How do you know if you're being overprotective?

13. What problems do we face in our Christian lives when personal ambition becomes an idol, like it did for Haydon?

14. After Haydon tried to kill Crystal, Gillian was so angry that she wanted to kill him. Is violence in this situation justified? Is it ever justified?

15. During one crisis in the story, Gillian was forced to turn to prayer and realized that she hadn't recently prayed in any

meaningful way. What is your prayer life like? Do you turn to God only when you face a crisis?

16. Marc and Gillian faced several struggles in their marriage. How does their relationship change by the end of the novel?

17. At the end of the novel, when Gillian left her letters at the graves of her twins, she realized that she had been talking to her dead babies more than she'd been talking to God. Is there anything in your life that you've substituted for intimacy with God?

ABOUT THE AUTHOR

WHILE GROWING UP IN a farmhouse, Michigan native Adam Blumer filled notebooks with pirate and fantasy stories and dreamed of being a novelist. Though he finished his first novel in high school, he pursued journalism in college and took every creative writing class he could. He graduated with honors from Bob Jones University with a degree in print journalism. While completing a newspaper internship during the Gulf War, Adam sensed that God had something other than print journalism in mind for his life.

For the next fourteen years, Adam served in editorial capacities at two ministries, Awana Clubs International and Northland Baptist Bible College. In 2006, Adam became a full-time freelance editor and writer. His work has been published in a variety of periodicals. *Fatal Illusions* is his first novel.

Adam met his wife, Kim, during a trip to the Holy Land. They have two daughters and live in Michigan's north woods, where Adam is hard at work on his next suspense novel. When he isn't working, Adam enjoys running, reading, watching true-crime TV shows, and hiking in the great outdoors with his family. For more information about Adam, visit www.adamblumerbooks.com.